Praise for the work of Leonard B. Scott

CHARLIE MIKE
"One of the finest novels yet written about the Vietnam War."
—*The Washington Post*

THE LAST RUN
"It's more *Charlie Mike*, but better. . . . The kind of book that leaves you wanting more."
—*Atlanta Journal & Constitution*

THE IRON MEN
"Superbly written . . . A very fine and fast-paced story, a sweeping and generational tale of murder and retribution, set against the headline events of the last half century."
—NELSON DEMILLE

FORGED IN HONOR
"This story is better than *Rambo* in any of his incarnations and flows smoother than many high-adventure yarns . . . [with] battles so spectacular that those who love adventure and great war scenes will jump for joy at reading this well-plotted novel."
—*Ocala Star Banner*

By Leonard B. Scott
Published by Ballantine Books:

CHARLIE MIKE
THE IRON MEN
THE HILL
THE LAST RUN
THE EXPENDABLES
FORGED IN HONOR
SOLEMN DUTY
DUTY BOUND

DUTY BOUND

Leonard B. Scott

BALLANTINE BOOKS • NEW YORK

A Ballantine Book
Published by The Ballantine Publishing Group
Copyright © 1998 by Leonard B. Scott

http://www.randomhouse.com

Library of Congress Catalog Card Number: 97-94243

ISBN 0-345-39189-6

Manufactured in the United States of America

First Edition: July 1998

10 9 8 7 6 5 4 3 2 1

CHAPTER 1

Sparks, Georgia

Not a breath of wind gave respite to the blistering heat. In the weeds alongside the dry, dusty peanut field, grasshoppers buzzed, disturbed by the grunts of a man bending over a dead monster. Sweat trickled down Virgil Washington's ebony face, and his arm and neck muscles bulged and veins stood out like blue cords as he strained to loosen the old tractor's rusted lug nut; the nut wouldn't budge. Virgil kicked the tractor's flat tire and threw down his wrench. Backing up from the forty-year-old John Deere relic, he glanced at the scorching midday sun. *You ain't beat me yet, ya bastard,* he said to himself. Taking in several deep breaths for strength, he was about to pick up the wrench and try again when footsteps sounded on the hard-packed clay road behind him. He turned. A big-muscled white guy was walking toward him, wearing tan shorts and a tight, dark blue T-shirt. *Now what we got here?* Virgil wondered as he faced the stranger he judged to be in his forties, a little over six feet, and probably at least 210. By the bulging muscles, crew cut, square face, and *don't give me no shit* look, the dude could have been one of those new breed of cops who pumped weights and ate bran flakes, but the faded khaki shorts and big diver's watch told Virgil something else. He had seen shorts like those before, when he'd conducted joint training in Panama with the Navy SEALs. You couldn't buy those kind of shorts at Wal-Mart or Sears; they were issued

1

by Uncle Sam to a select few. The man was in the machine, or had been.

Ted Faircloud halted a few feet from the stocky black man. *Yeah, I like him already,* Ted thought. Losers couldn't keep eye contact. The candidate hadn't even blinked; his gaze was steady, measuring him. He had the look. He hadn't allowed himself to be broken. Yeah, Virgil Washington still had his pride. "Hiya," Ted said, raising his hand.

"Ya lost?" Virgil spoke evenly.

Ted Faircloud kept his eyes on the prospect. "No, Sergeant Washington, I've been looking for you. I guess your time in the pen didn't hurt ya."

"It hurt me aw'right," Virgil said, thinking maybe he was wrong, Mr. Muscles might be a cop after all; he knew too much about him. "Leavenworth's not a 'pen' anymore; it's a maximum-security disciplinary barracks . . . heavy emphasis on the disciplinary part. What ya want?"

Ted's lips slowly crawled into a smile. "I'm what ya might call a recruiter. I want you, just like those recruiting posters where Uncle Sam is standing there pointing his finger. Today that's me, Uncle Sam, and I'm pointing at you."

Virgil relaxed a little because the smile on Mr. Muscles took some hardness off him. "You're wastin' your time," Virgil said. "I'm not interested in joinin' any militia or reserve outfit."

Ted Faircloud kept his smile. "You've got a felony conviction for attempted murder of that lieutenant at Fort Bragg. You couldn't join a reserve unit if you wanted."

Virgil now knew for sure the man was no cop. It was the way Muscles spoke his first sentence, like it was cool to be pinched for trying to do in an officer. Virgil shrugged. "It was a misunderstanding is all."

Ted nodded as if agreeing. "Yeah, and what about the guy you killed in Leavenworth; was that a misunderstanding, too?"

"Naw, that was different," Virgil said, wrinkling his brow. "That redneck says to me he didn't want a *buck nigger* workin' in the leather shop with him. I like leather; it smells good. I didn't want to do woodworkin' cause the damn wood dust makes me itch. And in automotive you're always greasy, so I told that redneck he'd have to deal with it because I wanted to learn to make belts and shit. He fucked up and made a move on me. I made a better one. The judge musta liked leather, too, 'cause he decided I was defending myself from bodily harm."

Ted motioned to the rusted tractor. "Maybe you would have learned somethin' in automotive?"

Virgil nodded as he glanced at the relic. "Yeah, but I got me some cool belts up at the house." He looked back at Ted. "I'll ask again. What do ya want?"

"I want you in my unit, Sergeant. I need experience, and you've got what I'm looking for: former Green Beret team sergeant, commo, demo, and weapons expert. Did a couple of tours down south, saw action in Grenada, Panama, and did your time in the desert. Yeah, you've got the experience I'm looking for. I've got an op going down in a couple weeks and need you in."

"What kind of operation are we talkin' about?"

Ted looked into Virgil's eyes. "The kind you were trained to do. . . . 'Course, it could get you dead, but it's also the kind that can make you a new start. We're goin' to score off a big drug player. We're goin' to hit 'em when they move a load of cash that's goin' to be laundered. It'll be away from civilians, and there ain't gonna be no law types comin' after us—these guys can't report the loss. You'll get twenty percent of the take . . . and the take is three million bucks. Before you answer, I gotta tell ya this ain't gonna be no cakewalk. It could get messy."

"You're shittin' me, right?"

"Nope, that's the deal, Sergeant. You'll be joining me and two others like yourself who have military experience. Think of it as a special detachment without the gung-ho bullshit. We're all vets and we have the best equipment and weapons money can buy. Yes, you'll do some training to get back up to speed, but no spit-shinin' boots or paintin' rocks. I call the shots, I do the plannin', and I say when it's over and you can go home. You screw with me, you're history. You do your duty, in a couple of weeks you'll have a good-size, tax-free stake in a safe-deposit box to jump-start a new life. That's the deal. You have a minute to decide."

Virgil looked over the man's shoulder at the distant run-down rented frame house that was in desperate need of a new roof and major repairs. His sixty-six-year-old mother sat rocking on the porch as her six grandchildren, all under twelve, played with broken toys in the dirt yard. One of his divorced sisters lived in the house, and the other had left her two kids and run off to Mobile. Six children and three adults living in a four-room house rented from a white farmer who charged them half their combined welfare checks—and Big Muscles was asking him if he wanted in?

Virgil straightened his back and shifted his gaze to Muscles. "I'm in, but I need an advance. I need to take care of my mother and family before I go."

Ted took a wad of bills wrapped in a rubber band from his pocket and tossed it to Virgil. "Ya got eight grand there and two cards. The first card is from the Dodge dealership in Valdosta. Go pick yourself out a good, used pickup under ten grand. Give 'em that card and they'll fill out the paper-work and it's yours. The second card has an address and directions and a company name where you can say you'll be workin' as a construction foreman. Be at that address in three days at 1000 hours.

"Be smart with that money. Don't flash it or lay down any big down payments on whatever you're goin' to do for your family. People may get suspicious and start askin' questions. You'll get another five grand when you arrive, and ten more after your refresher training. If somebody calls to check your employment, you'll be covered. And Sergeant Washington, show up on time and don't tell anyone about this. . . . There's no need in telling you what happens if you try and get slick on me."

Virgil looked into the big man's eyes. "I'll be there—but tell me something. Who are you?"

"Ted. That's all you need to know for now. See ya in

three days." Turning, Ted walked back toward the house, where his rental car was parked.

Virgil took a deep breath and looked across the peanut fields he'd worked for the past year. Exhaling slowly, he smiled; he wouldn't be eating dust anymore. In a few minutes he'd walk up to his mother and make her proud of her son again. He would give her what she hadn't had in over thirty years. Virgil Washington was going to give his mother and her grandchildren hope for the future.

One day later, Miami

Ted Faircloud was dressed in tan slacks and a Hawaiian shirt as he drove out of the Miami airport's National rental car parking lot. Fifteen minutes later he pulled to the curb of a run-down motel in Little Havana. He walked into a dimly lit office that stank of cigarette smoke and disinfectant. A woman in her fifties displaying a lot of cleavage sat on a stool behind the counter, reading a Spanish *Cosmo*. She looked up from the magazine and gave Ted the once-over before saying, "No rooms."

Ted casually leaned on the counter. "Señora, please tell Ramon I wish to speak to him."

The woman leaned over within two inches of his face and spoke, gushing her cigarette-laden breath on him. "You police, no?"

"No, I'm a businessman."

"D.O.H.?"

"No, not Department of Health, and I don't want a date, either. I only want to speak to Ramon."

Pressing a button under the counter, the woman slid off her stool and backed up, busying herself with looking through another Spanish magazine. A long moment later the door opened behind her. A youngish, short, suave, dark-haired pimp with a ponytail stepped into the small office. He was wearing pointy shoes, a shiny sharkskin suit, and a collarless shirt. Ted knew the duded-up Cuban was twenty-nine years old and had been a former Army Ranger and member of Delta Force. What he had not been prepared for was that the former Ranger could have doubled for Antonio Banderas. *Man, the guy is something in the pretty-face department. Too short, though. Probably messed up his chances of doing movies or posing in his underwear for magazines.*

Moving his left hand closer to his sharkskin jacket, Ramon Lopez looked the big man over. "Who are you, man?" he asked.

Still leaning on the counter, Ted looked into the short man's suspicious brown face. "I'm your salvation, Ramon. I'm here to offer you a job that will pay good money and get you out of this dump."

Ramon's left hand disappeared inside his jacket. "Who are you? I don't ask again."

"What, you goin' to pop me here, Ramon?" Ted asked with a smile. "I thought Delta guys were smart. You know you can't do me here. What you got there, a Glock? Man, that thing would make a big mess. All I want to do is talk to you. You listen, and if you don't like the deal, I'm gone. It's a simple thing, Ramon."

Ramon stood in silence, staring as if measuring Ted for a casket, before stepping closer and lifting the hinged countertop. He patted Ted down and said, "This better be good. You got ten minutes. Don't bore me."

Ted followed the small Cuban into the next room, where five washed-out working girls sat on two couches watching a Spanish game show on a small battered TV. Two weren't bad, Ted thought, but the others were past middle age, and all had their hair dyed in different shades of blond. *No way I'd pay for some of that.* He followed the Cuban into a spotless kitchen where an old woman was wiping off a table.

Ramon patted the woman's shoulder. *"Dos cervezas, por favor."* He motioned Ted to a chair. "Sit. You have nine minutes thirty seconds."

"I can't talk with her here," Ted said.

Ramon made a shooing motion to the woman and faced the big man. "Talk."

As soon as the old lady disappeared, Ted pulled up a chair and sat. "Ramon, I need your experience. I have a unit made up of two other men and me. I need one more man to bring me to full strength to pull off a score I've been workin' on for over six months. . . ."

He repeated what he'd told Virgil the day before and made the same offer of money. Finished, he looked into the Cuban's eyes and waited.

Ramon's fingers drummed the tabletop for a moment before he canted his head slightly. "How you find me, man?"

"I have friends who follow the action here in Miami, Ramon. I know you're into a player for ten G's and you can't even pay the vig. You can't hire out your normal services because they have you marked. That makes you a dead man in a week unless you get dumb and try and pull a one-man job, which means you're dead anyway. You're in a fix, Ramon, a kind of catch-22 where you end up dead no matter what you do. I'm offering an out. I'll pay off the debt you owe, but then you're mine. Don't give me that look. It won't be so bad. With your cut of the take you can pay off the debt to me and still pocket a bundle. Believe me, you're goin' to like workin' for me. I treat my people with respect. You're good at what you do, Ramon. I know, I checked you out. You're going to be a star in my outfit, a big-time star."

"You say you been working on the plan for six months, man. Why you need me now?" Ramon kept his eyes level with Ted's.

"I lost two of my detachment members last week. They had a car accident coming back from a recon. Funny how shit happens. They both were good and made no mistakes while workin' for me, but then Joe Bob, the driver, goes to sleep at the wheel, and wham, it's all she wrote. Swerved over into the oncoming lane and got it from a semi loaded with frozen chickens from Arkansas. Ramon, think about it. What's your future hold? I'll tell ya, you're goin' to be whacked, stuffed in a trunk, and dumped in the 'glades. I'd hate that . . . not a way to go out for a Delta guy. 'Course, goin' out with frozen chickens isn't any way to go, either, but at least they didn't know what hit 'em. What ya goin' to leave behind if you don't take my offer? That fake gold Rolex and your piece? Your mama might get what, two hundred for a Glock?"

Ramon studied the stranger's face for a moment. "You pay off my debt?"

"Yeah, and the vig."

Ramon drummed his fingers again. "You hooked up, man? If you're connected, I'm a dead man if I work for you."

"Come on, Ramon, do I look like a wise guy to you? You think if I was a guinea I'd be showin' my face here in Little Havana? I know the rules. I'm an independent who has friends is all. Are you in or out?"

Ramon lowered his head a long moment before looking at the big man. "I'll do it, man, but give me room. . . . If it feels wrong, I don't do the op." Ramon extended his finger and touched his forehead. "I can feel it, man, right here. I know when it feels right and I know when it's fucked up."

Ted took a wad of bills from his pants pocket and set it on the table. "This ought to *feel* right to you. There's a card attached to the first bill. Be at the address on the card in two days at 1000 hours. Use the money to buy yourself some wheels and some new clothes . . . no shiny shit, no pointed shoes, and lose the ponytail and fake Rolex. You're goin' to be with the best, so I want you to look it. And Ramon, be there or my people will come lookin' for you. Like I said, they're the best."

Ramon shrugged as he looked up from the money. "No sweat, man. And it isn't a Glock; it's a Beretta. Mama would have gotten at least three bills."

Ted drove his rental car into a South Miami marina parking lot and turned off the ignition. He got out and walked to the B pier, looking for his ride. Just as he stepped on the wood planks, two men stepped off a cigarette boat and gave him *hold it right there* looks.

Ted stopped, and a man came up behind him and said, "You're late."

Ted shrugged. "Traffic was bad."

"Yeah, I know; my guys been followin' you to make sure ya didn't pick up any tails. You ready?"

"Yeah, let's do it," Ted said.

Minutes later Ted was staring at his white knuckles as the cigarette boat bounced across Biscayne Bay, heading for the Atlantic. *Christ'a'mighty, this ain't fun,* he thought. *In Miami Vice it always looked like those guys skimmed over the water, but we sure as hell ain't skimmin'. Oh man, my stomach can't take this.*

Finally the sleek craft slowed and made a wide turn. The man who had escorted Ted aboard lifted binoculars and scanned back toward the distant shore. A full minute passed before he lowered his glasses and spoke to the man behind the wheel. "It's clear. Tell him we're on the way."

The driver increased power again and spoke into a hand-held radio. Ted braced himself for another pounding, but this time the boat did skim as it headed due south.

Five minutes later the cigarette boat came alongside a large Baycraft pleasure cruiser. Ted saw his old friend on the deck and raised his hand.

"Permission to come aboard."

The smiling, dark-haired man lifted his hand, holding a Heineken. "Come on, Teddy. You want a beer?"

Ted grabbed hold of the starboard ladder. "Have I ever turned down a beer, Gee?"

Vincent Genesse handed his old friend a bottle of Heineken as soon as Ted joined him on the deck. "Here ya go, Teddy. . . . You got your replacements yet?"

Ted glanced at the two bodyguards standing behind his former teammate. "You know the deal, Gee. I don't discuss business with your guys around."

Genesse motioned toward the cruiser's cabin. "Tommy, you and Al check out what's on the movie channel, huh."

Both men gave Ted *screw you* looks before slowly making their way to the cabin door.

Ted lifted an eyebrow. "Your guys need an attitude

adjustment, Gee. You should train 'em to snap to attention and do what ya say without the looks."

"They're civilians, Ted, what'd ya expect? So you get a crew together?"

"Yeah, Gee, I got 'em. Thanks for the info on the little Cuban ex-Ranger; he worked out."

"No sweat. Too bad about the boys you lost. I'm sorry, buddy."

"Thanks, Gee . . . but you didn't want to see me just to give me your condolences. What's up?"

Genesse gestured to the cushioned seats. "Sit down, Teddy; we have to talk about the op. Some things have happened recently . . . the situation has changed."

Ted's face hardened. "What d'ya mean, changed?"

"Relax, Teddy, my boss isn't going to back out on you. In fact he wants to make you a better offer. Sit down, will ya?"

Ted took a seat but kept a hard stare on his friend. "He don't make 'better offers' unless he wants somethin' in return."

Genesse took a sip of beer and leaned back in his seat. "Look, Teddy, you came to me six months ago wantin' help to get Mendez. I told you then what you wanted was impossible and—"

"Yeah, yeah, I know what ya said," Ted said impatiently. "Ya told me you guys had an agreement with the Latinos and ya couldn't do anything."

"But I did help you, didn't I, Teddy? I wanted that bastard as much as you for what he did to us. . . . I talked to the boss for you. He let me use some people to do some checking, and I found out about Mendez's laundering operation in Georgia. I knew it wasn't what you really wanted, but takin' a big score off Mendez was the next best thing . . . until now."

The hair on the back of Ted's neck stood up. "What are you sayin', Gee? Your boss goin' to help me get him now?"

Genesse leaned forward. "Teddy, we got real lucky last week. Call it fate, call it luck, but it looks like you're gonna get what ya want after all—a chance at Mendez."

"Keep talkin'; I'm listenin'."

"Look, Teddy, what I'm about to tell you will get us both popped if word gets out, you understand?"

"Come on, Gee, you're talkin' to me, here."

"Teddy, Mendez had him a honey on the side, a real looker. He played house with her on his yacht, and when his ol' lady was away he'd even take this babe to his estate to keep his bed warm. It was a nice arrangement for almost a year. Then last week Mendez tells her next time they meet he's goin' to have another babe join them to double the fun. Problem is, the looker isn't into that and says no way. Big mistake. Mendez tells her if she wants to keep her benefits she better play and love it. She sees she's in big trouble and tells him she'll love it. She lied. To make a long story short, the looker gets real scared and takes off. And guess what?"

Ted set down his beer bottle. "You got her."

"Yeah, it was a pure luck thing, but we got her. She went to the cops for protection. . . . Lucky for us it was a couple of guys we help out now and then."

"So because you got Mendez's broad, your boss changed his mind?"

"Ted, we've got the mother lode in this babe. She's no dummy; she kept her ears open when with Mendez. We now know Mendez goes to his yacht like clockwork to get his jollies off every Monday, Wednesday, and Friday evening. We also now know how many security people he has with him and where they're stationed. What I'm sayin' is, with this info we can get the bastard, and Ted, you're the man who can do it."

"Me? Wait a minute. We had a deal that I was going to score three million off Mendez. Are you tellin' me that's off and now you're goin' to help me pop him?"

Genesse smiled. "Teddy, I'm sayin' you can do both . . . score the money and take him out. The broad is going to help you."

"The broad? Are you shittin' me?"

"If you want Mendez you're goin' to need her."

"What is this, Gee? You're not tellin' me everything. Six months ago ya told me there was no way your boss would help me whack the bastard. Now all of a sudden he gives me a green light just because you got his bimbo? Uh-uh, I don't think so—you guys been watchin' Mendez and know his schedule. What's really going on here?"

Genesse sighed. "Okay, Teddy, I'll level with you. You're right, there is something else. Mendez is expanding his legit business here in town. Pretty soon the bastard will be steppin' on our toes. He's crossin' the line, Teddy. He's goin' to be usin' Latino construction and labor crews and keepin' our unions out. The boss can't let him do that. Mendez has to go. The problem is, we can't be involved in it. If the Latinos found out we contracted the hit on one of their big players, there'd be a war. And Teddy, you know we can't have that. We have to stay out of it. . . . You'll be on your own."

Ted shook his head in disbelief. "Wait a minute . . . ya want me to take him out but you guys aren't goin' to help?"

"Teddy, you'll have the woman, who will tell you everything you need to know to get him, and I've already arranged through third parties all the weapons and equipment you'll need. It's the best, but that's it; I can't do any more. The boss has put me in charge of this—nobody else in the organization knows. When you make the score and the hit, we've got to be clean. Nothing can be traced back to us. Not even a rumor."

"What about the money?" Ted asked. "You guys wanted half the take, remember?"

"You get it all, Teddy. We can't risk taking his cash. Once you make the score, Mendez will go ballistic: to a player like him, stealin' his money is worse than catchin' you screwin' his wife in his bed; it's the ultimate insult. All his people will be on the street, willing to pay big bucks to anyone who will rat out the crew that did it. We'll be suspected first. He'll find nothing because there's nobody who knows about this."

Ted studied his friend's face a moment. "You guys were the ones who were settin' up the score for me. How am I goin' to do it if I don't know how it's goin' to go down?"

"The broad, Teddy. Like I told you, she's smart, and the

important thing is, she knows computers. I have a computer geek who briefed her on all the details of the score. The geek says she's good to go."

"Christ'a'mighty, Gee, you told the bimbo about our score? You trust her that much?"

"Ted, she knows she'd be dead if we hadn't stepped in and helped her. This op is her only chance to live a normal life. With her split of the take, she can disappear for a long time. Anyway, it's the only way it can be done to keep us out of it. The setup of the score is complicated, and you gotta have her to do it."

"Give me the geek, Gee."

"Can't do that. He runs our sport-book spreadsheets— we're modernizing, Ted. The guy is a genius and we can't afford to lose him. Hey, trust me, the broad knows what she's doin'."

Ted lowered his head. "Looks like I don't have any choice . . . but I got a problem. I hired the new guys for a score, not a hit. I gotta find out if they want in—and if they do, I got to get 'em trained and up to speed."

Genesse smiled. "Ted, you were the best platoon leader the SEALs ever had—you'll get them up to speed. And remember, the score is now *six* million; they'll want in."

Raising his head, Ted frowned. "I'll talk to 'em and see. What else I need to know, Gee?"

Genesse picked up a thick manila folder from a side table. "In here are pictures of his yacht and blueprints we got from the company that made it. You also got maps and directions to two safe houses for when you come to town to do Mendez. The keys to the houses are in here, and there's a hundred grand for expenses, plus there's a new ID in there for you with the name Ted Wilson. Weapons and gear have already been shipped in care of the broad."

Genesse handed Ted the folder and took out an envelope from his pocket. "This is the address where the woman is. We got her out of here a couple of days ago and put her in a house near Lake Lanier, only about twenty minutes from your place. Third parties set it up, Ted, so you've got to stick to a cover. The story is, she's hiding out from her husband till the divorce comes through. Her name is Bonita Rogers, but the name she's using is Linda Stone. She's got a live-in maid and a local security guy who keeps her protected. You're a P.I. by the name of Ted Wilson and you've been hired by her to keep tabs on her soon-to-be ex. Use the new ID and buy yourself a car to look the part. She's expecting to see you as soon as you fly back into Atlanta."

Ted accepted the envelope but shook his head. "Jesus Christ, Gee, you sound like the CIA."

"I'm tryin' to keep her alive, Ted. Mendez has his people out searching for her. Look, this is it. After you leave, we don't see each other again for a long, long time. It's begun—I don't know you and I don't know about anything that's going on; we're out of it. If something happens and the op goes sour, you're on your own. If you get caught and gotta talk, tell 'em the broad is the one who hired you. She's the fall guy in this, you understand?"

"She know she's the one whose goin' to take the heat?"

"She knows if it goes bad she's dead anyway. She can't hurt us if she sings . . . she can only give up the two cops and two of my boys that I've already moved to Vegas."

"What about the geek? She could give him up."

"We keep him away from us . . . he's too weird. They can't make the connection to us, so we're covered."

Ted walked to the railing and looked out at swells. A long moment passed before he faced his friend again. "I want him, Gee. I've dreamed of nothin' else . . . the money doesn't matter to me; it's him I want."

Genesse set his beer bottle down and stood. "Teddy, I made you the offer because the boss wanted me to. I love you like a brother. I don't want you to accept the deal unless you think you can do it and get out in one piece. Mendez has to go one way or another. If you don't do it, we'll find an independent who's dumb enough to try. I want that son of a bitch as much as you do. I still dream of that fuckin' night. I can't get the screams out of my head, Teddy. I still hear the screams."

Ted put his hand on his friend's shoulder. "I know, Gee; I

still hear them, too. I'm in. Like I said, I have to talk to my crew, but I don't think it'll be a problem. Glenn wants him as bad as we do, and the new guys won't be able to turn down the big money."

Genesse lowered his head. "Teddy, I wanted to be there and help you put him away but I—"

"You've done enough, Gee. You've stuck your neck way out for me. You'll be there. The whole team will be there with me when I even the score. The screams will end, Gee. I promise."

Genesse hugged the bigger man to his chest. "Do it and get out safe, Teddy. I don't wanna be the last of Team Two-two. You hear me? Get out safe."

"He's goin' down, Gee." Ted stepped back, forcing a smile. "I guess I'd better get to the airport; I got a plane to catch. You take care, Gee."

Genesse waited until his former teammate made his way down to the cigarette boat before speaking. "Teddy, we were somethin', weren't we? We were the best, huh?"

Ted nodded. "Yeah, Gee, we was the best."

Key West, Florida

Seated in the shade of a banyan tree, Dr. Reese warily looked across the plastic table at the newly arrived doctor who was looking through his patient's medical records.

Dr. Sarah Laski set the documents down and took off her reading glasses. "So, the bottom line is you believe he should be released?"

"As I told your people three days ago, we've run every test and had numerous sessions with him. We found nothing abnormal."

"And his wounds?" Sarah asked.

"The head wound was superficial and has healed quite nicely. The arm wound will take a little more time because of muscle damage, but he is working very hard in physical therapy and should be almost a hundred percent by next week. As you will see shortly, he is not your average forty-seven-year-old male. He's in excellent physical condition, which I believe accounts for his rapid recovery."

Sarah picked up the folder again. "What about the depression you say he is suffering?"

Reese studied his hands a moment before looking at her. "We are the reason for his depression, Doctor. Since coming here, he has not been allowed to communicate with anyone outside the compound. For all intents and purposes, he is a prisoner, and prisoners tend to get depressed."

Sarah nodded as if in understanding. "The orders were necessary. The press made extraordinary efforts to find him, so we had to ensure the story did not get out."

"I don't like being involved in a cover-up, Doctor," Reese said with a glare.

Sarah met his glare with one of her own. "You were briefed on the sensitivity of the situation, Doctor. Public knowledge of the actual events that took place would have served no one's interests, especially not the patient's. The congressional oversight committee was briefed thoroughly, and they agreed unanimously with our decision to keep the case permanently closed to the public."

Reese relaxed his taut shoulders and lowered his head. "I'm sorry, Doctor. I fear I've grown too close to the patient to be objective anymore. I understand the concerns the Bureau had on this, but as you can see, our examinations lay those fears to rest. Special Agent Eli Tanner is physically and mentally fit for duty."

Sarah motioned to the file. "I was provided only his test and evaluation results. Could you fill me in on his past before I speak to him?"

Reese's face tightened. "It was communicated to me you were going to review our findings. Nothing was said about your interviewing my patient."

"You want him released, don't you, Doctor?" Sarah asked with a condescending smile. "I was sent here to make a final evaluation and I—"

"Don't play word games with me, Doctor. You doubt our

findings. Fine. Talk to him. I ask only that out of professional courtesy you tell me your conclusions after your talk. You asked about his past. I'll summarize for you. Our patient joined the military out of high school and attended the Army's Airborne and Ranger courses before going to Vietnam in 1972. In Vietnam he was a sergeant in the 101st Airborne Division and saw very heavy action. He was wounded badly and took quite some time to recover. Once released from the hospital, he was discharged from the Army and attended the University of Georgia, where he obtained a degree in criminal justice. Upon graduation he applied for and was accepted into the Bureau. I must point out here that he followed in his brother's footsteps. His older brother was in the Bureau at the time. Our patient graduated from the FBI Academy, and because of his military training and combat experience, he was assigned to the Bureau's then-new Special Operations unit. He was sent to many schools and became highly specialized in his field. His follow-on assignments kept him principally in special-operations assignments throughout the states. He was wounded while working on the drug task force in Miami in 1990 but fully recovered and continued his duties in special operations. Three months ago he was assigned as the resident special agent in charge of the Columbus, Georgia, office, and you know the rest—he began working the case that he closed a little over a month ago."

Sarah looked past the doctor toward the ocean. "I assume he's not married?"

"He was once. Divorced in 1988. The former wife is remarried and has a restraining order in place to keep him from seeing his son. He doesn't like talking about it."

"What else doesn't he like talking about?" Sarah asked.

Reese motioned toward the beach. "You'll find out very soon. That's him running toward us now." Reese rose and dipped his chin. "Please excuse me, Doctor. I'll leave you to your evaluation."

Sarah nodded in shocked silence as she kept her eyes on the approaching tanned, gleaming runner. Eli Tanner was not what she'd expected. For some reason, she had assumed

he would be taller and look older. Instead he was short, not
over five-nine, and had the body of a thirty-year-old athlete.
He was wearing only nylon shorts and running shoes, so she
could see that his chest was heavily developed, as were his
legs. Reese was right, she thought, he was certainly not your
typical forty-seven-year-old male. Prematurely gray hair
contrasted sharply with a rugged, tanned face that reminded
her of TV newsman Tom Brokaw; it was a friendly face.

Eli Tanner told himself to ignore the pain and push harder.
*Just another fifty yards, push, push, go man, pump your legs
faster, push it!*

In a full sprint, he crossed the imaginary line in the sand,
then slowed to a wobbly walk. Every muscle in his legs was
screaming. He bent over and held his knees to steady himself. Taking in several deep breaths, he felt the high coming
on. Yeaaaah *baby*!

"How far did you run, Agent Tanner?"

Eli glanced up. One look told him all he needed to know:
a shrink. He lowered his head again and spoke between
breaths. "Th-Three . . . miles."

"I'm Dr. Sarah Laski."

Eli stood erect, put his hands on his hips, and began slowly
walking back down the beach. "You the final inspector?" he
asked without looking at her.

She stepped out of her shoes and quickly caught up. "I'm
not sure what you mean."

"When you buy pants you find a little piece of paper in
the pocket that says 'Inspected by Number Four.' Are you
Inspector Four?"

Sarah gave him a side glance. "You might call me that.
Do you mind if I walk with you?"

Eli shook his head as he lowered his arms to his sides.
They walked in silence for a long moment before Sarah
gave him another glance. "Do *you* think you're ready to be
released?"

"Sure do, Doc."

"Please, call me Sarah."

"Doc, I was ready to be released two weeks ago. What-ever you want to ask me, get on with it."

"Do you think we've treated you unfairly?"

"You people have a job to do, and I understand that. You're worried that I might have problems. I don't think I have any problems other than my being here. You want to make sure I'm all right, and I want to convince you I am. I've taken tests, been asked a zillion questions, and I've tried to answer all of them honestly. Have I been treated unfairly? No. Am I ready to go? Hell yeah."

"Do you think about the men you killed?" Sarah asked as she stepped over a dead jellyfish.

"Not much."

"Does it bother you when you think about it?"

"Nope."

"Did you have to kill them? Couldn't you have wounded them instead?"

Eli stopped and faced her. "Doc, have you ever killed an animal?"

Sarah looked at him with a blank expression. "Not on purpose; I hit a dog once while driving."

"Well, Doc, ya have to understand humans are one of the hardest animals there is to kill. In the movies a guy shoots another guy and he goes down and just lies there. That's not what really happens. When bullets start flying, most people aren't even hit, but those that are are usually wounded, and they can still shoot back. Humans don't want to die; they fight to live and are very dangerous when hit. In Nam the ratio was one to nine. One killed for every nine wounded. Does that tell you something? It should tell you that if you're facing more than one armed assailant who intends on doing you bodily harm, you shoot them in the face or heart to make sure they stay down. It's a matter of survival."

"You killed five men and wounded two," she said matter-of-factly.

"My mistake on the two. I thought I killed them."

"Do you like killing, Agent Tanner?"

"No, Doc." Eli looked into her eyes. "I felt guilt and

remorse the first time I killed a man. It was in Vietnam. I agonized over it because that North Vietnamese trooper was just like me, a soldier doing his duty. I felt for him because I knew it could have just as well been me lying there. But I don't agonize over the armed assailants I've had to shoot, Doc. They're not like me. I don't feel anything for them. Do I like killing them? The answer is no. I don't like being in a situation where I might end up dead."

Sarah kept her gaze on him. "How do you cope with it?"

"I don't live in the past," he said as he started walking again. "I look ahead, not back."

"What about your son?"

Eli came to a halt with a pained frown and faced her again. "You don't play fair, Doc."

"I'm sorry, Agent Tanner, but I had to know if you were really that callous. Tell me about him."

"There's nothing to say. I haven't been able to see him. I wish I could say something. I really wish I could."

"Is it because you almost died that you want to see him?"

"I've always wanted to see him, Doc. But to answer your question honestly, I wasn't willing to beg his mother to let me see him before. I am now. I'm getting older, Doctor, and the job doesn't seem as important to me as it did before. It'd be nice to get things right again. I'd really like to have a chance to be with my son, do father things, let him know I care."

Sarah saw that the special agent's eyes were misting and lowered her head. "Agent Tanner, you'll be released in two days. I'm sorry it can't be sooner but it will take that long to brief my findings to those who were concerned."

Eli looked out at the ocean and closed his eyes. "So it's finally over."

Sarah turned to retrace her steps but stopped and looked over her shoulder at him. "I'll recommend you receive another week's leave, Agent Tanner. Perhaps it will give you time to make things right. Good-bye."

Eli nodded in silence as he stared out at the ocean. *Make things right,* he repeated to himself.

CHAPTER 2

Hartsfield International Airport, Atlanta

Glenn Henderson nervously scratched his bearded chin as the passengers from Miami walked by. He shifted his feet as he waited. *Come on, Teddy, where are you, damnit? You call and say meet me, we have to talk, then you hang up. Why'd you do that to me?*

Glenn sighed when his best friend finally exited. He forced a smile and raised his hand in greeting. "Hiya, Teddy, how was the trip?"

Ted Faircloud nodded toward the well-dressed man as he kept walking. "I got our crew . . . and I got an added mission from Gee."

Henderson quickly caught up and walked alongside his friend. "What do you mean, 'added mission'?"

"We're going to take out Mendez *after* we make the score," Ted whispered.

Shocked, Glenn came to a halt. "Jesus, Ted, are you serious?"

"I'm dead serious. Come on, keep walkin'. You gotta drop me by a used-car lot so I can get me a car."

"What's wrong with your pickup?"

"I've gotta play like I'm a P.I.; gotta see a woman Gee says is goin' to help us."

Again Glenn stopped. "A woman? What's going on?"

"Gee and his people are out of it. They can't be fingered. They've given the broad all the info on the score and she knows all about Mendez."

21

"Slow down. Jesus, Ted. What do you mean, she knows all about Mendez?"

"She's been bangin' him the past year; she was his sweet thing."

"My God, that means we've really got a chance to get him."

"Damn straight we do. And there's somethin' else, Glenn—we get to keep all the score."

"All six million? Gee doesn't want his half?"

"We get all of it—'course, we have to give the new guys and the broad their split, but that still leaves us plenty to get us new equipment and start that construction company we've been dreamin' about. The main thing, though, is we get Mendez. It's finally payback time."

"About damn time."

Ted pulled off the lake road into a private drive and came to a stop in front of a large ornate metal gate. A small box attached to a pole suddenly blurted, "State your business!"

Ted rolled down his window and spoke into the box. "I'm Ted Wilson, the private investigator working for the lady. I called. She's expectin' me."

"Drive in when the gate opens. Park in the circular drive by the cabin. I'll meet'cha."

The gate started rolling back and Ted put his '92 Lincoln Town Car into gear. He drove four hundred yards down a winding tree-lined asphalt road and did a double take when he saw the massive three-story log mansion sitting on a finger of land jutting out into the lake. *A cabin? The guy calls* that *a cabin? Christ'a'mighty, the logs alone cost a couple million. Looks like a ski resort.*

Ted parked in the drive and got out of the white Lincoln. The massive front door opened and a thin, balding man walked out wearing jeans, cowboy boots, and a leather shoulder holster holding a nickel-plated .357 Magnum. "You carrying, Mr. Wilson?" he asked. "The lady don't want anybody comin' inside who's packin'."

Ted lifted his arms and nodded toward the house. "Naw, I

ain't carryin' anything. You the one who called this thing a *cabin*?"

The man approached and patted Ted down. "Rich folks up here call 'em cabins; I just call it big. The lady is waitin' in the great room for ya. Mrs. White will show you in—and Wilson, I'd keep an eye on that damned dog the lady has, if I were you; he'll eat your ass up."

An old black woman appeared in the doorway. "He the dick, Duwane?"

"Yeah, Halley, it's Mr. Wilson. You can take him on in."

The tiny gray-haired woman looked Ted up and down as he walked toward the door. "Wipe yo' feet 'fo' ya come in here."

"Yes, ma'am," Ted said, wiping his feet on the mat. He noticed the little woman had snuff packed under her lower lip.

The old woman spat toward the driveway before motioning him inside. "Come on, I'se take ya to Mrs. Stone. Mind her dog now, ya hear? It one of them danged ol' foreign dogs. Meaner than a snake. Seen it eat up the cable man the other day. I warned him, yes, sir, I warned him, meaner than a snake."

Ted entered the foyer and came to an abrupt halt. *Man, the thin guy was right; it is big. Gotta be an old lodge or something.*

"You comin' or ain't ya?" the old woman said.

Ted strode across the spacious pine-floored foyer to catch up to his escort and glanced up at the exposed log beams. *How the hell they heat and cool such a big place?* It had to be forty feet up to the wood ceiling. All that wasted space had to cost a bundle to heat and cool. *Jesus, and the furniture. How the hell you supposed to get comfortable on log and willow furniture? Damn decorator must have been a Cherokee or something.* There were Indian blankets, feathered things, cow skulls, and Indian pictures everywhere.

The old woman halted in the hallway and gestured ahead. "She's just down there workin' on that machine a'hers. Lordy, like she need ta be worryin' about her weight. Go on, just mind that dog."

Directly in front of Ted three steps led down into the enormous sunken great room where four huge windows gave him a spectacular view of the lake fifty yards away. He was about to step down but heard a growl. Ted saw the dog and froze.

A voice said, "Come to mama, Baby. You Ted?"

"Yeah, I'm Ted." He looked in the direction the voice had come from. All he could see was an eight-foot partition covered with a colorful Indian blanket.

"Come on down. Baby won't bother you now," the voice said.

Thinking about the "ate up" cable man, Ted didn't move until the big, golden dog with the little head moved slowly toward the partition and disappeared behind it. Ted walked down the steps onto the Persian carpet and scanned the room, stopping when he saw the huge stone fireplace. *Jesus, you can walk into that thing.* He heard heavy breathing, turned, and froze again. Ten feet away, partly hidden behind the partition, a tall, glistening, deeply tanned blonde was working a StairMaster, her legs going up and down like pistons. Her back was to him and he couldn't see her face, but that didn't matter. What he could see made him immediately break out into a sweat. She was wearing a skintight white spandex exercise outfit.

Not looking at him, the blonde spoke over her shoulder. "Hand me a towel, will you?" The woman raised a hand from the bar and motioned to her right. "The towel is over here on the chair. Baby won't bother you."

What the hell, I'll just kick the stuffing outta the mutt if it makes a move on me, Ted thought. He walked over and picked up the towel. Taking in a breath, he stepped closer, turned his head away from the woman, and held out the towel. "Here ya go."

She took the towel as she kept pumping her legs, tossed it around her neck and looked him over. "So you're him, huh? You're not exactly what I expected."

Still keeping his head turned, Ted shrugged, having picked up the disappointment in her voice. "Yeah, well, you're not what I expected, either."

"What, you thought I'd be the Miss Chiquita Banana type?"

"The thought entered my mind, yeah."

"I have a degree in business. Well, almost . . . I only need seven more credit hours. Just because I was Carlos's friend doesn't make me a bimbo or a whore."

Ted looked out the window toward the lake, thinking, *This flaky dyed blonde is going to help me? Yeah, right.* He sighed, then said, "Why don't ya stop doin' that and put somethin' on. We've got business to discuss."

"I only have another minute to do. Why don't you get yourself something to drink. The bar is by the fireplace."

Ted walked back into the main room and stopped at another window, wondering how fast Genesse could find him somebody else who knew computers. Something touched his leg. He looked down. *Ohhh, shit!* The dog was sniffing his trouser legs. Taking another step closer, the animal started sniffing higher. Thinking of the cable man, Ted didn't move a muscle until the dog got to his crotch. *That's it!* "Down, dog!" Ted snapped.

To his surprise, the animal sat on his haunches and looked up at him as if saying *Huh*?

Ted pointed to the partition. "Get on back to your master."

The dog immediately hurried behind the wall, but came back seconds later wagging its tail. There was a worn tennis ball in its mouth.

"He wants to play," the woman said as she followed the animal.

Ted gulped. Big bust, narrow waist, wide hips, and long legs—all sheathed in see-through spandex. Ms. Rogers looked like a Las Vegas showgirl on her break.

The woman frowned. "You're staring at me like I'm lunch."

Embarrassed, Ted lowered his eyes to the carpet. "Put somethin' on, will ya?"

"You don't get out much, do you? This isn't any more revealing than what women athletes wore during the Olympics."

Ted raised his head, looking into her big hazel eyes. "I get out plenty, lady. You want to wear that thing to talk business in, that's fine." He leaned over, took the ball from the dog's mouth, and tossed it across the room. The dog became a blur.

The woman shook her head. "You started something. Baby loves chasing that nasty ball. You'll have to throw it a hundred times before he poops out."

As if making her point, Baby scampered back with the ball and dropped it at Ted's feet. He picked it up and gave it another toss. "What kind of dog is he?" Ted asked, just to say something and give himself time to get used to looking at the half-naked woman.

"He's a Rhodesian Ridgeback. They're originally from Africa and were bred to hunt lions. See the hair on the top of his back? It grows in the opposite direction from the rest of the hair on him. It's kind of like a giant cowlick. I'm Bonita Rogers, by the way."

Now genuinely interested in the animal, Ted dipped his chin toward the dog. "You call a *lion*-hunting dog *Baby*? That doesn't seem right."

"I thought you said you wanted to talk business?"

"Sure has a small head, doesn't he? How could he bring down a lion with such a little jaw?"

"Ask the cable man who came a couple of days ago," Bonita said as she walked to the coffee table. She leaned over and started to put on the jewelry she'd taken off prior to her workout.

Ted tossed the ball again and glanced at the mound of what looked like a small treasure. "Those the benefits of shacking up with Mendez?" he asked.

Bonita slipped on a four-carat diamond ring. "Look, Faircloud, you wouldn't understand, but I was a queen. I got everything I ever dreamed of having, okay?"

Ted nodded as if in understanding. "Yeah, and did your *king* give ya that busted lip, too?"

Bonita unconsciously raised her hand, touching the still

puffy lip. "He didn't do this. . . . I got it from Simon before I escaped."

Ted nodded again. "You escaped with your lion hunter and jewelry but no clothes, huh?"

"I got out alive, okay?"

Ted stared at her. "No, it's not okay. Ya see, I'm standin' here tryin' to figure out how a yacht queen gets away from her king. I mean, it's one thing doin' a swan dive off his boat and makin' a swim for it . . . but it's another when ya have time to take your dog and your benefits. I'm just a dumb ex-squid who doesn't have a degree in business, ya understand? How about you humoring me and tell me how you pulled off this *escape* of yours."

"What is it with the questions—you don't trust me?"

"I wanna hear your story, Miss Rogers." Ted gave her his best *don't mess with me* look.

Bonita took a step back. "It wasn't what you think. I had my own life. I was going to school and working part-time at KNJP, Channel 24, in Miami. I was a researcher for their newsroom. . . . I was doing so well they were about to promote me and—"

"Get to the escape part," Ted said.

"Okay, okay. I'd get beeped when he wanted me to come out to the boat or his place. His people would come and pick me up. Carlos was good to me, but then he started getting weird. I can take a lot of things, but I'm not into weird. I saw the handwriting on the wall, so when I got back to my place I started packing. But the servants called Carlos's people. One of his bodyguards, Simon, came over and asked where I thought I was going. I told him I was going to see my sick mother, and he says 'Sure,' then he hits me. That's how I got this. I thought he was going to kill me, so I shot him. . . . I had a pistol in my purse. He looked so stunned . . . like he just couldn't believe I would do it. He stood there, gasping like a goldfish out of water, bleeding on my white carpet, staring at me. I left him there, still standing and holding his stomach, afraid to move. Baby and most of my valuables and things were already in the car, so I ran out and left. That's what happened . . . it's the truth."

Ted wrinkled his brow. "You really shot the guy?"

"He hit me, Faircloud, and his face told me he wasn't finished. Yeah, I shot him."

"Where'd you learn to shoot people?"

"I was raised on a farm, and I hunted with my brothers. I know how to shoot . . . but I'd never shot a man before. It was awful."

Ted leaned over to pick up the ball. He gave it a toss and looked at the attractive woman again. *She's gotta be in her upper thirties, maybe early forties . . . shows in those big eyes of hers, eyes that say she's been around the block a couple of times. Gotta been a showgirl or big-time working girl.*

Ted said, "So, a friend of mine says you're goin' to help me. You've been briefed on everything and you're up to speed. He wasn't blowin' smoke, was he?"

"So you believe me now?" Bonita asked as if surprised.

"I never did *not* believe you—my friend would have checked you out. I asked 'cause I was curious is all."

Bonita's eyes narrowed. "You're a bastard, you know that? You scared me with that look of yours."

"I practice that look in the mirror, Miss Rogers. I guess it works. So are you up to speed on the op or not?"

Bonita began putting on a series of gold bracelets. "Yes, I'm 'up to speed' . . . but I want you to understand up front that I get a portion of the money you're going to steal from Carlos. Your friends said I'd have to negotiate the amount with you. I want a million."

"A million? Lady, you got a quarter of a million in rocks and gold there. You get 250 G's if we pull it off, and that's being real generous on my part."

Bonita snapped the clasp of the gold Rolex she'd just put on. "Do you know anything about computers, Mr. Faircloud? How about the Internet? Do you know how to go online? Do you know how to use e-mail? I didn't think so. How about this: Do you know how your friends were planning to make Carlos move his money so you can get to it?

No? Well, I know all those things, Mr. Faircloud. One million dollars. That's the deal for my help."

Ted tossed the ball again. "You still have that pistol you shot the guy with?"

Bonita lowered the thick gold chain with the diamond pendant she was about to put on. "Uh ... yes, it's in my purse. Why?"

" 'Cause you're goin' to need it. When I walk out of here, there ain't goin' to be no op. My friend will have to find somebody else to do it. And guess what? He won't need you anymore—you'll be on your own. Ya see, the way I look at it, I'm the guy who's goin' to take all the chances. You? You'll be *online*, whatever that is. The deal is you get a quarter million or I forget the whole thing and walk out of here."

"You're bluffing me."

Ted began walking toward the steps. "Let me give you some advice. Get yourself a lot more bullets, and when you shoot the next guy, shoot him in the face, not the stomach. It's kinda messy but they don't stand there lookin' at you."

"Okay, half a million and I'll help you."

"A quarter," Ted said, coming to a halt. "That's it."

"You're a bastard, Faircloud."

"And your butt is hangin' out, Miss Rogers. Deal?"

"Oh, all right. Deal. Help me with this clasp, will you?"

Ted rolled his eyes but stepped toward her as she turned her back to him, holding both ends of the necklace. He took the ends and attached the small clasp. *Oh man, nothing like the smell of a sweaty woman. What the hell you doin', Ted? Get the hell away from her, man; she's workin' on you. She's a pro, remember?*

Ted backed up quickly. "You'd better fill me in on the details of the score."

"What's the matter, Faircloud, haven't you been around a woman lately? You're acting as if I were going to bite you."

"I've been around plenty of women, lady, just not many half-dressed queens."

"Get used to it, Faircloud. I like it that it bothers you.

Come on, follow me; the computer is in the office just off the great room."

Ted followed her with the dog at his side.

Bonita sat behind a desk and motioned to the computer and monitor to her front. "This is called a com-pu-ter. It lets you into the information superhighway and what is known as cyberspace."

"I know what it is, Miss Rogers. Lighten up on me, will ya? Just tell me how you're goin' to help me."

"Okay, as long as you don't ask me any more questions about Carlos and me. You wouldn't understand anyway. And no more of those tough-guy looks."

"Fine, but I have to know one thing before we start. You said I wasn't what you expected—what did you mean by that?"

Bonita shrugged. "I don't know, I guess I had it in my mind you'd be like Al Pacino or Alec Baldwin—you know, dark hair, smooth, dressed well."

"Hey, these are new Dockers."

"Yeah, but did you get that flowered shirt at a garage sale? It's about ten years out of style."

"I just got off the plane from Miami, Miss Queen. It's wrinkled is all."

"You asked me what I expected, I told you. You look like an over-the-hill jock, not a hit man. Alec Baldwin you're not."

Alec Baldwin? I could take that lightweight pretty boy down with one hand. Taking in a breath, Ted spoke evenly. "Okay, Miss Rogers, I'm no Alec Baldwin. Please tell me about the score. I know it has something to do with a company and the bank in Dahlonega, but that's all I know. My friend was goin' to give me the details later."

Bonita motioned behind her. "Pull up a chair. Have you ever heard of a company here in Georgia known as the Yona Group?"

"Yona is the name of a mountain near Dahlonega—is it a group of tree huggers who want people to stay off the mountain?"

"Not even close. This group launders money for Carlos through their business."

"Here in Georgia?"

"In Dahlonega, Georgia, to be exact, and in the Dahlonega bank is just over six million dollars of Carlos's money. Your friend was very smart in figuring out how to make Carlos want to move it. It's simple really. The Yona Group is engaging in illegal business practices. They're monopolizing and price fixing, which are violations of antitrust laws. Your friends anonymously sent the information about the group's illegal practices to your Georgia senator, Stephen Goodnight, who happens to be on the Senate committee for fair trade. Your friends sent the information over the computer using e-mail—sent properly, it can't be traced. Anyway, it worked. The senator appointed a lawyer in his office, a Matthew Wentzel, who started a preliminary investigation. Wentzel confirmed that the information was accurate and just last week asked the FBI and the Federal Trade Commission to take over the investigation. We know all this because your friend kept in contact with the senator's investigator by e-mail, anonymously, of course. The investigator wanted your friend to come forward and reveal himself, but of course, that didn't happen. I'm now the one who keeps in contact with Matthew, the senator's investigator—look here at the screen. That's the message he left for me. I'm known only as C. Citizen; C for Concerned. See, Matthew says I should now contact Special Agent Paul Eddings with any additional information that might help the case. Eddings is in the Atlanta FBI field office, and these letters are the agent's e-mail address."

Ted paled. "Wait a minute. If the FBI moves on the Yona Group, they'll freeze all their assets. How is Mendez goin' to move his money?"

"Not a problem," Bonita said. "Your friends didn't give the investigator any information about Carlos's being in business with the Yona Group. You see how it works now? Matthew Wentzel, the investigator, only knows about the Yona Group's other illegal business practices; he doesn't know anything about their laundering Carlos's money. When the FBI starts questioning the group's leaders about their activities, Carlos will panic. He'll have to get his money out before the feds find out about the dirty money. That's when you take it—when it's on the move."

"How long before the feds make their move?" Ted asked. He was impressed by the plan and the woman's knowledge.

"According to the senator's investigator, the FBI just appointed Eddings as the case officer. It will be a week or so before Eddings actually takes over and gets the ball rolling."

"A week? I need more time than that to get my crew trained. And I still need the weapons and equipment."

Bonita swiveled her head around, looking at him in disbelief. "Don't tell me you're not ready. Your friends told me you were all set to do it."

"I *was* ready, but I lost two of my men last week in a car accident. I need more time."

"Well, the plan's not slowed down any; it's moving faster. Two days ago a truck arrived here with boxes marked 'Fishing Equipment.' I think it's the things you're looking for. I had the boxes put in storage in Cumming. You'd better give your boys the crash course and get them ready fast. Once Carlos learns about the investigation, that money is gone."

Ted looked up at the ceiling as if searching for divine guidance. A long moment passed before he lowered his gaze to Bonita. "We'll be ready."

Bonita studied his rugged face before speaking. "You really are going to do this, aren't you?"

Ted thought he saw pity in her eyes. "Yeah, I plan on doing it. Six million isn't chicken feed."

"I'm not talking about the money; I mean your taking on Carlos. It's suicide, you know. I told your friends it was impossible—he's too well protected."

Still feeling uncomfortable with her look, Ted averted his eyes to the monitor. "I thought you wanted him out of the picture so you could get on with your life?"

"With a quarter million I can go someplace he won't find me. I suggest you take the money and run, too, Faircloud. He'll kill you."

Ted shook his head. "There's no place we could go and truly be safe unless you don't mind living with Eskimos. Mendez won't rest until he finds out who took his money. It has to be that way for players like him. He has to make an example so others won't try it."

"You're a bigger fool than I thought, then," Bonita said.

Ted patted the dog's head. "Yeah, I've been told that before. I gotta go and get my buddy and check those boxes of fishing equipment. I'll drop by tomorrow and we'll go over what you know about Mendez. You want me to pick up some things for you, like maybe a robe or something?"

Bonita began to shake her head but instead said, "Movies. I really like movies. Would you rent some recent videos for me? The TV doesn't have HBO."

"Yeah, sure, no problem. I'll get the lion hunter here a couple of bones, too. See ya." Ted rose and began walking toward the door leading to the great room.

Bonita stood. "Hey, hold it a sec." She picked up a key from the desk and tossed it to him. "That's the key to the storage shed in the U-Store-It in Cumming. And I'm sorry about calling you a fool. Who am I to call anybody that, right? It's . . . it's just that I know Carlos. He's smart, Faircloud, very smart, and he's surrounded himself with men who know what they're doing."

Ted dipped his chin and was about to go when Bonita stepped closer. "I'm trying to apologize, Faircloud."

"Yeah, well, don't. You were right, I am a fool. And don't tell me how smart Mendez is—he can't be that smart if he thought he needed somebody other than you to make him happy."

"Are you saying that to make me feel better?" Bonita's face wore the beginning of a smile.

Ted shrugged and started walking toward the door again. "I was sayin' what I think Alec Baldwin woulda said. Pretty smooth, huh?"

Bonita watched him until he disappeared. She leaned over and patted Baby's head. "What d'ya think? Yeah, me, too. I think he's okay . . . for a damn fool."

CHAPTER 3

Duluth, Georgia

Virgil Washington took a dirt road that led to the river. A few minutes later he pulled into a sandy, tree-lined driveway and saw a trailer house just up ahead. Parking alongside a white Lincoln, he climbed out of his truck and walked to the wooden porch attached to the trailer.

Seated in a lawn chair on the porch, Ted smiled at Washington, who was dressed in overalls. He had guessed Washington would be the first to arrive. Virgil had a workingman's ethic; he knew what being responsible was.

Ted waited until Virgil reached the steps before getting up. "How come you didn't get a newer pickup? That Ford is ten years old."

Virgil glanced over his shoulder at the truck. "It'll do. I used the rest of the money you gave me for the down payment on the house for my mama."

"How much was the house?"

"Thirty-one five. It's air-conditioned, even got some trees and room for a garden. My mama likes to garden. I bought the little ones a swing set and built 'em a sandbox."

Ted shook Virgil's hand. "There's coffee inside in the kitchen, and some doughnuts. Help yourself. We're waitin' on another recruit like yourself."

Virgil paused and looked around. Nice, he thought. Huge pine trees, no underbrush, and the river only fifty yards away. The big trailer sat in the shade of a towering pine, and behind it was the poured-concrete foundation of what looked like a medium-size house. The wood-frame skeleton had already been partially assembled, and stacked wood sat nearby in neat piles.

"Nice big lot," Virgil said. "Nice and quiet, no neighbors. Whose house it gonna be?"

"It was going to be a lawyer's here in town but his ol' lady wanted one style and he wanted another. They argued for a year and finally divorced over it. He sold the place to me real cheap."

Nodding, Virgil disappeared inside the trailer. Minutes later he dipped a doughnut into his coffee cup as he sat in a lawn chair on the porch. He gave Ted a side glance. "What were you in the machine?" he asked.

Gazing out toward the river, Ted said, "The SEALs. It was good duty, but like you, I ran into a little trouble." Ted stood as a new Ford Ranger pickup pulled into the drive. "Looks like you're goin' to meet another member of the detachment."

"Is it the other new guy?" Virgil asked.

"Naw, it's Glenn. He's an old SEAL bud of mine. He quit his job a couple of months ago to help me run the op."

Glenn Henderson got out of his truck, shut the door, and walked toward the porch with a smile. "I hope you have coffee, Teddy. I need some java bad. This must be the SF guy you talked about?"

Ted motioned to Virgil. "Yeah, Glenn. Meet Virgil."

Virgil stood and shook the bearded man's hand. Like Ted, the guy was in good shape and in his forties, but those were the only things they had in common. Glenn had smart written all over him. His dark brown hair was styled, his beard was neatly trimmed, and he knew how to dress. Everything was understated, from the baggy off-brown slacks, belt with silver buckle, starched faded jean-style shirt, to loafers with no socks. Yeah, he had Mr. Casual GQ down perfect, Virgil thought.

"A distinct pleasure to meet you, Virgil," Glenn said.

"Same here," Virgil responded with a soft smile, because Mr. Casual's greeting came out genuine.

Ted threw his arm over the former SEAL's shoulder. "Which one you take home last night?"

Glenn frowned. "Come on, Ted. A gentleman doesn't talk about his lady friends."

Ted released his grip from his friend's shoulder. "Ah, hell, I bet it was that redhead. . . . Get yourself some coffee and join us. We're waiting on the last recruit to show up."

Glenn shook his head. "I'll take the coffee but then I better get up to Dahlonega and make a recon. After what you told me last night, I want to be ready."

Ted nodded, smiled. "You're going to check out the local action up there, too, aren't ya?"

"Come on, Teddy, you know I'm celibate."

"Yeah, you're celibate. That's like Madonna saying she's shy. Give me a break, this is Teddy, your pard."

Glenn sighed and gave Virgil a conspiratorial smile. "Teddy thinks all I care about is women. He's right, of course, but I put up with it because I know he can't help himself. It was a pleasure meeting you, Virgil. I'd better skip the coffee and go on before Teddy asks if I'm wearing clean underwear in case I'm in an accident. He was my platoon leader and real mother-hen type, always pecking." Glenn slapped Ted's chest and grinned. "I did put on clean underwear for the trip. See you, buddy."

Watching the pickup roll down the gravel drive, Virgil glanced at Ted. "I guess I shouldn't ask what that was about, huh?"

Ted shrugged. "Sure, you can ask. Glenn is goin' to recon our score sight. Dahlonega is just up the road about thirty miles. We got info that the score may go down in a week or so. We're getting ready."

Virgil glanced over his shoulder. "So this is where I'll be stayin' until it goes down?"

"This place? Naw, I got you somethin' better. You'll stay in Atlanta in a supernice apartment complex. Glenn lives there and really digs it."

"He sure dresses sharp . . . looks sophisticated. No wonder women want some of his action."

"Yeah, Glenn always dresses like that, but it's not just the clothes the women like. He's got a gift. I don't know what it is with him, but he can talk the talk that always works. Never could figure it out. We walk into a bar on a hunt and the damn guy scores every time without even tryin'. Me, I end up with the ones that only look good after five beers. Not Glenn; he gets a looker right off. The guy really pisses me sometimes for that, you know what I mean?"

Virgil nodded. "Yeah."

Ted shifted his gaze to his new recruit. "You a ladies' man, Virg?"

"Could never afford to be. I had an ol' lady when I was in the machine . . . picked her up during a tour in Korea. Man, don't make that mistake. Korean gals are out for one thing—more things. No sooner I get her to Fort Bragg, she wants her mama and sister to come over. Within six months I got a house full of her relatives all jabbering slope and eatin' kimche. Man, that stuff stinks. And party? Man, the woman could party hearty. America was too much for her . . . couldn't get enough of it. Big-screen TV, clothes, car, jewelry, she had to have it all. She didn't marry me for me, Ted, she married a ticket to ride on the American dream."

"So, what happened?"

"She OD'd on the U.S. of A. Read too much *Cosmo* and saw too much Oprah. She thought she could do better than a sergeant first class and started messin' with officers. One thing I draw the line at is messin' with officers. This 82nd Airborne West Point lieutenant thought she was foxy, right? He was sneakin' around snoopin' and poopin', thinkin' he was cool about it. But shit, man, I'm a bad SF team sergeant with years of experience snoopin' and poopin'. He was dumb, really dumb, thinkin' he was cool and could out-snoop me. I caught them in his new car, a Mustang convertible no less. You shoulda seen his face when I laid my Beretta barrel on his forehead. He shit his pants—not cool anymore, uh-uh, Mr. West Point wasn't cool anymore."

"Why didn't you pop him?"

"Couldn't do it. Mr. Cool fainted on me. I couldn't kill a

guy who had fainted on me. And anyways, the ol' lady was jumpin' around the seat like a chicken with its head cut off, 'cept she was screamin' slope. Never saw anything like it. There she was half naked, throwin' herself around, squealin' and screamin' and jumpin' this way and that. I couldn't get her to stay still long enough to punch her out. I thought, screw it, she deserved fainted Mr. Cool West Point."

"That's heavy, Virg. I can see it, you know. I can see the whole thing in my mind—but a Mustang? How'd they screw in a Mustang?"

Virgil shrugged. "She was double-jointed, could squat on a dime. I watched them for a while thinkin' to myself, Look at that, will ya? She was wantin' it bad from Lieutenant Cool in his shiny Mustang. What, she didn't have a big-screen TV already? She thinkin' Lieutenant Cool made more than a sergeant first class with seventeen years?"

"She stay with the lieutenant after they busted you?"

"Uh-uh, that officer got into big trouble, too."

"She go back to Korea?"

"What, and leave Oprah? Man, she wasn't goin' to leave the train. I heard when I was in the joint she married some leg first sergeant. She's ridin' that train again, her and her family all ridin' the dream train. Poor ol' top sergeant don't know, man. She'll ride him to death and get herself another ticket."

Sighing heavily, Ted shook his head. "That's sad, Virg. I'm sorry, man."

Virgil dunked his doughnut again. "It's all over. I got my own ride now, right? So tell me about your 'misunder-standing' when you were in the machine. You bust an officer or somethin'?"

"No, nothin' that cool. I was too gung ho for that. I was a badass leading petty officer. Six years ago we had a mission down south, one of those surveillance missions on a suspected drug runner. It was a joint thing, us, the DEA, and the Air Force. Problem was, the DEA was in charge. They don't know shit about military ops. Anyway, they tell me to make an insertion just off this island close to Hondo. It was a setup; when we got into the bay, the druggies were layin' for us. It was bad. Six guys in my platoon bought it and three others including me were wounded. Guess who the DEA said fucked up? Yeah, me. In the board of inquiry I told 'em the DEA set us up. The DEA head guy said it wasn't so. They believed the DEA guy, and I got court-martialed. The Navy knew I got screwed on the deal, but still had to make it look good. I was busted down a grade and had to forfeit two months' pay—no bad time, though. But it was still over for me in the SEALs after that. You know how it is? When you're the best, you can't go back to being just a blue-water sailor. I unassed the Navy rather than degrade myself. That's when my wife left me."

"Why'd she do that?" Virgil asked.

"The money, I guess. She stuck around as long as I brought home the bacon is all I can figure. As soon as I was charged, she forgot about that 'till death do us part' thing. She split faster than a speedin' bullet and took the kids with her. She remarried about two years ago, some cracker in Texas. I figure the cowboy must be deaf. No way she could land another fish with that whine she's got unless the guy was deaf. Real high-pitched whine, like, 'Teddeeeee, I neeeed some new clothes. Come on, Tedeeee, give meeeee some moneeeeey.' Drove me crazy, Virg."

"You're a ladies' man now, right?"

Ted let out a sigh. "Naw, I'm not cool like Glenn. I don't have the patience for the talk ya gotta talk. Once we're done, I'll go on the hunt for a classy broad. Little League and soccer fields is where ya find 'em."

"Little League and soccer fields?"

"It's a sure thing, Virg. Who do you think drops little Johnny off at practice? Yeah, Mommy. Man, there are so many divorced, rich, classy mommies in Atlanta you wouldn't believe it. The key is joinin' the right league. Get yourself into the league that comes from the rich side of town, you know, the big house additions. Mommies drive up in Lexuses and Mercedes there. Weather gets nice and

Mommy watches her Johnny play ball and you can scope out the possibles, you know, cull the fat ones, ugly ones, and those with an attitude. Johnny tells ya if he has a dad or not so you know who your prospects are. Oh, hiya, Mrs. Classy, Johnny is doing real good, he's pickin' up the grounders great, or Johnny sure can kick that ball. Johnny tells me you're divorced . . . that's too bad. Look, I know it must be tough, you havin' to drive Johnny to practice. I'd be glad to drop by and pick him up for you and drop him off after practice. Man, that line works like a charm, Virg. Gets you in the door, so to speak. I'm tellin' ya, Little League and soccer fields is where it's at."

Virgil pulled on his chin. "Yeah, but it's kind of seasonal, isn't it? And when you learn to play soccer?"

"I don't know shit about soccer, but how hard can it be? All ya gotta do is kick a ball."

Before Virgil could respond a dark green six-year-old Camaro pulled into the long drive. Ted lifted an eyebrow. "Looks like our pretty boy made it after all. You keep an eye on him for me, Virg. He's Cuban, and you know how they are. He's a former Ranger and Delta Force guy, so he has his act together, but he ran into trouble and got kicked out. I don't know what for, but maybe it's 'cause of that hot blood of his."

Virgil gave Ted a deadpan look. "Delta guys have to take a psychological examination. I know; I had buddies go into Delta. Delta guys stay in control, Latino or not."

Ted shrugged. "Let's find out." He stood just as Ramon Lopez stepped out of the Camaro. "Up here, Ramon. Hey, I thought I told ya to get some decent clothes."

Wearing sharkskin slacks and a white shirt without a collar, Ramon took off his Ray-Ban shades and motioned to himself. "This is good shit, man. Sears' best, on sale. Check out the watch, a real chronograph with all the little numbers and shit, man. And check out my Florsheim shoes. Do I pass or do I gotta go to Wal-Mart?"

"At least you lost the ponytail. Get up here and meet

Virgil. He's an ex–sergeant first class out of the SF. You two are going to be training together."

Ramon eyed the black man wearing overalls. "He don't look SF to me . . . looks like a dumbass farmer."

Unfazed, Virgil stuck out his hand. "Virgil Washington."

Ramon paused before taking his hand and spoke coldly. "Ramon Juan Delgado y Lopez."

Ted spoke up, thinking he had better explain Virgil's appearance. "Ramon, Virgil here was in Leavenworth for the past six years for a misunderstanding of sorts. They busted him for attempted murder of an officer. Virgil caught a lieutenant banging his wife in a Mustang convertible."

Ramon looked into Virgil's eyes and slowly shook his head. "In a Mustang? No way."

Virgil shrugged. "She was Korean, could squat on a dime."

"Attempted murder, man? Why didn't you do the L-tee?" Ramon asked.

"He fainted."

Ted motioned to the third lawn chair. "Sit, Ramon. We were just talkin' about you. Tell us what really happened that got you busted out."

Ramon gave Ted a pained expression. "Ah, man, I don't like talkin' about it."

"Come on, Ramon, we're all being honest here," Ted said.

Ramon sighed. "I . . . I got caught making it with the C.O.'s wife."

Ted grinned. "The commander's ol' lady? Come on. Don't shit us."

"It's not a war story, man. I was on my way up. I was going to be promoted to E-seven, but man, she was one hot lady."

"How in the hell you meet the C.O.'s wife?" Ted asked, not believing a word.

"I worked out a lot and she was there workin' out in the post gym, too. She was an aerobics instructor . . . lookin' good, man . . . had a body that made you sweat just lookin' at her. She came on to me, thought it was cool flirtin' with me, and her old man being the C.O. I couldn't help myself.

She was a lady, man . . . a real lady, but really fucked up in the head. I could tell, man. Dressed like a high school girl, ya know. Short skirts, tight blouses, always showin' off her body, and she had it to show, man. I'm talkin' tits out to here, man, and legs and ass you wouldn't believe. She got off on people starin' at her all the time. I should have known, man."

"The C.O. caught you doin' it to her?" Ted asked, warming up to the yarn.

"No, man, her *mama* caught us! Her mama drove down from Richmond a day early and walks into the house and hears her moanin' and groanin' while we're gettin it on in the bedroom. I'm just about to get it, and Mama walks in. Like I said, the foxy lady is *muy loco* 'cause she keeps humpin' me, man, like it doesn't make any difference to her. The mama is yelling for her to stop but she just pumps me faster. I'm tellin' ya, man, it was bad. I couldn't do anything but lay there and let her go for it. She finally gets off on me and then asks Mama if *she* wants some of my action. Mama says she's going to shoot me and leaves the room to find a gun. I booked, man. Left with only my pants."

"Oh, shit, then the C.O. finds out?" Ted asked.

"Oh, yeah. Mama ratted us out, but says I was raping her daughter. It was a done deal in two days, man. 'Course they couldn't pin the rape charge because she drove me to the house, but they had other shit they could use, conduct unbecoming and all that. I had a choice of court-martial or leave for the good of the service."

"Was she good?" Ted couldn't resist. "I mean she sure as hell had better been."

Ramon frowned and shook his head. "I could have been an E-seven and you askin' if she was good?"

Virgil patted the Cuban's arm. "Everything happens for the best . . . we're ridin' the train again, Ray. Big money and doin' what we do best. We gonna be ridin' high again."

Ramon gave the black man a cold stare. "You turn fag in the pen?"

Virgil wrinkled his brow. "Naw, Ray, I was an E-seven

sergeant first class, and it wasn't all that great is all. Ya didn't miss nothin' by not makin' the rank."

"My name is Ramon, not *Ray*, man. You got that?"

"I knew a Ramon in the pen. He *was* a fag," Virgil said, looking into the Cuban's eyes, showing he wasn't the least intimidated. "I can use one of your other names if you want. José, Juan, Julio—what were they again?"

Ramon saw he wasn't going to bluff the older man but still kept his bad-news stare on him. "You call me what you want, Farmer John."

Ted relaxed; it would be all right now. The jockeying for position in the pack was something he had expected, but not quite so soon. A little snarl here and a nip there was just their way of staking out ground. *Now I gotta know who wants to go all the way,* he said to himself as he stood.

"Guys, it's time we talked about the op. . . . I told both of you it was going to be a score. It is, but now we have a change—we've got an added mission. The good news for both of you is that upon successful completion of both jobs you're both gonna be very rich men. How's a million bucks sound?"

Virgil whistled but Ramon stared hard at Ted. "What's the added mission, man?"

Ted returned the stare. "We're going to knock off a big player."

"Who?" Ramon asked suspiciously.

"Carlos Mendez."

Ramon backed up with a look of shock. "Mendez? You fuckin' loco, man?"

Ted wrinkled his brow. "Naw, I'm not crazy. We got good intell on the guy, his schedule, location of guards, everything we need. We can do it."

Ramon threw up his hands. "Mendez? I knew this was too good to be true! And shit, I cut off my ponytail, too, man. No way, not even for a million bucks."

Virgil sat calmly in his chair and slowly turned, looking at Ted. "You sure the intell on this player is good?"

"Yeah, it's all recent stuff," Ted said.

Ramon stared at Virgil. "Don't listen to this squid, man. It doesn't matter what he has. Mendez has an army protecting him and they all carry serious shit, man. I know all about Mendez. I worked for a player who was Mendez's competitor. Mendez is big shit, man, the biggest in Miami. He has people on the payroll everywhere. Even if we make the hit we'll never get out alive. He lives in a walled-in estate on Key Biscayne that'd take a division to storm . . . no way we can get in."

"Yeah, but he's like you, Ramon," Ted said. "He's a sucker for strange poontang. He's got him some broads on the side he visits on his yacht. That's where we'll hit him."

Ramon smiled without humor. "You're crazy if you think that makes a difference. We'd still have to neutralize about twenty people to get to him. Where you goin' to get that kind of equipment and firepower, man?"

Ted motioned to the stacks of wood on the cement foundation. "Come on, let me show you somethin'." Without hesitation Ted began to walk toward the foundation. Virgil stood and patted Ramon's back. "I think for a chance at a million you ought to take a look at what the man has."

Ramon lowered his head and followed.

Ted stood on the foundation and pointed at a tarp as the two men approached. "I have some friends who gave me everything we might need to make the score. It's also enough to do the hit." He bent over and pulled back the tarp, revealing a trunk. He unlocked the padlock and swung back the lid. "This is just a sample of what we got."

Virgil whistled, but Ramon leaned over for closer inspection. He picked up a silenced Mac-10 and pulled back the charging handle. "It's new," he said, and looked at the other weapons and equipment. "You didn't get this stuff at an army surplus store, man; it's all illegal. Who are these friends of yours?"

"You don't need to know," Ted said.

Ramon put the submachine gun back in the trunk and shook his head. "You're connected, man. You lied to me."

Ted stepped closer to the Cuban. "I don't lie to my teammates, you get that straight right now. I am *not* connected; I have friends, I told you that. That's just a sample of the hardware. I also have claymores, grenades, smoke, frags, incendiary, and gas. We've got demo, electric and nonelectric blasting caps, det cord, the newest night-vision gear, and all the soft gear we'll need. We've got good intell and I have the makings of a plan that'll be finalized in a week. So, are you in or out?"

Ramon looked into Ted's eyes. "What about the score? You got a good plan?"

"It's a pure military operation that we can handle with no problem. The hit is different; like I said, I don't lie. Hitting Mendez is goin' to take pros with balls. In two days you both will have new IDs and a passport. Once it's over you can skate to wherever you wanna go 'cause you don't exist anymore. Now, I'll ask one more time—are you in or out?"

Virgil put his hand on the Cuban's shoulder. "It's goin' to be a ride, Ray. Don't miss this train."

Ramon stared at the trunk a moment before raising his head. "I'm in."

Ted shifted his eyes to Virgil. "And you? You have any second thoughts?"

"Me? I told ya, I'm ridin' this train. I like the benefits. Hey, Ray, Ted here is puttin' us up in some nice apartments in Atlanta. Isn't that right, Ted?"

"Yeah, they're nice all right. The place has a pool and hot tub, and Glenn says it's crawling with career ladies. Nothin' but the best for my team; we go first class. But enough on that for now. We got work to do. We gotta go and get passport photos made for your new IDs. Then when we get back I've got manuals for you to look over on the newest stuff we got—laser sights and the new lightweight night-vision gear and the individual commo gear you'll have. It's high-speed gear, guys; you gotta know it inside and out. We'll start trainin' on the stuff tomorrow."

Ramon motioned to Virgil. "What about Farmer John, here? You goin' to get him some threads, man? The dude looks like he fell off the turnip truck."

Virgil patted Ramon's back. "Check out Ted, Ray—you think he knows about clothes? Look at that Hi-wiian shirt. Is that an antique or what? Uh-uh, I'm gonna wait and have Glenn square me away on threads. Glenn is definitely a clothes man."

"Glenn? Who is he, man?" Ramon asked.

Ted motioned to the trunk. "You'll meet him tonight at the apartments. He's second in command of this team. Grab that and load it in the back of my Lincoln; we got work to do."

Ramon sighed as he leaned over to grab one end of the trunk. "Guess I'm a buck-ass private again, Virg."

Virgil smiled as he picked up the other end. "Yeah, but you goin' to be one *rich-ass* private, Ray. This train is takin' us to the promised land."

CHAPTER 4

One week later

Sitting at the trailer kitchen table eating a sandwich, Glenn Henderson heard footsteps behind him and turned.

Ted approached with a quizzical frown. "You're still here? . . . Ahh, man, did you use the last of the mayonnaise?"

"I had some catching up to do," Glenn said around a mouthful of ham sandwich.

"Like what, eat up the rest of my food? Christ'a'mighty, Glenn, it's past seven. Why didn't you go back to Atlanta with the guys?"

Glenn swallowed and shifted around in his chair. "I stuck around so I could talk to you when they weren't around."

Ted smiled as he leaned against the counter. "I know what you want to talk about. . . . They're doin' really good, aren't they? Today they proved to me they knew their gear inside and out—they're ready. I think we can slack off on the training and let 'em relax a little. When you get back to the apartments, you can tell 'em tomorrow is free time—they can go shoppin' or take in a flick or something."

Glenn nodded. "They're getting real tight, Teddy. Looks like just the right chemistry because those two have become really close. Maybe them both being Army grunts is it—you know, done a lot of the same things and seen the same places. Whatever it is, we don't have to worry about them not working together; I can hardly separate them."

"We're a team, Glenn. I knew they'd gel once we got

47

started with the training. Go on home, and tomorrow you take the day off too."

Ted pushed off the counter, heading for the door, but Glenn reached out and touched his friend's arm. "I didn't stick around to talk about the guys, Teddy. I stuck around to talk to you about that woman. You're going up to see her again, aren't you?"

Ted came to a halt in front of the door. "I'm going up to talk to her about the plans of the yacht, Glenn."

Sniffing the air, Glenn said, "You're wearing cologne— you *never* wear cologne. Don't bullshit me, Teddy. You've been up to see her every evening for the past week. You're getting hooked on her, aren't you?"

"Look, Glenn, I gotta know everything there is to know about Mendez. It's business, not pleasure. Anyway, a looker like her ain't goin' to mess around with an old ex-squid like me."

"Business, huh? I stayed around last night after you left, Teddy. I was reading the stuff Gee gave you on Mendez and must have dropped off. I woke up around midnight on the couch, and guess what? You weren't back. That tells me she's either a really slow talker or you're up there playing house with the Mendez bimbo."

"She's no bimbo. Don't ever say that again," Ted snarled.

Glenn held up his hands as if surrendering. "Sorry, but as your friend I have to warn you about her. I haven't seen this woman but I know all I need to know about her if she was Mendez's sweetie pie. She's a pro, Teddy. Women like her are like mistletoe—they feed off a host to live . . . they'll say and do anything to keep attached to whatever will keep them alive."

"Christ'a'mighty, Glenn, mistletoe? Why would she attach herself to me?"

"I'm just telling you, don't believe a word she says if she's making eyes and puts moves on you. Mistletoe types don't have feelings; it's only about survival to them."

"What is this all really about, Glenn? You worried I'm goin' to violate operational security? Come on, you know me better than that. I've never said a word to her about you or the guys. She doesn't know anything about the team and never will."

Glenn pinned his friend with a stare. "You said yourself, Gee was using her as the fall guy if the op goes sour. She'll give you up in a heartbeat, Teddy. She's the only one outside of Gee and his people who knows you're in this. Don't get close to her; it could be fatal."

Ted raised his index finger. "One, the op ain't goin' sour. Two, she hasn't made any eyes or moves on me. And three, it's not what you think. Yeah, I go up there a lot . . . I like being around her. . . . Ahh, now don't give me that look. We talk and watch movies is all . . . it's nothin'. I don't know how to explain it. I feel comfortable around her, ya know? Yeah, she looks good, but it's not that. It's—It's just nice sittin' and talkin' to her."

Glenn rose from his chair. "Teddy, think a minute. She was Mendez's honey. You think for a second she was forced to stay with him? Come on, she's a pro, Teddy, and pros are all actresses. They make you feel like there's nobody else in the world. And even if that's not enough to make you keep your distance, think about this: If the op gets blown, Gee can't let her live . . . she knows too much. I'm telling you as a friend, keep your distance from her . . . nothing good can happen."

Ted grasped the door handle. "I'll see ya day after tomorrow. You and the guys are off tomorrow. And Glenn, I know she's a pro . . . it's just nice bein' nice, too, for a change."

Ted opened the door and walked out.

Lake Lanier

"Hiya, Mr. Teddy," the tiny black woman said as Ted entered the foyer.

"Hello, Halley. Here's that can of Skoal you wanted." Ted took the snuff can from the shopping bag he was holding.

"Ain't ya sweet for rememberin' . . . 'preciate that, Mr. Teddy. Mrs. Stone waitin' on ya in the great room. Ya had your supper?"

"I stopped off and ate before comin' up, Halley, thanks. Guess I'd better not keep her waitin'."

"Mr. Teddy, talk to her, will ya? She was out sunnin' herself on the deck today in her birthday suit again. Gets Duwane all flustered when she does that . . . 'sides, it ain't proper. Talk to her please . . . it jus' ain't proper layin' out there naked as a jaybird."

Ted sighed. "I'll try, Halley."

Still holding the bag, Ted strode down the hallway. Once at the steps, he saw the dog coming and leaned over. "Glad to see me, huh? Oh, you wanna know what's in the bag, huh? Some damn lion hunter you are—lion hunters shouldn't want poodle treats. Okay, okay, here."

"You've spoiled him rotten," Bonita said as she rose from the couch. "He bugs me all day for those damn treats."

Ted walked down into the room, taking two videos from the bag. "I rented some really good flicks for you tonight."

"I hope you didn't get more Arnold Schwarzenegger stuff. I really wanted to see *Sleepless in Seattle* again."

"Come on, Bonita, you just saw it two days ago and cried all through the ending. Looky here, I got ya Arnold in *Predator*, *and* I got the sequel, *Predator II*."

Bonita winced. Ted grinned as he handed her the two cases. "Just kiddin'. They're both chick flicks. Yeah, and one of 'em is *Sleepless*."

Bonita kissed his cheek. "You're a pussycat, Teddy Faircloud. Thank you."

The heat already beginning to build inside him, Ted quickly backed away.

"Come and sit beside me, Teddy. I've got popcorn and a beer all ready," Bonita said as she walked toward the couch.

"Bonita, I gotta go."

"What?" Bonita said, turning toward him with a hurt look.

"I can't stay around like I have the past week. I need to finish some work on the plan."

Bonita studied his eyes. "What's going on, Teddy? Have you got a girlfriend you haven't told me about?"

"I have work to do is all," Ted said, forcing himself to keep eye contact.

She held his eyes for a long moment before finally lowering her head. "You've got that X-ray look, Teddy, like you're trying to look through me. What is it? You having second thoughts about me again?"

"Naw, it's not that, Bonita. It's just I've been hangin' around too much. I gotta stay more focused is all."

"Am I distracting you from business, Teddy?"

Backing up a step, Ted stammered, "Uh . . . I . . . well, yeah, sometimes you do."

She moved closer. "What do I do that distracts you, Teddy?"

"You're doin' it now with that look you're givin' me. Stop it, will ya?"

"This look? What kind of look is it, Teddy?"

"You know."

"No, I don't. Tell me," she said, standing just inches away, looking into his eyes.

Ted backed up another step. "Lonely . . . it's a lonely look," he said, vowing to himself to regain control.

"I am lonely, Teddy. And I was wrong about you . . . you *are* smooth, very smooth, in your own way. I like it; I like it a lot."

Exhaling, Ted reached out, took hold of her shoulders, spun her around, and began walking her toward the couch. "Uh-uh, you sit down and watch your movies. I'm leavin'."

She angrily shook off his grip. "What is it with you? I thought we had something going."

"We do, an op."

"That's not what I meant and you know it."

"See ya." Ted was feeling good about taking charge.

As he began walking away, Bonita said, "Don't you want to know about the message I got from the FBI agent?"

Ted stopped and turned around. "What are you talking about?"

"A message. He left it for me. I'm *C. Citizen*, remember?"

"He can track it back to you?"

"No, he doesn't know my e-mail address. He left the message for me in a closet, a room that only I can get into because I know the password. Anyway, you'd better start watching that bank. His questions tell me they're about to move on the Yona Group. He wants me to meet him in person, and he guarantees my safety."

"It's started? Okay, I'll get my guys watchin' it."

Bonita moved toward him with a questioning stare. "It's not about the money, is it?"

"Huh?"

"We've talked every night for the past week and you've never mentioned the money once. What is it, Ted; why are you doing this?"

Ted turned away from her and walked toward the hallway.

Bonita followed him. "Why, Ted? It's going to get you killed. You know that, don't you?"

Ted stopped when he reached the steps, and faced her again. "Money isn't everything, Bonita. Look at your exboyfriend. He has enough to buy Florida, but he can't live like other people. The asshole needs an army to protect him."

Bonita searched his eyes as she moved closer. "Why, Teddy? Why are you putting your life in danger to try and kill him if it's not for the money?"

Ted avoided her stare for a moment by leaning over and patting Baby's head. "Enjoy the movies, Bonita, and don't forget to rewind them. They charged me a fee last time. I'll see ya tomorrow."

Ted turned, but Bonita was close enough now to grab his arm. "Don't go, Teddy. Please stay awhile. I'm sorry. I won't ask any more questions. Just stay with me awhile."

Ted looked into her pleading eyes.

Bonita suddenly released her grip and narrowed her welling eyes. "Go on, Faircloud. I can see it in your face. You think all I care about is the money. You're right, damn you. It is *all* I care about. I'm just what you thought I was, an over-the-hill whore. Wait, take these." Bonita stormed over to the coffee table, picked up the two video cassettes, marched back, and slammed them into his chest. "Take these with you! Don't do anything nice for me again. I'm just a whore; don't waste your time!"

"Ah, come on, Bonita, don't get—"

"To hell with you, Faircloud! Baby, come here! Get away from him. Go on, Faircloud, and don't worry—I'll do my job. You just do yours and don't screw it up. I want my money."

Not knowing what to say or do, Ted turned and walked up the steps, thinking to himself, *Uh-oh, I don't think that was acting.*

CHAPTER 5

11:10 A.M., Apalachicola River, Northern Florida

Stephen Goodnight, freshman senator from Georgia, patted his eldest son's shoulder as he stepped back to let him take the wheel of the forty-two-foot cruiser. "Keep her speed down, son; no telling what's around the next bend."

Twenty-six-year-old Chad Goodnight struck a stiff pose and elevated his chin. "Aye-aye, Captain Hornblower! Keep her slow as she goes. Ahoy, all hands, French fleet about! Beat to quarters! Clear the quarterdeck! Open the gun ports and sand the decks. Mr. Mike, fire as the guns bear!"

Mike Goodnight, at twenty-two the youngest son of the senator, rolled his eyes and stepped up beside his father. "Dad, I think the sun has gotten to Chad; or maybe it's the beer."

Chad glanced over his shoulder at his younger brother with narrowed eyes. "Belay that talk, Mr. Goodnight. Have you never read the Hornblower series? I'll not be havin' insubordination on the captain's ship. Captain, I think the ensign needs a good keelhauling."

The senator grinned. "Aye, and the cat-'o-nine-tails might lick his back as well."

Seated on the leisure deck behind the three men, Chad's wife, Susan, leaned closer to her mother-in-law and asked, "Is this a guy thing?"

Mary Rigney Goodnight, the senator's wife of thirty years, smiled and patted the attractive young woman's bare leg. "They're having a good time, Sue. It's good to see

Stephen smiling and laughing again. After a year in Washington I was afraid he had forgotten how."

Janice, Mike's girlfriend, scooted closer to the two women. "I had my doubts about this trip, Mary, but I think they all needed it. Just look at them. They're sunburned and acting like fools—it's wonderful. I'm glad the senator insisted we all come."

Mary held her smile. "I told Stephen we should all go to Disney World if he wanted us to get away for a while, but he was set on this 'expedition,' as he calls it. He said it would be just like the jungle cruise in Disney World but it would last three days instead of thirty minutes. I think he was right. We haven't seen another living soul or any semblance of civilization since we broke camp this morning. I don't know about you girls, but I'm in desperate need of at least the sight of a shopping mall. Heck, I'd settle for a 7-Eleven."

Janice laughed and put her hand to her forehead as she looked toward the banks of the river. "Not even a golden arch."

Drawn by the laughter, the senator turned and stepped down to the deck, where the women were sunning themselves. Dressed in tennis shorts and a dirty University of Georgia T-shirt, he flopped down by his wife and gave her a gentle hug. "Are we havin' fun or what?"

Mary rolled her eyes. "Oh, yeah, lots of fun. Are you checkin' up on the rest of your crew, Captain Hornblower?"

"Aye, that I am, matey. Me and the lads be gettin' hungry and be wantin' to know what the wenches be cookin' after we sink the French fleet."

Mary shrugged. "As I remember, good Captain, you said *you* and your lads would be catching fish on this expedition. Well, where are they?"

Stephen's smile faded. "Ahh, heck, Mare, the darn fish are all Democrats and won't bite. How about puttin' some steaks out and marinating them? We'll put in about ten miles downriver and set up camp."

Janice canted her head. "We were thinking more along

the lines of pizza, Senator. Any towns up ahead where we could stop for carryout?"

The senator gave her a fake scowl. "No, fair wench, no towns up ahead. You don't eat *pizza* on an expedition. Just look out there at those tree-lined banks and this unpolluted river. You're witness to true, unspoiled native America; how could you possibly think of pizza?"

Janice shrugged as she did what she was told and looked toward the far bank. "Okay, how about a Long John Silver fish'o'more meal with french fries?"

The senator stood and barked, "Lads, they're talking insurrection here. Prepare the keelhaul lines!"

11:28 A.M., Georgetown, Washington, D.C.

Thirty-four-year-old Matthew Wentzel, staffer for Senator Stephen Goodnight, rolled off his assistant and tried to catch his breath. He was nude and his body gleamed with sweat.

Dana Cooper smiled as she ran her fingers over his damp chest. "Now, wasn't that better than walking along the canal?"

Matthew spoke between gasps. "A . . . a lot . . . better. Aren't . . . you winded?"

"You did all the work," she said huskily. "And it was great work, I might add."

Matthew was about to respond when a man's voice said, "I thought you two would never stop. Have you got everything, Dana?"

Before Matthew could react, a fat man stepped up and pressed a pistol barrel to his forehead. "Easy, Matt. Just lie back down and stay nice and quiet. You need your rest after all that rutting. Thata boy."

Matthew shook uncontrollably as he stared at the silenced pistol.

Glaring at the obese man but not the least embarrassed about being nude, Dana got up from the bed. "It took you long enough. He wanted to go for a stroll!"

The man wrinkled his brow as if apologetic. "I didn't want to walk in during the action—just didn't seem right. So, do you have everything?"

Dana nodded as she picked up her bra. "I have it all on disks. I erased the hard drives and the backups in the office, just the way you showed me."

"What about the paper files and documents?"

"All of it is in my car. They won't find anything about the investigation . . . I made sure of it. I even checked the computer here in his apartment, erased it, and reformatted all his disks. It's done; let's get out of here."

Trembling, Matthew tried to speak. "Wh-What is . . . is going on? Dana, what have you done?"

The fat man sighed. "You've been screwed, Matt. And you thought you were the screwer, didn't you? It doesn't work that way." The fat man squeezed the trigger. Matthew's head jerked back into the pillow from the impact of a .22 bullet that blew through his left eye. The killer casually lifted the weapon and pointed the barrel at Dana. "Sorry, honey, but I don't need you anymore."

The weapon coughed. With her hands still behind her to fasten the bra, she crumpled to the floor. The man stepped closer and fired another bullet into her head. He looked around the room, slid the pistol into his belt, picked up Dana's purse with his gloved hands, and seconds later had her car keys. Putting the purse back on the dresser, he put the keys in his pocket, pulled his pistol from his belt, and began unscrewing the silencer. A minute later he shut the apartment door and began walking down the steps, shaking his head in disgust.

Women, they're ten times worse than men. And they always talk about how much more sensitive they are. Dana gives me the key to his place, boffs the guy, and tells him how wonderful he is, knowing full well he's going to be offed, and that's sensitive? Not a tear for the guy, not even a wince when I pop him. She didn't even look, just kept putting on her bra as if he were nothing. She should have winced at least.

11:32 A.M., Apalachicola River, Northern Florida

Chad Goodnight steered the cruiser around the bend. A large bass boat lay up ahead just off a small island in mid-channel. On the craft's deck two men were waving their arms. "Dad, looks like we've got company on the river after all."

The senator nodded as he held his gaze steady on the distant boat. "Looks like they're in trouble; they've got their motor pulled out of the water . . . probably a busted prop."

Hearing the conversation, Mary rose from her cushioned seat. "What is it, dear?" she asked, putting her hand to her forehead to block the glare.

The senator motioned ahead. "A couple of fishermen who ran out of luck. We're going to stop and see if we can help them."

On the cruiser bow, Mike Goodnight yelled toward the fishermen, "What's the problem, guys?"

A tall, thin blond in his early thirties motioned to the motor. "The prop is fouled with wire. Sure glad you guys came by when you did. We were getting worried. Can I borrow a pair of pliers? I dropped mine in the river when I was trying to pull the wire free."

Chad reversed the engine to decrease their speed even more as Mike nodded and yelled back, "Sure, no sweat. Y'all catch anything?"

The blond grinned. "We've caught some nice stripers. We'll give you some for helping us."

Mike looked over his shoulder at his brother and father. "Looks like we can forget the steaks. Janice gets her fish'o'more after all."

The senator walked toward the cushioned seats. "I'll get the toolbox."

Janice got up so the senator could lift the hinged top of the seat and she headed for the cabin door. "I'll put the steaks back in the fridge. Mary, Sue, you want anything while I'm in the cabin?"

Mary lifted her empty bottle. "I'll take one more wine cooler while you're up."

Sue shook her head. "Nothing for me, thanks."

Janice opened the narrow hatchway door and stepped down into the cabin.

Paddling closer to the cruiser, the blond man placed a bag over his shoulder and lifted a stringer with eight stripers.

Mike tossed down a line to the sunburned blond and whistled. "Man, those are huge. What kind of bait are you using?"

"I'll show you. It's a new spinner. Here, take the stringer."

Mike took the stringer of fish from the man's hand and set them on the deck. He then offered his hand to the fisherman. "I'll help you up."

Smiling, the man grasped Mike's hand and swung himself up on deck just as the senator walked forward with a pair of pliers. Still smiling, the fisherman took the bag off his shoulder. "These new spinners make the fish go nuts. . . ." He reached in the bag, grasped a small Tech-9 machine pistol, and fired through the material. The burst of three rounds hit Mike in the chest, knocking him off the bow into the water. Turning, the killer shot Stephen Goodnight in the face with another burst. The back of the senator's head exploded outward, showering the Fiberglas deck with blood, brains, and skull fragments.

In the bass boat the other fisherman raised a Tech-9 and pointed it at Chad, who was frozen in horror. When he realized the weapon was aimed at him, Chad lunged for the throttle, but was suddenly thrown back as the gunman shot him in the neck. Blood gushed out of his wound as he staggered back toward the two women on the lower deck. Screaming, Mary stood and was showered with her oldest son's blood.

Sue saw the blond-haired killer running toward them and dove overboard just as he fired. Too afraid to move, Mary jerked spasmodically as bullets stitched her from crotch to neck. The killer looked over the side to finish the younger woman, but his companion was already shooting.

As soon as she surfaced, the water churned around Sue as if she were being pursued by piranha. Seconds later she floated facedown, her light brown hair billowing in the water as though caught in watery wind.

Stepping over Chad, who lay on the deck shaking in his final death throes, the blond man kicked in the hatchway door and stepped down into the cabin. Swinging his machine pistol left then right with his gaze, he saw no one, but sensed the presence of another. He leaned over, looked under the table, then began to rise. He heard a noise coming from the closet beside him, spun, and fired a burst into the door.

The first bullet missed, but the second creased Janice Ayers's forehead. The third entered the back of her head and exited above her left ear.

The blond man swung the door back, ready to fire again, but one look at the limp, bloody body told him the job was done. Lowering his weapon, he walked to the refrigerator and took out a beer.

As she knelt in the closet with her head resting against the interior wall, Janice Ayers understood what was going on. She had heard men talking as they dragged things into the cabin that had made soft thuds on the hatchway steps. Someone had even poked at her, but that had happened minutes ago or maybe hours, she wasn't sure as she tried to sit up. She felt so strange, almost as if she were floating underwater. She knew she was moving the way her mind had commanded, but it seemed as if her body was in slow motion and in a cloud. She was standing now in the cabin but couldn't remember how she got there. Something warm rolled over feet. Wiping the blood from her eyes, she saw it was water and it was already to her ankles. It was such a strange color, she thought, reddish like. . . . Slowly, she rolled her head and saw them lying stacked on top of one another on the cruiser's cabin floor. It took several long seconds before it registered it was really people and not pale mannequins. *Yes, there's Mike,* she thought. *I picked out those Nike shorts for him . . . and Mary, she was wearing that blouse . . . and the senator, he was wearing tennis shorts, wasn't he? Oh, there's poor Sue, and Chad . . . they should have at least put them together. So sad . . . so . . . sad.* Turning, Janice waded toward the cabin hatchway but saw that it was blocked by a mattress. "They don't want the bodies to float out," she said in a whisper. "I suppose I should die with them . . . yes . . . I should. I really should."

Janice touched her forehead then stared at the blood on her fingers. Her footing was becoming more difficult. *The stern is sinking,* she said to herself. *The boat is sinking and I can't get out. No, I don't want to die here. I want to live. I want to live. Must get this mattress out of the way first . . . there. Now try the door . . . good, it opens. Wait, Janice. WAIT! They may be out there watching. Think now, think. Stay by the door, and when the water comes up, push out and stay by the seat cushions that will float. Keep yourself submerged and just keep your nose and mouth above water, close to the cushions, so they won't see you. I can do this . . . I can do this.*

It was almost midnight, and the full moon cast a pale glow on the slow-moving river as an old ski boat made its way up the channel. Mounted on the bow of the boat, a spotlight shined close to the near bank. Seated behind the steering wheel on a plastic bucket, Tucker held a .22 rifle across his lap. He spat brown tobacco juice over the side, which partly splattered the dead, nine-foot alligator tied to the port cleats. "Nat, ya reckon we oughta start headin' back?"

Nat spoke over his shoulder as he shined the light farther upriver, looking for the telltale glow of an alligator's eyes. "Head toward that small island. We'll swing around it and check the other bank, then check out the mouth of Dead Lake . . . always gators hangin' 'round them banks. Get us just one more an' we'll be sittin' purty. Hand me some chaw, will— What the . . . ya see that?"

Tucker followed the beam of light that shone toward the island and gasped. "Oh, Lord." He throttled forward and steered toward the island, where the beam was shining on a partially nude white woman standing on the bank as if in a stupor.

Nat kept his light focused on the woman. "Ya reckon she's one of them crazies escaped outta that nuthouse upriver?"

"Could be . . . oh, Jesus, look at her face. She's dead and don't know it."

CHAPTER 6

Sunday, Columbus, Georgia

Special Agent Ashley Sutton slapped twice at the ringing phone before finding the handset. Rising slightly from her pillow, she looked at the digital clock on the nightstand and moaned. It was only a little past five A.M.. She spoke sleepily. "Ms. Sutton."

"Morning, Sutton, this is Tanner. We—"

"Eli! You're back!" she blurted in surprise as she sat up in bed. "How come you—"

"We've got a situation. Get dressed and get down here," he said. "I'm at Lawson Army Air Field at Fort Benning. The SAC has ordered us to chopper down to a small town in northern Florida to conduct a search for Senator Stephen Goodnight and his family. It's backwater country, so dress accordingly. I'll fill you in when you get here. Move it, Sutton; we're waitin'!"

Ashley began to respond but a click told her he'd hung up. Her face reddened in anger.

She threw back the sheet, got up, and hurried for the bathroom.

Fort Benning, Lawson Army Air Field, Flight Operations

Captain Alsop stood outside flight ops with his copilot, who motioned toward the parking lot. "That must be her, Tony. The agent said she was small."

Tony Alsop frowned as the short strawberry blonde stepped out of a Jeep Renegade that had just pulled into a parking space. *Ahh, hell, she's a wannabe for sure,* Alsop said to himself in disgust. The FBI baseball cap pulled over her short hair was the first indication, and the big black Casio on her wrist was the second. *Jesus, what a waste,* he thought. He knew the kind all too well: the Jeep, man's watch, man's clothes, absence of jewelry and makeup, and the walk were the signs. She was definitely a wannabe: she wanted to be a man. The Army was full of such women, lady jocks who thought they could do anything a man could do and were always looking for a way to prove it.

Eyes hidden behind his aviator sunglasses, Alsop studied the woman as she strode toward him. Jesus, all she had to do was lose the hat, unbutton a few buttons, use some makeup to highlight her cheeks, wear some earrings, slow the walk, swing her butt a little, put on a smile, and presto, you had Miss Foxy Federal Agent instead of Miss G-man wannabe. *Who goes out with her type?* he wondered. *Hell, nobody, that's who. I'd be afraid to. Jesus, she'd probably wanna arm wrestle or talk about guns or crimes or whatever they talk about in the FBI. Oh, man, what a waste.*

"You must be Special Agent Sutton?" Alsop said, wearing his most innocent smile when Ashley stood before him.

She didn't return even a hint of a smile as she responded. "Yes. Is Special Agent Tanner here?"

Alsop maintained his smile despite her obvious attempt at being the cool professional. "Yes, ma'am, he's on the phone to your people in Atlanta. The others are in the waiting room."

Ashley canted her head with a look of surprise. "Others?"

"Yes, ma'am. Sergeant Major Murphy and a gentleman named Hilbert are waiting for you inside. I'll escort you to them, then Jim and I will wait in the aircraft. We'll be ready to depart as soon as you all are on board."

Ashley's face tightened as she followed the two pilots inside the building. In the waiting area she saw the camouflage-fatigued form of Dan Murphy sitting at a table, his massive hands wrapped around a mug of coffee. She marched straight for him. "What the hell is going on, Dan?"

Murphy lifted a bushy eyebrow. "Nice to see you again, too, Agent Sutton."

"Where is he?"

Dan raised his hand. "Hey, give me a break, will ya? He called and said he needed me here, so I'm here. I saw him for just a sec when he came in, and you coulda cooked eggs on him—he was hot. Your boss in Atlanta screwed things up, and he's tryin' to unscrew them."

Ashley lost her scowl and stepped closer, patting the soldier on the shoulder apologetically. "Sorry, Dan, it just surprised me when he called this morning. I didn't expect him back from recovery leave for another week. I haven't heard from him for over a month and he—"

"Welcome to the club," the thin sergeant major said as he stood. He gave her a consoling pat on the shoulder. "He didn't call me, either. He's been in town two days, been stayin' with Jerome and Millie, 'keepin' a low profile,' he says to me. Personally, I don't think he's recovered worth a damn—he looks like hell."

Ashley's eyes narrowed in renewed shock and anger. "Two days? He's been back two days?"

A middle-aged man wearing a dark suit stepped up and tapped Ashley's shoulder. "Are you Agent Sutton?"

Ashley turned and eyed the pale-faced man whose eyes were filled with worry. "Yes, are you Mr. Hilbert?"

Hilbert extended his hand. "A pleasure, Agent Sutton. Yes, I'm Gary Hilbert, Senator Goodnight's chief staff assistant. I was briefing the agent in the other room as he was on the phone. He asked me to tell you and the sergeant major that we should go on out to the helicopter. He'll be right out. I certainly hope we can clear this up quickly. I'm sure the senator has probably just run aground on some sandbar and—"

Ashley tuned Hilbert out as she stared at the door he had obviously come through. She took a step toward the portal but Murphy grasped her arm. "We'd better do what he says.

You can light into him later, and leave a little for me, too. Can't believe he didn't call you either."

Ashley allowed herself to be escorted out the back entrance along with Hilbert only because she wanted some time to get her thoughts together. What had she done to deserve the silent treatment from Tanner? Why hadn't he called? It wasn't her fault they had made her leave Washington after the case was closed. She had wanted to stay with him at the hospital, but they wouldn't allow anyone to see him. Damn him, two *days*? He'd been back two *days*?

The helicopter crew chief met them halfway down the sloping sidewalk leading to the tarmac, where a large Blackhawk helicopter sat, huge rotor blades slowly turning. The crew chief spoke loudly, to be heard over the whine of the engines. "Folks, I'm required to give you a safety briefing prior to boarding. The aircraft is equipped with . . ."

Ashley turned and looked back toward the building. A dark figure was striding toward her. Although he was backlit by the sun and she couldn't make out his face, she knew it was Tanner. Sensing the onset of tears, she sniffed them back and told herself he was a bastard for not contacting her. No possible excuse justified shutting her out so completely. Trembling, she brought her hand up to block the glare. Dan was wrong, she thought; Eli Tanner looked wonderful to her. The damn fool had almost gotten himself killed a month before trying to free her when she'd been held hostage. The red and purple bullet scar that ran into his hairline, and the small scar on his left arm, were obvious reminders of what he had endured to save her.

Despite being angry with Tanner, Ashley stepped out to greet him; she couldn't help herself. He stopped a few feet away and dipped his head. Able to see him clearly, she sensed something was wrong; the mischievous glint in his eyes was gone.

"Good morning, Agent Sutton. Nice to see you again," Eli said softly. Without waiting for a response, he continued past her and, smiling, clasped Dan Murphy's shoulder.

"Dan, my man, it's goin' to be like the old days gettin' on that bird. Ya ready?"

Upset and disappointed that he had saved his infectious smile for his Army buddy rather than her, Ashley turned and faced him. "All I get is a 'Good morning,' Tanner? What the hell is going on?" she blurted.

Eli's indifferent look froze her in place. He motioned everyone toward the chopper. "Let's load up. Mr. Hilbert, have you ridden on one of these before?"

The staffer shook his head. "Not one this loud."

"No sweat, sir; the crew chief will give you earplugs once we're on board," Eli said. "I want you in the middle seat, and we'll get you a headset so we can talk. Come on, follow me and I'll get you squared away. Agent Sutton, you coming?"

Still feeling the hollow aftereffects of his look, Ashley turned and followed in silence.

Inside the cabin, Eli checked Gary Hilbert's seat belt, then sat down beside Ashley, who was still fumbling with the ends of hers. He took both ends from her, buckled the belt in place, then tightened the straps. She looked into his steel-gray eyes and almost had to yell to be heard over the whining engine. "You okay?"

He sat down and yelled back as he buckled his belt. "Yep." He handed her a headset and put his on.

Immediately her voice came through the headset speakers pressed against his ears. "Why didn't you at least call me?"

"I did," he answered as the bird lifted from the ground and shot forward.

"When?"

"The first Saturday after you left me in Washington. When I didn't get you, I called Regina and she said you and Agent Watkins were on a date."

Ashley twisted in her seat, looking at him as if she'd been slugged. "Agent Watkins took me to dinner so we could get acquainted. It wasn't a date, Tanner!"

"Regina said it was a date." Eli avoided looking at her.

"Let me remind you, Tanner, Ms. Washington is our sec-retary. I can't believe you'd ask her if I was on a date."

"I didn't ask; she told me. Drop it. I need to tell you what—"

Ashley was shaking with anger. "You didn't call again because you thought I was on a *date*?"

Eli's brow wrinkled and he gave her a look that said it was a dumb question. "Agent Sutton, I don't know what you're all hot about but drop it, will ya? When they took me to Key West, I was in a place where I couldn't call anybody. Can we get on to business now?"

"It wasn't a date, Tanner."

"Fine, it wasn't a date. Agent Sutton, I don't care what you do on your personal time; you're a big girl. You asked why I didn't call. I did call; that's the end of that discussion. Let's get down to business here. We're choppering down to a small town in northern Florida called Wewahitchka. It's near Dead Lake, which feeds into the Apalachicola River. Fishermen found a white female in her early twenties on the river only about five hours ago. She's alive but appears to have sustained gunshot wounds to the head. Mr. Hilbert, here, is Senator Stephen Goodnight's congressional assis-tant. It seems the senator and his family set out from Columbus on Friday on a cabin cruiser down the Chatta-hoochee River with an intended destination of Apalachicola on the coast. I'm told it's a three-day trip. The senator called Hilbert Friday night on his cell phone to check in, but the senator did not make his scheduled call last night. We wouldn't have been concerned, but yesterday something else happened that now has us very worried. Late yesterday afternoon two of Senator Goodnight's staffers were found dead in a Georgetown apartment. It was a double homicide. That's bad enough, but the female found on the river last night matches the description of one of the females in the senator's party. The senator's family includes his two sons, wife, a daughter-in-law, and a young woman who is the younger son's girlfriend. The woman found on the river had no identification on her person and was in no condition to tell anyone her name, but she does match the description of the girlfriend of the senator's son, a Miss Janice Ayers. Since the senator is from Columbus, the lead is going to the Atlanta office. They're sending down a team to take charge of the search. The Tallahassee resident office is also responding as we speak, but right now they can't get helicopter support from Eglin Air Force Base because the birds are fogged in. They'll be conducting a search of the river for the cruiser. Since we're the closest who can respond, the SAC wants us to positively ID the female and, if at all possible, to talk to her. A local doctor is with her now, and he reports she's stable."

Ashley glared at him. "What's this about your being in town two days?"

Ignoring her, Eli motioned toward the ruddy sergeant major seated on the other side of him. "I brought Dan along because he knows the Apalachicola River. He says the Chattahoochee and the Apalachicola are one and the same but the name changes once you cross the state line into Florida. He says it's about three hundred miles from Columbus to Apalachicola, on the coast. This place, We-watchamacallit where we're heading, is about two-thirds down the river. It's backwater country, nothing but gators, snakes, and mosquitoes, but damn good fishin', he says."

"Did you hear what I asked, Tanner? How come you didn't tell me you were back?"

"Will you please listen to me? I haven't turned on Hilbert's headset device yet. He doesn't know I brought him along in case there are bodies to ID. Right now, it doesn't look good for the senator or his family. The girl's condition tells us that. I'm going to show Hilbert how to work his headset so he can fill us in, but I'm not going to play it straight with him until we arrive and I get a look at that girl and talk to the doc. If it *is* Janice Ayers, and if they *are* gunshot wounds, we're going to have our hands full. We're probably going to be the first agents to arrive. You stay with the girl once we try to talk to her, and go with her on the chopper that takes her to Eglin's base hospital. I'm going to help coordinate the military and local support for the search for the others. When I talk to Hilbert, you'll be able to listen, and I'd like you to take notes for me. Okay?"

"Wait a minute, Tanner. You just said we're not lead on this. Why are you going to start coordinating stuff?"

Eli looked at her impatiently. "The Atlanta crew won't be there for another couple of hours, so tell me who's going to coordinate the support and search until they arrive?"

Ashley sighed and slowly nodded. "Okay. I see your point. You're probably right, but just remember we're in a supporting role on this, okay?"

Eli reached over and flipped the toggle on the little device attached to Hilbert's headset. "Sir, can you hear me now? No, sir, I can't hear you unless you hold down that little black transmit button. Once you're through talking, release the transmit button."

"Can you hear me now?" Hilbert asked, pushing the button.

"Yes, sir. We are on the bird's intercom so Agent Sutton and myself can hear you. Please tell us why the senator took this trip, sir."

"Yes, of course, it was a getaway, actually. Stephen has been under a lot of pressure in Washington . . . more than he had bargained for when he ran for office, I can tell you. Nobody can prepare you for that. . . . Anyway, he started planning this trip some months ago. It was going to be his chance to have his family with him for a while—not your typical vacation, you understand. He wanted them really to be together without distractions. He felt he needed to spend some real quality time with them all. He had heard about the river trip from friends in Columbus and decided it would meet his needs perfectly. I helped with the 'preplanning,' getting him the necessary books and navigation maps, and he took care of obtaining the cruiser from a friend in town. The hard part was coordinating his schedule with his two sons'. Both of them balked at the idea at first, but I talked to them and explained it was important to Stephen. Agent Tanner, I know they're all perfectly fine, probably run aground somewhere or have had problems with the boat motor or something. The cell phone doesn't work all that well when away from civilization, you know?"

Eli nodded. "Yes, sir, you're probably right. Sir, can you tell me about an investigation the senator was conducting?"

Hilbert shifted in the seat. "I guess it's all right to tell the FBI. You all were involved, after all. Among other committees, Stephen was on the Senate Judiciary Subcommittee on Antitrust, Monopoly, and Business Rights. That one was where he planned to make a difference. You see, he had gathered numerous complaints of shady dealings in northern Georgia that branched out to at least five other states. He talked to Congressman Richards of the Fourth District about the complaints because they were principally coming out of his district, but Richards told him it wasn't a problem and not to be worried about it. Stephen wasn't happy with the polite snub and decided to do some checking on his own. Agent Tanner, please understand, I was not privy to his investigation. I work the medicare and welfare issues along with military construction, housing, and arms procurement for his other committees. But I can tell you this much: Stephen has spent enormous energy working on the investigation. Special Agent Eddings from your Atlanta office is working with him on it and I'm sure he can provide you with more detail. And, of course, you can talk to the staffer who is in charge of the investigation, Matthew Wentzel. He's an attorney and lives in Washington and works with the senator at the Sam Rayburn Building. Matthew lives in Georgetown, I believe."

Surprised that Hilbert still had not been notified about Wentzel's death, Eli exchanged glances with Ashley. Then he looked back at Hilbert and pushed his transmit button. "Sir, how was the senator planning to get back to Columbus? Was he going to turn around after arriving at Apalachicola and return by cruiser?"

"No, he didn't have time for that. A friend, John Fine, was going to meet him when he arrived. John has a twin-engine Beechcraft and had made arrangements for the senator and his family to be flown back to Columbus. John is to take the boat back himself. John is quite the fisherman. He's the one who suggested the trip in the first place."

Eli nodded again and glanced at Ashley, who had her notebook out and was writing furiously. Hilbert touched Eli's arm. "I'm really sorry about calling you all in on this; I know it's all right, but I just couldn't take any chances. Stephen is a good friend. He's one of the new breed, you know; he planned on only two terms, then . . ."

Leaning back in his seat, Eli tuned the staffer out. He hoped that Stephen Goodnight and his family were only having boat problems.

Wewahitchka, Florida

The state troopers turned their backs to hurricanelike winds and the clouds of dust churned up by the helicopter. Then the crew chief slid back the Blackhawk's door. Eli hopped to the ground and strode to the closest trooper, who was brushing dirt and sand from his uniform. Eli showed his ID. "I'm Agent Tanner, sir."

"I'm Trooper Vickery," the trooper drawled. "The little gal and doc are up the road a piece in a house owned by the proprietor of a bait shop. Not much in Wewahitchka. It's the best we could do. I'll take y'all there."

Eli motioned for the others and raised an eyebrow. "How's she doin'?"

The trooper sighed and began walking toward his cruiser. "Physically, better than ya'd expect . . . mentally, she's fishin' without a pole. Too bad . . . she was probably a cute little ol' gal—bullets messed her up purty good. You'll see."

"Can she talk?"

"Oh, yeah, she's a' talkin' aw'right, but ain't makin' a lick a'sense. Just keeps sayin' over and over again somethin' about 'They shoulda put 'em together.' She still hasn't told anyone who she is."

*   *   *

Eli stepped into the small kitchen followed by a small bespectacled man with a stethoscope around his neck. He approached Gary Hilbert, who was staring at him with a horrified look. Eli spoke softly. "Sir, the young lady is in the next room. The doctor here says she is in no danger of dying; the wounds are ugly but not life-threatening. I've explained to the doctor the gravity of the situation and he's going to allow Agent Sutton and myself to talk to her before she's medevacked out. Sir, I need you to come with me and please tell me if the young lady is in fact Miss Janice Ayers."

Hilbert lowered his eyes and stared at his hands. "If . . . if it is Janice, it . . . it means . . ."

"Yes, sir, it does," Eli said as he stepped closer.

Tears began to trickle down Hilbert's pale cheeks. He shook his head slowly as he stood. "I . . . I'm not sure I can walk."

Ashley pushed away from the wall she'd been leaning on and took Hilbert's arm. "I'll help you, sir."

Seconds later Hilbert stood in front of a small bed where the young woman was sitting up, her back and head resting on pillows. He opened his eyes and winced. "Oh, my God, Janice, what have they done to you?"

Eli motioned to the doctor to take Hilbert out of the room, then sat down beside the young woman, who looked at him through swollen eyes. "Janice? No, please don't look away from me. Look at me, please. I'm Eli Tanner from the FBI and this lady on the other side of you is Agent Ashley Sutton. Janice, we need you to talk to us. We need to know what happened. Look at me . . . that's it, Janice. Tell us what happened."

Janice lifted her hand as if in slow motion and touched her bandaged forehead. "They shot me . . . they shot us all."

Eli took her hand into his own. "Who shot you, Janice?"

"They shot me and I pretended I was dead. . . . I pretended . . . then the boat began to sink. . . . I didn't want to die there. I didn't want to die, but I didn't want to leave them. I didn't want to die."

Eli stroked her hand. "You did the right thing, Janice.

There was nothing you could have done . . . but you *can* do something now. I want you to shut your eyes. I know it will be difficult, but I want you to think about what happened. Clear your mind and think of yourself as looking through a camcorder. You were on the boat with the others. . . . Pretend you're looking through the camcorder viewer and tell me what you see and hear. Keep your eyes closed but look through the camera, Janice. . . . That's right . . . close your eyes now. . . . You are on the boat and . . ."

"I was talking to Mary . . . then Chad said to the senator, 'Look, there's a boat ahead of us.' I stood and looked down the river. . . . It was a green boat, a bass boat like my brother's, but nicer. There were two men on it but we were too far away to see their faces. Wait . . . one had blond hair, I remember now. Yes, he was tall and thin and had blond wavy hair, because it caught the sun. The other was wearing a baseball cap."

"So they were both Caucasians?" Eli asked softly.

Janice began sobbing. "They . . . they shot everybody; the noise was so terrible and I didn't know what to do. . . . After I saw the boat, I went into the cabin to put up the steaks we had put out to marinate. I heard Mike talking to them. Yes, they were white . . . I heard one talking . . . he had a Spanish accent, though. Later, after the shooting, I heard them talking. They were all speaking Spanish very fast. I heard three, maybe four voices, all Spanish. I . . . I never saw any of their faces."

Eli patted her hand. "You're doing very well, Janice. Now please close your eyes again and look through the viewfinder. When you saw the green bass boat, do you remember where you were on the river? Was there anything you remember that would help us find the cruiser?"

Janice suddenly grabbed his hand in a viselike grip and sat up. "The island! We were close to an island. When the boat sank I floated out the cabin door and hid beneath the water. I used the seat cushions to hide my face. I . . . I drifted with the current and heard the boats going away. . . . I was afraid to stop drifting but my feet touched bottom. . . . I remember thanking God, and then I remember praying to God they wouldn't come back."

"Janice, you said 'boats.' Does that mean you heard more than one?"

Janice closed her eyes a moment and slowly nodded. "Yes, two boats. One started, then a closer one started. They went downriver the way I was drifting. Two boats."

Eli motioned Ashley to take his place and stood. Leaning over, he patted the young woman's arm. "You've helped us quite a lot, Janice. Agent Sutton is going to sit here beside you now. In a few minutes you'll be taken by helicopter to a hospital and she'll be going with you. We'll notify your parents and make arrangements for them to come and see you. The worst is over."

His jaw muscles working, Eli gave Janice a last look and strode out the door. Seconds later he stepped out on the front porch where the state troopers and Dan Murphy waited.

Eli looked past the troopers; two young black men were seated on the ground in the shade of a rusted pickup.

Trooper Vickery motioned to the men. "Those are the two who found the little gal."

Dan stepped closer and spoke in a whisper. "They're probably gator poachers, Tan. Best tell 'em up front they're not in any trouble or you won't get much."

Eli took in a breath and slowly let it out before speaking to Vickery. "Sir, please bring them over here and let's get started." He turned to the other troopers and pointed at the nearest one. "Sir, please take out your notepad and write down the following information. Once I'm finished giving you the info, call your headquarters and give it to them so they can begin the hunt."

The trooper hurriedly pulled his small pad from his back pocket and took out a pen. "Ready," he said.

Eli began pacing. "There were three, possibly four assailants. Two boats were used. Victim ID'd one as a bass boat, green. One assailant was tall, thin, and blond. All spoke Spanish. Assailants fled south down the river. Tell your headquarters this has all the appearances of a planned hit;

we'll know more once the cruiser and bodies are recovered. Go ahead, sir, make that call now."

Eli pointed at the next trooper, who already had his notebook out. "Sir, I want you to radio your headquarters and get four waterborne search teams and two dive teams here as quickly as possible. If need be, I'll provide you helicopter support to bring the crews in. We'll also need a recovery crew with whatever equipment is necessary to raise a sunken cruiser from the river. I'll need the M.E. here and also a team from your State Bureau of Investigation and a crime scene crew, along with a support unit and commo van. Tell your people to get on that for me and that you'll get back to them in a few minutes with where the command post will be located. Go ahead, sir, make the call."

Eli turned to the two young black men. "Gentlemen, I am Agent Tanner of the FBI. I want to thank you on behalf of the young lady you found last night. You undoubtedly saved her life. I now need both of you to help me. The lady mentioned an island in the river. Is there an island anywhere near where you found her?"

The two men looked at one another, then the one with a bulging jaw nodded. "Yes, sir, she was standin' on its banks when we shined her. It be the onlyiest island till ya gets downriver for purt' near four mile."

Eli stepped closer to the young man. "We're going to be mounting a recovery and search operation and need to establish a command post as close to this island as we can. Can you tell me where the best place would be? It needs to have access for putting in boats and recovery equipment."

Before either could speak, the old gray-haired black man who'd been rocking on the porch spoke up. "Ain't no place. Ain't no roads south of here . . . all backwater. Ya best make that post of y'alls over in the park just down the road a piece. Park's got ramps goin' inta the lake for them boats y'all be needin' to start searchin'."

Wearing overalls and white shirt, the old man stood and motioned to the distant lake. "I been livin' here for over sixty years, Mr. Agent. I knows Dead Lake and the river up and down. I thinks ya best get in one of them whirlybirds and fly over the bar y'all is callin' an island. That sunk boat gonna be makin' a oil or gas slick sure as I'se standin' here. It a big boat?"

Eli smiled; he had found a gem. He nodded. "Yes, sir, a cabin cruiser."

"If them boys who hurt that child had 'em a depth finder on their boat they'd haveta sink that cruiser just north of the bar in the west channel . . . cuts deeper there. Anywhere else it'd be too shallow. Reckon ya know them gator, gar, and turtles ain't gonna leave much for ya if ya wait too long in findin' 'em?"

Eli pushed the gruesome thoughts of what they would find out of his mind and patted the old man's shoulder. "Sir, have you ridden in a chopper before?"

The old man shook his head with a twinkle in his eyes. "Don't reckon so, but if y'all needin' the best guide knowin' that river, y'all lookin' at him."

CHAPTER 7

Lake Lanier, Georgia

Ted Faircloud stepped through the front door of the huge house and handed the old black woman his baseball cap.

"Where is she, Halley?" he asked.

"She in the great room watchin' TV with her dog, Mr. Teddy. She been waitin' a long time for ya. She been actin' real upset . . . didn't even have no dinner."

"Fix her something, Halley, and I'll see that she eats. Bring it when it's ready, okay?"

"Sure, Mr. Teddy, I'll fix her up somethin'."

Seconds later Ted strode down the steps into the great room and was confronted by Baby, who held the tennis ball in his mouth. Ted gave the animal a quick pat and faced Bonita, who sat on the couch watching a big-screen television by the fireplace.

Trembling, Bonita broke her gaze from the screen. "It's on CNN, Teddy . . . they're saying Senator Goodnight and his family are missing. . . . It's Carlos, Teddy, he's killed them."

"What in the hell are you talkin' about?"

Bonita rose and pointed at the television screen. "That's what I'm talking about. Look at it!"

Ted shifted his gaze to the screen and shrugged. "Looks like an aerial view of the 'glades to me."

"It's a CNN reporter in a helicopter showing what he sees of the search for the senator. Haven't you heard about it?"

78

"I was up in Dahlonega with my guys, takin' turns watchin' the bank. . . . Who you say is missin'?"

Bonita shook her head as if dealing with a third grader. "Senator Goodnight, as in the same Senator Goodnight who was running the investigation of the Yona Group."

"Ooh shit." Ted's knees suddenly weakened.

"He knows, Teddy. Carlos must have found out about the investigation. Your mob friends didn't think this thing out, did they? They just wanted Carlos dead and didn't think about what else he could do. . . . Well, he's doing something, all right. My God, Teddy, Carlos will kill them all."

Ted held up his hand. "Now wait a minute, are you sayin' you think Mendez is behind this?"

Bonita glared at him. "You don't get it, do you? You're no better than your mob friends. All you cared about was taking out Carlos. You didn't know—nobody knew—what he was capable of. The *investigation*, Teddy! It's all about Senator Goodnight's investigation into the Yona Group. Carlos must be in deeper than anyone thought. Don't you see? The senator isn't missing . . . Carlos had him killed, and he'll have everyone else killed who knows he's involved with the group."

Ted's eyes quickly came back into focus. "Come on, Mendez isn't dumb enough to order Goodnight killed. Christ'a'mighty, we're talkin' about a United States senator. Mendez would try other ways to convince the senator to back off."

Bonita shook her head with a vacant stare. "I know him, Teddy. Oh God . . . oh God, I should have known this would happen."

Ted tried to put his arm around her shoulder but she backed away from him like a frightened child. "Don't touch me! You and your friends caused this, and now I'm responsible, too. . . . Oh God, what have I done?"

"Jesus, Bonita, get hold of yourself. The TV says the senator is *missing*. You're jumpin' to wild-ass conclusions. Take a deep breath and relax a minute."

"Relax? Are you that stupid? I'll tell you what I'm going to do. I'm getting out of here right now!"

Ted grabbed her arm. "You leave here, Mendez will find you and you'll be fish food. Okay, *relax* was the wrong word. Just calm down a minute and talk to me without takin' my head off. Tell me why you're so sure Mendez is behind this."

Bonita sank onto the couch. "A month ago I overheard Carlos talking to Raul on the yacht. We were in bed sleeping when Raul came in and woke Carlos and said he had to talk to him. They talked in the passageway and didn't think I could hear them. Raul told Carlos their friend in the DEA had called and said DEA agents were going to pick up several people in the used-car business who were laundering money for Carlos. Carlos told Raul to eliminate the problem."

Bonita raised her eyes to Ted. "I swear I thought Carlos meant for Raul to get rid of the money . . . but a day later I heard on the news that the owners of two big used-car lots had been murdered along with their families. Don't you see, Ted? Carlos must have thought the senator was another 'problem.' "

Ted sat down beside her. "Who is Raul?"

"He's Carlos's brother-in-law . . . they call him the chief of staff. Carlos runs everything like he was in the army. Raul is really his do-it man. If Carlos wants something done, he tells Raul to do it."

Ted looked into Bonita's eyes. "And you stayed with Mendez even though you knew he was ordering people whacked?"

"I was too scared to leave him, Teddy. I tried, God knows I tried to leave. . . . I made up excuses about why I couldn't come over when he'd call me, but he wouldn't listen—he'd send one of his bodyguards over to get me."

Ted's face hardened as he shifted his gaze to the television. "Maybe you're right . . . but just maybe the senator is lost. The only thing we can do is wait and hope they find him."

"It's not just the senator, Ted. They say he was on a boat with his whole family."

Ted closed his eyes. "Jesus."

Baby began to growl, and seconds later Halley appeared at the top of the steps holding a tray. "I got some supper for you, Mrs. Stone."

Ted got up and took the tray from the elderly woman. "Thanks, Halley. I'll make sure she eats."

"Everything all right, Mr. Teddy?"

"Yeah, Halley, everything is just fine."

Wewahitchka, Florida

It was almost nine P.M. when Ashley hopped down from the helicopter. In a park next to the lake just outside the once sleepy town of Wewahitchka, portable road construction lights had turned night into day around a huge collection of National Guard, state, and federal vehicles of every type and description. Like a wagon train, the trucks, vans, and cars encircled a lighted tent city where soldiers, state troopers, divers, crime scene technicians, and federal agents moved purposefully from the lakeshore to the tents. Despite the sticky heat, it looked as if it were snowing within the lighted area. But as Ashley drew closer she could see that the snowflakes were millions of moths and insects drawn to the huge lights. Walking past clusters of black families that had come to watch the only show in town, she showed her ID to a soldier and entered the new tent city. Gas generators hummed loudly and metal trays clanked where men sat eating near a tent. She stopped for a moment in awe of the power of her profession; Eli Tanner had been able to summon all she saw just by saying it was needed. Walking again, she saw men taking soggy equipment out of boats dragged up on the shore, while other men were replacing their diving gear in the back of a truck. Someone tapped her shoulder.

"You're back, I see," Sergeant Major Dan Murphy said.

Ashley smiled. "You don't know how happy I am to see you, Dan. This place is a madhouse. Where's Tanner? I have us a ride home—the chopper is heading back to Fort Benning in thirty minutes."

Dan motioned toward the lake. "He should be comin' up from the site in a little while, but I don't think he'll be leavin' anytime soon. The guy you call the case agent in charge made him his assistant at the site. Come with me to the CP. I just ate and got to get back on duty."

"Duty?" she asked, taking his arm as he walked toward a large tent.

"Yeah, I've been helpin' coordinate the military-support side of this operation. Helluva note, Tan asks me to come along 'cause I know a little somethin' about the river, and I end up workin' my ass off as a damn REMF. Hell, I never got close to the river."

Ashley knew better than to ask the old vet, but did anyway. "What's an REMF, Dan?"

"Rear echelon motherfrigger ... but it ain't really 'frigger.' It's what we called the rear support weenies in da Nam. Us line dogs didn't care for 'em much 'cause they got three hots a day and slept in real beds. They got to go to the USO shows and play checkers with the Red Cross doughnut dollies while we were humpin' the boonies, snoopin' and poopin' for Charles."

Ashley couldn't help but smile, and squeezed his arm. "So now it's Dan the REMF who's got three hots and a cot?"

Dan slapped at her shoulder. "I shouldn't even be talkin' to ya. You damn FBI people don't know shit about takin' care of your own."

"What are you talking about, Dan?"

Murphy's eyes narrowed. "I'm talking about how they treated Tan. I talked to him while we were waitin' for the support units to get in. You should have told me, Ashley. I woulda busted him out ... I swear I would have."

Ashley felt a sinking sensation but held her eyes on him. "Dan, I don't know what you're talking about."

Murphy looked at her a moment then took her arm and began walking again. "Come with me; I'll tell ya in the CP."

Stepping over cables and wires, they entered a large open-sided tent that smelled of sweat, stale coffee, and wet canvas. The sergeant major approached a long table filled with communications equipment. Seated at the table wearing headsets or with telephones pressed to their ears were Army, state, and federal men who received, analyzed, and transmitted information to others. Murphy spoke to a young sergeant. "It goin' smooth?"

The sergeant nodded. "Yes, Sergeant Major. They closed the search down a few minutes ago and will pick it up again tomorrow at oh-dark-thirty. The mess hall has been notified and we have a platoon erecting a couple more sleeping tents for the search teams."

Murphy waved his hand. "You're doin' so good I'm gonna let ya keep doin' it for another half hour. I'm goin' to be talkin' to the lady."

The sergeant grinned and bobbed his head. "Thank you, Sergeant Major."

Shaking his head, Dan led Ashley to the corner of the tent, speaking out of the side of his mouth. "Young ones don't know when they're gettin' scammed."

Overhead, Coleman lanterns hissed and cast yellow light on maps and charts taped to the tent frame as Murphy pulled up two folding chairs. He sat down heavily and shook his head as Ashley sat down on the other chair. "When they took Tan to Key West, it wasn't for any damn recovery leave; they took him to a damn loony bin."

Ashley began to shake her head, but the sergeant major's eyes locked on her. "Some people in your Bureau thought he had a death wish. Others thought the case had pushed him over the edge. Jesus Christ, Ashley, after all he went through and all he did, *that's* how you people treat him? Ya lock him up in a loony bin and sic shrinks on him?"

Lowering her head, Ashley spoke in a whisper. "I didn't know, Dan."

Seeing she meant it, Murphy leaned closer. "Ashley, why

would they do that? You and I both know he hates hospitals. It's a damn wonder he didn't really go nuts on them."

Ashley slowly raised her eyes to him. "Dan, you're not going to like it or understand, but I think I know why. I guess I should have known when they questioned me during the debrief and wouldn't let me see him. It all makes sense now. Dan, you have to understand he killed five men and wounded two others in less than a minute. The operation looked like a suicide mission to everybody. They had to be sure he got through it all right without . . . well, you know. It's standard policy—after an agent kills an assailant, they're to be checked out by a shrink—and I guess in this case they thought they were doing him a favor by sending him to Key West."

"Bullshit, now you're condoning what happened," Dan blurted. "A month of gettin' drilled by shrinks didn't do him any favors."

"I don't condone it but I understand why it was done. Dan, Eli does things that make people feel very uneasy. No, don't give me that look—it's true. Maybe it's his time in Vietnam or in Special Ops, but it's there; I've seen and felt it. When a situation heats up, he changes into somebody else. I saw it with my own eyes. It's like he doesn't feel the tension or fear that everybody else is feeling. That's the part that makes people uneasy when they're with him. You wonder if he cares. What makes it worse, he seems to like it. I mean, he seems to feed off others' worries and fears, and it seems only to make him calmer. It drives you nuts to watch him think so clearly and spout commands like a damn machine while you're worrying about this and that and forget half of what you were supposed to be doing. Dan, I'm telling you it's scary. . . . You wonder . . . and I'm sure some people did wonder about him after the op went down."

Murphy sighed and lowered his head as if very tired. "You know, Ashley, I'm as dumb as dirt . . . never made it past high school, and that was a struggle. But I'm goin' to tell ya a fact that's in no damn book and never was taught or even talked about in all my trainin' in the Army. I figgered you people in the FBI was better than us military types, but I guess you're no better than us. Ya see, I learned in Nam that some men have somethin' that others don't. I may be dumb, but I saw it right off. You ask any grunt who ever humped a ruck if what I'm tellin' ya isn't true. In every platoon you'll find one, maybe two, who have the gift. These men are special because they sense trouble comin'. In da Nam every grunt was tested sooner or later, and those that had it, knew it . . . believe me. They wanted to be the point men, ya know why? 'Cause they knew they were safer out front of everybody than they were being led by somebody that didn't have it. I'm tellin' ya all this because Eli had it. . . . You saying you felt uneasy tells me he still has it. We all felt uneasy being around him. We'd watch everything he'd do and pray 'today' wasn't the day he'd see, hear, or feel somethin' we didn't . . . because if he did, we knew trouble was comin'. The Tan man was what we called him, and it wasn't just another handle . . . it was out of respect. When you got scared, you looked to the Tan man. He was all calm like and all business and you knew he was figuring out a way to get us all out alive."

Murphy leaned forward, looking into her eyes. "He's not crazy or even close to it; he's just different and handles pucker time differently than most. I know I sound like some old drunk in a VFW tellin' war stories, but believe me when I tell ya it's no drunken war story; it's real. All of us who been out there in a life-or-death situation know—we know men like Eli have a gift—and you just pray to God that the enemy don't have one like him."

Ashley lowered her head. "I . . . I guess I knew. He's told me in his own way about it, but I wasn't listening. My dad was like him, you know. . . . Of course you don't, but he always said he had a special knack. Dan, my dad died one night in an alley. He was a detective, and he and his partner walked into the alley responding to a possible drug buy. Dad didn't come out alive . . . his knack wasn't enough. I believe what you're saying, but gift or not, Eli has used up his nine lives. He was lucky on our last op. It *was* a suicide mission, and everybody knows it."

Murphy stood and raised an eyebrow. "The one thing I learned about a fight, Agent Sutton, is there is no such thing as luck. It's all about experience, training, and skill. The best wins. If I were you I wouldn't be countin' the Tan man out just yet. He may be gettin' gray and he might even be thinkin' he's over the hill, but I don't think the men he killed and wounded would agree with you that it was just luck."

"Why's he angry at me, Dan?"

Murphy looked down at her a moment before replying. "He's not angry at you, Ashley . . . he's just feelin' different about a lot of things. Almost dyin' does that to ya, you know? You think about life a little differently, and I think them damn shrinks got to him, makin' it even worse. After they released him he went to see his son. . . . Guess it was a waste of time. His ex wouldn't even let him get close, let alone talk to the boy. Tan wanted to make amends to his ex and try to work out a way where he could see his son, but I guess she didn't want to hear it, 'cause she called her lawyer. He's down, Ashley, real down. He came back to work early 'cause he said he needed to work and feel like he was doin' somethin' useful. It's all he knows, Ashley—the job. It's all he's got, and he wants to hold on for as long as he can."

Murphy leaned over and patted her leg with a tired smile. "This operation has been good for him. Ya ought to have seen him in action this afternoon. Christ, ya woulda thought he was Patton, givin' orders the way he was doin'. Look at this. He did it all, got all this organized and the search goin' without a single snag. The damn shrinks told him to take it easy and reflect on life! Bullshit, they don't know him. *This* is what he needed, action, somethin' to make him get those wheels in his head turnin' and the adrenaline flowin' again. Hey, speak of the devil! There he is, just walked in. Don't let on I told you what happened to him—I had to pry it out, and it wasn't easy."

Ashley patted the sergeant's arm. "My lips are sealed. And Dan, thanks."

Ashley tilted in her seat to look at Eli, and felt the all too familiar goose bumps run up her arms and a tingling sensation in her stomach. Dan was right; it had been good for him. He looked tired but good. His tan slacks and chukka boots were caked with mud, and his sweaty khaki shirt clung to him like a second skin, showing the definition of his heavily muscled chest. His rugged face was splattered with mud, and on his head, pushed back, exposing his forehead, was a blue baseball cap with the letters FBI across the front. He looked tired but satisfied.

Eli saw Murphy waving and tiredly walked toward him. He saw Ashley a second later.

She pulled another chair over. "I got relieved from my duty once the Atlanta rep arrived at the hospital—Janice is doing fine. How did it go at the recovery site?"

Eli sat down wearily and looked up at the hissing lantern. "We found the boat at about three, but the divers had a hard time because of the low water visibility and later the darkness. It was a struggle for them because the hatchway was facing the current. It took a lot of work but the divers got the last body out about an hour ago. They'll refloat the boat tomorrow at first light."

A man wearing a thin plastic rain suit approached and lifted a clipboard. "Agent Tanner, I've got the prelim you wanted."

Eli nodded with his eyes closed. "Go ahead, Doc."

The M.E. spoke quietly. "All five of the victims were ID'd by Mr. Hilbert. Four of the five victims were shot repeatedly. I'd say based on the pattern of the wounds, it looks like automatic weapons were used. It also appears the wounds were the cause of death of each of the victims. It appears none of them died as a result of drowning. In the young female victim's back, we found one complete nine-millimeter bullet that was not damaged. The bodies are being moved now to a helicopter, and I'll be able to tell you more after the autopsies are conducted. I do want to tell you, however, unlike the others, the senator took a burst in the face. It's my opinion whoever your killers are, they made sure with him. Too bad . . . he was one of the good ones. We'll start work as soon as we get back. I expect we'll have more details for you by tomorrow."

Eli nodded. "Thanks, Doc. Please fax your findings to the Atlanta office. I'll pass on your report to the case agent as soon as he finishes closing down the site."

Ashley waited until the medical examiner had left before speaking. "Tanner, this is bad, isn't it?"

Eli exhaled and shifted his eyes to her. "Yeah, it's going to be big-time."

Ashley nodded in silence; confirmation of the senator's death had just elevated the case to the number one priority of the FBI. "Big-time" was an understatement.

A tall agent wearing suit slacks, white button-down shirt, and regimental tie walked up and tapped Eli's shoulder. "You're Agent Tanner, correct?"

"Yeah," Eli said warily.

The agent extended his hand without smiling. "I'm Agent Frost, Tampa office. I'm relieving you effective immediately. Headquarters has directed our office to finish up here. You along with all the Atlanta office agents including the case agent in charge are being relieved by our office. I've already been backbriefed by the CAC, and he told me you are to leave immediately for Columbus. Tomorrow you and any agents you may have brought with you are to report to the Atlanta office at 1000 hours for a meeting with the deputy director, who's flying in from Washington for the briefing. There's a Blackhawk helicopter waiting, Agent Tanner. Your job is done here."

"What about me?" Murphy asked. "I came along 'cause Tanner told me he needed me. I'm relieved, too, right?"

Before the tall agent could respond, Eli stood and put his arm around his friend's shoulder. "Come on, I'm not leaving you with these tanned Tampa dudes . . . unless of course you wanna stay and do some fishin'?"

Ashley lowered her head, thinking he'd forgotten her,

when she felt herself being pulled up. Eli grinned and patted her back. "Come on, pard, you heard the clean man, we're outta here. Time to saddle up."

Ashley smiled, seeing that the glint in his eyes was back. Once outside, they walked straight for the distant helicopter. A black family sat in lawn chairs just outside the lighted area, and a small boy Ashley judged to be about eleven pointed and said excitedly, "Looky, Mama, an FBI man!"

Eli slowed his steps and veered off from Ashley and the sergeant major. He stopped in front of the boy and kneeled down. "What's your name, son?"

The boy looked at his mother, then back to Eli, and lowered his head as if embarrassed. "My . . . my name is Amos. . . . I'm twelve."

Eli took off his cap and put it on the boy's head. "Well, now you're Agent Amos of the FBI. You're assigned to take care of your mama and your small sisters and brothers."

The boy's eyes widened and he looked at his mother. "Mama, look, I'se a FBI man."

Eli patted the boy's shoulder and walked back to the others. Ashley looked away when she saw a tear trickling down his cheek. She followed him in silence, knowing he was wishing he had been able to give his son the hat and seen the same smile.

CHAPTER 8

5:45 A.M., Monday, Lake Lanier, Georgia

Ted leaned over the couch and gently shook the sleeping woman's shoulder. Bonita's eyes slowly opened.

Ted lowered his head and backed away. "A report just came on a minute ago. . . . The senator and his family were found. They're all dead."

Bonita closed her eyes. "Oh God . . . please forgive me."

"Don't do that, Bonita," Ted said as he turned off the television. "Stop blaming yourself. Wasn't your fault . . . wasn't mine, either. Your lover boy ordered the hit . . . the son of a bitch."

"We caused it, Teddy. We're responsible," Bonita said, sitting up, her eyes beginning to well.

"Look, Bonita, I've been sittin' here all night thinkin' about this. I've been over it in my mind and I keep rememberin' what you said about that conversation you overheard. You said this Raul guy told Mendez their DEA *friend* called and warned them about other DEA agents goin' to pick up those used-car guys. This *friend* in the DEA has got to be their snitch."

"What's that got to do with—"

"It's got everything to do with it. It means this DEA snitch probably told Mendez about the investigation the senator was running."

"What are you saying, Teddy?"

"I'm saying we did what any good citizen does when he knows somebody is dirty—he turns them in. We did that.

We knew the Yona Group was price-fixing, and we told the right people who could do something about it. Problem is, the system is broke. Mendez has corrupted it by having a paid snitch on the inside."

Bonita shook her head. "You're just trying to justify what we did. We only told them because we wanted to steal Carlos's money."

"Think a minute, would ya? What would have happened if we hadn't even known about the money? I'll tell you, the senator would have been killed anyway. Bonita, we may have given the senator the information, but we sure as hell aren't responsible for his death. The DEA snitch, a damn fed, who's supposed to be workin' for the people, sold the senator out. Mendez and the snitch are the ones who are responsible. Mendez ordered the hit, for Christ's sake."

Bonita slowly lowered her head. "I—I guess you're right . . . but I don't feel any better about . . . Oh my God! The others! We've got to warn Matthew Wentzel, the senator's investigator, and the FBI agent who took over from him. Carlos will kill them!"

"Whoa now . . . you're right, but we gotta be smart about it. We can't just call 'em and say, 'You're in some really deep shit.' We can't let 'em know who we are or we'll be in serious trouble ourselves."

Bonita sprang up from the couch. "E-mail. I'll warn them by e-mail . . . they won't know who it came from."

Ted followed her into the office. "You sure they can't find out who sent it?"

"Trust me," she said as she sat down behind her computer.

"Bonita, listen to me now," Ted said, seeing her click the mouse. "We gotta be smart on this so we don't blow our op. Tell 'em they're in grave danger. Say a big drug player is tryin' to knock 'em off, but don't tell them who it is or how exactly he's involved with the Yona Group."

Bonita swiveled around in her chair, looking at up him as if in disbelief. "You're still planning to steal the money after what's happened?"

"I can't take out Mendez unless I have the money to pay

my team . . . and you won't get your split, either. How long can you hide out with what you've got? You want to live, don't you?"

Bonita turned back to the computer. "Please, God, forgive me . . . what do I say again?"

Minutes later Bonita pushed back from the desk but kept her eyes on the monitor. "Something is wrong. The FBI agent received the message, but not Wentzel."

"How do you know that?"

"It says right there on the screen whether their computer got the message or not. Wentzel's computer won't accept it. Something is wrong. It's always accepted my messages before."

"Maybe his computer is turned off," Ted offered.

"Uh-uh, that doesn't matter. I'm going to call him."

"You can't do that. A phone call is traceable . . . they keep records."

Bonita picked up a cell phone from the desk. "I'm not stupid, Faircloud. Your friends gave me this cell phone to use. I used it to call you yesterday. They called it a safe phone . . . it's got a number to somebody in Texas . . . can't be traced here." She pushed the keys and put the phone to her ear. A long moment passed before she lowered the device and gave Ted a worried look. "He's not answering. . . . He wouldn't have already gone to work this early; he should be there. Something is wrong. Oh God, do you think . . ."

"I don't know," Ted said, patting her shoulder. "Keep tryin' . . . I've got to get back to my guys. I gotta feelin' Mendez is goin' to be movin' that money real soon."

As Ted turned to go, Bonita grabbed his hand. "Teddy, what are we going to do if Carlos has already got to Wentzel?"

"Do?" Ted repeated. "There's nothin' we can do, at least for now. But once I get his money I'm goin' to do something. . . . I'm puttin' that son of a bitch away permanently."

Bonita kept her grip. "What happens if you don't kill Carlos?"

"I'll be dead then, Bonita. And so will you."

"That's right, we'll all be dead and Carlos will have won. I can't let that happen. . . . If I die, I want to die with a clear conscience. I know somebody, Teddy, a TV news investigator from a station in Atlanta. She came to our station in Miami a year ago and did some research on a story she was working on. I'm going to send her an e-mail and tell her about the Yona Group. . . . Don't worry, I won't name Carlos, but I'll give her enough to get started. She'll eventually piece it together and expose him."

Ted frowned. "You could get her dead, too. You think about that?"

"She's good, Teddy. I'll warn her and she'll know what to do. Please . . . we have to make sure Carlos doesn't get away with what he's done."

"I'm goin' to do my part, Bonita; I'm gettin' him . . . but go ahead, do what ya gotta do if it'll make you feel better."

Bonita forced a smile. "Take care of yourself, Teddy. I'll be waiting for your call."

10:02 A.M., FBI field office, Atlanta

Seated in the large conference room with other resident office chiefs and agents, Eli Tanner lowered his eyes and looked at his hands as the projector clicked and flashed pictures of dead bodies on the screen. Seated beside him, Ashley doodled on her notepad, having seen enough after the first picture of the body of the senator. A minute later the lights came on and Don Farrel, the special agent in charge of the Atlanta office, looked at the deputy director of the Bureau, who was seated beside him at the head of the table.

"Sir, the senator's cruiser was raised from the river early this morning. Nine-millimeter shell casings were found inside the cabin and on the deck, corroborating the statement of the survivor, Miss Ayers, and the M.E.'s conclusion that automatic weapons were used. Also, sir, local Florida sheriff's deputies found three abandoned bass boats this morning in Apalachicola Bay. One was green, matching the description from Miss Ayers. Our people have already made a search of the boats and found nothing—they were wiped clean."

The deputy lowered his head, looking at his hands. "Automatic weapons and three boats used. I assume we've concluded this is a hit?"

The SAC spoke evenly. "Yes, sir. Based on the evidence we have so far, we believe the attack was a hurriedly planned assassination of the senator . . . and because of the method and weapon used, we also believe the murders of two staffers in Washington were hits as well. We believe the Goodnight assassins were on a short-fuse timetable and had little time for planning. We believe this because if the assassins had more time, they could have easily made their attempt on the senator while he was in Washington, where it is common knowledge he jogs alone every morning."

The deputy director nodded. "I agree it had to be short-fused, but why did they take out the senator's family? A sniper hidden on the bank could have done it with one shot."

"Sir, we believe the assassins had to ensure the senator was killed. Placing marksmen on the river bank would have been too risky in that the senator may have been out of sight, in the cabin, when the cruiser passed them. The only way to ensure his death was to be within point-blank range. Sir, the attack does tell us something, however, about their timetable. We believe the assassins had only twenty-four to thirty-six hours of planning time. We came to this conclusion because if they had more time they could have made the attempt on the senator in Columbus before he left for the trip. He jogged alone Friday morning before going to the cruiser to join his family."

"Yes, that seems logical," the deputy director said. "It would have been less risky for them rather than staging their daylight attack. Have we got anything on why the senator would be subject to assassination?"

"Sir, we learned this morning from the Washington office that all of the computers in the senator's offices had their hard drives erased and all their disks had been blanked. Paper files are also missing, and a check of Wentzel's residence and private office revealed the same—the computers were erased of all data, disks were blanked, and files are missing."

Farrel paused a moment and leaned forward in his chair. "Sir, we believe there is a connection between the murders and the destruction and removal of the files. At this time I will have Special Agent Paul Eddings continue the briefing. I've assigned him as the case agent in charge of this case, and he will explain the connection."

Seated at the opposite end of the long table, Eli drew in a breath and shifted his eyes from the SAC to the big, good-looking former all-American special agent who stood, then moved to the right side of the screen. Eli knew Paul Eddings only by reputation and from having watched him on television years ago. Eddings had been a star halfback for the University of Alabama.

Eddings dipped his chin to the deputy and nodded to the computer operator, who touched the keyboard, causing another slide to be projected to the screen. It was a color map of Georgia and its bordering states.

Eddings extended his pocket pointer but kept it at his side as he spoke. "Sir, as you are aware, Senator Goodnight requested the Federal Trade Commission and the Bureau to investigate a business here in Georgia known as the Yona Group. The senator had received numerous complaints from constituents that this group was using unfair business practices within the northern region of the state. The senator had also received an anonymous e-mail message a month before containing very specific information, laying out the unfair business practices being conducted by the group. Using the information, Senator Goodnight made a preliminary investigation under the leadership of his staffer, Matthew Wentzel. Mr. Wentzel found within a few weeks that the group was indeed engaging in price-fixing and in violation of antitrust laws. He contacted the Federal Trade Commission to report his findings but they were unable to look into the matter for some time. He then contacted the Bureau, and as you know I was assigned to look into the matter. Six days ago I met with the senator and Mr. Wentzel for the first time, and they showed me what they had uncovered. Sir, I must point out that Matthew Wentzel was an attorney who was very thorough. He had done extensive legwork and had conducted interviews with several witnesses who he had managed to locate. After reading the document and witness statements, I concluded there was enough evidence to warrant our involvement. Sir, it was clear the Yona Group was engaging in an illegal monopoly of the conversion van, boat, and truck industry of the southeast region."

"Conversion industry?" the deputy director asked.

Eddings stepped closer to the table. "Sir, I'm talking about an industry that customizes vehicles and boats, dramatically enhancing their appearance and comfort. A customized van, for example, on average has seven thousand dollars' worth of accessories, paint, and parts installed on the finished product. Everything that is attached to a boat other than the motor and standard equipment also falls into the category, and nowadays pickups and even semis are being converted. We are talking about an industry that brings in just over a billion dollars a year in annual revenue. Not IBM, Xerox, or General Foods, but substantial nevertheless. The conversion industry encompasses more small companies and employees and affects more of the general population in northern Georgia and the surrounding region than many of the large corporations taken together. The companies and businesses that make up the industry are for the most part small and rural, employing, on average, only ten employees. The Yona Group is the exception, sir. They are quite large and at present employ well over six hundred workers. They bought out many of the smaller companies and have forced many others out of business through the use of unfair business practices. When one of these small company owners is given a choice of whether to join the Yona Group or be forced out of business, the decision is simple. In most cases the owners opt to survive. Those who chose to ignore the Yona Group's proposal quickly found suppliers of needed materials would not respond to orders. If that was not enough, frivolous lawsuits were filed against their products for being unsafe or causing injury. Last-resort tactics included owners having 'accidents.' The bottom line is that Senator Goodnight's investigation was about to bust open a can of worms."

The deputy director stiffened. "You said 'was,' Agent Eddings?"

Eddings frowned as he collapsed his pointer. "Sir, as I said, I had just started on the case. I had not yet had the opportunity to collect and copy the information that Mr. Wentzel had acquired. The Washington field office search of his office and Wentzel's residence has turned up none of the paper or computer-generated records, reports, and statements. And there is more bad news, sir. Whoever stole the files now knows the identity of the witnesses who came forward. In light of the events of past days, we can assume those witnesses will be contacted and threatened into silence, or worse."

The deputy leaned back in his chair with a disbelieving frown. "Are you telling me you believe the motive behind the murder of the senator and the others is his investigation into the Yona Group?"

Eddings held the deputy's eyes. "Sir, I'm saying the senator and his two staff members had collected information that would have exposed a monopoly whose benefactors, if exposed, would lose roughly twelve million dollars in profits this year alone. And the senator's investigation had only scratched the surface. Wentzel had not yet expanded his investigation into the bordering states—that's why he wanted the Federal Trade Commission and the Bureau's involvement. It was going to be my recommendation that we form a special task force and—"

"Yes, I understand, Agent Eddings," the deputy said. "Please forgive me for cutting you off, but discussing recommendations of what we *were* going to do doesn't help us. I find it difficult to believe state authorities were not aware of the Yona Group's activities. What does the Georgia Bureau of Investigation say they have on them?"

"Sir, I have not talked to GBI as yet. We only found out a few hours ago that the missing files were those on the Yona Group investigation."

"I suggest you do that very soon, Agent Eddings. Also based on the amount of profits this group is generating, I'm sure the IRS will be of some assistance to us, and I also want the Federal Trade Commission brought in."

Before Eddings could respond, the deputy director shifted in his seat, pinning the SAC with a stare. "Don, this motive theory of Agent Eddings's seems very thin to me. I know it's all we've got to run with for now, but I have to tell you I have some problems with it. I find it difficult to believe the leaders of this group would hire assassins to kill a United States senator in order to stop an investigation concerning unfair business practices. We've seen price-fixing and monopolizing before in much larger corporations, and we both know they are nonfelony offenses. Even if they had been convicted, the leaders of the group would have suffered only fines and hard slaps on the wrists. There has to be more."

The SAC's face tightened with resolve. "Sir, myself and Agent Eddings agree with you. I assure you we will dig deeper and find out what else, if anything, the group is involved in."

"I know you will, Don. Now, what are you going to need from me, besides my people handling the media? I'm sure you've got a plan prepared."

"Yes, sir, we do. We're organizing a task force, but I'll need your permission to strip the resident offices to minimums and bring in the rest to man the task force. Agent Eddings has already made up a straw-man organization chart. I'll also need forty more agents from other offices for a period of at least a month, and of course we'll need your experts from headquarters and Quantico."

The deputy nodded and stood. "Done. Anything else?"

Farrel looked into the deputy's eyes. "A word with you alone, sir. It's sensitive in nature."

The deputy frowned. "Somehow I knew you were going to say that. I'll meet you in your office. Go ahead and finish briefing your people and I'll go on up and have a cup of coffee."

Once the deputy departed with his two assistants, Farrel looked down the table at his agents. "Okay, people, right now it looks bleak, but there's bound to be light somewhere. Find it. I'll let Agent Eddings brief you on how you're going to be organized. There is no need for me to underscore how important this case is. One note of warning to you all. As you know, the press has the story about the murders, and the reporters are outside the front entrance right now. All of the Atlanta television news crews are setting up camp. Remember, no one is to make any statements about this case. Presently, the press does not know of the two staffers murdered in Washington, and for now we want to keep it that way. Refer all press to our media spokesmen. That's it for me. Agent Eddings has suggested we take a five-minute break for coffee then return and get down to business. Thank you."

Eli stood, as did everyone else, until the SAC disappeared out the door. Stretching, Eli was about to ask Ashley what she thought about the meeting when he saw the Alabama halfback walking toward him with a smile.

Eli was about to introduce himself but saw that Eddings's eyes were not on him, but on Ashley.

"Ashley, you look absolutely wonderful," Eddings said as he drew closer.

Eli winced and waited for the fireworks to begin. No *male* agent dared called Special Agent Sutton by her Christian name. Eli had witnessed firsthand her response to those who had made the fatal error, and he knew what would be coming.

Waiting for the verbal blow, Eli was shocked to find that she was blushing like a schoolgirl. Then she smiled and said, "You're looking pretty good yourself, Paul."

Eli nearly fell over in shock. Special Agent Sutton blushing? And calling the jock *Paul*? And *smiling* at him? What in the hell was going on? he wondered.

Eddings stepped closer, looking into her eyes as if nobody else was in the conference room. "I knew you were going to be here. I saw your name on the list. I . . . I've missed you, Ashley."

Ashley blushed again and bashfully lowered her eyes. "I've missed you, too, Paul."

Eli shook his head, but she was still standing there, looking like the pretty wallflower just asked to the prom by the best-looking hunk in school.

Eddings patted Ashley's shoulder. "I have to get some charts from my office for the meeting, but I'm not letting you go again until we talk. After the meeting I'll take you to lunch so we can catch up. Don't say no, Ashley, I really want us to talk."

Feeling like he was watching an episode on a soap, Eli quickly shifted his eyes to Ashley to await her response. She smiled coyly. "I'd love to have lunch with you, Paul. I'd like to catch up, too."

Eddings's eyes lingered on her for a long moment, then he turned and walked toward the door.

Eli tried to pin her with a questioning stare, but she didn't notice because she was watching the all-American walk away. Finally, when he was out of sight, she exhaled and shot a glare at Eli. "What?" she snapped.

Eli backed up a step and lifted his hand. "Nothin'. I was just wondering if you were feelin' all right?"

She gathered up her purse, swung it over her shoulder, and strode for the door. "I'm going to visit the ladies' room. . . . I'll be back."

Stunned by the sudden transformation of Ashley Sutton, Eli sank back into his chair. Three minutes later he got another shock as Ashley walked through the conference room doorway along with the other agents—she was smiling. Special Agent Sutton did not smile, ever, when in the presence of agents; she assumed all male Bureau personnel hated female agents. And that wasn't all. Ashley had brushed her hair, put on lipstick, and applied some blusher to her cheeks. Eli stared at her. *Ashley, is that really you?* He forced himself to look away just before she got to her seat. Then he caught the scent of her perfume, which she had never worn before, and knew he was in trouble. The new Special Agent Sutton was making him very uncomfortable. He liked the other version better. Yes, she could be bitchy, and yes, at times she was hard to work with, but at least before he had known what to expect. This new person sitting beside him was a strange creature who bewildered and surprised him and smelled too good. It wasn't fair. The additional makeup, maybe; the smile was okay; but the perfume was too much. Hell, she smelled like a woman, not an agent. How in the hell could he think and act naturally with that damn smell going through his head, triggering all kinds of crazy thoughts? Not fair.

At the head of the table Agent Paul Eddings said, "Let's get started. The Washington office will be responsible for investigating the Wentzel and Cooper homicides and the theft of the records. Our task force will have responsibility for everything else. First slide, please. Here, as you can see, is how we will be organized. Note, Team A will have responsibility for continuing the investigation on finding the assailants of the senator and his family. Team B, the larger team, will be responsible for reconstructing the investigation that Mr. Matthew Wentzel had started. Included in Team B will be representatives from the Georgia Bureau of Investigation, Federal Trade Commission investigators, and the IRS. The team chiefs have been appointed and have already given me a list of positions that will need to be filled. You can see on the chart where each of you is assigned and what positions are still vacant and will be filled by the additional support the deputy director approved earlier. Please note the room assignments for each team because I propose we break up into our teams and allow the team leaders to further brief you on what your specific duties will be. Staff meetings will be conducted every day at ten A.M.

and at three P.M., to exchange progress reports. Thank you in advance for your support. Please adjourn to your team rooms."

Eli's jaw muscles twitched as he looked at the chart and saw his name below Ashley's, both of them listed as special assistants to Paul Eddings. Yeah, right, Eli thought, now he'd have to watch the two of them play goo-goo eyes and pitty-pat for however long the investigation took. *No way, I'm not going to be an REMF for Mr. All-American.*

Ashley poked Eli in the side. "Come on, we have to go to Paul's office."

Eli slowly collected his notepad and spoke through clenched teeth. "Yeah, I wouldn't want 'Paul' to have to wait."

She eyed Eli as she swung her purse over her shoulder. "Tanner, Paul is like a brother to me. We went through the Academy together, and we helped each other get through the tough times."

Standing, Eli sniffed the air. "You smell anything different?"

Red-faced, she turned her back on him and marched toward the door. He nodded to himself and said silently, *Yeah, that's what I thought, too. Like a brother, my ass.*

Minutes later Eli walked into the small office of Agent Eddings and saw the ex-jock and Ashley seated beside each other, all smiles. Eddings rose and extended his hand. "Agent Tanner, Ashley has been saying good things about you. I'm very happy to finally meet you. . . . I know we'll make a great team. We were just about to head out to have a bite of lunch. Please join us and we can all become acquainted and I'll explain how you'll be assisting me with the case."

Eli wrinkled his brow as he shook the ex–football player's hand. "Agent Eddings, I'm sorry, but I'm not the assistant type. If it's all the same to you, I'd like to fill the open position in Team B that liaisons with the GBI. I have friends in the Georgia State Bureau and I think I can do a lot more good there. And as far as lunch is concerned, I appreciate the offer but it's a little early for me to eat, plus I think it would be better if you two caught up on old times by yourselves."

Caught off guard by the rejection, Eddings let his smile dissolve. He motioned toward a large folder on his desk. "I should have been honest with you up front. I read your personnel file and saw that you had been assigned to the Miami office and were a member of the organized-crime division. I need your help. I need your expertise in looking into the possibility the Yona Group is connected to organized crime."

Eli shook his head. "That'd be a waste of time. The way I heard it in the meeting, the group uses local labor with no union connection. If there's no unions involved, then you forget about the wise guys being involved."

Eddings raised his chin slightly. "I wasn't referring to the mob, Agent Tanner . . . I was referring to the Yona Group possibly being involved with Miami drug players."

Eli gave Eddings a questioning stare. "What makes you think players are involved?"

Eddings handed the folder to Eli. "What you heard in the meeting earlier was only part of what we have. I received an anonymous e-mail this morning saying a player was connected with the Yona Group. . . . The message also said this unnamed player was responsible for the killing of Senator Goodnight."

"Why didn't you mention this in the meeting?" Eli asked.

"It's on a need-to-know basis, Agent Tanner. The SAC is briefing the deputy on it as we speak. And there's something else that came up recently that could possibly be a connection. That file you're holding is a copy of what our Miami office has on the major drug players. The DEA has the lead on them and provided an update. A couple of weeks ago one of our Miami office C.I.'s told an agent a player was laundering big money here in Georgia."

"How reliable is this confidential informant?"

"According to our Miami people, he's very reliable. The information he gave is all there in a report in the file. The

SAC assigned me as the case officer to check out the information relating to laundering here in the state, but that was before the senator's murder. The Goodnight case has of course taken priority. I wanted you to assist me by looking at the file and seeing if you thought there might be a possible connection."

"No, thanks," Eli said, setting the folder back on the desk. "I only worked in organized crime for seven months, and that was eight years ago. You've got agents a lot more qualified than me you can pick from to help you. I'll just take the job as the liaison with the GBI."

Ashley stood. "Tanner, you can't refuse Paul on this. He needs your help."

Eli shrugged. "Oh yeah, I can. I spent the last three months with the O.C. Division in a Miami hospital. . . . I got shot and lost a partner working a case on a player. Agent Eddings needs the best to help him, and that's not me. I suggest he get the Miami office hotshot O.C. agent to do it."

Showing his disappointment, Eddings walked behind his desk and let out a sigh. "I'll assign you as the liaison to the GBI, Agent Tanner. And I'll take your advice and request an agent from the Miami office. Thank you."

Eli turned to Ashley. "Give me the keys to the van so I can get my stuff. I presume you're going to be working with Agent Eddings, so I'll rent myself a car while I'm up here."

Ashley gave him her best evil glare as she dug in her purse. "You take the van, Tanner. Paul will provide me transportation. I'll get my things out before Paul and I go to lunch, which will be in just a few minutes."

"Fine," Eli said, taking the keys from her. He dipped his chin to the all-American. "Thanks for letting me take the liaison job."

Walking out of the office, Eli congratulated himself on how he had managed to escape the assignment. *Man, that was close! I could just see me having to put up with watching those two working together. Yeah, gettin' out of that assignment was the best thing I could have done. Ashley is going to be happy working with Paul baby, and*

I'm going to be happy workin' with the state boys. Yeah, now we're both happy. He stopped in front of the elevator doors and pushed the button. *Damn her!*

The elevator doors opened and he stepped inside and smashed the ground-floor button. His stomach was rumbling and sending a bad taste up into his throat.

The elevator door opened on the ground floor, and Eli stepped out into the hallway and immediately knew it was not his day. The large foyer was filled with reporters and cameramen all making their way toward the building's glass double doors. More of them were coming out of the room to his right, and he realized a press conference must have just concluded. One class of people he disliked more than lawyers and car salesmen was the media. In his experience, they were nothing but sharks hunting for something to attack and chew up. Eli stayed on the fringe of the man-eaters, willing himself to be patient because they'd be gone in minutes. Then he saw her.

Eli Tanner knew he had weaknesses, and he'd always tried to face and beat them, but when it came to Stacy Starr, she was a weakness he never minded. And there she was, only ten feet away. Miss Georgia, 1972. He wouldn't have known another Miss Georgia if she'd paraded before him with a sign, but Stacy Starr was different. When he'd been serving in Vietnam, his hometown VFW had sent him a large envelope with a small Georgia flag enclosed, along with letters of support and a signed eight-by-ten color glossy of the new Miss Georgia, Stacy Starr. He had received the VFW packet his fourth month in Nam, while his company was patrolling in the mountains of the Central Highlands. He had not seen a woman in three months, so the picture of the smiling young Miss Georgia in her bathing suit had been a very special treat. There was something about him being young and in a foreign land where people were trying to kill him. He had missed home terribly, and for some reason the picture of Stacy was like being home again—she seemed to represent the girl next door. Something in her smile made him feel special, as if it was just for him. He had fallen completely and absolutely in love with her.

Eli couldn't help but smile, thinking of the little blurb on the back of the picture. He had memorized it, repeating it to himself over and over again when he was humping the mountains.

Miss Georgia, 1972, Stacy Starr, our Georgia peach from Waycross. A former cheerleader at Waycross High School, she received a scholarship to attend the University of Georgia, where she is majoring in journalism. Her hobbies include music, tennis, and staying in shape. Miss Starr plans to become a broadcast news journalist. On behalf of Stacy and the people of Georgia, we salute our boys who serve us so proudly.

Eli smiled. He still recalled every word. But it was no wonder, he thought. He had put her picture in plastic and kept it in his helmet and slept with her every night in his dreams. After returning from Nam and recovering from his wounds, he'd followed her career in the newspapers. She had achieved her goal and become one of the top broadcast journalists in the state. Later she moved up to work for ABC network news. She had lasted only three years there, but Eli rarely missed a broadcast in all that time. It had been like watching a dream. A messy divorce and the loss of her two girls to her former husband on the grounds that she'd been an unfit mother helped to knock her out of the big leagues, but in Georgia they forgave their own; she returned and won back her old job with Atlanta's Channel 2.

Eli sighed as he watched her talking to her cameraman. On his scale of one to five, she was a seven. Age had only made her more beautiful. Only an inch or so shorter than he was, she looked like Princess Di and had her regal bearing. Her skin was milky smooth and her large brown eyes were huge pools that made you want to get naked so you could jump into them and splash around and never leave. Streaks of gray splashed her brunette hair and added elegance, but didn't age her a bit, he thought. Her willowy figure was still intact and she still had that smile that he'd always thought special.

Eli was about to look away when her eyes slowly moved to him and locked onto his. His heart quit beating for an instant, but suddenly thumped like a snare drum when she began walking toward him. Having made the same mistake already once today, he looked behind him to see if she was looking at someone else, but there was nothing there but the wall.

"Agent Tanner, I'm happy to see you recovered fully from your wounds," she said, stopping in front of him, her eyes studying the scar on his forehead.

Eli was dumbfounded. She saw his confusion and smiled as she touched his arm. "I'm sorry, I'm Stacy Starr, Channel 2 news. I covered the story about the terrorists a month ago. I was in Washington and was at the hospital when they brought you in. I must tell you that you intrigued me, Agent Tanner. Of course, I received the FBI's version of what happened, but we both know that was bull. I checked you out, Agent Tanner. I managed to secure a file on you. You are a very interesting man."

Eli wanted her to keep talking even though he wasn't really listening to what she was saying. Watching her expression and the movement of her lips was what he focused on, and he was trying to memorize every detail, putting them all in his imaginary helmet for safekeeping. Realizing she was waiting for a response, he raised an eyebrow. "Ditto, Miss Starr, I know something about you as well. You probably don't remember, but in 1972, when you were Miss Georgia, you signed photos for us Georgia boys in Nam."

Her eyes seemed to sadden for a moment, then she looked at him in a different way. "It's Eli, isn't it?"

"Yes, ma'am."

"Eli, I feel as if I know you. The FBI's files are very informative. . . . Tell me something please, off the record, of course. Did you really kill all five of those terrorists?"

Eli lowered his head, knowing she couldn't help herself. The smile, the pat on the arm, the innocent searching stare, were all calculated moves. She was media. It was always the story to them, and even though she'd said it was off the record, he knew better.

Eli spoke softly. "Miss Starr, you know I can't comment on the case."

Her eyes sparkled as she reached out and patted his arm again. "I know what happened, Eli ... but don't worry; your secret is safe with me. Terrible thing about the senator and his family, isn't it?"

Now she's getting to it, Eli thought, knowing all the rest had been nothing but foreplay. She wanted the current story, not old history. He nodded. "Yes, Miss Starr, it is terrible."

"Are you involved in the case?"

"Miss Starr, you know I can't answer that."

She gave him a little bit of a smile. "I heard you were involved in the recovery of the bodies. I have my sources, Eli. Do you think the deaths of Matthew Wentzel and Dana Cooper are connected to the Goodnight murders?"

So much for the media not knowing about the others. He gave her a look that said he couldn't respond.

She nodded and slightly shrugged her shoulders. "I understand," she said softly.

Eli motioned to the now clear open doorway and surprised himself when he reached out and took her hand. "Miss Starr. It was a genuine pleasure meeting you. I really mean it. I guess I'd better get going now."

She seemed shocked by his touch and looked at his hand, then up into his eyes. "I'll walk with you, if you don't mind," she said, and turned and rattled to the cameraman, "Have the boys set up outside the entrance for an intro to the piece. I'll be there in a sec."

Eli tried to tune out the warning bells clanging inside his head as they walked toward the doors together. Her shoulder lightly brushed his and he knew she would try a different tack, but he didn't care. Being with a dream was too good to pass up.

"You're from Columbus, aren't you?" she asked.

"Yes, and you're from Waycross. You were a cheerleader and your hobbies were music, tennis, and staying in shape. You're still staying in shape, I see."

"Thanks, Eli. I'll take that as a compliment. I see you're not wearing a ring. Still haven't remarried?"

"Nope. How about you?" he asked as he opened the glass door for her.

"No, once was enough . . . but you know about that, too, don't you?"

"Sure do. But I'm getting older and smarter, Miss Starr. I'm beginning to think being alone isn't all that great. I think people really do need other people to be whole."

She looked at him for a moment before reaching out and taking his arm, bringing him to a halt. "Eli, I know this may sound awfully direct, but do you think we could possibly have dinner this evening?"

Eli allowed himself a smile he didn't feel. "Miss Starr, I can't do that. We're both working and I'd just disappoint you . . . I wouldn't discuss my work. I do appreciate the offer, though. Under different circumstances I . . . I . . . hell, it doesn't matter. We both know you wouldn't have asked."

She stepped closer, looking into his eyes. "No, that's not true, Eli. Ever since I saw you on that stretcher and heard what you had been through that day, I've wanted to meet you. Come on, give me the chance to fulfill a dream. I want to have dinner with a fellow Georgian who in my book happens to be a hero."

A young man holding a video camera walked up to the couple. "Stacy, ya want to set up here?"

She ignored the young man and kept her gaze on Eli. "What do you say, Eli? Dinner at nine, my place?"

Eli shook his head. "Sorry, Miss Starr, but it's impossible. Like I said, I'd just disappoint you; I'm no hero. Looks like your crew is waiting for you. Good-bye." He turned and walked down the sidewalk, focusing on the parking lot thirty yards ahead of him, but he really wasn't seeing anything.

Still standing on the sidewalk, in a stupor at finally actually meeting his dream girl, Eli shook his head. Everything suddenly came into focus and sounds and sights assaulted his dulled senses. He realized the parking lot was a madhouse. TV news vans and cars were parked haphazardly behind the office employees' cars in the first two rows, and many workers wanted out to go to lunch. The hungry office workers were bitching at the TV van drivers, who were not listening. TV crew members were shouting to other crew members asking what equipment was needed and arguing where their live shots should be conducted. Eli shook his head again, thinking he wasn't the only idiot. The sharks were really at it.

"Eli, please reconsider."

He turned as Stacy approached with a look that melted his insides. "Eli, if you can't make it tonight, let's at least exchange telephone numbers . . . maybe we can have dinner some other time."

Eli saw she was serious, and he was about to respond when over her shoulder he saw Paul Eddings step out the front entrance of the office building with Ashley following a half step behind. His stomach rumbled a warning and he felt himself getting angry all over again, but he told himself to focus. He looked into Stacy's liquid brown eyes and opened his mouth to speak when a loud cracking sound instinctively made him duck. Dropping into a crouch, he pulled a pistol from his back holster. To his horror, he saw Paul Eddings reeling back. Ashley was falling, too, her face and neck showered with blood. Eli spun as another shot was fired and was joined by a rattling staccato of submachine-gun fire that drowned out the screams and shouting from the horrified news crews and people exiting the office building. A thunderous boom came from somewhere in the parking lot, followed by an all too familiar swooshing noise. Eli dove toward Stacy, who stood like a frightened girl with her hands up under her chin. Knocking her down, he landed on top of her just as a rocket swooshed over the top of them and impacted ten feet above the building's doorway, exploding in a roar. Glass shattered, people screamed, concrete pieces of the wall turned into tearing shrapnel, and another rocket swooshed over Eli's head, leaving a spiraling white smoke trail. Again the building seem to shudder with the impact, and dust and dark smoke began turning day to dusk.

Eli screamed *"Stay down!"* to Stacy as he rolled off her and broke into a dead run into the parking lot. Immediately he saw a dark-haired man standing on top of a Buick's trunk, raising an M-72 antitank rocket launcher to his shoulder. Eli chambered a round, flicked off the safety, and lifted his pistol to fire, but a running wide-eyed cameraman slammed into his shoulder, spinning him around. Eli bounced off the side of a Mazda, caught his balance, lifted his pistol, and fired just as the dark-haired man was about to depress the firing button. The man's head snapped back and he toppled off the trunk. Eli ran toward the body, but a tall blond man holding a scoped rifle hopped down from the back of a camper shell on a pickup only ten feet away. The blond man saw him and raised his rifle. Eli fired. The man reeled back with the bullet's impact, which struck him above the bridge of his nose. Eli spun toward the sound of more shooting and saw men firing Mac-10s at the office entrance as they ran toward a white conversion van. He raised his pistol, but from the open sliding door of the van a small man appeared holding a chattering Mac-10. Bullets seemed to chew up the pavement just to the left of Eli's feet. He dove behind a station wagon, popped up and fired four quick rounds, ducked down, ran four steps to the front of the wagon, and popped up again. The van lurched forward, struck the back bumper of a new Lexus but kept going, pushing the new car sideways into another vehicle. Eli aimed and squeezed the trigger again and again as the van continued on. Its rear door window spiderwebbed with one of his bullets, then spiderwebbed again. A body tumbled out of the still-open sliding door as the vehicle squealed around the corner, missed it, and jumped the curb into a flower bed. Still going, the van bucked wildly as it sped down over the curb onto the road again. Not slowing at the exit, the speeding van struck the back end of a Toyota, knocking the small vehicle into the curb and up into another flower bed. The van, with its front bumper hanging on only one side, continued on, leaving a trail of sparks where the bumper was dragging on the pavement.

Eli spun, looking for any shooters left behind, but saw only other agents running toward him, holding their pistols up with both hands in the ready position. Breaking into a run, Eli headed straight for the building entrance, where people were still screaming and the dust and smoke lingered in a thick mist. The smell of the cordite and blood filled his nostrils as he dodged those lying on the ground, afraid to move, and those who lay in puddles of blood, beyond pain and fear. Crystallized glass lay like sparkling carpet beneath his feet as he pushed on, praying somehow she had lived. He slowed and prepared himself for the worst as he approached the kneeling people around the bodies at the entrance. A middle-aged secretary knelt in an expanding pool of blood by Paul Eddings. She was brushing shards of glass from his pale face. Eli saw the bullet hole in the agent's forehead and continued on to the others kneeling by Ashley's still form. Closing his eyes just for a moment for strength, he stepped closer and leaned over to see her. "Oh God, no," he murmured as he sank to his knees. She was lying perfectly still, her hair, face, and neck matted with blood and brain tissue. Suddenly she jerked and her jaw and lips began quivering.

Eli leaned over her. "Ashley, it's me, Eli; can you hear me?" he said as he quickly inspected her for wounds.

"I don't think she was hit; I couldn't find any wounds," said a blood-spattered man kneeling on the opposite side of her. "I was just behind her and saw Eddings knock her back as he fell. We were lucky; the entrance overhang protected us from most of the glass and debris of the blast. What was it, a bomb?"

Eli cradled Ashley's head in his lap and with a shaking hand lightly brushed the gore and small crystals of glass from her eyelids. He felt something in the corner of her right eye that wouldn't move. He lightly touched the protruding sliver, and she jerked and moaned in pain.

"I'm sorry, Ashley, lie still. Don't move your eyelids . . . you've got something in your eye . . . you're going to be fine, Ashley . . . you're going to be fine. I'm here . . . I won't leave you . . . I'm here."

Eli heard sirens in the distance above the din of confusion and shouting of people rushing to help those wounded by gunfire or hurt by the debris, and he heard other sounds, whirring and clicking. Cameramen were snapping pictures of him and the bodies lying about. He glanced up just for a moment and saw Stacy Starr standing only five feet away. Her hose had holes and runs, and blood ran down from one of her knees. The dress she wore was ripped at the sleeve, her hair was mussed and sticking up on one side, and she held her arm as if it were injured. And despite being in obvious physical pain, Eli heard her tell the video cameraman at her side to get a wider-angle shot. *The sharks are feasting,* Eli thought as he wiped the blood from his fingers on his shirt and began pushing more away from Ashley's forehead. "I'm here," he whispered to her. "Just lie still . . . the paramedics are on their way. Just lie still . . . I'm here."

CHAPTER 9

Dahlonega, Georgia

Ted got into the blue conversion van and slid the door shut.

Seated in the driver's captain's chair, eating Fritos, Glenn Henderson glanced in the rearview mirror at his friend before shifting his gaze out the front window toward the distant bank. "Where have you been?"

"Calming the lady down. Glenn, I think Mendez had Senator Goodnight popped."

Glenn nodded. "I was afraid of that when I heard it on the radio. That asshole doesn't mess around, does he?"

"No, he don't. The lady tried sendin' an e-mail to the senator's investigator, but his computer won't accept it. She tried calling, too. Nothin'."

"Like I said, Ted, he's not messing around. They'll be comin' for the money soon."

"Yeah, that's what I thought, too. Anything so far?"

Glenn dipped his chin toward the front window. "Quiet as a mouse . . . nothing but locals going in and out."

"Where's Virg and Ramon?"

Glenn looked at his watch. "Virg ought to be relieving me in a few minutes. Ramon is probably racked out back in the motel room. I let them make a run to Atlanta to go shopping for clothes yesterday evening after the bank closed. Don't give me that look. I watched the bank, and they both had cell phones if I needed them."

"Christ'a'mighty, Glenn, what woulda happened if they moved the money when they were off in Atlanta?"

"Relax, Ted. They couldn't have moved it last night. A city road crew blocked the street off down there and did some patch work . . . took most of the night. Anyway, the guys were back by nine."

Suddenly the van door opened and in stepped Virgil and Ramon. *What the hell is goin' on?* Ted wondered as he looked both men over. They were almost identically dressed, same color and style expensive slacks, same color belts, and even the same style and color tasseled loafers. The only thing different about their clothes was that Virgil was wearing a dark blue polo shirt and Ramon was wearing a black one.

"Who the hell are you guys supposed to be, the Blues Brothers?" Ted asked.

Virgil Washington got in the front passenger seat as Ramon settled in the rear seat. Virgil pushed his new teardrop-shaped glasses farther back on his nose and lifted his chin. "Well, what do ya think, Ted?"

"Huh? What d'ya mean, what do I think?"

"My new look. What do ya think of it?"

Ted softened his glare as he studied Virgil's closely cropped hair and new clothing. "Eh . . . yeah, I kinda like it. You really look different, but I didn't know you wore glasses."

Pulling down the sun visor, Virgil tilted his head one way then another as he looked at himself in the vanity mirror. "I *don't* wear 'em. Glenn gave me and Ray some advice on lookin' sophisticated. These aren't prescription, they're clear, but they do something, don't they? I mean it makes me look like a professor or somethin', don't you think?"

"Yeah, you have that Christopher Darden look, you know, the black lawyer that had O.J. put on the gloves. I like the clothes, too, real *GQ* stuff," Ted said.

"How about me, man?" Ramon asked. "Glenn told me about these socks. They're so thin it's like wearing nothing at all."

Ted glanced down at Ramon's ankle then shook his head. "How about lettin' me know next time you guys are dressin' up. I'm feelin' kinda bad just wearin' these jeans and T-shirt here. I mean shit, here I got two sophisticated dudes dressed to kill, and I look like a hick. But, gee, guys, I hate to break it to ya, but we're supposed to be construction guys, remember? Dressed as Mr. GQs don't fit."

"We're cool construction guys," Virgil said as he adjusted the new glasses. "Me and Ray are doin' it in style from now on. Right, Ray?"

"There it is, Virg, we're sophisticated guys from now on," Ramon said, leaning back in the seat again.

Ted sighed. "It's about broads, isn't it? You guys meet some career ladies in the apartments?"

Virgil flipped up the sun visor and shrugged. "We met a few when we were off the other day. Ray and me worked out in the apartment workout room and we met a couple of real lookers. No big deal."

"And you need Glenn here to help you score with 'em?" Ted gave Glenn a conspiratorial wink.

"I asked him to help us a little 'cause we didn't do so hot with them," Virgil said. "Glenn knows his shit, Ted. Just look at how the man dresses. He's cool, man. Well, now so are we. He says we need to work on our language skills, but other than that we should be good to go with the ladies." Virgil looked over his shoulder at Ramon. "Right, Ray, we're ready for action, huh?"

"There it is, Virg. We're ready for the ladies now, man."

Ted rolled his eyes. "Yeah, right, two Army paratroopers made into sophisticated guys with glasses and socks, sure. Listen to me, you two, you'd better keep a good eye on that bank tonight. I think Mendez is goin' to be movin' that money real soon."

"Why you thinkin' that, boss?" Virgil asked.

"Remember I told you guys how this was all set up? Well, we think Mendez had Senator Goodnight whacked. If he did contract the hit, that means he knows about the investigation and that means he's gotta move his money."

Virgil slowly shook his head. "Mendez must be really bad news to be takin' out a senator—gotta have balls to do that."

"I told you the man was bad," Ramon said, sitting up again. "I saw it on the news—they did the senator's family, too. That's Mendez, all right . . . he takes out everybody to teach a lesson."

Ted got up and grasped the door handle. "The point is, keep your eyes peeled. Ya see people go into that bank after hours, call me on the cell phone and me and Glenn will be here in five minutes."

Glenn slid out of the front seat and was about to follow Ted out the side door when Virgil motioned to the sack of Fritos in his hand.

"Ya gonna leave those for us, aren't ya?"

Atlanta, Georgia

It was just past ten in the evening when Don Farrel approached the fifth-floor nurse's station where a young agent stood waiting. The agent handed a clipboard to the SAC. "Sir, here's a list of our people and the status of their current conditions. We lost Tompkins an hour ago. The doctors did all they could, but his wounds were too massive. His death brings the number to seven of our people. Mrs. Sweeney is still critical, but as you can see, the others are all stable."

Farrel looked down the list of ten names; two were agents, two were legal analysts, and the rest were secretaries or administrative employees. After reading the status of each, he handed the clipboard back. "How many were treated and released?"

"Nineteen of ours. Mostly lacerations from the glass. There were about the same number of press people and other office workers. Last count was six of them were killed and fourteen others are hospitalized throughout the city."

Farrel shook his head. "Those damn antitank rockets that hit the building did most of it. The explosions shattered most of the office windows facing the parking lot. . . . I saw on Agent Sutton's update that she's doing all right. Is Agent Tanner with her, by chance?"

The agent looked at the clipboard to refresh his memory. "Sutton . . . Sutton . . . oh yes, the female agent. She had the skull fragment lodged in her right eye. I don't recall the agent's name, but he has premature gray hair. He's been with her since she arrived. While she was in surgery I got him a scrub shirt from a nurse so he could get rid of the shirt he was wearing—pretty gruesome with the blood and all. He's with her now if you want to see him, sir. Room 314."

Farrel motioned to the clipboard. "The status report didn't say if Agent Sutton's eye could be saved or not."

"Oh no, sir, she's not going to lose it. I talked to the doctors who operated on her. The fragment lodged in the lower portion of her right eye and didn't do any damage to the pupil or lens. The fibrous sclera, the white of the eyes, was slightly punctured, as was the cornea, and there was some slight damage to connecting eye muscle. The surgeon assured me after her surgery that she would have no difficulty seeing from the injured eye within a couple of weeks."

"Thank God for that. I want you to stay here for a while because I expect the deputy director to come by. If he does, show him the updates and tell him I'm visiting my people. I'll start with Agent Sutton. And thanks, you did a good job collecting the information. I appreciate it."

The young agent nodded. "I'm glad I could be useful. And sir, when you talk to Agent Sutton, it was a glass shard that was removed . . . the doctors didn't tell her it was a fragment of Agent Eddings's skull."

"I understand," Farrel said. "Let's keep it that way."

Seconds later the SAC entered Room 314 and saw Eli sitting next to the bed with his head resting on the rail. He was holding Ashley's hand.

Eli heard his footsteps and began to rise, but Farrel waved him down and whispered, "Stay put; how is she?"

"I'm doing fine," Ashley said softly as she slightly lifted her head from the pillow.

"No, please lie back down, Agent Sutton. I just stopped by to ensure you were doing all right and also to find Agent

Tanner." He stepped closer and patted her shoulder. "I'm very glad to hear the surgery went well and that you'll be on your feet soon."

"Yes, sir, that's what they tell me," she said just above a whisper.

Eli stood but kept hold of her hand. "She's still a little doped up, sir."

Farrel leaned over to Eli and whispered, "Does she know about Eddings and the others?"

Eli nodded. Ashley shook her bandaged head from side to side. "No whispering, please . . . I want to know what happened to the assailants, sir. Agent Tanner is being his typical self and won't tell me anything. Sir, I must know, please tell me. Did we get them?"

Farrel exchanged glances with Eli, then patted Ashley's shoulder again. "Agent Tanner shot three of them, Agent Sutton. Two were killed and one was wounded and is in Grady. Three fled the scene, but we found blood in their abandoned van in a shopping mall where they changed vehicles. It appears Agent Tanner may have wounded another when he fired at their fleeing vehicle. We ID'd only one of the dead, a mechanic-for-hire named Jorge Orlando. The others didn't come up on the computer and probably won't. It appears they're Cuban. The Miami office sent us a list of those who were known to run with Orlando, and most entered the country illegally. We believe they were hired to assassinate Paul and then do as much damage as possible in the thirty seconds they had allotted themselves for the hit. The wounded assailant hasn't talked, but plans and photos were found in the assailant's van. We also found a map of the Apalachicola River in the van. It looks like they were the same crew that made the hit on the senator and his family."

Ashley's eyes shifted to Eli then back to Farrel. "Did our people find anything on who let the contracts?"

"No," Farrel said, shaking his head, "and I don't think the wounded assailant will tell us. Maybe we'll get lucky when we collar the others. It's just a matter of time."

Ashley's unbandaged eye began watering. "They . . . they can't get away with this, sir. The people who let the contracts have to burn."

Farrel patted her shoulder. "They will. . . . Whoever ordered the hits made a tactical error, thinking that killing Paul and the others would slow us down. The deputy is sending in one hundred agents to help us renew the investigation. We'll get them."

Eli handed Ashley a Kleenex. "Try and sleep now, pard. I'll be right here."

Farrel touched Eli's arm and whispered, "You've got statements to make and—"

Eli cut him off by lifting his hand. "I'm staying with my partner, sir. I'll make the statements and talk to the shrink right here. I've already surrendered my weapon to Agent Giles and given him a brief statement of the events as I saw them."

Farrel's eyes narrowed slightly. "Don't interrupt me, Tanner. I was going to say get some rest is all. You don't need to see a shrink—you did a good job out there today. I'll talk to the hospital staff and have them bring a cot or something so you can get some rest. See you later."

Farrel looked once again at Ashley, then walked out the door.

Ashley squeezed Eli's hand. "You should have told me you got some of them."

"I knew you'd just get upset with me. Ya told me to take it easy, remember?"

A tear trickled down her cheek. "You hate hospitals, Tanner; why are you staying with me?"

"I don't have a ride. Our van is still at headquarters, and even if it were here, you know how I hate driving. Hey, get some rest, will ya? You can play twenty questions tomorrow."

"Tanner . . . thank you for staying."

"Yeah, no sweat. Now get some rack time. I'll be here."

Eli reached up, turned out the light above her bed, and was about to sit down in his chair when a nurse walked in the room. "Agent Tanner?"

"Yes?"

"Agent Tanner, Miss Stacy Starr is in the second-floor waiting room and she asked if you would please come down and speak to her a moment. I believe she wants to thank you for saving her life."

Eli sat down and shook his head. "Please tell Miss Starr I'm not available."

The nurse stepped closer. "Agent Tanner, she was treated for a dislocated elbow. . . . She says it's really important that she see you."

Eli shifted his eyes to the woman. "And this is important to me, ma'am."

Seeing his expression, the nurse left in silence.

"Is that Stacy Starr of Channel 2, Tanner?" Ashley asked with her eye closed.

"Yeah. She was out front when the shooting started."

"Do you know her?"

"Kinda, from a long time ago."

"Maybe you should go, then."

"She's media . . . you know what I think about them."

"Yeah, Tanner . . . they're up there with hospitals and driving, right?"

"Yep. Go to sleep, pard."

Eli rested his head on the railing. Closing his eyes, he gathered all the memories of Stacy Starr from the scrapbook in his mind and let them slowly fade away. He knew she was a dream no longer worth keeping. As with so many things that had seemed important to him, it was time to let the past go.

Midnight, Days Inn, Dahlonega, Georgia

Lying on the bed watching television, Ted heard a light knock on his door. He got up and walked to the door thinking it was Virgil or Glenn. He opened the door and blinked, not believing who he saw.

Before she could speak, Ted grabbed her arm, pulled her into the room, and closed the door. "Christ'a'mighty, Bonita! What the hell you doin' here?"

Seeming unfazed by his anger, she motioned with a trembling hand toward the television. "You saw it, didn't you? "An . . . an earlier report said several agents were killed. One of them, they said, was Agent Eddings . . . the one who was working with Wentzel. Carlos did it, didn't he?"

"Yeah, it sure looks like it. Jesus, Bonita, you can't be here; one of my guys is in the next room. How'd you get here?"

"After I saw it on the news, I borrowed Duwane's car and drove up to find you. I've been driving around for an hour trying to find your Lincoln, and saw it out front of the room and—"

"Christ'a'mighty, did you knock on all the motel's doors?"

"No, I saw you through the window."

Ted hurried to the window and pulled the curtains closed. "Dumb, Bonita. This is really dumb. You could blow our operational security by—"

Bonita began crying. "Don't do it, Teddy. It's out of control. Carlos is killing everybody . . . you saw what happened, all those poor people. My God, we can't go through with this."

Ted softened his stare, walked over, and put his arm around her shoulders. "Come on, Bo, get hold of yourself. We can't quit now. The money is your only chance to get out of this alive."

"I can't do it, Teddy. I don't care about the money; I just want it to end."

"You're upset, Bo. Sit down a minute." Ted led her to the bed and sat down beside her. "Take in a deep breath and listen to me. Mendez is goin' to be movin' the money anytime now. Me and my guys are ready . . . we'll get the money. When we do, we'll do just like we planned. I'll call you on your cell phone and tell you where your share is hidden. You borrow Duwane's car again, pick up the cash, and buy yourself a used car from the papers. Return Duwane's car, then take a cab to your car and head for Kansas. You hear me, Kansas. Go to a town called Hutchinson and call Henry Duggin; he's a friend of mine. He'll hide you out and get you a new ID. I'll call him and set it all up for you. His name is Henry Duggin. Now you say it."

"Henry Duggin."

"That's right. Once things blow over, then you can get yourself an airline ticket and go anywhere you want. I'm uppin' your share—you'll get a half million, so pick someplace nice."

Bonita looked into his eyes. "Why, Teddy? Why is going after Carlos so important to you?"

"It's personal, Bo."

"He'll kill you. I . . . I don't want that to happen. Don't do it. Leave with me right now and let's run off together."

"I can't do that, Bo. I got a promise to keep . . . it's a duty."

"A duty? Ted, it's suicide. I told you about the number of guards he has around him when he's on his yacht—there's no way you can get to him."

"I know a way, Bo. I'm a SEAL, remember?"

"I'm never going to see you again, am I?" she asked.

"It wouldn't be smart."

"Teddy, make love to me."

"What?"

"You heard me. I don't want to leave you without you ever holding me. I . . . I care for you. I liked us . . . I liked us being able to talk and watch movies together. No, don't look away from me. Can you look me in the eyes and tell me you don't have feelings for me? Well? Can you?"

"No, Bo, I can't lie to you, but it's not going to happen. You gotta go right now. Come on, get up."

Bonita allowed him to pull her to her feet. She cupped his chin. "Promise me something, Teddy, then I'll go. Promise me you'll get out of this alive."

"Of course I will. Now come on . . . I'll walk out first and see if anybody is in the lot." He began to open the door when she stepped closer and kissed him. A long moment passed before she stepped back.

"You're no Alec Baldwin, Teddy Faircloud, but you sure have a way about you. I'll never forget us." She forced a smile, turned, opened the door, and walked out into the darkness.

CHAPTER 10

7:20 A.M., Tuesday, hospital cafeteria

Eli sat at a corner table drinking coffee and reading the paper when he heard someone approaching. The SAC, Don Farrel, set his coffee cup on the table and took a seat. "Did you get any sleep last night, Tanner?" he asked.

Eli put his paper down, looking at his disheveled boss. "Yes, sir, a little, but it looks like you didn't."

Farrel nodded tiredly. "Yeah, it was a long night. I had Tom Bowlan take over for Eddings as the case officer. We went over Paul's organization charts for the task force. . . . I saw where he penciled you in as the liaison with the GBI."

"Yes, sir. I volunteered for the job."

"Tom made a few changes to the organization, but you're still the liaison. We faxed what we had to the GBI this morning and told them you'd be over this afternoon for a sit-down. I suggest if you know somebody over there, you request him to be your point of contact. They can be a pretty chilly bunch when it comes to supporting us feds. Our relationship with them has never been the best."

"I understand, sir. I'll make the call," Eli said.

Farrel glanced at the newspaper headlines. "The media don't like being targets, do they?"

"They took a heavy hit, sir. Paper says the Channel 2 guy didn't make it. . . . That makes eight of them that bought it."

Farrel closed his eyes a moment. "They're taking it personally. All the big names are coming into town to cover the story . . . Tom Brokaw, Rather, Jennings. I don't need that right now. We did get a couple of breaks last night, though. Our people picked up one of the hitters at the airport, and we got another trying to rent a car. All we're missing is the wounded one."

Eli waited for more news but saw his boss staring vacantly at his coffee cup. "Sir, you said there were a *couple* of breaks?"

Farrel nodded as if to himself. "I'm sorry, yes, the other break came from the Washington office. It appears the female, Dana Cooper, the assistant to Wentzel who was murdered, was the one who erased the computer hard drives and blanked the disks. Her prints were found on the computers and she was the last one to sign out of the office the day before the murders took place. A search of her apartment turned up an airplane ticket for Paris—she was scheduled to depart the afternoon she was killed. They also found a faked passport in the name of Delia Beckman, along with IDs and credit cards and twenty thousand dollars in travelers checks. They're checking her finances now, and I suspect we'll find she has big money deposited somewhere."

Eli's face tightened. "It's getting uglier by the minute, sir. Whoever is running the show has money to burn and is taking no chances with loose ends. . . . Who is the player, sir?"

Farrel raised his eyes. "What?"

Eli met his superior's stare. "You can cut the crap with me, sir. Last night you told me they ID'd the blond shooter I shot—his name was Orlando, a Cuban. And yesterday, ten minutes before the attack, Agent Eddings told me about the anonymous e-mail he'd received saying a player was involved with the Yona Group. Come on, sir, I'm not stupid. A hired Cuban hit crew stinks of a connection. . . . Who is the player?"

Farrel's eyes narrowed. "Eddings shouldn't have told you about that e-mail message, Tanner. Don't breathe a damn word of it or I'll have your ass, you understand me?"

"No, sir, I don't understand. What the hell is goin' on? Why are you keeping the player connection secret?"

Farrel studied Eli's face a moment before lowering his eyes and speaking in almost a whisper. "The DEA has the lead on the possible connection, not us. The deputy isn't happy about it, either, but it's orders from the top—the DEA has it and we're to provide support."

Surprised by Farrel's words, Eli leaned closer. "The DEA has a suspect?"

"I don't know . . . their case agent in charge is flying up from Miami and briefing us this afternoon on what they have. In the meantime we're to keep working on reconstructing the senator's investigation into the Yona Group."

"This is bullshit," Eli said angrily.

"I know it's bullshit, Tanner, but I've got my orders and we'll all do as we're told. Now drop it; this conversation didn't happen. . . . Have you seen Agent Sutton this morning?"

Trying to calm himself, Eli nodded slowly. "Yes, sir, she's feeling a lot better. They're going to release her sometime today if the shrink clears her."

"Good. She's a tough little thing, isn't she?"

"Yes, sir, she is."

"I had my doubts about her. Hell, I admit it. I didn't like her . . . a damn admin wirehead, and a feminist to boot, but I have to give credit where credit is due. She's done all right as a field agent. Well, guess I'd better make the rounds and see our people. Damn, it's hard, Tanner; it's hard seeing them lying there all beat to hell. Hardest damn part of the job is doing this. . . . Damnit! They've got to get the asshole responsible for this."

Eli was about to agree but froze. Despite the blue canvas sling around her neck, Stacy Starr looked stunning even at that early hour.

Stacy smiled when she stopped only a few feet away from their table. "It looks like it's my lucky day. I've found the two men I've been looking for. How are you, Donny?"

Farrel dipped his chin. "I'm doing okay under the circumstances, Miss Starr. How's your arm?"

"I'm alive, thanks to Agent Tanner," she said, then pinned

Farrel with a glare. "Donny, what's this about a Washington public affairs officer taking over as your office spokesman?"

"It's too big for my people to handle, Miss Starr. You can understand that."

"I do if you tell him to work with us locals on an equal basis. If he grants one interview with a national before he talks to us, you'll have hell to pay."

"He knows how it's played, Miss Starr. How's your sound man doing?"

Stacy stepped closer as she pulled a piece of paper from her oversize purse. "Like me, he was treated and released last night. I thought I'd better show you this. It was on my e-mail when I got back home from the hospital. It was sent yesterday morning."

Farrel took the paper and began reading. His head snapped up. "Where did you get this?"

"As I just said, on my e-mail. I take it by your response it's not just a weirdo who got my personal e-mail address?"

"Don't you dare use my reaction as confirmation. You ambushed me. Now where did it come from?" Farrel asked as he handed the paper to Eli, who quickly read the one paragraph.

To Stacy Starr, Channel 2:
The attack on Senator Goodnight and his family was ordered by a major Cuban drug player in Miami. The reason was to stop the investigation into the Yona Group of Dahlonega, Georgia. This information will give you a start in the right direction, but you must be very careful and don't trust anyone until you go public. Your life is in extreme danger now that you have this information.

Concerned Georgia Citizen

"Come on, Donny, you know I can't reveal sources . . . and I don't know anyway," Stacy said. "There was no return e-mail address. When I saw what it said, I downloaded it and ran a couple of copies. That's your copy. You can keep it, but you should know I'm already working on it."

"Sit down!" Farrel growled.

Stacy rolled her eyes but pulled up a chair. Farrel leaned close to her. "What you got cannot be released to the public, do you understand? It will jeopardize our case. I'm not being overly dramatic here, Miss Starr; I'm serious. Whoever sent this to you must be deeply involved. I can't tell you any more than that, but believe me, I can't allow you to go public with what you have."

Stacy shrugged. "You're obviously tired, Donny, and aren't thinking. Whoever sent me the information wants it to get out. If I don't follow up on it, the source will just send the information to some other station or paper until he or she gets what they want. I called around and did some checking and no other station or paper received that message. It looks like the source wanted the best reporter on it and gave it to me."

"Christ," Farrel said, lowering his head, "I don't need this."

Stacy smiled as she patted his hand. "Don't worry, Donny, I'll cooperate fully with you. I already found out one of the shooters killed in the parking lot was ID'd by your people. He was a Cuban named Jorge Orlando. I checked with some friends in Miami and found out this Orlando was a mechanic-for-hire for the drug boys. I also ran a check on the Yona Group to see what business they were in. I must admit that part of the e-mail didn't make sense to me—when I found out they owned a bunch of smaller companies that just do conversions of vans and boats. But Donny, when I ran a check and saw who was running the group and who the partners were, then I smelled a whopper of a story. Tell me, Donny, have you picked up the leaders of the Yona Group for questioning yet?"

Farrel looked into her eyes for a long moment before responding. "Miss Starr, we're going to need some time . . . you're way ahead of us on this."

Stacy returned his stare for a moment before her eyes widened. "You do know who runs the Yona Group, don't you?"

Farrel's face screwed up as if in pain. "Look, you were there yesterday. You know Agent Eddings was killed, but you probably didn't know he was my case agent in charge. Don't quote me on that and don't say a damn word about Orlando or his possible connection to the Yona Group. We know who the group's leaders are, and we're investigating, but we need more time. You'll have to sit on your information for at least a day to allow us to catch up. Promise me."

Stacy held his gaze a long moment before lowering her chin. "Okay, but I want to be told when you do move. And Donny, I want to be told about anything else that breaks on this case two hours before it's officially released. That's the deal for my cooperation."

"One hour," Farrel said.

Stacy's eyes fell on Eli. "Okay, Donny, but one more thing and we've got a deal. I want you to please tell Agent Tanner to be at my place at nine tonight for dinner. It's my way of thanking him for saving my life. Do we have a deal?"

Farrel looked at Eli as if saying, *Don't give me a hard time on this.* Eli nodded. "Sir, I would be honored to have dinner with Miss Starr this evening."

"Deal, Miss Starr," Farrel said. "But don't tell a living soul we're giving you preferential treatment."

She got up and bowed her head. "Always a pleasure seeing you, Donny. And Agent Tanner, dress casual tonight. Good day, gentlemen."

As soon as Stacy walked away, Farrel wearily shook his head. "Goddamn it! That's all I needed . . . the damn media involved."

Eli shrugged. "At least she was nice about it. Most of the sharks wouldn't have shown you that message—they would have run with what they had."

"Nice? Tanner, Stacy Starr is a lot of things, but *nice* isn't one of them. She's got me by the balls and knows it. You can bet she smells a Pulitzer in this story. You'd better call the GBI and move up the meeting time. I need what they have on the Yona Group. . . . I wasn't all that honest with Starr. Eddings was going to run a check on the group's leaders yesterday. Maybe the GBI has something on them and can save us time. Plus I don't want the GBI thinking this is an all-fed show."

"I'll call now, sir," Eli said, getting up. He handed the e-mail message back to his boss. "The source says the player was Cuban and that he ordered the hits."

"I read it, Tanner. Forget you saw it. I'll give the message to the DEA and see if they might know who the source is. And Tanner, I'm sorry about the dinner thing with Starr. She had me in a box."

Eli sighed. "No problem, sir. Anything for the Bureau."

Ten minutes later Eli walked into Ashley's hospital room and was surprised to see her sitting in a chair, fully dressed. She rose as soon as he entered. "Where have you been? Come on, let's get out of here," she said.

"Whoa, Sutton. You're not going anywhere until the docs say you can go."

Ashley motioned to her dressing. "Look, they changed the bandage and gave me an appointment for next week. I've been cleared for limited duty, so let's get out of here."

Eli still blocked the door. "You're supposed to see a shrink."

"She just left, Tanner. Now if you don't mind, I want out of here. I've been around you too much, I guess; I've picked up your aversion to hospitals."

Eli put his arm up to stop her from grasping the door-knob. "Wait a minute, Sutton, I'm working. I've got to be at the GBI headquarters in thirty minutes for a meeting. I can't drive you back to Columbus right now."

She pushed his arm down. "Fine, I'll go with you. Give me the keys; I'll drive."

"Slow down, will ya? Can you drive with your eye bandaged that way?"

"Tanner, I'm not riding with you if *you* drive, so it's me driving or me taking a cab to the GBI. Decide."

Eli handed her the van keys. Fifteen minutes later Ashley was driving down Peachtree Street listening as Eli filled her in on Stacy Starr's e-mail and the SAC's deal with her to keep a lid on the information. Eli left out the last part of the deal, the dinner date.

Ashley shook her head when he had finished. "The SAC shouldn't have made the deal."

"You don't get it, Sutton. Starr is a shark and that e-mail pointed her in the direction of fresh blood. What do you think would happen if she reported on the national news that she had received information from an unnamed source incriminating the Yona Group as being connected to the murders of Senator Goodnight and his family? And then she says that the FBI would not confirm or deny that the company is in fact under investigation? Come on, Sutton, tell me what would happen then?"

Ashley's shoulders sagged. "Okay, okay, I see your point. If she released the information, the rest of the media would have pounced on it and started their own investigations of the group. Yeah, I see what you mean. They'd get to the suspects and friends and family before we would and really screw things up."

"Right," Eli said.

Ashley's face constricted. "Maybe we should let her release what she has. The media will fry them if they're dirty. The sharks will make sure the bastards get what they deserve."

Eli looked at her a moment before shifting his gaze toward the road. "That's not the way to run an investigation. The source is running the show, and you have to ask yourself what's behind it."

Ashley clenched the steering wheel tighter. "Maybe the bastards killed somebody the source cared about, Tanner. They know how slow we move. Maybe they wanted justice now."

"Attack by the media isn't justice, Sutton," Eli said softly.

"Just as long as they get eaten, Tanner. Media or us, it doesn't matter to me just as long as the bastards go down."

Eli said nothing; obviously his partner had been hurt from more than the eye wound.

8:30 A.M., Washington, D.C.

Georgia Congressman Bradley Richards held his brief-case and the *Washington Post* as he walked toward his Cadillac parked in the town-house parking lot. A fat man in a silk suit came up alongside him and said, "We need to talk, Congressman."

Richards slowed his steps. "Do I know you?"

"No, Brad, but we have a mutual friend who's been let-ting you use his cash to make yourself a lot of money."

Richards came to an abrupt halt. "What do you want?" he asked, unable to hide the tension in his voice.

"It's not about what I want, Brad. It's about what our mutual friend wants. You need to make a call. Here, please use my cell phone. Call the Dahlonega bank and release the money to a Mr. Inez, who is in the bank and waiting for the release. I know it's early, but believe me, he's there and so is your banker friend. Just do it."

Richards's forehead began glistening with nervous per-spiration. "Wh-Why?"

"Come on, Brad. You know why. Very soon you and your buddies are going to be investigated. Our friend is a cau-tious man, and cautious men always think ahead to avoid problems. Just make the call and make our friend happy for me."

"In-Investigated? Why?"

"Ah, come on, Brad, don't give me that 'I don't know what you're talking about' look. You and your friends have been greedy. We've tried to keep you out of trouble, but it's beyond that now. All we can do is stall them for a while while we divest ourselves of you guys. Make the call."

"It . . . it wouldn't do any good for me to call the banker. He doesn't know I'm involved with the company."

The fat man nodded. "That was smart of you, Brad. Okay,

then call your buddy Henry Cobb. He can release the money, can't he?"

Trembling, Richards carefully put down his briefcase and took the phone. His hands were shaking so badly that it took two tries to punch in the right sequence of numbers.

"Good morning, please put Henry on the line. It's Brad Richards . . . Hello, Henry . . . Yes, I know it's early, but we have a problem. I have a gentleman standing beside me who says our principal investor is concerned and wants to pull out right now . . . I know, Henry, I know, but I believe it would be in our best interests to do so. Please call the bank and authorize the release to a Mr. Inez, who is already there . . . Henry, I know the bank isn't open yet, but make the call. He's there. We'll talk again in an hour or so and discuss other options for us . . . Yes, Henry, I think it is that important that we act now . . . Yes, thank you. I'll call again soon, good-bye."

Richards handed the small phone back to the fat man. "Are you satisfied?"

"We'll see," the obese man said, replacing the phone inside his suit jacket pocket. "We're going to have to sit awhile and wait. It's not that I don't trust you, Brad, but I have to make sure the money is released without any complications. Once I get the call from Mr. Inez that everything is okay, I'll leave and you'll never see me again. Come with me."

Richards backed up a step. "If you think I'm going anywhere with you, think again."

"Ahh, Brad, is that any way to talk?" the fat man said. He nodded toward the dark Buick parked to his front. Immediately the car doors opened and two well-dressed men stepped out.

The fat man said, "Don't make a scene, Brad. Get in the Buick. We'll wait there for the call."

Richards looked around the parking lot, hoping someone was there to yell out to, but there wasn't a soul. The two men stepped closer and the fat man took hold of Richards's arm. "Relax. If you don't try to pull anything funny, you'll be on your way in no time."

8:35 A.M., Dahlonega, Georgia

Seated in the van two blocks from the bank, Ted shook his head in frustration. "Something's wrong, Glenn. They've been sittin' there for over a half hour and nothin' is happenin'. Maybe it's not them."

Glenn kept his eyes on the bank as he spoke. "Uh-uh, it's them. That one guy went into the bank with the banker, and that Winnebago and two Suburbans parked in the alley have Florida plates. . . . Wait, the side door just opened. . . . Look, the rest of them are getting out of the vehicles and going into the bank."

"Shit, Glenn, I don't like this. I can't believe they're getting the damn money in broad daylight. This screws up everything . . . there's going to be too much traffic on the road."

Seated behind the steering wheel, Glenn shook his head. "Relax, Ted, there won't be any civilians around the detour we're going to make them take. Your plan is a good one, and the guys know what to do. . . . Look, they're beginning to load the money."

Ted lifted a small handheld radio to his mouth. "Tango Two, the runner is coming to the plate. Runner will be in a large tan Winnebago and has two black Suburbans as escorts. Be advised the runner should be advancing to first base in a few minutes. Over."

Ted's radio speaker crackled, then Virgil's voice came over the speaker. "Roger, Tango One. We roger a Winnebago and two escorts . . . runner will be advancing soon. We are in position and ready. Out."

Glenn smiled as he watched the distant men toting trunks from the bank entrance to the Winnebago. "Look at that, will you. They look like pissants at a picnic, but instead of crumbs, those ants are toting trunks full of soon-to-be-our money. . . . Jesus, seven . . . eight . . . nine . . . ten trunks! How much are they takin' out?"

Ted had counted, too, and shook his head. "I . . . I don't know . . . I thought it was six million. Maybe they spread the cash out in the ten trunks. I count eight guys. Is that what you got?"

"Yes, I count eight too. . . . Hold it. Look, two guys are escorting the banker into the Winnebago. He doesn't look happy about it."

"Ya wanna bet they're goin' to do him?"

"Uh-huh, the expression on his face told me he thinks the same thing. Okay, they're closing the bank door . . . they must be finished. Here we go . . . they're all getting back into their vehicles."

Ted raised his radio again. "Tango Two, the runner is heading for first. Over."

"Roger, out."

Glenn had begun to pull the van away from the curb when Ted lifted his hand. "Hold it. Look, they're turning around. What the . . . Oh shit, they're heading north, not south like we thought."

"Goddamnit, Teddy, are they lost? There's only one way in and of town, Highway 19. If they stay heading north, they'll end up in North Carolina."

Ted watched the large recreational vehicle pass by and threw up his hands in frustration. "Christ'a'mighty, they've screwed up everything. Follow 'em! Keep your distance, but don't let 'em out of your sight." He quickly raised his radio. "Tango Two, be advised the runner is not advancing to first base. I say again, he's *not* advancing to first . . . he's going to third on us. Come to home base immediately and take 19 north until you find us. You copy?"

"Roger, we're on the way. Out."

Ted lowered the radio. "Shit! I can't believe they're taking the money north instead of heading toward Florida."

"Ted, it could be the best thing that could have happened. They're heading into the mountains . . . Chattahoochee National Forest begins a few miles up. Once Virgil and Ramon get ahead of them, there will be plenty of good places to set up the ambush site . . . not much traffic, either."

"Yeah, yeah, but I don't like surprises, and those assholes just surprised me. There's gotta be a reason they're headin' north. Oh shit, maybe there's an airstrip somewhere up ahead. They could have a chopper or plane waiting."

Glenn winced. "Oooh shit."

8:47 A.M., Washington, D.C.

Congressman Brad Richards jumped when the cell phone held by the fat man rang. The obese man lifted the phone to his ear. "Yes, I'm here . . . Good. I'll pass on the good news." He pushed the terminate button and looked at Richards with a smile. "You've done well, Brad. Mr. Inez says he has the money in his possession. You can go now. . . . Oh, and Brad. You know to never tell anyone you did business with our friend, don't you?"

Richards was so relieved to be getting out of the car he could only nod. Seated in the backseat between the two suited men had been the worst experience of his life. He had sat the whole time wondering which one would kill him. The man to his right opened his door and got out. Richards slid toward the open door but saw out of the corner of his eye the other man reach inside his jacket. The car door suddenly closed, blocking his escape. Richards shut his eyes.

Hearing the coughing sound, the fat man turned and saw the congressman fall forward. The other man got back in the car and pushed the body over onto the floor.

The fat man started the engine and spoke over his shoulder. "Get that garbage bag over his head before he ruins the carpet."

CHAPTER 11

Georgia Bureau Detective Ed Faraday walked into the small conference room and gave Eli a scowl. Seeing Ashley, he changed his expression and extended his hand to her. "Good to see you again, Agent Sutton. I'm very sorry for what happened."

Ashley kept her seat at the table as she took his hand. "Thanks, Ed, it's good to see you again, too."

"That eye going to be all right?"

"Bandage comes off in two weeks and I should be one hundred percent."

"That's good news," Faraday said, then his faced turned sour again. "Cover your ears for a minute for me." The detective turned and pointed his finger at Eli's face. "Ya son of a bitch. How come ya requested me to head up our side?"

Eli shrugged. "Because you're the best, Ed."

"Horseshit, Tanner. You don't know any other GBI detectives but me."

"I know ya like country music and Bubba's ribs . . . what else is there to know?"

Faraday's scowl slowly faded. "Yeah, ya got a point there, I guess."

Eli stood and patted the stocky detective's shoulder. "Look, Ed, you did a helluva job on that last case we worked together. I need your help on this. It's big-time."

Ed's face soured again. "Yeah, sure, you need our help. You feds are screwin' up already by treatin' us state boys like ugly stepchildren. What I hear on the news and read in the papers this mornin'? Over a hundred fifty federal agents are going to be working the case? And not one damn word in any report about GBI involvement. Sounds to me and my pissed-off bosses like you feds don't need anything from us except for us to stay out of the way."

"Ed, seven of our people were killed yesterday. Our Public Affairs mouthpiece was posturing for the benefit of the press."

"Posturing? That what you feds call it? My bosses call it snubbing. I'm here, Tanner. You got what you wanted. The governor told my director to cooperate fully with you guys, but I'm tellin' ya up front—because we're friends— my boss is not happy, and neither is the rest of the crew in the GBI."

Eli wrinkled his brow. "I'm sorry, Ed, I'm just dense, I guess. I don't understand why your boss and you are so upset."

Faraday stared back, searching Eli's eyes. He then looked at Ashley. "You two really don't know, do you?"

Ashley shrugged her shoulders and Eli shook his head.

Motioning Eli to sit back down, Faraday drew up a chair, but only used its back to lean on. "Let me give it to you two straight, then. The problem is this: It looks like you feds think us state boys fell down on the job or worse, the way we looked on this Yona Group. My bosses read the stuff your people faxed over early this morning, and none of the dirty business in northern Georgia is new news to us. We've known about the Yona Group for about six months. Hell, we got all kinds of complaints from locals saying this Yona bunch was movin' in on their businesses. Six months ago the boss sent a couple of our detectives up to check out the complaints, and it didn't take long for them to see the Yona Group was playin' dirty. We took what we had to the State Attorney to get approval for a full investigation, but he said we didn't have enough to warrant further investigation—he killed it, Tanner; he wouldn't do a damn thing. Look, I'm going to tell you both something that stays right here in this room. My boss was a close friend of Senator Goodnight. He told him he was havin' problems with the state attorney's office on the matter. The senator said he would get you feds involved, and that's where it all ended for us. We thought you feds were on it and sooner or later would come to us on what we had."

Eli exchanged looks with Ashley before regarding Faraday. "The senator did bring us in, but I'm afraid it was too late. Agent Eddings from our office was assigned to the case. He'd only begun a preliminary investigation when the senator, his family, and two of his staffers were hit . . . and yesterday Agent Eddings was killed in the attack."

Faraday shook his head. "Jesus, I knew it was bad but I didn't know your case agent bought it, too. I'm sorry, Tanner. . . . What do you need from us?"

"We need to know everything your people found out about the Yona Group. All we know is that the company was in the conversion business. Did you all check out the partners and leadership of the company?"

"Yeah, sure. We found out who they were, but the State Attorney stopped us before we could dig deeper. Look, Tanner, I read the stuff your people sent over, and I see where you feds are goin' with this. You think the leadership had something to do with contracting the hits. I'm tellin' you right now you guys are barkin' up the wrong tree. Sure they're engaged in some shady dealings, but as far as we could tell, none of it would even get 'em a felony conviction. Tanner, we're talkin' about unfair business practices . . . *monopolizing*, for Christ's sake. The most they'd get for a conviction is fined, a couple thousand dollars for each count."

"Who are they, Ed? Who is runnin' this Yona Group?"

"Big money people," Faraday said. "Big money and big political connections. All of them are from old moneyed families here in the state, your basic country club good ol' boys, except these guys aren't old. They're all under forty

and got in to make easy money. Their leader is Congressman Brad Richards of the Fourth District. He's the one who
came up with the idea, but he's kept himself out of the
actual running of the business. What he gets in return is
the others' campaign support by way of funds, people, organization, and an almost guarantee of keeping his seat in
Congress. The day-to-day honcho of the group is Henry
Cobb. He's the CEO, and his is a real old family; his great-
grandfather was a big general in the Civil War. It's Henry
who keeps the locals in line. The best we could tell, he had
hired about four local boys, all ex-football-player types with
lots of muscle. They're the enforcers and do the roughing up
when necessary. We ID'd most of them. A few had priors,
but most are just big and stupid, but the kind that can take
orders and—"

"Whoa, Ed," Eli said, raising his hand. "You've lost me. I
don't know what you're talking about when you say
'enforcers' and keeping the locals in line. What kind of
business are we talking about here?"

Ed looked at Ashley, then Eli. "I thought you feds knew
all about this?"

"We don't know how the business is actually run,"
Ashley said.

Ed nodded. "Okay, let's start from the beginning. The first
thing you gotta understand is that the actual conversions
are mostly done by mom-and-pop companies. We're talkin'
about a cottage industry with little overhead ... at least
that's the way it used to be. Let me explain. Let's say you're
in the market for a full-size conversion van. Where do you
go to buy one? You go to a Dodge, Ford, or Chevy dealership, that's where. Now you see one you like, but the interior colors are all wrong. You say to the salesman, 'I'd take
this one if the interior was blue instead of maroon.' The
salesman says, 'No problem, I can get you a van with what
you want by next week. Just come in and sign the paperwork and give me a deposit.' The salesman then calls the
mom-and-pop company in Toccoa, Georgia, that sold the
dealership the van and says, 'I need Model 123 with blue

interior by next week.' Pop says, 'No sweat.' He hangs up, goes to the bank, borrows the money, buys a basic van from the local dealer, then drives it to a relative who stocks all the conversion parts. Pop buys what he needs, then drives to his barn, where Mom and Pop and maybe their older kids start work. They cut off the metal roof and put on a new sloped Fiberglas one. They cut out panels in the van walls and put in windows. They take out the seats, lay blue carpet, install new blue captain's chairs and a blue backseat that folds down into a bed. They screw in panels that are covered with light blue material and install indirect lighting and make the van cherry in three days, then drive it to another relative who does the paint and striping work. In five days the van is finished and is driven to the car dealership, which pays the wholesale price for it, then calls you and says your van is ready to be picked up. That's the way the system worked up until about a year ago."

Ashley lifted her hand. "I don't get it. Why doesn't the Ford company make conversion vans if people want them?"

Faraday smiled. "Unions, Agent Sutton. If they converted their vans, they'd have to pay union wages for the work. The van I just talked about would cost at least a grand more. A union guy gets paid twenty-five bucks an hour to cut off the roof. Mom and Pop can do it for six. Plus, if you wanted a blue interior instead of maroon, Mom and Pop can deliver in a week. Ford would take months."

"Go on, Ed," Eli said. "You said that's the way it *used* to be."

"Yeah, now it's changed because the Yona Group figured out there was big money to be made. A group rep goes to Mom and Pop and says, 'Look, you're makin' some money but it's seasonal and isn't steady, plus others are cutting into your profit. Right now you convert thirty vans a year. You work for us and we guarantee you fifty vans a year. We sell the vans for you, so there's no lost days driving to dealers, plus when you go to our warehouse, it's a one-shop stop. You get the van and all the accessories, and we do the painting and striping in our shop. You get everything from us and we pay you on time for your work. You still get to work your hours in your barn, and your company name goes on the van even though we sell it.'

"Mom and Pop like the idea, but there's a catch. Ya see, before, Pop made five hundred dollars profit on each van he sold, but now he'll make only three hundred and seventy, eighty-five, per van. But the deal still looks good because he's guaranteed a steady income. But let's say Mom and Pop said no deal. They like working for themselves and plan on expanding. Now this is where the group rep plays rough. He tells Pop he won't be able to get the vans or accessories because the group is buying all the stock. Pop either joins the group or doesn't work at all. Now what I just told you goes for all the other mom and pops who convert boats, pickups, and any other small business owners who buy accessories and do the installing. In the case of the vans, the group clears about a two and half grand on every van sold to a dealer. Boats are a little less, depending on size. When you think about over seventy thousand vans being sold in the Southeast region a year, and about the same in boats, you're talking big money. Now add some other things. The group now owns the dealerships that sell the basic vans, and one of the group's big boys owns the warehouses where the accessories are kept. Add something else. The group is playing hardball with the small companies that make the accessories. They guarantee the number of products they'll buy. If the company owners don't agree to sell only to them, their raw materials are cut off or nobody buys their products because the group has all the converters working for them. Independents can't compete with the group because it can make a better deal with the car and boat dealers. Once the independents are gone, then the group has no real competition, raises its prices to the dealers, and makes even more of a profit."

"So much for the American way," Eli said.

Ashley canted her head. "It doesn't sound that hard to prove they're shaking down Mom and Pop."

Faraday nodded. "You'd be right if Mom and Pop were

screaming foul, but most of them are satisfied with the deal. They're making steady incomes for a change. The ones who didn't take the deal are too scared to talk. They know the group doesn't play by the rules, and they figure silence is better than having their legs broken, or worse."

"But some did talk," Ashley said. "Wentzel had witness statements."

Faraday nodded with a frown. "Yeah, and now the group knows who they are. I'll bet there's already been a rash of 'accidents' up there."

Eli looked into Faraday's eyes. "And you still don't believe they put the contract out on the Goodnights?"

Ed shook his head. "Nope. These country club boys don't kill their own. Goodnight was old family. Plus, why would they? The state attorney explained to us the takeover of the small mom-and-pop operations is considered normal business practice for an expanding company ... except the group got a little carried away is all. He wouldn't touch it because all we had was misdemeanors. The Yona Group lawyers would tie it up in court for years and would just end up settling out of court."

"That's it? The state attorney wouldn't go after them because they were only breaking the laws a little bit?" Eli asked.

"You have to understand, Tanner, the group partners are millionaires and very powerful men in this state. It appeared to us that Henry Cobb was the only one heavily involved in making the decisions of the company. The others were silent partners who let their accountants take care of the bottom lines. I doubt if the silent partners knew what was going on. But Cobb, unlike the others, is not moneyed. His family once was, but his father lost most of the family's liquid assets during the savings-and-loan fiasco in the eighties. The Yona Group is Cobb's chance to get back in the black. We had Cobb pegged as a principal as well as Richards. We got the company's phone records and saw where the good congressman was in daily contact with Cobb. We were zeroing in on Cobb and Richards when the state attorney pulled the plug on us."

"Is Cobb capable of putting out the contract on Good-night and the others?"

"Naw, Tanner, I don't buy that. He wouldn't have been worried if we had made a case against him on unfair business practices. His lawyers would have hushed it all up and settled the whole thing out of court."

Eli leaned back in his chair but kept his eyes on the detective. "Ed, did your people find anything that might suggest the Yona Group was money laundering?"

"Money laundering? Jesus, where did you get that?"

"I take it that's a no?"

"Tanner, our people were lookin' into unfair business practices . . . they weren't lookin' into money laundering. What have you got? Are you sayin' you feds think they're involved with somebody else?"

Eli shook his head. "We don't have anything right now, Ed. We have bits of information that point to their possible involvement is all. It's a long shot we'll have to check out."

Faraday raised an eyebrow. "You just said *we'll* have to check it out. That mean we're going to work on this together?"

Eli smiled as he rose from his chair. "You're pretty quick for a state guy. Thanks for the information, Ed. I've got to get back and tell the SAC what you told me."

"Wait a minute, Tanner. Why don't you let me tell him. My boss would feel better knowing we're involved in the case."

"Sure, come on."

"First, come clean with me, Tanner. What have you got that makes you all think the Yona Group has dirty friends?"

Eli motioned to his stomach. "It's my gut telling me, Ed."

Faraday's eyes narrowed. "I know you, Tanner. I trust your instincts, but you're keepin' somethin' from me, aren't you?"

Eli looked into his friend's eyes. "You're right, Ed, I am. You'll just have to trust me on this for now."

Faraday studied Eli's face a moment before nodding. "Let's go."

Dahlonega, Georgia

Henry Cobb dabbed his perspiring forehead with a hand-kerchief as he tried to concentrate. He stared at the pad of legal paper on his desk where he had written down numbers. He had calculated that the sudden withdrawal of money would cost the group at least a million in projected earnings for the quarter.

Hearing a loud clanging noise, Cobb looked up. His office door swung open and his secretary gave him an apologetic look. "It's the fire alarm, Mr. Cobb."

"What the hell?"

The secretary was about to shrug but an excited voice yelled from the hallway, "There's smoke coming from the second floor!"

Cobb stood and hurried toward the door. "Call the fire department and I'll go see what's going on."

Striding down the hall past scurrying people from other offices, Cobb reached the steps leading down to the second floor. He was about to start down but felt the presence of someone behind him. He was going to turn but never made it. A second later his body was tumbling down the stairs.

Twelve miles north of the Yona Group office building, Ted paced nervously beside the van that was parked under trees just off Highway 19.

Glenn touched Ted's arm and nodded toward the two men approaching them.

Ted closed his eyes for a moment, praying they had good news.

Virgil smiled as he halted in front of his team leader. "You're one lucky squid, Ted." He turned and motioned up the road. "Up ahead and around the bend they pulled off the highway onto a dirt road that goes up about four hundred yards to an old cabin. Ray and me saw 'em pull off and drove on past. Good thing we did 'cause they dropped off two guys at the road intersection. We pulled off the road a half mile up and humped back through the woods and spotted 'em at the cabin. They were unloadin' trunks and haulin' 'em inside."

Ramon took over as he stepped closer. "We snooped and pooped up closer to 'em. They're Cuban, man, I heard 'em talkin', and they're plannin' on stayin' a few days. They're waiting on more people to show up and take the money. They don't wanna take the chance of moving all the bread at once. Others are going to come and take out a million at a time."

Relieved, Ted relaxed his taut shoulders. "Any place a chopper could land around the cabin?" he asked.

Ramon shook his head. "No way, man, it's all forest along the road and around the cabin. And the cabin sits just below a mountain, so there's no way out except that dirt road. They've boxed themselves in."

Virgil smiled. "It'll be a piece of cake for us, Ted. They've got the two guards hidden in the tree line just back from the intersection, but the rest of 'em was smokin' and jokin' after they unloaded the dough. I figger we can go in tonight usin' our night-vision gear and get the money with no sweat."

Ted looked up the road in thought. Finally he turned. "Ramon, go on back to your vehicle and get the cell phone and radio. You'll stay and keep an eye on them. The rest of us will go back and get the gear we'll need. We'll come back and do a daylight recon, and once it's dark we'll do another one. If it looks good, we'll make the raid just before dawn. Let's go; we've got work to do."

9:30 A.M., FBI office, Atlanta

The SAC, Don Farrel, sat in a small conference room along with Agent Bowlan, the case agent in charge. Both men listened to Detective Ed Faraday as he briefed them on what the GBI had found on the Yona Group.

". . . so in conclusion, sir, I don't believe the Yona Group partners had sufficient motive to—"

The conference room door opened and the SAC's secretary quickly walked in, holding a piece of paper. She went straight to her boss. "Sir, I'm sorry to disturb you, but I just received this message from the director of the GBI. He is waiting on line two to discuss it further."

Farrel read the note. His facial muscles tightened and he snatched up the phone beside him. "Charley, it's Don ... Yeah, I just read it ... Yeah, I'll send my people up there ASAP ... Yes, we'll have to take it over, but I want your people assisting us. What about Congressman Richards? ... I was afraid of that. I'll call the Washington office and see if they're on it ... Right, I'll get back to you."

Farrel hung up the phone and looked at the people across the table. "Looks like we're too late ... Henry Cobb was shot in the back of the head just thirty minutes ago. It appears it was a pro. A small-caliber weapon was used and nobody heard the weapon's report. Firemen found his body before the office building became an inferno."

Eli exchanged looks with Ashley. "What about Congressman Richards, sir?"

The SAC looked up at his secretary. "Doris, get the Washington office SAC on the phone for me." As she hurried from the room, Farrel's gaze fell on Faraday. "He's missing ... he hasn't showed up at his office this morning."

Farrel turned to Agent Bowlan. "Get our people to the scene in Dahlonega and seize all the Yona Group's records, if there are any left. You'll also need to get hold of the U.S. Attorney and tell him what's happened. We'll need an okay to pick up all the partners for questioning."

Bowlan stood and strode toward the door. Ed Faraday stood, too, and leaned over, looking at the SAC with a glare. "Sir, what the hell is goin' on here? Were Cobb and Congressman Richards connected?"

Farrel leaned back in his chair with a distant stare. "We don't know."

"Sir, excuse me, but I don't buy that. Something is going on here. The two men who could have answered questions about the Yona Group's business affairs are dead or missing.

I'm just a state dick, but that tells me somebody didn't want them questioned. It seems logical to me, then, that they were both involved with that somebody—and I think you know who that somebody is."

The SAC kept his face expressionless. "Detective Faraday, I told you what I know. Thank you for coming over and filling us in on the group's leaders. Now, if you'll excuse me, I have work to do."

Faraday kept a hard look on the SAC for a long moment before finally turning and facing Eli. "So much for sharing information, huh? I'll wait outside for you two."

The SAC waited until the detective had left before looking at the two remaining agents. "Agent Tanner, I want you to check Agent Sutton into a hotel so she can rest. She's got no business working so soon."

Ashley began to protest, but Farrel growled, "That's an order, young lady; don't argue with me." Farrel shifted his glare to Eli. "Once you've taken care of your partner, talk to the GBI again and try and smooth their feathers. We're going to need their assistance on the case."

Eli raised an eyebrow. "Sir, you were pretty rough on Ed. He was right—it's obvious somebody else is involved. We can't keep him and the GBI in the dark and expect cooperation."

"Handle it, Tanner. My hands are tied, damnit! Do the best you can, but don't tell them about the player connection. Now get out of here."

Eli and Ashley left in silence and met Faraday in the hallway. The fuming detective motioned toward the SAC's door. "Does he think I'm a damn idiot?"

Eli gave his friend a consoling pat on the shoulder. "Ed, he's under a lot of strain . . . he's got a murdered senator and a missing congressman to deal with."

"They're *my* senator and congressman, Tanner. You don't think the GBI isn't under pressure to find out who's knockin' off our Georgia boys?"

"Ed, we're all under pressure. Just believe me when I tell ya that the SAC is doing all he can."

"Yeah, I'm sure he is, Tanner, but I also think you feds are hiding something. Come on, what is it?"

Eli began to shake his head when Ashley spoke up. "Ed, there might be a connection with a drug player out of Miami."

"A drug player? Connected to Cobb and Richards? How?"

Despite the glare Eli was giving her, Ashley said, "Money laundering. The conversion van business is perfect for it—high turnover of vans and boats. They buy the basic boats, vans, parts, and accessories with the dirty money. . . . When the vehicle sells, they get back clean money."

"Who's the player?" Faraday asked.

Eli spoke before Ashley could respond. "That we honestly don't know, Ed, and neither does the SAC. The DEA has the lead on the case and is working the player connection angle . . . we're only in the support role."

Faraday shook his head. "Jesus, you feds are unbelievable. My senator is dead, along with his whole family, and a congressman is missing, and you feds are playing turf games. I know, I know, it's not your fault it's run this way, but it still doesn't make it any easier to swallow. . . . Thanks for telling me. At least now I understand what we're up against. So what's the deal? Are we supposed to wait and let the DEA get the player?"

"No," Eli said. "Agent Bowlan is driving on with the investigation; we're not standing still on this."

"What part are we going to play?" Faraday asked.

Eli sighed. "Sorry, Ed, we're just gofers. As liaisons, we pass each other info on what our investigators come up with."

The stocky detective's shoulders sagged. "We're not gofer types, Tanner. We should be doin' somethin' real to get the bastards."

"Not our job, Ed. Right now I've got orders to check Sutton into a hotel so she can rest. How about tomorrow morning we get together at your office and I'll show you everything we've got so far."

Faraday nodded. "Fine. Hey, since you guys are in town,

we might as well have dinner together tonight. I know a couple of joints that have good ribs."

Ashley was about to nod, but to her shock saw Eli shaking his head. "Sorry, I can't, Ed. I have a date tonight."

"A date?" Ashley said, giving her partner a disbelieving look.

"Yeah, I told you about it."

"You didn't tell me you had a *date*, Tanner. That I'd remember."

Eli's face reddened. "Oh . . . guess I just thought I did. It's not a real date; it's kind of a *have to* thing. Stacy Starr made a deal with the SAC, and part of the deal was that I—"

"Take her on a date?" Faraday asked with a smile. "You expect me and Ashley to believe that?"

Eli held up his hand. "Scout's honor, guys. It really is a duty."

Ashley gave him a disapproving glare. "Tough duty, huh, Tanner?"

Before Eli could respond, Faraday stepped closer to Ashley. "What d'ya say I take you to dinner, then? We'll just happen to go to the same place Tanner takes the news lady and we'll see firsthand how tough Tanner's duty really is."

"Sorry, guys," Eli said. "We're having dinner at her place."

"Her place?" Ashley croaked. "What's going on, Tanner? Her place?"

Eli was beginning to enjoy her anger. "Look, Sutton, I'm just following orders, just like I have orders to check you into a hotel. Drop it, okay?"

Faraday lifted his hand. "Hey, as much as I'd like to stay and watch you two claw each other up, I've got to get back to the office. I'll see you guys tomorrow." Faraday began walking down the hall, and spoke over his shoulder with a smile. "And Tanner, good luck with your duty tonight."

Ashley rolled her eyes and began walking in the opposite direction. Eli barked, "Where you goin'? I've got orders, remember?"

"I'll meet you in the van. I've got to pick up something first."

Minutes later in the parking lot, Ashley got into the van holding her briefcase. Seated in the passenger seat, Eli held up his cell phone. "I got us reservations at the Marriott and I called Regina. She's going over to your place and pack you a few things. Tom will drive the stuff up this evening so you'll be more comfortable."

Ashley nodded in silence as she kept her gaze on the front entrance of the office building. A single tear rolled down her cheek. Eli was about to ask what was wrong but she held up her hand and growled, "I'm fine." She started the engine and quickly backed out.

Dahlonega

Ted held his breath as the Georgia highway patrol car sped around the van with its lights flashing. As he sat behind the steering wheel, Glenn sighed in relief; the patrol car continued on. "Oh man, I thought we'd had it," he said, shaking his head.

Ted looked over his shoulder at the pickup following them. "I bet Virgil shit his pants seeing that county Mountie come up behind him."

Glenn motioned ahead. "Look, that's what that cop was in such a hurry about—there's a fire someplace in town. See that smoke cloud?"

Entering the outskirts of the community, Ted glanced at the distant billowing gray-black cloud and was about to comment when he saw two GBI cars parked at a gas station on the corner of an intersection. "Uh-oh."

Glenn glanced at the two cars and winced. "You think they're here because of the missing money?"

"I don't know. Better drive on past the motel and let's see if they're stakin' it out."

"God, Teddy, you think somebody ratted us out?"

"We haven't done anything yet. Christ'a'mighty, don't get paranoid on me now."

"I'm paranoid because if they pull us over and search us, they'll find enough illegal weapons and demo in the back of this thing to put us away for twenty years!"

"Take it easy, Glenn. The motel is just ahead. Look, the parking lot is almost empty; nobody is waitin' for us. Relax now, will ya?"

Glenn pulled into the motel parking lot and brought the van to a halt beside a small Hertz rental truck.

Ted got out and smiled at his friend. "See, nothin' to worry about." He turned as Virgil parked and got out of his truck.

"You guys see the GBI vehicles back there?" Virgil asked, getting out of the pickup.

Ted was about to respond when a blue sedan pulled into the lot and stopped in front of the motel office. Three men got out, all wearing blue windbreakers with big gold letters on the back saying FBI.

Ted froze, Virgil closed his eyes, and Glenn began trembling.

None of the agents even glanced in the three men's direction as they walked toward the office door, which suddenly opened, revealing a gray-haired woman. "Hiya. Agent Bowlan called and said you boys would be over to sign for rooms. I told him none of 'em was cleaned yet."

The agent in the lead smiled. "That's no problem, ma'am, we just wanted to get them reserved for us. We'll need all the rooms you have available."

"All of 'em? That's twenty-one rooms."

"We'll take them all, ma'am."

"All of 'em? You sayin' you want all of 'em?"

"Yes, ma'am. We have more agents coming."

"This all about that fire over there at the Yona company building? I heard somebody died over there, that right?"

"Yes, ma'am, it's about the fire. We need to get back to the scene. Could we make the arrangements for the rooms now, please?"

" 'Course, you boys come in . . . y'all goin' to pay with credit cards, aren't ya?"

As soon as the agents disappeared inside the office, Ted spun around and faced Virgil. "Get in your truck and follow us. We've got to get the weapons and gear hidden outside of town." He turned to Glenn and held out his hand. "Give me the keys to the rental truck and I'll drive it and follow you guys."

Glenn's face sagged. "Ramon has the keys."

"No, don't tell me that." Ted shook his head. "The night-vision and tactical gear is in the back of the rental."

"Okay, Ted, I won't tell you Ramon has the fucking keys, but guess what? Virgil and I don't have them, do you?"

Ted looked up at the blue sky. "Why are you doin' this to me, Lord? Are you tryin' to tell me somethin'?"

Virgil worriedly glanced toward the office before looking back to his leader. "Ted, we gotta get the hell out of here before this place turns into an FBI convention."

"Let me think a minute," Ted said, lifting his hand. "All right, I got it. We drive our two vehicles out nice and slow and easy. We find a nice secluded spot and hide the weapons. Once we're clean, we get the keys from Ramon then come back and get the rental truck."

Glenn motioned toward the office. "Once the feds leave I'll check us all out of the motel."

"No," Ted said quickly. "If we check out now it would look too suspicious. If the feds know about the missing money, they'll be looking for the crew that took it."

"Ted's right," Virgil said, patting Glenn's shoulder. "We gotta stay here again tonight and be cool."

"But what about the money?" Glenn asked.

"Most of it will still be there," Ted said as he opened the van door. "Ramon said they were going to take it out a million at a time, remember? Come on, we gotta hide our weapons and get those keys."

Atlanta

It was a little after noon as Ashley sat in the Marriott's lounge holding a gin and tonic. Eli walked in, saw her sitting at a corner table, and sat down beside her. He handed her a card key. "Your room number is 204. I'm in 206."

Seemingly ignoring him, Ashley raised her hand toward a passing waitress. "Another one, please, but make it a double." She shifted her eyes to Eli. "I'm going to get myself drunk, Tanner. When I get where I can't sit up, just take me to my room, okay?"

Eli saw the warning signs in her eyes. "What's wrong?" he asked softly.

She lowered her eyes to the empty glass. "I can smell the blood on my clothes. They washed them, but I . . ."

He saw the tears coming and reached over, taking her hand. "Come on, let's go shopping and get you out of those things." Eli stood and took her arm to help her to her feet but felt her trembling.

She looked up at him as if in terrible pain. "I'm not very good at this, am I? I should be stronger . . . I'm an FBI agent, right?"

"You're doing better than most I know, Sutton, but maybe you should talk to the shrink again."

She tried to stand but sank back into the chair. "Give me a minute. . . . I didn't like her, Tanner. She acted like she understood, but she didn't. You understand, though, don't you?"

Sitting down beside her, Eli put his arm over her shoulder and gave her a gentle squeeze. "Yeah, I understand, pard. It'll take a while but you won't think about it as much. There was nothing you could have done. It happened; nothing will change it."

"Paul was a good guy, Tanner. I really liked him."

"I know."

"I had feelings for him when we were in Quantico, but I never told him or did anything to make him think we weren't just good friends. I always regretted not telling him.

When he looked at me yesterday that first time, I knew, I felt it, you know? I knew he felt the same way."

Eli squeezed her shoulder again but didn't speak. She stared blankly at the glass and shook her head. "It's not fair, Tanner. It's like I'm being punished for even thinking something would have happened between us. He . . . he was married, Tanner . . . and I didn't care. I thought . . . no, that's not right. I didn't think. I was so high from his reaction to seeing me, I didn't even think about his wife and children. I didn't care about them. I only cared about me and what I thought was going to happen between Paul and me."

The waitress set the drink on the table and began to speak but saw Ashley's tears. She gave Eli a consoling look and walked away.

Ashley looked into Eli's eyes. "I'm pretty pitiful, aren't I?"

He wrinkled his brow as he handed her a cocktail napkin. "No. You've been through a lot is all. I think once we get you some new clothes and you get your mind on other things, you'll start healing faster than you think."

"Work is your answer to fixing everything, isn't it, Tanner? I mean, you have to have it to keep going, don't you?"

"I dream, too, Sutton. I wish a lot of things were different but they're not. Work is real and it's now. Maybe one of these days I won't need it, but right now . . . yeah, it's all I've got. You ready to go?"

She stood and gave him a sad look. "I think we're both pretty pitiful, Tanner."

He put a ten-dollar bill on the table and walked her toward the door without responding. She was right, and that hurt.

CHAPTER 12

Dahlonega, Georgia

Lying on the embankment of a heavily vegetated stream bed, Ted lowered his binoculars and looked at the angry, small man beside him. "Ahh, Ramon, stop pissin' and moanin' about it. We'll just have to wait until tomorrow to hit 'em. Tonight we'll make a night recon and make any adjustments we need for tomorrow evening's score."

Ramon spoke between clenched teeth. "You're screwin' up, man. Tomorrow might be too late. The money will be gone."

"No way. The guys comin' for the money are gonna see the town is crawlin' with FBI and have to wait just like us." Ted motioned to his watch. "It's 1600 hours, Ramon. You know we couldn't do a good recon by nightfall."

"Maybe you squids couldn't do it, but me and Virg could make the recon, man."

Ted scooted back and gave the Cuban his best glare. "Who's runnin' this op?"

Ramon stared back for a moment before finally lowering his eyes. "You are."

"Yeah. Now tell me what ya think the best approach is."

Crawling back up to the edge of the embankment, Ramon pointed and whispered. "The crew is usin' the cabin's porch as their smokin' and jokin' area. They're eating and sleeping in the Winnebago. The best approach is from the east—too much thick vegetation to the west; they'd hear us."

Ted raised his binoculars, scanning the cabin and terrain

to the east. "Yeah, I see what ya mean . . . the east is the best." He lowered his glasses and motioned to the gravel road. "What about the two sentries they posted down by the highway?"

"No sweat, man. I checked 'em out a couple of hours ago. They're bitchin' about the heat and tellin' each other lies about how many women they've laid. They're not expecting any trouble."

Satisfied at what he saw, Ted backed up and handed Ramon the binoculars. "Okay, I'll have Virg come out and relieve you as soon as I get back. The rest of us will come out about midnight for the recon. Give me a call on the cell phone if anything changes."

Ramon nodded toward the bag Ted had brought. "Thanks for the drinks and sandwiches, man."

Ted winked as he crawled back farther. "Gotta take care of my team. See ya in an hour or so."

9:00 P.M., Atlanta

Stacy Starr opened the door and smiled. "Are you always so punctual?"

Standing on the porch wearing his blazer, new shirt, and tie, and holding a bottle of wine and a small bouquet of flowers, Eli gave her an embarrassed smile. "It's been a while since I've been on a date. I wanted to get it right."

Stacy backed up and swung the door open. "Come in, Eli. I guess I should tell you it's been a long time for me, too. Don't mind the mess. I just got home a few minutes ago. Donny was true to his word and kept me informed of events; it's been a madhouse trying to keep up. Come on, let's go back to the kitchen."

Eli slowed his steps as he looked around. "It's beautiful, Miss Starr," he said, and meant it. Like the outside, the interior of the small plantation-style house was picture-perfect. He had thumbed through *Southern Living* magazines while at the hospital, and he thought Stacy's place would have qualified for the cover of the next issue. The exterior of the house was all wood and painted white, with a covered veranda surounding it. He could just see her in a bonnet, sitting in the porch swing sipping a mint julep. The inside was even better. High ceilings, lots of windows, wood floors, and Stacy Starr's classy touch everywhere. The furniture was all antique. Because fresh-cut flowers were everywhere, the foyer and front sitting room had the look and smell of a lush outdoors. He liked it, he liked it a lot, although somehow he wasn't surprised.

Stacy saw his look and came to a halt. "You like the house?"

"It's like you, Miss Starr, very warm and charming." *Ahh hell, did I just say that? Damn, Tanner, it's duty, remember?*

Stacy took the wine bottle from his hand with a smile and spoke with an exaggerated drawl. "My my, aren't you the one with compliments, Agent Tanner. It does make a girl's head swim. I do declare, if I didn't know better, I'd believe you were trying to woo me."

Eli couldn't help himself. He bowed and presented the flowers. "Miss Starr, a gentleman does not *woo* on his first date with a lovely lady such as yourself. He merely states the facts as he sees them."

She fanned herself with her hand. "My my, a gentleman indeed. My mama always warned me to beware of proper gentlemen. She said they'd steal your heart."

"Stealing is a felony, Miss Starr. I'm a federal officer and would never *steal*."

"In that case, I will assume I'm safe for the moment. Come on back to the kitchen and let's see what Cecila has prepared for the occasion. I told her I wanted a special meal for a special guest."

Eli followed, telling himself to stop having such a good time.

"Eli, I would like to present Miss Cecila Thomas. She is almost my second mama."

A smiling, very, very heavy black woman wearing a flowered dress and white apron stepped forward. "Ahh now, missy . . . oh my, isn't he a handsome thing? You was right, missy, he somethin' special all right. Give me those flowers; they need to be put in water. Y'all go on out to the back veranda, now. Dinner will be ready in fifteen minutes."

Eli smiled at the short, rotund woman. "It's a pleasure meeting you, Miss Cecila."

The woman winked at Stacy. "He's a gentleman, too, missy. You'd better watch yourself."

Stacy led Eli out the back door onto the veranda, where she walked to the railing and took a deep breath. "You smell that, Eli? That's the end of summer coming. . . . I do like the fall, but I always enjoy summer best."

Eli joined her and looked out over the small manicured lawn surrounded by pines and festooned with plants. "Summer is my favorite time, too, Miss Starr. I always liked nights like this as a boy. My brother and I would chase fireflies while my mama churned that ol' ice-cream maker. . . . That was the best ice cream I've ever had."

Stacy regarded him a moment. "It's hard to imagine you as a boy, Eli. Were you a handful?"

"Not really, I was just a kid like everybody else. In those days baseball was my passion, and mama always knew where to find my brother and me—in Parker's lot shagging flies and grounders. Things were different in those days, simpler for kids, I guess. I think there was only one television station back then."

"What about your father? What did he do?"

"Dad worked for the railroad. He worked long and hard but he was always there for us. He passed away when I was fourteen. It was an accident . . . robbed us all of him. He was a good man."

Stacy touched his arm. "He would have been proud of you, Eli."

The meal was wonderful, but Eli had a hard time enjoying it because he was waiting for Stacy to start asking questions about the investigation. It was just a matter of time, he kept telling himself. *Damn, I feel like a cat locked in a room with twenty old guys in rocking chairs.*

After dessert, Stacy suggested they once again sit on the back porch to enjoy the evening. When Eli sat on the porch swing and she took a seat beside him, the warning bells in his head began clanging. Stacy had not once mentioned her work nor asked him any questions about his. Although he kept telling himself she was a shark, it was getting more and more difficult to think of her as one. He told himself the duty was done, he could leave, but he really didn't want to go. She was everything he had imagined in his dreams, and more. He liked listening to her talk, the homey little expressions she used, and especially her eyes. They told him everything, and that was what worried him most. They were telling him she liked his company as much as he was enjoying hers. But there was an even bigger problem. She was also sending other signals, not intentional but there nevertheless. The light touches, her closeness, and that damn intoxicating scent of hers were driving him crazy. It was heat emanating from her, pure sexual, sensual, steaming heat, and it was melting all his mental defenses. His dream was winning and he knew it.

Stacy patted his hand. "I lost you there for a moment. What were you thinking about?"

Eli sighed and lowered his head. "I was thinking how nice this is. I was also thinking I should go."

"You're scared, aren't you?"

"Uh . . . well, I hate to admit it, but yes. I'm scared to death because I like it *too* much. That doesn't make sense, does it?"

She patted his hand again. "I understand because I was thinking the same thing. I think we're alike, Eli. I think it's been a long time and we're scared of what could be. My work is everything to me, but right now, sitting here like this it makes me wonder. Maybe it isn't so important after all."

Eli took her hand in his. "I have this thing; it's something inside me that tells me things. I can't explain it, Stacy; it's just there. And it tells me when something is right and when it's wrong. It's telling me now I ought to go but it also says don't go away for long. It says to me it's good, what's happening, and I should do it again."

She squeezed his hand as she looked into his eyes. "Then I think we both should listen to this inner voice of yours. Now let me tell you what my inner voice says. It's telling me, Stacy, so far so good, but you don't know one of the things about this man that's important to you. Does he play tennis? I know that sounds strange but I happen to be addicted to the sport. It's so bad I couldn't possibly consider a relationship with a man unless he played. I'm sorry, Eli, I know it's terrible of me but I have gotten so set in my ways. . . . Do you play?"

Eli rose and bowed his head. "Miss Starr, it has truly been a delightful evening. And to answer your question, get us a court sometime after your elbow heals and I'll show off for you. I'm pretty darn good for an old guy."

She smiled coyly. "I know, I checked you out, remember? I was just setting you up and it worked. Give me your cell phone number and I'll call you about playing as soon as I'm healed."

Eli rolled his eyes as he reached for his billfold. "And here I was just thinking how sweet you are and you go and get slick on me. Fine, Miss Starr, for that I'll whip you badly on the court to teach you a lesson. Here's my card. Call me when you're ready for a lesson in humility."

She accepted the card and rose. "The one thing you will have to learn about me, Agent Tanner, is that I work very hard for what I want. And right now I want to beat your butt on the court. I'm delighted you enjoyed the dinner. You may kiss me good night now, and the deal I made with Donny is complete."

"What if I don't want to kiss you?"

"Then I'll call Donny and tell him you didn't show up."

Eli nodded. "Well, I guess I'd better do it, then, huh?"

"I guess you'd better."

Eli stepped closer and gently took hold of her shoulders. He had every intention of making it a short good-night kiss, but as soon as his lips touched hers, he forgot everything. It felt so damn right he couldn't stop. It was like he knew how she would feel when she pressed herself against him. It was *supposed* to happen; his body told him so. He was trembling and couldn't stop and didn't want to. Every fiber in his being seemed to tingle and want more of her. Deeper and deeper he kissed her, feeling as if there were no end to his desire to consume all of her. Two seconds passed, then five; he didn't care, he couldn't let her go. Finally, he began shaking so badly he had to release her. Embarrassed and feeling guilty, he stepped back. "I . . . I'm sorry. I didn't mean to—"

"Shush," she said as she pressed herself against him again. "I'm not letting you go just yet."

She kissed him. And Eli thought, *Tanner, my man, dreams really can come true.*

Dahlonega, Georgia

Dressed in black fatigues, their faces smeared with dark camouflage face paint, the four men sat in a ravine two hundred yards from the cabin. Ted whispered, "I've seen enough; how about you guys?"

Virgil nodded as he reached up and turned off the night-vision goggles perched on top of his head. "It'll be a piece of cake with these babies."

Ramon bobbed his head. "Looks good, man, but remember to plan on Murph. If somethin' can go wrong, it will."

Glenn looked back toward the cabin. "They're all heavily armed . . . that worries me. Maybe we should hit them at about one or two in the morning when most of them are sleeping. It would give us the darkness to escape in."

Ted took off his night-vision goggles. "Two in the morning sounds good to me. Everybody agree?"

The other three nodded. "Two it is, then. Okay, Virg, you stay and keep your eye on the place. The rest of us will head back to the motel and get some rest. Glenn will relieve you in three hours. Keep your cell phone by you and call me if something comes up I need to know about. All right, let's get going. Tomorrow is going to be a big day."

Ramon whispered, "I'll hang out here with Virg, man. It's a nice evening. I'll rack out right here."

"Suit yourself, just don't get to bullshitting and get too loud."

Ramon hissed. "We're sophisticated Army dudes, Ted. We don't fuck up ops. We make 'em happen, right, Virg?"

"There it is, Ray."

Ted grinned in the darkness and patted Glenn's arm. "It's gettin' deep; let's get outta here. See ya, guys."

Once they had traveled a hundred yards, Ted turned to Glenn and whispered, "Ya know something? I really like those guys."

"Me, too."

Marriott Hotel, Atlanta

Eli took out his card key as he walked down the hallway toward his room. Reaching his door, he saw a note taped to the lock.

Tanner, knock on my door as soon as you return. Important!
                                                    Sutton

Eli walked down to the next door and was about to knock when he saw it was already open a couple of inches. He knocked as he entered. "Sutton, are you all right?"

He walked past the bathroom and saw her seated on the bed with papers lying scattered over the blanket beside her. She looked at her watch, then up to him. "It's almost one, Tanner. You kind of went beyond the call of duty, didn't you?"

His face reddening, Eli shrugged. "Uh . . . I stopped off and had a few beers in the lounge before coming up."

Ashley stared at him a long moment, got up, walked past him into the bathroom, and immediately came out holding a box of tissues. "Oh really, a couple of beers, huh? Was it the waitress who left the lipstick all over your face for tipping her or was it Miss Shark showing you her teeth?" She slammed the box into his stomach. "You should have gotten rid of the evidence, Agent."

She stomped back to the bed and resumed her previous position.

Eli quickly wiped his face and began to speak, but she shook her head. "Now the right side of your neck. You check for fang marks before you left her?"

"Look, Sutton, you're not my mama or my keeper, so don't sit there giving me that look."

"Hey, Tanner, I don't care what you do. As I recall, you said those exact words to me not long ago. Well, I'm saying them back to you. You're a big boy . . . but a dumb one if you think she's not after something, but that's not my concern. I just didn't want you standing there with lipstick all over your face and neck while I told you I found something. I think I know who the DEA's suspect is. Unlike you, I worked tonight. This is the file Paul wanted you to look at. When we talked today about laundering, I thought of it and went back to his office and got it."

Eli stepped closer to the bed. "What did you find?"

"I don't know; you'll have to tell me. You remember Paul told you the Miami office had a confidential informant that came forward? Well, I read the statements he made to our people. . . . The informant was on the mark. It gets interesting when he says a buddy of his and two unnamed colleagues engaged in a moonlight job two weeks ago. They had heard of a big-money haul that their chief competitor was making so they tried to make a score. Trouble was, they made the raid but there wasn't any money. The C.I.'s buddy beat up the driver to convince him to tell them where the money was. The driver said they had it all wrong. They had already delivered the dirty money to a bank in Georgia and were coming back empty. The buddy then got very angry and beat up the driver a little more. The driver swore all he did was drive the truck to Georgia and drop off trunks. He said he and eight others dropped off four trunks to a bank in Dahlonega."

Eli's eyes widened. "Trunks?"

"That's what he said, trunks. I figure a trunk holds at least a million in cash. Wait, it gets better." Ashley picked up another piece of paper. "I think this next part tells us who the DEA's suspect is. The C.I. stated his buddy said the driver of the truck worked for a big player by the name of Carlos Mendez."

Eli slowly raised his eyes to her. "You sure the guy said Carlos Mendez?"

"Yes, it's right here in black and white, Carlos Mendez. Do you know him?"

Eli lowered his head. A full ten seconds passed before he nodded. "Yeah, I know him. When I was with the Miami office, I was the AIC of an investigation on him—it got my partner killed and three others wounded, including me. Yeah, I know him."

"You've never mentioned it before," Ashley said.

Eli spoke as if very tired. "I screwed it up, Sutton. I didn't mention it because I don't like to think about it."

Her eyes locked on him, Ashley scooted closer, holding out the informant's statement. "Tanner, this could be it. This is the connection we've been looking for. If Mendez was laundering, he has to be the one who ordered the hits to cover up his involvement with the Yona Group. He's our man."

Eli shook his head. "He's the DEA's man." Rising from the chair, he walked toward the door.

"Where are you going, Tanner? We've got to call the SAC and tell him we know who the player is."

Eli halted and faced Ashley with an uncharacteristic frown. "I don't want anything to do with it, Sutton. You call the SAC. I'm sure he'll be impressed."

"What's wrong with you, Tanner?" Ashley blurted. "Now we know who let the contracts. We can help the DEA get Mendez."

"Get Mendez?" Eli said, shaking his head. "No, it's not

that easy. Once I thought it would be easy, too, but he's smarter than that, Sutton. Think a minute. Who is going to testify that Mendez was involved with the Yona Group? Henry Cobb? Congressman Richards? They're dead or missing, remember? Strike one. Next question. Who is going to testify that Mendez let the contract? Orlando? No, I killed him. What about the other hitters? No, they'll never say a word, but even if they do talk they don't know who gave them the contract. That's strike two. So, what have you got left? What else links Mendez to any of this? I'll tell you—nothing. That's strike three, Agent. You're out, and so is the DEA and anybody else who tries to get Mendez."

Ashley looked into Eli's eyes. "You're forgetting something, Tanner. The money. Four trunks delivered to a bank in Dahlonega, remember? Don't you think Mendez will want to recover his investment?"

"He'll write it off, Sutton. It's nothing but a small business expense to him."

"You'd be right if he thought we had his money, Tanner, but he doesn't think we know about the money. He had Cobb, Richards, Paul, and all the others killed to protect his investment and his involvement with the group. He thinks he's accomplished his mission of keeping the money and his involvement a secret."

Eli returned her stare for a moment before dipping his chin. "You may be right. . . . It'd be like him to try and get his money right out from under our noses."

Ashley picked up her cell phone from the bed and offered it to Eli. "Call the SAC and tell him what've we got."

"Me? You're the one who thinks we might still have a chance to nail him. You call him. I'm out of it."

Ashley licked a finger and rubbed his chin. "You missed a little evidence there, Tanner. Aren't you in this with me?"

"You want me in on this?" Eli asked. "I'm the dumb guy, remember?"

"Yes, of course I want you in; you're my partner. I'm just a white-collar wirehead and you're a field guy. I need you." She held the phone out. "Make the call."

CHAPTER 13

9:30 A.M., Thursday, Atlanta

Ashley held Eli's arm as they walked down the chapel steps. When she saw the black hearse parked alongside the curb, she dabbed at her good eye with a Kleenex.

Eli gave her arm a gentle squeeze. "You doing okay?"

She nodded. "I'm fine, really. It was nice, wasn't it? The SAC did a good job with Paul's eulogy."

Eli slowed, seeing Stacy Starr across the street with her camera crew. Ashley saw her at the same time and spoke through clenched teeth. "She never rests, does she? Damnit, why can't they stay out of people's lives?"

"She's just doing her job, Sutton."

The SAC caught up to the couple and tapped Eli's shoulder. "Tanner, you and Agent Sutton be in my office in an hour. We'll discuss what you told me last night."

"You did a wonderful job with the eulogy, sir," Ashley said.

Farrel lowered his head. "Paul was a damn fine agent. I'm going to miss him. . . . Well, I'd better get back to the office. See you two in a little while."

Minutes later Ashley started the van. She was about to shift into reverse but regarded her passenger a moment. "Thanks for coming with me, Tanner. I know now it would have never worked. Paul wouldn't have let it."

Not knowing what to say, Eli gazed out the window in silence. The one thing he did know was that he didn't know his partner as well as he'd thought. Ashley's feelings toward

Eddings had caught him completely off guard. He knew Ashley was capable of feelings like everybody else, but he'd never thought she could direct those feelings toward a fellow agent and be so open about it.

Misreading him, Ashley patted his arm. "You all right?"

"Yeah, I was just thinking is all. I haven't been to one of these since my Miami partner died. I'd forgotten how much they hurt and yet are so . . . so . . ."

"Settling?"

"Yes, that's a good word for it. The hard part is seeing Paul's kids. Gus had kids, too. That was the toughest thing for me . . . talking to his boys. Alice, his wife, wanted me to explain he wouldn't be coming home again. . . . It was the toughest duty I've ever had to do."

"Were you and Gus close?"

"As close as two guys can get. The job was actually fun with him. I didn't mind going to work, knowing he'd be there, bitching like he always did. He was always complaining about the hours. . . . He wanted to be with his family more. He kept things in perspective for me, kind of like you do, Sutton."

"Are you saying I bitch a lot, Tanner?"

"Do I get to count last night?"

She pushed the gearshift into reverse. "Never mind, Tanner. You want to get something to eat before we go to the meeting?"

"Sure, but none of those light salad lunch places. I need real food for a change. I'm up for a big greasy burger smothered in grilled onions."

"Tanner, I'm driving, so I pick the place; that's the deal."

"Uh-uh. That's not fair because you always drive. I get even days and you get odd. Today it's real food. Tomorrow you get the salad brought by the guys with the ponytails."

"So you get the greasy burger brought by the girl in a short skirt? Is that it?"

"It's real food, Sutton. I don't care who brings it to the table as long as they bring lots of it. I'm starved just thinking about it. Come on. Find me a burger joint where we can sit down."

"Tanner, it's an *odd* day, so guess what? Yeah . . . ponytail time!"

Eli smirked and shook his head as if defeated, but inside he knew he'd won a victory. He had gotten Ashley Sutton to smile again. Trouble was, he really could taste that burger.

Don Farrel read the informant's statement before looking at the two people seated on the other side of his desk. "It's thin but I want you two to get up to Dahlonega and work with Agent Bowlan on this. We need to find the money if it's there. Agent Sutton, you were White Collar and know how the division works. Work with Bowlan's White Collar people and find out what bank the Yona Group did business with. And Tanner, you'd better talk to the GBI and tell them what's going on; we'll need their help in getting cooperation from the locals. I'll call their director and let him know you're coming over for a chat. Once you're done I'll have a chopper waiting here to take you and a GBI rep up to Dahlonega, to Bowlan's CP."

Eli raised an eyebrow. "Sir, what about the DEA? Are you going to bring them in on this possible money laundering angle?"

"Not until I know for sure there is actually dirty money involved. All we've got is this hearsay statement from the C.I. If we prove the Yona Group was laundering, then I'll give them a call and tell them what we have."

"They won't like being left out, sir."

"That's too bad, isn't it?"

Ashley stood. "We'll head over to the GBI office now, sir."

Farrel gave her a long look before speaking. "You doing okay, Agent Sutton?"

"Yes, sir, my eye is giving me no problems."

"I wasn't referring to your eye. I know you and Agent Eddings were close."

"Sir, I hope you are referring to 'close' as in the professional sense."

"I am, Agent Sutton, but I'm not blind. It was obvious to me you had feelings for Paul. I'm asking if this is personal to you. Tell me now. You know I can't allow you to become involved in this case if it is."

Ashley stood rigid and lifted her chin. "Sir, I assure you it's not personal."

"Very well, I'll accept that. Agent Tanner, have Agent Bowlan give me a call once you two have briefed him on what we've discussed. Good luck."

Once in the hallway and walking to the elevators, Ashley took hold of Eli's arm and brought him to a halt. "What was that in there? I wasn't that obvious, was I?"

Eli patted her shoulder. "Look, Sutton, I'm your pard, so I'm going to be straight with you. Yes, it was *that* obvious. You glowed when you talked to Paul. You don't do that with the rest of us, so of course everybody noticed."

"Glowed? What's that mean?"

"You ever see that movie *Casablanca* with Bogie?"

"Yes, of course."

"You remember the scene where the girl is looking at Bogie when the black guy is playing 'As Time Goes By'? That's what glowing is, and that was you."

Ashley lowered her head. "I—I didn't realize I . . ."

"Forget it, pard. Nothing to be ashamed of. It looked good on you. A little disturbing maybe . . . but it said you were a real person, not just a hard case agent. That perfume you put on is what got me. . . . What was it?"

"I . . . I don't know. I was in the ladies' rest room and a secretary was putting some on and I asked if I could borrow a squirt."

"It was nice, pard . . . but don't do it again. It really drove me nuts."

Ashley began walking again. "I'll pass that on to that lady shark friend of yours."

Eli growled. "Let that alone, will ya?"

She stopped and looked over her shoulder at him. "I'm just trying to help you out, Tanner. Pards, remember?"

"Yeah, well, don't do me any favors in that department, Sutton. I can do for myself just fine."

"Touchy, huh? You like her, don't you?"

"I'm not answering that, Sutton."

"I'll let the evidence of last night speak for itself, Tanner. In my book you're guilty as charged."

Eli stomped past her. "Let's get goin'. We've got work to do."

Ashley smiled to herself; she had gotten him angry. *Good, he deserves it,* she said to herself. *He can't fall for a shark. Uh-uh, he can do better than that.*

Georgia Bureau of Investigation

Detective Ed Faraday knew he was going to be tagged as soon as he walked into his director's office and saw the two FBI agents seated at the table. The GBI director motioned to a chair. "Sit down, Ed. I believe you know these two special agents."

Ed wrinkled his brow as he took a seat. "Yes, sir, I'm afraid so."

"Good, because you'll be working with them. They've just told me an interesting story about the possibility of dirty money in Dahlonega. The SAC has been kind enough to include us in on the investigation, and these two agents have asked for you by name. Do you have a problem with representing our interests in this?"

Faraday took a breath and let it out slowly. "No, sir. But I guess this means I can forget about going to the Falcon game this weekend, huh?"

The director's eyes lit up. "Where are your seats?"

"Thirty-five yard line, sir. But I paid seventy-five apiece for the two."

"You got it. I'll write you a check right now."

Faraday glared at Eli. "You'd better have a damn good reason for this, Tanner."

3:40 P.M., Dahlonega

The blackened brick walls and charred remains of the Yona Group's headquarters office building sat as a backdrop behind a newly erected blue-and-white-striped tent. Under the canopy, Special Agent James Bowlan, the case agent in charge, sat behind a small desk speaking to the three people who had just reported for duty. He leaned back in his chair and motioned toward the destroyed building.

"As you can see, there's not much left; the fire was no accident. Our people found pieces of four ignitors. And the water to the building was turned off just before the fire, making the ceiling sprinklers useless. We've concluded there was definitely more than one arsonist involved and that they were pros. All the company's records were destroyed in the fire . . . but based on the SAC's call, we did some checking with the group's personnel department and we've found which bank the group dealt with. I ordered printouts of the group's phone records."

Bowlan picked up a thick stack of computer hard copy from his desk and passed it to Ashley. "Look at this. This is a record of calls Henry Cobb, the CEO, made the day he was murdered. The third call I highlighted is the one he made to a local bank. In just a second we'll confirm the bank for you . . . ahh, here's our confirmation now."

Bowlan rose as two agents escorted into the tent a small woman who looked to be in her late forties.

"Please take a seat, Mrs. Gilcrest." Bowlan motioned to an empty chair. "I understand you were the personal secretary to the group's CEO, Henry Cobb."

"Yes, I worked for Mr. Cobb for a little more than a year," the woman said, taking her seat.

"Mrs. Gilcrest, we have a printout that shows Mr. Cobb made a call to a local bank here in town only an hour before he was killed. Do you know who Mr. Cobb would have talked to?"

"Yes, that would be Harold Lynch, the owner of the bank. Mr. Cobb and Mr. Lynch were golfing buddies, and Harold handled all the group's banking needs. But I believe you're mistaken about the call. Henry was killed before ten, and the bank doesn't open till ten."

"Does Mr. Lynch live in town?" Bowlan asked.

"Yes, but he's not home or at the bank. I called him at the bank the day of the murder to inform him of the tragedy, but his secretary said he had left on a vacation. It was all very sudden and she was worried about him. He had left a note on her desk saying he was leaving. Mr. Lynch is all business, you must understand. It's not like him to just leave."

Eli exchanged looks with Ashley and Faraday as Bowlan nodded. "Just one more question, Mrs. Gilcrest. Did the group deal with any other banks or savings and loans?"

"No, just Dahlonega First National. As I said, Mr. Cobb and Harold were friends. Henry trusted Harold with all the group's banking transactions."

Bowlan rose again. "Thank you, Mrs. Gilcrest. You've been most helpful."

As soon as the secretary left the tent, Bowlan frowned. "You want to bet that Mr. Lynch is dead?"

Ashley was already on her feet. "It also means we're too late; Mendez has already gotten his money. We'd better get down to the bank and see what the employees know."

Bowlan headed in the opposite direction, speaking over his shoulder. "I'll get the search warrant and have the White Collar crew down there in fifteen minutes."

Still seated in his chair, Ed Faraday gave Eli an accusing stare. "You said we were gonna find trunks of money, Tanner. Sounds to me like we're gonna find zip."

Eli rose and offered his hand to pull his friend up. "No, Ed, not zip. If the money was there, then we'll know for sure the group was involved in laundering. We'll have our motive for the contracted hits."

The detective took Eli's hand and allowed himself to be

pulled to his feet. He softened his expression. "Where's that going to leave us?"

"It leaves us with one suspect . . . Carlos Mendez," Eli said as he walked toward the van.

"What do you mean, you don't know what was in the vault?" Ashley Sutton pinned the young bank assistant manager with a glare.

The assistant winced. "I . . . I didn't get involved with Mr. Lynch's affairs. All I know is he had this new vault built a year ago and nobody but himself was allowed to enter. He said it was because of security and that was the way our number one customer wanted it."

Ashley motioned to the open vault door. "Why is it open?"

"I assume because Mr. Lynch opened it. We were afraid to close it because we don't have the combination to open it again. And it's empty, as you can see, so we really felt no need."

"What was in there?"

"Like I told you before, I really don't know, Agent Sutton. I came to work yesterday morning and it was open just like it is now."

"And you didn't think this extra vault was strange?"

"Agent Sutton, I've been working for Mr. Lynch a year and I thought many things he did were strange, but he told me the Yona Group account was the reason we were doing so well. He said they had very strict security needs that he was forced to abide by in order to keep their business. Please understand, Mr. Lynch worked extremely long hours keeping our number one account happy."

"Do you know where Mr. Lynch went on vacation?"

"No, but I'm worried about him. It's not like him to leave, especially to leave with the vault door open. He never mentioned to me he was going on vacation. I know he recently was divorced and he was down about that, but I can't imagine him leaving without giving me instructions first."

Faraday studied the vault door. "Wasn't this thing rigged with alarms?"

"Yes, but they were deactivated. Mr. Lynch had the sequence code to do that."

Tired of the games, Eli took out his FBI identification card and held it up in front of the assistant manager's face. "Bud, what do the big letters on this card say?"

"FBI."

"Right, you think that means Funny, Blind, and Incompetent?"

"Of course not."

"Really? 'Cause you're standing there shucking us like we're stupid. We're not stupid, bud. We hear all kinds of stories and see all kinds of slick people like you who think we're dumb. We're not. We know you were involved because an operation this big can't be run by just one man. Think about that. It's common sense, isn't it? You make, what, thirty, forty grand in salary a year?"

"Thirty-six." The young man was beginning to sweat very heavily.

"Now, what's it going to mean to us when the White Collar boys find out you have a lot of money in one of those safety deposit boxes? But you may be smarter than that. You might have put your cut into an offshore bank. But we'll know that because we'll check. Are you getting the picture here? We know you were involved. And it's just a matter of time before we find out how much. The key word you need to be thinking of right now is the word *co-op-er-ation*. Because if you cooperate with us right now, we'll be grateful, and that means opening the possibility of dealing down to lesser charges. Look at me. No, look me right in the eyes. Good. Now I'm going to Mirandize you. That means I think you're a suspect. It also means when I'm finished you'd better start cooperating with us because you know and I know you're involved. Do you understand?"

The young man's eyes filled with tears, then he sank down to his knees. "Oh, God, I told him we couldn't keep doing it . . . I told him."

"You have the right to an attorney. If you cannot afford an attorney . . ."

Once he'd finished, Eli helped the young man up to his feet. "Okay, I see you're going to be smart and cooperate with us. First tell us what was in the vault."

"Ten million, six hundred and fifty-two thousand dollars."

"In trunks."

"Yes. The money was in twenties, fifties, and hundreds. We received a little over four million two weeks ago in addition to the six we already had."

"Where's the money?"

"I don't know, and that's the God's honest truth. I came in early yesterday morning and found the vault door open. I also found the note from Mr. Lynch saying he was leaving on vacation. Everything is gone, our books, all our records, everything that we used to manage the Yona account."

"Who else was involved in the recordkeeping—now don't start getting stupid on me. That kind of money takes more than two people to manage. Who else?"

Ashley stood tapping her foot as two handcuffed female bank employees and the young assistant manager were placed in waiting cars. She stared at Eli, who was looking through the notes he'd made. Feeling the heat from her eyes, he looked up at her.

"How did you know others were involved?" she asked.

"Because, just like I told him, one guy couldn't handle all the accounting. And you can't keep that much money a secret from key employees; they had to bring them in to keep them quiet."

"You were lucky, Tanner; you pushed him too hard. If he had lawyered up, we would have got nothing."

"Sutton, I knew he wanted to come clean; it was written all over him."

Ed Faraday smiled. "I liked that look you gave him. It said, 'I'll tear your heart out and eat it if you don't talk to me.' Is that look legal?"

Ashley kept her gaze on her partner. "Agent Tanner's methods are not by the book, Detective. He seems to have his own rules."

Faraday lifted an eyebrow. "Did you believe their story that they didn't know it was dirty money?"

Eli nodded. "I believe that's what they wanted to believe; if they knew who delivered the money and picked it up, they'd be like their boss . . . on *vacation*."

"You think they killed him?" Ashley asked.

"Oh, yeah, that's a for-sure," Eli said. "He knew too much. Mendez is making sure there are no loose ends. It's how he does business."

"How is it you know so much about this Mendez player, Tanner?" Faraday asked.

Eli lowered his head and was silent a long moment before finally responding. "Eight years ago in Miami, I was the agent in charge of a case similar to this. We suspected Mendez was laundering through a guy who owned a chain of grocery stores. The guy finally got the guilts and came to us. We thought we had Mendez put away, but our grocery guy was whacked a day later, along with his entire family. That was just the beginning. Over the next two days eight others who were involved were also killed—every material witness we had. My partner and I got smart on how Mendez worked and tried to set him up, but we weren't as smart as we thought. We walked into an ambush. Gus, my partner, was killed and three other agents were wounded, including myself. Mendez was in another country at the time. End of story. We lost—the bastard was better than me."

Faraday gave Eli a consoling pat on the shoulder. "We'll get him this time, Tanner. Is he Colombian?"

"Cuban," Eli said, finally raising his head. "He was Castro's secret police operations officer for five years before he decided to defect and put his training and expertise to work for him here in the States. Once he arrived, it didn't take him long to acquire the services of ex-Cuban military types who had defected. They went into the drug-running business and became very successful, but he realized the real money was in distribution and sales. When he became strong enough, he eliminated the people he was working for and took over their operation. It was just the beginning. He later knocked off their chief competitors and expanded his business until he became one of the major players in Miami. He even became the Colombian cartels' U.S. distribution front man. When the cartels' major players went down, he alone survived the Drug Task Force's shakedown. That should tell you something about his survival abilities. The guy is good."

"We're better," Ashley said.

Eli looked at her for a long moment before lowering his head in silence.

Key Biscayne, Florida

Within the huge estate facing the bay, Raul Ortega quickly walked down the marbled hallway to the polished-oak door where two bodyguards stood on duty. Ortega nodded to the bigger man. "Is he working or is he talking to them again?"

The bigger guard spoke as he opened the door. "He's with them again. . . . I think they're talking back this time."

Raul rolled his eyes and entered the huge office. He strode past the conference table and his boss's desk to the double glass doors of the large adjoining greenhouse. Pausing at the doors, Ortega unbuttoned his suit jacket and set his shoulders. He hated going into his boss's playroom because the heat and humidity always ruined his shirts. He wondered why his boss couldn't have had a hobby like stamp or coin collecting. Why did it have to be tropical plants?

Raul took a deep breath, opened the doors, and stepped into a small glass-enclosed anteroom that was ten degrees warmer than the office. To his front was another set of glass doors. Exhaling, Ortega thought the name his boss had given the office greenhouse was inappropriate. Carlos Mendez called the place his Green Heaven. To Ortega it should have been

called Green Hell because it was always hot as hell and
looked like a jungle right out of one of those black-and-
white Tarzan movies. Hell or heaven, one thing was for
sure: Stamps would have been a cheaper hobby. His boss
had spared no expense in obtaining all kinds of species from
every tropical jungle and forest in the world. According to
the accountant, his boss had spent more than ten million
perfecting his heaven.

Raul Ortega sighed; he would never understand what his
boss saw in the plants. They were green, big deal. Granted
they were every shade of green, but green just the same.
There were green ferns, green bushes, green trees, green
long spidery plants, and little green leafy things, but they
were all green, so what was the point?

Raul opened the second set of doors and entered his
boss's green obsession. A strange bird cawed. Raul shook
his head as he began his search. It wasn't a real bird, just the
computer sound system re-creation of birdcalls and the
sounds of a waterfall and wild animals. The quack plant
doctor who sold the system to his boss had said the sounds
made the plants feel as if they were in their native home.
Right, Ortega thought. The plants really could hear the birds
and the waterfall. But the boss thought the idea worked, and
if the boss thought it worked, then it worked.

The glassed-in computer by the entrance had cost the
boss fifty grand. The damn thing looked like one of those
computers in the ads for fifteen hundred bucks at Radio
Shack, but of course *those* computers couldn't automati-
cally turn on the mist spray and keep the temperature a constant 78 degrees and the humidity high and make bird sounds
and bug sounds and waterfall sounds and wild animal sounds.
No, this fifty-grand computer talked to plants . . . right. Raul
walked down a path in the small world of Carlos Mendez,
who knew every plant's name and how it was faring. They
were Carlos Mendez's children, his green children.

Raul wound his way around some huge ferns and finally
caught sight of Mendez as he stooped over some little green
something that looked as if it had hair.

"Colonel, we think we found her," Raul said.

Fifty-four years old, slightly overweight, but still raven-haired, Carlos Mendez stroked the plant's leaf. "See my new baby? It's a Sigma dahlia—very rare."

Raul wanted to say, *Yeah. And it's green like the others, boss.* Instead he nodded and said, "It's very nice, Colonel. You were right—the dog gave us the lead. A woman fitting Bonita's description took her Rhodesian Ridgeback to a vet in north Atlanta. I have the Fat Man visiting the clinic now. We'll soon have her address."

"Northern Thailand, that's where this beauty is from. It's very delicate and sensitive," Mendez said. He stroked the plant one more time before standing erect. "Such a pity my lovely Bonita is not a plant. I would place her here with my children. She was such a joy to me. What instructions did you give to our friend on how I want her handled?"

"I told him to question her and find out if she had spoken to anyone in addition to the police. And, of course, to find out who hid her from us."

Mendez smiled. "Come, Raul, you know as well as I who would gain by taking my beautiful blond flower. They are such fools. I will be most interested in what she tells our friend. Ensure he keeps her lovely. I will need her as proof the Italians are violating the truce. Once our friends hear her story from her own mouth, we'll strike first and teach their organization a lesson they will not soon forget."

Raul nodded. "I've already instructed several of our unit leaders to start planning the strike. I have other news from Georgia—our investment is safe and is only waiting for transport. The delay is being caused by the large number of police and FBI in the area. It seems there are very few access roads. Tonight we'll begin the transfer. I have Logan and his unit going in for a pickup."

Mendez nodded as he bent over another plant. "Excellent. Do you see this one here? It is a rare orchid from Burma. Beautiful, no?"

"Yes, Colonel, it's . . . it's a beautiful green. What color will its flower be?"

"A very light green."

Figures, Ortega thought, backing up. "I'll report back to you as soon as the Fat Man calls and says he has Bonita. It shouldn't be long."

Mendez glanced up. "Remind our friend that I want my wayward flower returned to me without damage. Later, once she has told our associates of the competition's treachery, we will deal with her disloyalty."

Ortega raised an eyebrow. "How do you want it done?"

"Painfully. Very painfully."

Raul nodded and made for the glass door. Bonita Rogers had made a tragic error in taking her dog to the vet.

6:30 P.M., Lake Lanier, Georgia

"State your business," said a voice over the small speaker.

The Fat Man leaned out the car window. "I'm doctor Tony Rawlins, veterinarian of Buckhead Animal Clinic. I've come to see Mrs. Stone about her dog, Baby."

"You have an appointment?"

"No, I'm sorry. I tried calling but always got a busy signal. They have found rabid skunks in this area, and I felt I should stop by and give Baby a rabies shot to ensure his safety. I'm sure Mrs. Stone will want to see me."

"Rabid skunks? Eh . . . yeah, okay. When the gate opens drive in to the cabin entrance. I'll meet you out front."

The Fat Man smiled as he pressed the button causing his window to close. He turned slightly and glanced at the two men in the backseat. "Stay down till I tell you. I'll take out whoever meets us while you cover me. Once the target is down, go for the door and get inside. We take out everyone but the blonde . . . and watch out for the dog. Kill it on sight."

Bonita stepped down from the stair climber machine and was about to pick up a towel when she heard Duwane calling for her from the hallway.

She scooped up the towel and walked from behind the partition. "What is it, Duwane?"

"Ma'am, your vet is drivin' in to give your dawg a rabies shot. He says he tried callin' for an appointment but the phone was busy. Says there's rabid skunks runnin' around."

"My vet?"

"Yeah, a Doc Tony . . . Tony . . . ah shit, forgot his last name."

Bonita dropped her towel and stopped dead in her tracks. "*His* last name? Was it a man?"

" 'Course it was a man. I know a man's voice when I hear it."

"Oh God! Toni Rawlins is a woman. They've found me!"

"Now don't get riled, ma'am. I won't let 'em in the house. Shit, I'm sorry. I'll make it right. I'll . . . I'll tell your ex you ain't here and to get off the property."

Bonita ran to her purse and pulled out her small pistol. "You don't understand. He's going to kill me. He'll kill you, too, as soon as you open that door."

"Kill me? Hey, them guys who hired me said nothin' about your ex being a nutcase. What's goin' on?"

"Duwane, there's no time to explain. We're all going to be dead unless we can get out of here right now. Where's Halley?"

"Gone to get groceries—what d'ya mean dead?"

"Talk to me, Duwane. Is there another way out except for the road?"

"The lake. There's a ski boat in the boathouse down by the pier."

Bonita spun around and looked out the huge windows toward the pier. She spun again. "You take Baby and get the boat ready. I'll be down once I slow them down. I'll be coming on the run so be ready to haul ass."

"Not with that little peashooter you ain't," Duwane said. He pulled out his nickel-plated .357 from his shoulder holster. "You take this. It's got the kick of a horse, but it'll stop an elephant. Pump a few rounds into his car when he pulls up. That'll make him stop and think."

Bonita took the big weapon from Duwane's hand. "Get going!"

The Fat Man eased the Buick to a stop and spoke calmly. "Okay, it's party time. I don't see anybody yet. I'm going to get out and meet whoever comes out. You two stay down but be ready to move."

Bonita had opened the front door a crack and held her breath, seeing the Buick's front driver's door open. *Oh God, please help me do this,* she prayed. The driver, a large, obese man, stepped out of the car and lowered a pistol to the side of his leg. Bonita exhaled slowly, pushed the door open with her foot, raised the heavy pistol, aimed, and squeezed the trigger. The heavy weapon bucked in her hand. *Oh God,* she thought, *Ted was right; you hit them in the face and they go down.*

Lowering the pistol to her new target, she fired again and again. The Buick's front windshield spiderwebbed. A rear door opened. Bonita shifted her stance, fired into the door, and heard a man grunt. The other passenger door opened and a large man jumped out with a small submachine gun resembling those she'd seen in the movies. *I'm dead,* she told herself. Suddenly there was a thunderous *ka-bloom* sound and the man was flying toward her. Too scared to move, Bonita watched in fascination and horror as he crumpled onto the steps in front of her.

Duwane stepped away from the corner of the cabin holding a shotgun. He approached the Buick cautiously and barked, "Don't move, shithead, or I'll blow your ass away! Get your hands where I can see 'em!"

Getting no response, Duwane stepped closer and looked into the backseat. He shook his head and backed up. "Looks like you got him in the neck. He ain't gonna make it by the look of the blood he's losin'."

Too weak to stand, Bonita sank to her knees and found herself looking into the lifeless eyes of the man on the steps. The expanding pool of blood beneath his head sickened her, and she closed her eyes for a moment to try to regain her strength.

Still holding the shotgun, Duwane sat down on the steps beside her. "It didn't set well, me leavin' ya—thought maybe I should help ya. Didn't think that damned ol' boat motor would start anyway. So, you gonna tell me what the hell I got myself into?"

8:00 P.M., Days Inn motel, Dahlonega, Georgia

Ted pointed at the large sketch on the bed. ". . . and once they're all down, I call Ramon, who books to the truck and brings it in. We load it, then skate. Any questions?"

Ramon yawned and leaned back in his chair. "We've gone over it a hundred times, man."

"Yeah, well, that's the way we SEALs do things." Ted glared at the Cuban. "Virg, you got any questions?"

"Nope; it's a piece of cake."

"Glenn, you have any?"

"No; it looks good to me."

Ted nodded. "Okay, then, we'll allow ourselves an hour and a half for chow, then come back and rest for an hour, then leave. We'll dress out in our gear at the base camp and recheck all our equipment. I want all radios working five-by-five and us in position by one."

Key Biscayne, Florida

Carlos Mendez sat behind his ornate desk and pinned Raul Ortega with a questioning stare as he entered the office. "Well?"

Raul shook his head. "It's not good news, Colonel. The Fat Man and his two associates are dead. One of our representatives confirmed it a few minutes ago with local authorities."

Mendez bolted out of his chair. "How could this happen? Where is Bonita?"

Raul backed up a step. "Colonel, it appears a security guard was guarding her and—"

"Where is she?"

"She's gone, Colonel. The local authorities are looking for her. The guard told the police she was taken by the Italians. It appears the guard believes the Fat Man and his associates were working for them as well."

Seething, Mendez slammed his fist on the desk. "Find her!"

Raul held his ground. "Colonel, I've already notified all our friends and given them her description. If she tries to leave the country we'll have her."

Mendez closed his eyes and took in a deep breath to calm himself. Exhaling, he stared at the glass doors leading to his Green Heaven. "I am becoming concerned about this, Raul. I don't want to feel the feelings I'm having. My stomach is upset, my blood is running cold through my veins. Find her. It is the medicine I need."

Raul nodded. "We will, Colonel."

Tinker's Bar and Grill, Dahlonega, Georgia

"How's your salad, Sutton?" Eli saw that she was only picking at the bowl.

"I told them a little dressing, and *look* at this. It's soaked. And it's the cheap, bottled stuff."

Faraday looked across the small table at Eli. "Does she always complain like this?"

"She's usually worse, Ed. She's really been kinda quiet tonight."

"Knock it off, you two. I can't believe you're both having ribs. You always have ribs; it's all you two ever talk about. Haven't you ever heard of variety in your diet? It's not healthy, always eating meat."

Eli rolled his eyes. "Here she goes on the health thing now, Ed. She'll start in on the harmful effects of barbecuing, then quote us chapter and verse on the most recent findings from some new health book she's read."

Ashley folded her arms across her chest. "I'm not saying another word to you two."

Eli raised his hand to a passing waitress. "Ma'am, could you please get the lady another salad? And please put the dressing on the side."

Ed nodded. "And ma'am, we ordered drinks ten minutes ago and still haven't got—"

"Have you looked around, hon? We're kind of busy tonight. If I was y'all, I'd get them drinks myself. The bar is right over there. I got six orders up and only two hands." The waitress kept walking.

Eli stood. "I'll get us the drinks. Ed, watch out for her; I bet she tries to make you into a vegetarian while I'm gone."

Ashley glared. "I'm not talking to you two, remember?"

Eli waved his hand. "Yeah, yeah." He weaved around the tables and approached the crowded bar.

Minutes later he returned to the table with three bottles of Dr Pepper. Ashley glanced at the bottle in front of her, then pinned Eli with a stare as he sat down. "What's this?"

"What it looks like, Dr Pepper."

"Dr Pepper? You know I only drink Diet Coke."

"They didn't have any Diet Coke, Sutton. Guess people up here aren't worried about their weight. It was Dr Pepper or an RC Cola; I opted for the Dr Pepper."

The waitress walked up with a tray. "Who gets the ribs?"

Eli was about to motion to himself when another woman walked up to the table. "Hi, Eli. What brings you up here?"

Eli rose with a smile. "Hi, Miss Starr. I might ask you the same thing."

"Rib dinner here, and the pasta goes to the lady," Faraday said to the waitress. "Put the other ribs in this guy's place."

Eli turned. "Miss Starr, I would like you to meet Detective Ed Faraday and Special Agent Ashley Sutton."

"We've met," Faraday said, sticking his napkin under his chin.

Ashley just dipped her chin. The reporter didn't have a hair out of place. It was bad enough that Starr looked as if she'd stepped out of *Vogue* magazine, but the way the woman was looking at Eli really upset her. It was a look that said, *Come on, invite me to join you.*

Stacy returned a nod to Ashley. "A pleasure to meet you, Agent Sutton."

"So, Stacy, what does bring you up here?" Eli asked, feeling uncomfortable with his tablemates' reception of his dream.

"Work, of course. It seems this is where all the action is on the case, but you all know that, don't you?"

Eli shrugged. "We can't comment, Miss Starr."

"That's all right, I know it is. We did a forty-second live spot in front of what's left of the Yona Group headquarters at six. Did you see it?"

"We were busy."

"Too bad, Eli. You would have been proud of me. Well, I can see your friends would like to eat so I'll let you go. I guess I should warn you, my arm is feeling much better. I'll be calling soon about that game you promised to play with me. Nice to see you again, Ed. Agent Sutton, please take good care of your partner; he's special to me. Good-bye, Eli."

Eli sat down again as soon as she walked away, and knew it was going to be quick but didn't know from whom.

"Game you promised to play with her, Tanner?" Ashley asked. "What kind of game . . . or is that something Ed and I shouldn't hear about?"

"No, I *wanna* hear about it," Ed said with a wolfish grin.

Eli tore a rib off with his hands and shook it at Ashley. "Sutton, she was talking about a tennis match. Drop it."

"Tennis?" Faraday repeated as if disappointed. "Hell, I thought we were talkin' about somethin' more . . . more . . . well, you know, somethin' involving physical contact."

Eli shook the rib at Faraday. "Don't you start on me, too, Ed."

"Okay, Tan, after all you are *special* to her."

"That's it. I'm eating at the bar unless you two let it go."

Ashley canted her head toward Faraday. "How do you know her? You said you'd met."

"Yeah, I know her all right. She steamrolled into one of my crime scenes once and I had to physically remove her. It wasn't all that bad, if you know what I mean."

Ashley shook her head in disgust. "You're as bad as Tanner, Ed."

"Hey, I just meant she's pretty darn firm for a little gal is all. I thought she'd be more soft, ya know?"

Ashley shifted her cold gaze to Eli, who was trying to ignore them. "Well, I'm sure it's probably the tennis that keeps her in shape. That and all the running she does after a story. I'm sure Agent Tanner can tell us what kind of shape she's in."

Eli decided he couldn't let that one go. "Nope, I can't. I haven't played her yet. Ed, pass me the sauce, will ya?"

Ashley picked up her fork and stabbed at her salad.

Ted came to an abrupt halt in the motel parking lot. The three men behind him saw what had caught his attention and froze.

Ted blinked, hoping his eyes were deceiving him, but she was still standing there in front of his room door with the dog at her side.

Bonita pushed away from the door. "Thank God, I thought you had already gone. I . . . I didn't know what I was going to do."

"Christ'a'mighty, what are you doin' here?" Ted said angrily.

"They found me, Teddy—I shot two of them and—"

"Oh shit," Ted blurted, feeling the questioning stares from his teammates.

Ted gave Bonita's shoulder a gentle squeeze before getting up from the bed. Seated on the other bed, Glenn looked up at his friend. "What are we going to do now?"

Ted glanced at Ramon and Virgil seated at the small table. "We can't leave her here alone. . . . She goes on the op with us."

Glenn stood with a look of disbelief. "On the op? Are you nuts?"

"You got a better idea?" Ted said with a glare. "We wouldn't even be makin' this score unless Bonita had helped us."

Virgil stood. "Come on, Glenn. The way I see it, Ted's right. The lady has been part of the team—we just didn't know it till Ted explained it to us a few minutes ago. We can't leave a team member behind."

Ramon nodded. "Yeah, I say the lady goes, too, man. She can stay in the rental truck till it's over. Once it's done she gets her share and books."

Glenn stared hard at Bonita. "You guys don't get it—she can make us all. If she talks, we'll never be able to spend a dime of the score."

Bonita stared back. "You want to kill me? Go ahead, get in line. I didn't want this to happen. I didn't have any other place to go."

"What about the security guard you said helped you?" Glenn asked, hardening his stare. "What did you tell him?"

"I told him my ex was in the Mafia and the men we killed were his goons. I gave him all my jewelry as payment for the story he would tell the cops."

"What's the story again?" Glenn asked.

"The goons came and got me. He tried to stop them and even shot three of them, but others already had me in the car and got away."

"What about the computer you used?" Glenn asked.

"I deleted everything from it, completely wrote over the hard disk, then had Duwane drop it in the lake. I've got the disks here in my purse. The cops won't find anything about us."

"And how did you get here, walk?"

"Halley, the live-in cook, drove me up and dropped me off. Don't give me that look . . . I had her drop me at the bus station. She thinks I'm on a Greyhound to California. She got my gold Rolex and a twenty-four-karat bracelet for her trouble. She won't talk."

"But what about Ted? The security guard and this Halley lady can make him if the cops ask who visited you at the house."

"I told Duwane and Halley to say nobody visited me while I was at the cabin. They think this is all related to me being a mob wife, remember? They're just as scared as I am. They know if they talk about Ted, it'll only cause them more trouble. Anyway, they liked Ted. They won't tell the cops about him."

"Smart," Virgil said, bobbing his head. "The lady has smarts. The story sounds good to me. Back off, Glenn; she's in with us. She's a team member."

Glenn gave Bonita a last look before backing up and nodding. "Okay, I'll back off. The story should buy us enough time."

Relieved, Ted patted Baby's head. "We got work to do. Everybody pack up; it's time to move to our base camp and get ready for action."

CHAPTER 14

2:00 A.M., Friday

Feeling very confident about taking out the two guards, who were both sleeping soundly, Ramon crawled forward between two pines. Closing to within a couple feet of the two men, he silently pulled the buck knife from the sheath on his web belt. Lifting his other hand, holding the silenced Beretta, he slowly rose and stepped closer. Bending over, he held the knife close to one man's neck and gently nudged the other's temple with the silencer. Then he whispered in Spanish, "You fucked up, people. Shouldn't sleep on duty. You move, asshole, I'll slit your throat. You feel the steel? You, get down on your belly now. Good. Now you. Good. Now both of you put your face in the dirt. Good. Now put your hands behind you. Do it, fuckups!"

Minutes later, his work complete, Ramon glanced at the two bound and gagged men lying at his feet as he pushed the small radio mike to the front of his lips. "Blue, this is Red. Over," he whispered.

Four hundred yards away, having heard the call in his earphone, Ted swung the boom mike around to his lips. He whispered, "Red, this is Blue. Over."

"Blue, I have a bingo, over."

"Roger, Red, understand you have a bingo. Collect the prize. Over."

"Roger, Blue. Out."

Ted lowered the mike to his chin and nodded to the black-clad men behind him. "Ramon has done it. It's our turn." He pulled his hood into place, then crept toward the porch. Virgil and Glenn followed.

A Coleman lantern hissed, hanging from beneath the porch overhang where two men sat at a table beneath the light playing gin. One guard set his cards on the table with a grin. "Check it out. I got your ass again. Gin."

"Shit, you're cheatin', man. No fuckin' body is that fuckin' lucky. I wanna play somethin' else."

The other man shrugged. "Like what, pig or old maid or—" He froze when a dark figure materialized out of the darkness, but he knew better than to move, because of the huge pistol pointed at his head. Another dark figure had already pressed a pistol against his companion's temple.

The bigger of the black-clad men whispered harshly, "You speak, you die. On your stomachs. Now!"

Eight minutes later Ted crept toward the Winnebago. Grasping the door handle, he waited until Virgil was behind him before slowly opening the portal. Silenced Beretta ready, he took the steps up into the cabin and nodded toward the two men sleeping on the fold-out couch. Virgil stepped toward the two men and nodded to Ted, who continued to the back room, where the other two were sleeping. Virgil was already counting, and when he got to ten he said aloud, "Sur-prise, boys!"

Inside the old wooden cabin, Ted took in a deep breath and exhaled slowly. Lifting a pry bar, he inserted the tip into the loop of the lock and with a quick jerk snapped out the entire hinged lock. Looking at the other two men standing in front of the trunk, he grasped the lid. "Guys, get ready to see what we've come for." He opened the lid and grinned. "Ta da!"

Virgil sank to his knees and ran his hand over the banded stacks. "Man oh man . . . we in the money. This ride is somethin'."

Glenn smiled as he picked up one of the banded bundles and fanned himself with it. "Ted, you've outdone yourself. There's gotta be a helluva lot more than six million here."

He looked at the other nine trunks and sighed. "Is this sweet or what?"

Ted was about to respond when a phone rang. All three men jumped, then went for the pistols in their holsters. Realizing what the sound was, Ted stopped himself and walked quickly outside to the porch, where the cell phone lay on the table.

"What do we do?" Virgil asked.

"Ignore it. Let's get the trunks out and we'll load 'em as soon as Ramon gets here."

Ted walked back inside and was about to take hold of a trunk handle when his earphone crackled with Ramon's excited voice. "Blue, this is Red! Two Suburbans are heading your way. They just pulled onto the gravel road and are moving fast, man!"

Ted spun and barked to Glenn and Virgil, "We got company! Virg, get to the clackers; two Suburbans are coming up the road! Glenn, when the claymores go off we'll rush and finish off what's left."

Ten seconds later Virgil lay behind a tree, holding the two prepositioned electrical detonators. The wire from each led to its claymore mine, which had been set up alongside the road thirty feet away. Virgil heard the vehicles approaching but could make out only their headlight beams. Heart thudding in his chest, he rose to his knees, holding a clacker in each hand. *Okay, Virgil, be cool; you got to ride this train out. Be cool, be cool, be cool,* he whispered to himself.

The first dark Suburban appeared, followed closely by the second. Virgil pressed himself against the tree, lifted his right hand, and waited for one more second to ensure the lead vehicle was in the kill zone, then he squeezed. For an instant night became day in a brilliant, blinding flash of light. Then the world seemed to end. The violent, ear-shattering explosion ripped through the forest like a monstrous screaming runaway train. The first Suburban disappeared in the debris cloud. Then Virgil squeezed the second clacker.

As soon as they heard the second explosion, Ted and Glenn got to their feet. The ground still shook beneath them.

Holding their pistols, they ran into the choking dust cloud. The first Suburban had run off the road into a tree. The vehicle's right side was peppered and all its windows were shattered by the claymore mine's hail of steel ball bearings. Ted swung open the left passenger door, where a screaming man was trying to get out. Ted jerked the blinded man out and was ready to fire at any surviving passengers but he saw none that were a threat. The two men who had been seated on the right side had taken the full effects of the mine and were dead. The driver was bleeding from the face and neck and was shaking as if having a fit. Holding his breath because of the overwhelming reek of C-4, blood, urine, and feces, Ted grabbed the driver and pulled him from the vehicle.

Inside the second Suburban, Glenn held his breath as he swung his Beretta and minimag flashlight left then right, checking each occupant. Two were dead, two were wounded and stunned. Both were bleeding from the shattered glass. He grabbed the first and dragged him out of the stink and blood. Virgil appeared out of the darkness and pulled out the second moaning man. Vehicle headlights suddenly sliced through the darkness and the smoke.

Ted yelled, "Don't shoot; it's ours coming in. Can he get by that Chevy?"

Glenn yelled back, "Yes, it's off the road. We've got two live ones here."

"And I've got two here. Get 'em tied up, then get to the cabin to load!"

Still wearing their black hoods, all four men were soaked in sweat as they loaded the last trunk into the rental truck. Bonita walked up to the men and motioned to the wounded men trussed up beside the cabin. "We can't just leave them here like that."

Ted grabbed her arm and marched back to the truck. "I told you to stay in the damn cab—Jesus, they've seen you now."

Bonita worriedly looked over her shoulder at the wounded. "You're not like them, Teddy. Don't kill them."

"Just get in the damn truck—we're not goin' to hurt them." Once she was in the cab with Baby, he walked over to the first wounded man and nudged him with his boot. "Yo, shithead, we're leaving you all here. None of ya look like you'll bleed to death. You're lucky we're not like you and your buddies or we'd cut your throats. We'll call the police in about thirty minutes and tell them where you are so you'll get medical attention. I know you won't tell them about us because it would mean you'd have to explain what happened, and you can't do that, can you? I guess you can say you were ambushed by deer hunters. The police will love that one." Ted turned and patted Glenn's shoulder. "Get me their cell phone there on the porch. I'll use it to make the call to the police. Let's get out of here, people. Time to move!"

Minutes later, seated in the back of the truck, Ramon looked at the stacked trunks before shifting his gaze to Virgil. "Virg, are they all really full of cash, man?"

Virgil smiled. "I told ya this train had better benefits, Ray. We're ridin' high and fast now."

"Ohh, man! I was scared shitless when I saw them coming down the road, man. I had just got to the truck when I saw them drive by. Good thing we planned for a Murphy, huh?"

"Piece of cake, Ray. Those claymores stopped 'em cold."

"Man, the next op isn't going to be a piece of cake, I can tell you that. Carlos has serious people who don't smoke and joke, you know what I mean?"

"Yeah, Ray, but we're sophisticated dudes who don't smoke or joke either. The C-man is goin' down."

Ramon shifted his gaze back to the trunks and spoke in a whisper. "No piece of cake next time, man. Uh-uh."

3:10 A.M.

In the darkness, an FBI agent walked with a roll of yellow crime-scene tape toward a tree to begin sealing off the area.

Near the cabin, local police and FBI vehicles were parked with their headlights shining toward a line of handcuffed men all seated on the ground. On the road, ambulance lights flashed while paramedics worked on the wounded. Just off the gravel road, Ashley and Ed Faraday followed Eli, who was using a mini flashlight to examine the faces of the dead men laid out on the road embankment. Eli stopped and leaned over the last body.

"I don't know any of them."

Ashley shined her light into the dead man's face. "This one is a Caucasian."

"Mendez must believe in equal opportunity employment." Eli turned off his minilight.

Ed Faraday stepped closer. "What in the hell are all these armed guys doin' out here?"

Eli motioned to the handcuffed men seated on the ground in front of the cabin. "Let's see if Bowlan has found the answer to that."

Agent Bowlan, the case agent in charge, met the three people as soon as they walked into the headlight beams. "None of them are talking, and neither are the wounded. They all have fake IDs, and we found automatic weapons in the vehicles and in the cabin."

Eli motioned toward the bodies. "It looks to me like a hit went down here. But what I don't understand is why the rest of these guys are still alive. It isn't these types' style to leave people who could talk."

Bowlan nodded toward the cabin. "You'd better take a look at what we found. I think I know what the raiders were after."

Inside the cabin, Bowlan pointed at the broken hinge on the floor. "I'd say that's a trunk hinge and lock, and take a look at those scratch marks. Doesn't that look like somebody dragged heavy objects toward the door?"

Eli squatted down, shining his light on the lock hinge, then the scratches. "They dragged something heavy all right . . . yeah, I think you're right. The money from the bank was here."

Bowlan nodded. "There's more. Just outside on the road, we've found four sets of fresh impressions made from military-style boots. And get this. There's another set that appears to be made from a pair of woman's Reeboks."

"A woman's shoe prints? Are they sure?" Ashley asked.

"My boys tell me the impressions were made by fairly new women's size-eight shoes. Based on the depth of the impression, the wearer weighed somewhere between 115 and 130 pounds—it was a woman, all right, or a small guy with narrow feet."

"Do you think a competitor of Mendez made the hit and took the money?" Ashley asked.

Bowlan shook his head. "Agent Tanner was right. A competing rival would have capped everybody. But I'll say this—whoever made the raid was good and knew what they were doing. My military vets tell me it was claymore mines that hit those two vehicles where we found the bodies."

"Claymore mines?" Ashley repeated, as if not understanding.

"They're directional mines," Eli said. "Electrically detonated by a handheld trigger mechanism called a clacker. Each mine is crescent-shaped, with a plastic plate of steel ball bearings laid over C-4 explosive. When it's detonated, the blast blows the balls out in a fan-shaped pattern. You saw what it did."

Faraday pulled on his chin. "Looks like we have some independents in the game that we didn't know about . . . and I'd say it's pretty obvious the fellas outside didn't know about them, either."

Ashley leaned over, studying the scratches. "Whoever they are, they must know how Mendez operates; they knew where his money was and knew when to strike."

Bowlan looked at Eli with a worried frown. "Could it be a mob score?"

"Maybe," Eli said. "They've got crews that are capable of doing something like this. Trouble is, the mob is like the Latinos—they wouldn't have left anybody who could talk. The other thing is, I don't think the wise guys would start a war with the Latinos over ten or eleven million dollars—it's chicken feed. Plus the mob wouldn't use a woman on something like this; they're still into sexual discrimination. I think Ed hit on it when he said independents. The only trouble is, how'd they get the information about Mendez's laundry operation? They'd have to have an inside man."

"Or inside woman," Ashley added.

"What about locals?" Ed Faraday asked. "Could be the Yona guys weren't very discreet about having the player's money. Could be local cowboys found out about it and decided to make a lot of easy money."

"I don't think so, Detective," Bowlan said. "We've learned that Henry Cobb and Congressman Richards were very discreet about their secret dealings with Mendez. Nobody else in the group nor anyone in their families knew about the money laundering. And I don't think locals would have attempted taking down eight armed men. This score was done by pros who planned and executed a near-perfect operation. The claymore mines tell us they even had a contingency plan. I'd say we've got an independent crew made up of four men and a woman who know what they're—"

Bowlan looked out the open door and growled. "Ahh shit, not now." He stormed out the door and barked, "Agent Hardy, stop that damn news crew vehicle! Sheriff Owens, what happened to your road guard? I told you not to let anybody into the crime scene area, damnit!"

Eli walked to the door just as the Channel 2 van door slid open. He wasn't surprised when Stacy Starr stepped out with a cameraman and a light man. She pointed and commanded, "Pan those shattered Suburbans and get those men seated on the ground, and get those bodies over there." Stacy lifted a handheld mike as Agent Hardy approached her. "Can you tell us what happened here, Officer?" She jabbed the mike up toward his face.

Hardy stopped dead in his tracks, looking at the mike as if it were a pistol barrel. "Ma'am, get back in the van. Hey, stop filming, you! Both of you get back—I said stop shooting!"

Bowlan stepped in front of the video camera, covering the lens with his hand. "You heard my agent. Get back into the van; this is an FBI crime scene."

Stacy held up the mike in front of him. "What happened here, Agent?"

"No comment. Please get back into the van this instant or I'll charge you with interfering with the investigation."

Stacy backed up but held up her mike. "Is this connected to the money missing from the Dahlonega bank?"

Bowlan's face tightened. "I don't know what you're talking about."

"Yes, you do, Agent. We talked to the husband whose wife was arrested this morning at the bank. He said she called him and said she was in trouble because millions of dollars are missing from the bank. What is your response to that? Is this crime scene connected to that missing money? Was the bank laundering that money, Agent?"

Hearing Stacy's barrage of questions, Eli approached and took hold of her arm. "Come on, Stacy, you know he can't respond to your questions. Please do as he says and get back into the van."

"Well, if it isn't Agent Tanner himself. Okay, Eli, we'll back off. I have enough for a spot anyway. Get in the van, John. . . . Eli, I talked to the assistant bank manager's wife. She said her husband had told her he believed the dirty money was drug money from Miami. If it was drug money then I have to assume the e-mail I received was correct—it was a Cuban player who ordered the deaths of Senator Goodnight and all the others to cover his involvement with the Yona Group."

"I can't comment on that, Stacy."

"I have contacts in Miami, Eli. I'll find out in a matter of hours the most likely Cuban candidates capable of letting the contracts."

Eli stepped closer, pinning her with his eyes. "Stacy, you'll get yourself onto very dangerous ground if you start asking questions about those people. Listen to me, I know what I'm talking about. The players take it personally when anyone digs into their lives, and that goes double for the media. Some of your colleagues have tried before, but they all backed off when members of their teams began disappearing. The players don't mess around, and they don't warn you first."

Stacy patted his arm. "Thank you for the warning. I'll be careful." She walked back, got in the van, and commanded, "Back it out, Fred. John, keep shooting through the window."

Bowlan stepped up beside Eli as the van began backing up. "You know she'll do it anyway, don't you?"

"Yeah, she smells a Pulitzer in this one—I saw it in her eyes."

"I'll call the SAC and warn him she's not listening. A team will have to keep her shadowed."

Ashley heard the conversation and stepped closer. "Do you both really think she could get herself into danger by just talking to her contacts?"

Bowlan exchanged glances with Eli before responding. "Agent Sutton, she doesn't understand who she's dealing with. Mendez and the others like him all survive because they're invisible to the public, and even to us for the most part. It's a very small and very sensitive community. They know when somebody starts asking questions. To answer your question more directly, if she pursues the leads she thinks she has, yes, she could be in great danger. I'm going to make that call to the SAC and brief him on what we found here and also warn him about Miss Starr."

Bowlan pulled a cell phone from his jacket pocket and was about to push the keys when an oncoming car's headlights blinded him. "Jesus Christ, now who's driving into my scene? Sheriff Owens!"

The small Ford stopped and four men got out. The tallest of the men growled, "Who's in charge here?"

Bowlan stepped forward. "Me, and who the hell are you?"

"Sanders, DEA. What have we got here?"

Bowlan shook his head. "This is *my* scene, so don't say *we*."

Ignoring Bowlan, Sanders slipped a minimag from his shirt pocket and, with the three other DEA agents, approached the prisoners. He nodded as soon as he shined his light into the first man's face. "You got yourself a Cuban crew here. This one is Inez and that one there is Palmia. Let's see . . . no, I don't make any of the others. They're not talking, correct?"

Bowlan made a shooing motion. "Go on and check the dead and wounded by the road and see if you can ID any of them. I've got a call to make to my SAC."

Sanders raised his chin. "Good. You can tell him we'll take over from here."

"What?"

"You heard me. The administration has the lead on player involvement. Don't worry, I'll cooperate fully with you, but I must insist you turn over the scene to me."

"Horseshit! Look, Sanders, you go look all you want but don't touch a damn thing. This is my scene and I call the shots."

Sanders glared at Bowlan as he took out his cell phone. "We'll see about that," he said as he pushed at the keys.

Not to be outdone, Bowlan hurriedly did the same to his phone.

Eli backed away with Ashley and Faraday, then whispered, "This ought to be good, a turf fight over who gets the scene."

"Who's going to win?" Ashley asked.

"Possession gives us the advantage, but they have the drug players' cases. I'd say it's too close to call."

Three minutes later Bowlan's jaw muscles rippled as he lowered his phone in defeat. Sanders smiled broadly. "Agent Bowlan, be so kind as to inform your people that I am now in charge of the scene. I'd like each of the agents and local officers who first arrived to meet me on that cabin porch so I can go over notes they may have taken. I also would like you to give me a quick rundown on what you think happened here."

Bowlan hissed, "I don't think. I know what happened here."

"Okay, what happened?"

"An unidentified crew of raiders made up of four men and possibly a woman snuck in and caught those eight over there off guard. Then the crew in the two Suburbans showed up, but the raiders were ready for them and blew claymores in an ambush and stopped them in their tracks. Then the raiders took the money and left."

Sanders's eyes widened. "A woman—and what money?"

Bowlan threw up his hands. "I knew it! I knew you damn guys didn't know. The money, Mr. DEA! The money from the Dahlonega bank . . . the money, like in eleven million in trunks."

"What are you talking about?"

"Shit," Bowlan said in disgust. "Agent Hardy, get over here and please tell the DEA what the hell is going on! I'm calling the SAC again. Agent Tanner, you and Detective Faraday keep me posted on the search for the raider's vehicle."

Left standing in the dark, Sanders barked, "Trunks of dirty money? *Trunks?* Did you say *trunks?*"

5:10 A.M.

Bonita held the flashlight as Ted moved the last rock in place to cover two of the trunks. He backed up from beneath the stone outcrop, wiping his hands on the back of his fatigues. "That ought to do it."

Bonita turned off the light. "Am I the reason the guys went off in different directions to hide their money—they don't trust me?"

"Naw, it was always the plan," Ted said. "Everybody is hiding their own money because if one of them is caught and made to talk, he can't tell where the rest is hidden."

Bonita looked into Ted's eyes. "But your money is here, Ted. I know where you've hidden it. What happens if they catch me?"

"You're not gettin' caught, Bonita. You'll be safe in Kansas. You got yourself two million dollars—I upped your split. Ramon has to drive back to Atlanta and turn in the rental truck. When he does, I'll have him stop and get you some big suitcases to hold your share. He'll also get you a good used car, then I want you to drive straight to Hutchinson and stay with Henry Duggin."

Bonita stepped closer to him. "Why did you bring me with you to hide your share?"

Ted leaned over and patted Baby's head. "Look, Bonita, I know I'm askin' a lot of you, but if I don't make it back, then—"

"I knew it. You wanted me to know where you hid it." She sniffed back her tears.

"Ahh, Bo, don't start leakin' on me. If the op goes bad and I don't make it, wait a couple of months, then come back here and get the money. Send my sis a million—she's all the family I got. You can keep the rest—her no-good husband will just squander the money anyway."

Bonita turned her back to him to hide her tears. "You . . . you don't think you're coming back, do you?"

Ted put his arm around her shoulders. "Bo, I told ya I was good at what I do—I'm not plannin' on dyin'. I brought you up here as kind of an insurance policy. You never know what could happen. I just don't want the money rotting away if something goes wrong. Will ya do it for me?"

Bonita wiped the tears from her cheeks. "If something happens to you, I'll make sure your sister gets the money, but promise me you won't let anything happen—promise me you'll come back."

Ted walked her toward the nearby dirt road. "Sure, Bo, I promise. Come on, we've got to get back to the linkup site. I gave the guys an hour to hide their share and time is about up. Come on, lion hunter, you can't stay with my money."

Ten minutes later Ted pulled off the highway onto a side

road that led to a small park. Parking by the other team vehicles, he and Bonita got out and approached a picnic table where the rest of the team sat waiting.

Glenn stepped forward. "We're all good to go, Ted. We've got all the weapons and gear packed in our vehicles, and the rental is clean and ready for turn-in. We wiped your Lincoln clean and ran it off into a ravine. . . . We're ready to roll."

"Where's Bonita's money?" Ted asked.

Ramon motioned to the two duffel bags beside him. "It's all here, Ted, two million."

"Load 'em in the rental," Ted said. "As you all know, it's only ten minutes to the interstate. We'll follow the plan with one exception. Ramon, when you drive the rental into Atlanta to turn it in, you'll also take Bonita and the hunter. Stop at a store and get her some suitcases for the money, then help her pick out a good used car off a lot. Once she's on her way, turn in the truck and meet us at stop two of phase two. Anybody have any questions?"

Glenn looked into Bonita's eyes. "We're trusting you to be smart. If you get dumb with that money, we're all dead. You understand?"

"She knows what's at stake, Glenn; back off," Ted growled.

Bonita's eyes misted as she returned Glenn's stare. "And I'm trusting you to take care of yourselves and bring Ted back in one piece."

Glenn held her gaze for a long moment before nodding. "We're all making it back."

Ted put his arm around Bonita's shoulders and led her to the rental truck. "Be careful, Bo. Don't stop at any motels; rest at rest stops in the car. Once you get to Henry, follow his instructions to the letter. When he says you can go, cut and dye your hair, and dye the hunter too . . . make him look like a Labrador or something."

"Teddy, I want to see you again—I don't want it to end like this between us."

"Bo, it's gotta be this way. I'll call Henry once the op is

over. If he doesn't hear from me in a week, you'll know I failed. Wait at least a month before coming for the money. Now get in the truck, Bo."

Bonita climbed up into the cab. Ted patted Baby's head, then Bonita's shoulder. "You both take care of yourselves . . . I'm gonna miss ya."

CHAPTER 15

7:10 A.M., Friday, Key Biscayne

Raul paused before opening the second glass door. Taking a breath, he strode inside into the heat, stink, and all that green. He heard a peacock in one corner of the glassed-in structure, then heard another return the call from the other corner. *Great, now the computer is running mating calls. Do horny peacocks turn the plants on and make them greener?* he wondered. Raul found his boss seconds later squatting over a leafed plant that looked like it had fingers. "Colonel, I'm sorry to disturb you, but our DEA contact just called and—"

"They found her?"

"No, Colonel, our friend was not calling about Bonita; he called to tell us—"

"This is a Digital begonia from the tropical rain forest of the Amazon," Mendez said, bending over the plant again. "Within ten years it could be extinct."

"Colonel, the investment capital we had in Georgia could be extinct right now."

Mendez shot up. "What?"

"Sir, our DEA informer says Logan is dead and Inez's squad is in cust—"

"Where's my money?"

"It's gone. An unidentified crew took it."

Mendez dropped the mist bottle he was holding. "Unidentified?"

"Yes, at least for now. Our attorneys talked to those who

207

are in custody. The crew that stole our investment were wearing hoods but were obvious professionals. Inez and his people were taken by surprise and tied up, and it seems Logan and his people arrived but were ambushed. Logan and another were killed; the rest of his men were wounded."

Mendez spoke between clenched teeth. "Surprised? Inez was surprised? You are telling me he is alive?"

"Yes, Colonel. He was taken into custody along with the others."

"No, Raul, he is dead. All of them are dead for being lax with my money. Make sure of that, but not now, later. Now, we must find who has insulted me."

Raul took in another breath before speaking. "Colonel, our DEA friend says Inez and the others were identified as past employees of ours. And Colonel, the authorities are aware of the missing investment."

"Inez and the others *were* employees of one of my companies, Raul. You must learn to think like an attorney," Mendez said. He stepped away from his plant. "They have no proof, no witnesses, and no evidence of our being involved with the group—they have nothing."

Raul nodded as if in agreement. "Yes, Colonel, you are right about the authorities, they have nothing, but I am very concerned about these raiders who took the money. Inez told our attorney that he saw four men—and a woman."

Mendez took a step back as if slapped. "A woman? A woman and only four men stole my money?"

"Colonel, I believe the woman was Bonita."

"Impossible!"

"Sir, Inez described the woman to our attorney and told him he saw a dog as well."

"Bonita knew nothing of our affairs with the Yona Group!"

"We don't know what Bonita overheard when she was with you, Colonel. She may have not been what she seemed. Perhaps she was working for someone. I did some checking and it is too much of a coincidence that the lake house where she was staying is only thirty miles from Dahlonega."

Mendez viciously kicked the mist bottle by his foot. "That whore will pay! Find her!"

Raul nodded. "Colonel, I sent a team to Georgia to have a talk with the security guard who killed the Fat Man and his associates. Once they convince him to talk, we'll know what Bonita was doing in the lake house and who she talked to. We'll find who the raiders are—but, sir, with eleven million dollars in cash, they could disappear for quite some time."

Mendez closed his eyes for a moment before lowering his head. "She and the four men are our first priority. They must be found. Call a meeting of our associates, and I will ask their help in finding her—she cannot do this to me."

"There is another possible problem for us, Colonel. A media person from Georgia, a television news investigator from an Atlanta television station, has called some of our friends and is making inquiries. She is aware of the missing investment and is attempting to find who had dealings with the Yona Group. She is flying down tomorrow to conduct interviews for her investigation."

Mendez shook his head irritably. "The media are like jackals—they don't leave their prey until every bone is gnawed white. Have Vargas eliminate the problem."

"This person is quite well known, Colonel. It is Miss Stacy Starr, formerly of Channel—"

"Stacy Starr?" Carlos said. "I remember her. Yes, I remember her beauty. Make arrangements for her to meet with me—secretly, of course."

"Uh . . . Colonel, that would not be a wise course of action. She doesn't know of our involvement and—"

"True beauty is a rarity, Raul. It must be seen and touched to be appreciated. We will use her—such a pity. It is time to give the authorities what they want—those responsible for the killing of the senator and all the others. Miss Starr will help us accomplish what we want. Just ensure we send our best—I don't want her damaged in any way; that will come later."

Raul smiled. "There are the bothersome Colombians;

they would be perfect for our needs. It will take me no more than a day to brief our friends on what should be leaked—I will also have the necessary evidence planted."

Mendez leaned over his plant again. "I want it to be a lesson. A very loud and destructive lesson to those who seek glory at my expense. The authorities who pursue the Colombians must find they made a fatal error in underestimating their capabilities. I should think a rather large, destructive device would do it."

Raul felt a chill run up his spine as he nodded. "I will send Vargas—he knows what is required."

11:20 A.M., Dahlonega, Georgia

Eli knocked on the motel room door and backed up a step. A few seconds later the door opened, but only a crack. A sleepy voice said, "You, already? What time is it?"

"Almost noon, Sutton. Aren't you dressed?"

"Tanner, we just got back from the scene three hours ago. Let me sleep a little longer."

"You want me to tell Agent Bowlan you needed more sleep? I don't think so, Sutton."

"Okay, okay, give me ten—no, you'd better give me twenty minutes."

Eli sighed. "Okay, Ed and I will be at the diner across the street having lunch. You want me to order you a big salad?"

"For breakfast? No, just coffee and—"

"Sutton, I just told ya it's almost noon. You missed breakfast. Never mind, you can order when you get there." He turned and began to walk toward the diner.

"A tuna salad sandwich on toast. Wheat toast, not burned, and lettuce and mayo," Ashley blurted. She suddenly realized she was hungry.

He nodded as he kept walking. "Yeah, and a diet Coke. I know."

Twenty-five minutes later Ashley took a seat in front of her tuna sandwich and Coke. Ed Faraday took the toothpick out of his mouth and exchanged looks with Eli. "You want to tell her, or me?"

Eli pushed his empty plate away. "You tell her, Ed. She's not a morning person, has a tendency to get bitchy with me."

Ashley picked up half her sandwich. "Tell me what?"

Faraday raised an eyebrow. "Yesterday a security guard shot and killed three men at a Lake Lanier cabin. The guard said he was looking after a woman who was hiding out, waiting for her divorce to go through from her mobbed-up husband. The guard's story is the woman was taken by wise guys and he shot three of them who lingered behind."

Having taken a bite of the sandwich, Ashley spoke with her mouth full. "Anybody believe him?"

"No, but he's stickin' with the story. The interesting part is our guys checked out the house. Guess what? The missing woman wears a size eight shoe. They found all kinds of her shoes but no sneakers . . . and get this—the guard said the woman worked out all the time. She's some kind of physical fitness nut. Tell me, you work out in flats or pumps, Agent Sutton?"

Ashley put down her sandwich. "This is getting more interesting."

Faraday took the toothpick from his mouth. "Funny, that's what Agent Bowlan thought, too. He's teamin' you and me up, and we're goin' to the lake house along with some of your lab folks. Bowlan wants us to have a little chat with the security guard and the elderly lady who also worked for the missing woman."

"You and me? What about Tanner?" Ashley asked.

Faraday shook his head as if distressed. "I'm afraid your SAC has personally selected poor ol' Tan for a different and very difficult assignment."

Ashley waited for more information but Ed kept shaking his head. She shifted her unbandaged eye to Eli, who was gazing out the diner window with a vacant stare. "What are you going to be doing, Tanner?"

Eli sighed. "Tell her, Ed."

Faraday shrugged. "He's been ordered to have a talk with Miss Starr and try and convince her not to ask questions about our player. If she doesn't listen, ol' Tan has been told to stick to the lady reporter like hide glue."

Ashley's eye narrowed into a slit. "You volunteered for the duty, didn't you, Tanner?"

"Me, *volunteer*?" Eli said, motioning to himself. "Sutton, the first rule I learned when I joined the Army was never volunteer for anything. The same goes for the boo."

"You watching Miss Glamour News is like a fox watching the henhouse. You volunteered for the duty, and I know it." She glared at him.

Faraday shook his head. "I don't think he did, Agent Sutton. I was with him when he got the call from your SAC. Seems Miss Starr is flying down to Miami tomorrow to interview some people for her story. The SAC is very worried, and since ol' Tan seems to have rapport with the lady, he got the tag. You should have heard Tan bitch and try to get out of the assignment."

"I'll bet." Ashley was eyeing Eli with suspicion. "So when does this *duty* start?"

Eli finally spoke as he rose from his chair. "My ride just pulled in. Bowlan is taking me to the little airport outside of town. They're flying me to Miami today so I can talk to the guys in the Miami office and also get brought up to speed by the DEA. Ed, keep an eye on my partner and don't let her feed you too many salads. See you all later."

Eli turned to leave but stopped and put his hand on Ashley's shoulder. "You take care, huh?"

She nodded but wouldn't look at him. He headed for the door. She waited a long moment before lifting her head. "Tanner!"

"Yes?"

"Take care of yourself, too, okay?"

Eli smiled, turned, and walked out the door.

Ashley couldn't help but smile as she sat in the passenger seat of the car.

Faraday glanced at her as he started the engine. "Why you grinnin'?"

"It's the first time I've gotten to ride as a passenger in a long time. Tanner hates driving."

Faraday backed the Ford up then slipped the gearshift into drive. "You like Tan, don't you?"

"He's a good agent, if that's what you mean."

"Yeah, that's what I meant, but you like him, too. I can tell."

Ashley turned so her good eye was fixed directly on him.

Faraday shrugged his thick shoulders. "Hey, I'm just statin' the facts as I see them."

"You're blind then, Detective."

Faraday nodded as he watched the road ahead. "Okay, I'll drop it. It's about a thirty-minute drive to the cabin."

"Where did you get the impression I *liked* Tanner?"

"Because you two fight all the time."

"Is that Georgia logic, Ed?"

"Kinda. Y'all fight but never go over the line, you know, say things that hurt each other's feelings. It's been fun watching you two bite and swipe each other—reminds me of younger days when I was courtin' the missus. She was a fighter like you, Agent Sutton. She gave as good as she got."

"Detective Faraday, I assure you I have no feelings toward Agent Tanner other than those of a federal officer who respects her fellow officer. We are partners, and this 'fighting,' as you call it, is our way of relieving the boredom of the job, that's all."

Faraday gave her a quick glance before looking back toward the road. "Sorry, Agent Sutton. I guess I shouldn't have said anything. It's probably just wishful thinking on my part—I like the guy. And even though ya have a spot of mayonnaise on ya chin, you're okay, too."

Feeling very uncomfortable, Ashley wiped her chin. She looked out her window and tried to sound as if the previous conversation had never happened: "So, Ed, tell me more about this missing woman."

Days Inn Motel, Brunswick, Georgia

Ramon knocked on the room door and waited only a few seconds before the door was opened. Ted smiled. "You made good time."

Long-faced, Ramon motioned behind him. "I tried, man, but she wouldn't listen to me."

Ted's eyes narrowed as he stepped out the doorway and saw the dog and Bonita walking up the sidewalk.

"It's not my fault, Ted," Ramon said, raising his hands as if protecting himself from a blow. "She wouldn't go. I told her I'd leave her but I . . . I couldn't do it."

Ted ignored the dog that licked his hand. He growled at Bonita, "What the hell you doin' here?"

"I thought about it, Teddy. It's safer for everyone if I stay with the team," Bonita said, halting two paces away. "Don't give me that look; I'm right and you know it. I know more about Carlos than anyone, and I sure know his yacht. You need me."

Hearing the conversation from inside the room, Glenn walked to the door. "I knew it. I knew she was going to be trouble."

Ted took Bonita's arm and led her inside. "Get in here before you're seen. Ramon, go to a store and get some dog food and dog treats. When you get back, get some rest— we're leavin' tonight and drivin' straight through to Miami."

Bonita glared at Glenn. "You should be happy now . . . you don't have to worry about me giving you up."

Glenn avoided her accusing eyes by walking over and turning off the television. "Yeah, I'm thrilled. The question now is, what the hell we're going to do with you." He turned to Ted. "And don't tell me she's going on the op."

Ted rolled his eyes. "Knock it off, Glenn. We sure as hell can't leave her here. She'll go with us to the Miami safe house, then we'll figure out what to do with her."

Bonita folded her arms across her chest. "Forget about sending me off to Kansas. You need me."

"Christ'a'mighty, Bonita, be reasonable for a change and—"

Bonita ignored him and instead said to Glenn: "You know I'm right. You're the one who's always worried about operational security. Me being with the team eliminates the problem. And you know I know more about Carlos than anyone—you need me. Come on, tell him. Tell him I'm right."

Glenn returned her stare. "If the op goes sour, you're going to be dead as us."

"So what else is new? They've already tried to kill me, remember? No, I'm safer with the team—we make it together or we die together."

Glenn sighed, and walked to the door. "She's right, Ted. It is safer for all of us to stay together. . . . I'm going to gas up the vehicles."

As soon as Glenn closed the door, Bonita faced Ted. "Looks like you're stuck with me. I missed you, Teddy."

"I didn't want it to be this way, Bo—I wanted you to be safe and out of all this."

"I'm in it, Teddy, for better or worse. . . . Come here and give me a hug. I need you to hold me."

Putting his arm around her shoulder, Ted gave her a gentle squeeze. "It could get a lot worse, Bo."

"That's okay, Teddy . . . it's okay."

1:30 P.M., Lake Lanier, Georgia

Ashley and Detective Faraday walked toward the entrance of the huge cabin and were met by a GBI detective wearing a cowboy hat. "Hi, Ed, how ya like workin' with the feds?"

Faraday shrugged. "Not as bad as I thought, LeRoy—what ya got?"

The detective motioned to the chalk lines on the drive. "That's where the armed bad boys bought it yesterday. One was in the car that was parked here."

"Anything on who they were?"

"Yeah, on one of 'em. Fingerprints IDed him. His name was Fred Sweet. According to his rap sheet, Freddy was a bad motor scooter, real bad. Mostly assaults with deadlies, but he had only one conviction, in eighty-six. Seems he'd been clean since then or got better at what he did and wasn't caught."

"Sweet doesn't sound like a wise-guy name to me," Faraday said.

"Yeah. We checked with the feds on whether he'd been associated with the mob, and they said he wasn't on their sheet . . . but he was on the other list—they got him on occasion workin' for the Latinos outta Miami. Seems Freddy worked out of D.C. as a salesman for an import company, Hispanic owned."

"What about the other dead men?" Ashley asked.

"Nothin'. At least nothin' from their prints. Their IDs were faked and they were carryin' new Uzis. We found airline tickets on all of them . . . they'd come in from D.C. The feds are checkin' the import company with photos of the dead guys to see if they worked there."

Ed glanced around. "Don't see any bullet holes. Any of them get off any shots?"

The detective shook his head. "The security guard says he walked up behind them from over there. He saw them carrying and told 'em to drop their weapons. He says the fat guy, Freddy, tried to blast him, and that's what started the shooting. 'Course it doesn't fit, but it sounds good. Freddy bought it right there without getting off a shot. A .357 bullet through the head. The other guy got it in the neck with the same weapon, but the third guy, over there, got blown away with a twelve-gauge pump. The security guard said he was holdin' both the .357 and the shotgun. Trouble is, the first two got it from about here. The third guy was hit in the back from over there at the side of the house."

"How's the guard explain what happened?" Faraday asked.

"He says it all happened so fast he doesn't remember how

it went down. He's hangin' tough with his story. He's an ex–local cop so he knows to keep it vague. There were no witnesses, so he also knows he's got us over a barrel."

"What about the black woman? I understand she worked for the missing female," Ashley said.

"She wasn't here during the shooting. And she's acting really dumb about the missing lady. I'd say the two of them are hiding somethin', but we sure as hell haven't gotten 'em to come clean. They're inside, so be my guest. Maybe you can get them to tell us what really happened."

Duwane shook his head. "Look, ma'am, you asked me that already and I already told you, I was down at the pier and heard the lady's dog barkin'. I came up and saw a car drivin' out of the drive. I saw Mrs. Stone in the backseat with a dark-haired man beside her. Then I heard a car door open and I walked up and saw a fat man standing in the drive holdin' a pistol."

Ashley held up her hand. "Okay, I see you've got that part of your story memorized. Let's talk about Mrs. Stone. You said she was blond and about five-eight or -nine and weighed about 120 pounds. Is that right?"

"Yep, that's right. She took real good care of herself. Worked out every day."

"What else did she do to pass the time?"

"Well, she stayed a lot in the office . . . and she watched a lot of movies on TV."

"What did she do in the office?" Ashley asked.

"I told you, ma'am, she had a mean-ass dog that didn't let me get none too close. I don't know what she did in there."

"And you're sure no one visited her while she was here?"

"That's what I told ya."

"And she didn't call anybody?"

"I don't know."

Ashley shifted her gaze to the elderly black woman. "And you still say you don't know what she did while she was in the house?"

"I cook and cleans. Dat white lady be a job is all. I'se paid ta cook an' cleans, not be watchin' what dat white lady doin'."

Ashley walked over to Faraday and the GBI detective, who still wore his cowboy hat. She whispered, "We're getting nowhere with these two. Have the crime scene guys found anything I can use for leverage?"

Faraday shook his head. "Not yet. The old lady must do a good job of cleanin'—the place is clean. They've got prints, but right now they're all from these two and one other— probably the Stone woman. And they didn't find anything incriminating in the stuff she left behind . . . but they did say it was strange that in the office there's a computer printer and scanner but no computer. They say there was one there because the jacks and cords are all there as if it was just unplugged."

"Phone records?" Ashley asked.

"No outside calls on the hard line except a couple to a vet in Atlanta and three or four to a catalog place in Miami. Your CS boys did confirm the Stone woman was blond, and a real one at that, from hair they found on a brush in the bathroom. One thing more—she was loaded. The clothes and makeup she left behind are very expensive, designer stuff."

The other detective lifted his hand, holding a photograph. "This is the only photo we found in the things she left behind."

Ashley studied the picture a moment before looking up. "What kind of dog is it?"

"Rhodesian Ridgeback, kind of a rare breed . . . You see what's in the background of the picture?"

Ashley nodded as she handed the picture back. "It looks like palm trees."

"Royal palms to be exact, but it doesn't help us . . . picture could have been taken anywhere south of Georgia."

Tired of the whispering, Duwane stood and spoke impatiently. "You all charging me with anything? If not, me and Halley are leavin'. I know the law; you can't hold us here any longer. You asked us to come back today and we did."

The GBI detective looked at Ashley, who shook her head. The detective motioned toward the hallway. "Go on, but don't plan on going on any vacations real soon. We'll pick you up at your house tomorrow and take you to our head-quarters to look through mug shots."

"What for?"

"You said you saw a dark-haired man sitting beside Mrs. Stone in the backseat of the car, remember?"

"Yeah, and I told ya all I saw was the back of his head, too. I told ya everything I know. Come on, Halley, we're gettin' out of here."

Ashley stepped in front of the thin security guard. "Sir, officers will take you home. You'll also have an officer staying outside your residence for your protection. When you get home, think long and hard about the statements you gave us. Tomorrow, after the lab guys are through, I'll give you a chance to tell us what *really* happened. I suggest you take my advice. If we find you have perjured yourself, we'll charge you—it's a felony offense."

Duwane smiled. "Ma'am, you'll be talkin' to my lawyer tomorrow. I've told ya all I know. Have a nice day."

As soon as the couple left, Ashley faced Faraday. "It stinks. They're covering up something."

Faraday wrinkled his brow. "Yeah, but what, and why?"

2:30 P.M., DEA field office, Miami

Sitting alone in a small conference room, Eli held a plastic cup half-filled with coffee. A forty-something DEA agent wearing blue suspenders entered the room, placed a folder in front of Eli, and took a seat. He pushed heavy black-frame glasses farther up his nose and said, "That's everything we have on Mendez. I just ran it off from our original file so you can keep the folder."

Eli opened the file. "Thanks, Stew."

Agent Steward Hines leaned back in his chair and canted his head. "You're wasting your time, you know."

Eli shifted his gaze to the partially bald agent. "What d'ya mean?"

"Mendez retired four years ago from the heavy action—we hear he had some medical problems related to stress. His doctor told him to avoid stressful situations and find something relaxing to do. Mendez took the doctor's advice and picked up golf and got into tropical plants."

Eli closed the folder. "What are you telling me, Stew?"

"I'm telling you my boss says he's not the one."

"Your boss read the report on all those guys we found up in Dahlonega? They worked for Mendez."

"He read it and so did I, Tanner. Both those crews worked for lots of players. It's changed since you were in Miami. The players got smarter and don't keep crews around that could later finger them. Those people could have been working for any one of eight players who run big laundry operations outside the state."

Eli's jaw muscles rippled. "Stew, what's going on? I came here for an update from you guys and all I'm getting is jerked around. You give me Mendez's file then sit there and tell me you guys don't think he's the one. I thought you had him as your number one."

"No, Tanner, *you* guys had him as *your* number one; we didn't."

"I saw the C.I.'s statement naming Mendez."

"So did we, and we forgot about it. This so-called informant who talked to your people pulled the name out of a hat, Tanner. Do you think for a moment a low-level scuzzball is going to know the details of his boss's competitor's laundry operation? Come on, give me a break. Your C.I. was lookin' for a paycheck is all."

"So who is *your* number one, Stew?"

"We don't have one yet; we're still workin' it."

Eli nodded. "Great. I tell you what. Since I'm here, why don't you update me on Mendez anyway. My gut says he's our boy."

"Your gut isn't tellin' you that—it's your trigger finger tellin' you. I went to the scene, remember? I saw you lyin' there with that bullet in the chest. I went to your partner's funeral, too. Your wanting it to be Mendez doesn't make it so."

Eli stared into the agent's eyes. "Talk to me, Stew."

The agent returned the stare for a long moment before slowly lowering his eyes. "Like I told you, Mendez retired . . . well, at least he's semiretired. He quit the running and distribution side completely four years ago and started going legit. He could afford to. We figure he cleared somewhere over a quarter billion. Problem was, most of it was very dirty. He's still tryin' to clean it. He's into real estate, construction, and importing goods from down south, mostly Argentine beef and leather and some designer coffee blends from Colombia."

"Where's he living now?"

"He's got him an estate on Key Biscayne. It's only a house down from the old Nixon compound—you know, the place Nixon would hang to chill when he was president? You ought to see the Mendez place—it's a five-acre walled-in fortress with a view of the bay. Talk about nice, the place is really first-class. The guy has it made; he's a member of that swanky country club there on the key—plays golf on the best course on the East Coast and rubs shoulders with all the big-money blue bloods of the club."

Eli shifted in his chair, hating what he was hearing. "And the members don't mind a druggie being in their club?"

"He owns a piece of it. Most of the members don't even know he owns the piece, and those that do don't care. In their eyes, Mendez is for all intents and purposes a very successful legit businessman. Hell, he's got a Bell Ranger chopper right on the estate that takes him wherever he wants. Like I told you, the guy has it made. He owns a huge yacht that stays out on the bay, and he's got him two other major places. One is another big estate on an island off the Georgia coast, and he's got himself another one in the Caymans. He doesn't visit those other places much anymore, though—like I told you, he's into tropical plants now, brings them in from all over the world. Sure keeps us busy working with the Customs boys, checking them out."

"Tropical plants?" Eli repeated.

Steward nodded. "Yeah, as in rare species—he collects them. Built himself a big greenhouse on his Key Biscayne estate a couple of years ago right up against the house. We talked to the construction guys who built it. Like everything else he does, it's first-class. Hard to believe, isn't it, Mendez with a green thumb?"

"Sounds like age has mellowed him out," Eli said. "He's become a regular family man, huh?"

Steward smiled without humor. "Mendez mellow out? No way, and he's far from being a family man. The plants must be helpin' his hormones. He's got himself a regular harem on his yacht, which he visits three nights a week. His wife must know 'cause she stays gone most of the time. Got her a big apartment in New York overlooking Central Park. The daughter is going to school there, some big-money music school. Anyway, the wife is doing her own thing. Loves spending his money and doing her personal fitness trainer—*he* likes telling us how good she is in bed. Sick reading, if you have the time and the stomach for it. Bottom line is, he's doing his thing and she's doing hers; they're not a typical family by a long shot."

Eli leaned forward in his chair. "You've told me about plants and harems but nothing on what you've got on his laundering operations."

"Yeah, and for good reason—we don't have anything. He's gotten wiser in his old age and covers his tracks with lots of middlemen who don't even know who they're workin' for. The boss has pretty much given up on him; our priorities are on those we *can* bring down."

"Given up on him?" Eli repeated angrily. "The son of a bitch killed—"

The door to the conference room opened and a dark-haired man stepped inside. Eli turned and gave the well-dressed intruder the once-over. The man looked like he just got off a shoot with *GQ* magazine. He was wearing tan loafers, slacks, and a silk shirt buttoned to the throat, and had on a lime-green lightweight blazer with lots of gold buttons. His dark hair was slicked and swept back, and from the corner of his mouth half an unlit cigar protruded. He gave Eli a cold stare before shifting his look to Steward. "How about wrapping up? I've got a meeting in here in five minutes."

Steward rose. "Boss, this is Agent Tanner from the Atlanta FBI office. I was updating him on our progress. Tanner, this is the chief of the division, Sam Ortiz."

Eli extended his hand, but Ortiz just nodded, took the unlit cigar from his mouth, and used it to motion with. "You people in the Bureau shouldn't have jumped on this without talking to us first. You've been spinning your wheels for nothing."

"Sir, I thought we had been talking to you."

"Your people have been talking, all right, but not listening. We don't need the Bureau telling us how to do our job."

"Sir, I'm sure we're all doing our jobs—Stew tells me you don't believe Mendez is the one."

"That's what I mean right there. You people came up with Mendez, but he's inactive! If you people would just let us do our jobs we'll get the one responsible."

Ortiz stuck the cigar back in the corner of his mouth and eyed Steward. "I want this room cleared in four minutes." He turned and walked out.

"Nice guy," Eli said.

Steward retook his seat. "Intense is more like it. He took it personally when he saw the Bureau was leaning toward Mendez as the suspect. Sam has been in charge of the division for two years now. He gets results."

"Stew, you were workin' here when I was here in Miami. . . . I'd rather know what you think, not what your chief thinks. You really believe Mendez is out of this?"

Steward sighed and shook his head. "I honestly don't know—he may be retired but he's got too much dirty money stashed around not to be involved in trying to clean it. And Tanner, you and I both know that takes some work. But I do know this: If he is involved, we're not going to be able to prove a damn thing. He's been around too long to suddenly get stupid. He's covering himself, Tanner; he's covering himself even better than before. He knows how we operate and is way ahead of us. It's a dead end no matter what you or I think."

Eli's shoulders slumped as he shook his head in frustration. "After all these years, Stew—all these years and we haven't been able to come up with anything? Something is wrong."

Steward rose from his chair. "I try not to think about it anymore, Tanner; it drives me nuts when I do. You lost a partner; I've lost four friends who tried to get him. Believe me, I know what you're feeling. Let it go—he's beaten us. Time to move on."

Steward took a step and put his hand on Eli's shoulder. "It was good seeing you again, Tanner. You need help covering the news lady while she's in town?"

"No, Stew, the local office is providing me support. I'm going to talk to Miss Starr once she arrives tomorrow and lay most of it out for her. Hopefully she'll understand and back off."

"Can you trust her with the truth?"

"It'll all be off the record. Starr is eager but she won't go over the line."

Steward gave Eli's shoulder a final pat. "Get her to back off, Tanner . . . she's in over her head. None of the players mess around when it comes to having their lives looked into. You'd best be real careful. If she stays and tries to find the guy, you'd best take care of yourself out there."

Minutes later Eli stepped outside and took a deep breath to calm his upset stomach as his Miami field office partner, Howard Parker, walked up. "You all done with the DEA?"

"Yeah, they laid it out for me."

"They don't have much, do they?"

"No, not much. Looks like we're losing this one."

"Yes, we've all pretty much come to that conclusion. You want to get a bite to eat before we check you into a motel?"

Eli closed his eyes for a moment to gather his strength. "No, Howard, I've got to make a visit first and pay my respects. The wife of my old partner still lives here in Miami, and I promised I'd drop by if I ever came to town."

Parker lowered his head. "I guess you're talking about Gus's wife."

Eli nodded. "I haven't seen Alice in years, but we still exchange Christmas cards and letters. Still hasn't remarried, huh?"

"Alice? You've got to be kidding. She knows I hold the old Mendez case file, and calls me every month to see if anything new has come up. She won't let it go."

"She hasn't changed, then." Eli was steeling himself for the meeting. "She asks me in every letter and card she sends what's being done to get him."

"Are you going to tell her why you're here?"

"Yes, just to let her know we haven't forgotten. But I'm also going to tell her the truth. She deserves to know we're still trying but it doesn't look good."

Parker looked at his new partner with concern. "She won't like hearing it."

Lake Lanier, Georgia

Ashley sat at the cabin's dining room table typing the finishing touches to her report on her laptop when Faraday walked up and put his hand on her shoulder.

"We gotta go. We just got a call—the cop guarding the security guy is dead and so is the security guard's wife. Our boy Duwane is missing. Looks like there was a struggle; he was bleeding when he was taken from the house."

Ashley's face paled as she stood. "My God, Ed."

"Yeah, it doesn't look good for him . . . but there is some good news. There was no attempt on the old black woman.

We've got extra officers with her now, and your people are on the way to move her to your headquarters. Maybe she'll want to talk to us now. And there's somethin' else. We got the report back on the missing female's prints. Bonita Rogers. White, age forty, had two priors in 1980. Seems she was an exotic dancer some years back in Miami and on occasion got too exotic. She moved up, though. In eighty-five she was picked up for prostitution in Miami, but later the charges were dropped. Must have had a high-class clientele. Here's the good part, though. She came up on the DEA's list of known associates of one Carlos Mendez. She was suspected of being his honey for the past year."

Ashley closed her laptop and quickly put it in the case. "Ed, we've got a real problem here—how did Mendez know about the security guard? The press didn't have the story."

Faraday took the case from her and put it over his shoulder. "I think we've got a leak somewhere up the chain—it's the only explanation. Come on, we'll call Tanner and Agent Bowlan in the car and tell them what we've got and what happened. We gotta warn them that somebody on our side is spillin' everything we find."

Ashley strode toward the door. "We've got to find Bonita Rogers before Mendez's people find her. She's the key. It's obvious she knows his operation. If we find her first, then we've got Mendez."

Faraday shook his head. "Don't get your hopes up on that one. Remember, she and the four guys who wore boots split eleven million bucks. I bet she's already out of the country and right now she's lyin' on a beach somewhere countin' her money and drinkin' one of those colored drinks that has one of them little umbrellas in it."

Ashley slowed her steps. "We'll find her . . . we have to."

Key Biscayne Country Club

Carlos Mendez was putting for par when Raul drove up to the green in a golf cart.

Mendez took a dime from his pocket and placed it behind the ball. "Go ahead, James, you try to sink your twelve-footer while I speak with my associate."

Mendez picked up his ball and walked toward Raul. Closing the distance, he whispered, "I hope you have good news for me."

"I do, Colonel. We know Bonita was involved in taking the money. The security guard told our interrogation team Bonita once borrowed the guard's car and asked for directions to Dahlonega. He also said a man visited her almost every evening while she was in the cabin."

"Who was he?" Mendez asked impatiently.

"The guard said he was a private investigator, a Ted Wilson. The team has his description as well as his vehicle's description. They're now checking the local investigators in the area."

"What else did this guard tell them?"

"He expired during the latter part of the interrogation, Colonel. He was very stubborn at the beginning, and required the cruder methods. But at least we are certain Bonita was involved."

Carlos's face tightened. "We must find Bonita and the others."

"Colonel, I have everyone available looking for her and have advised our friends of our situation. They, too, are helping. We also have help from the FBI and DEA. They are aware of her involvement and have begun a manhunt. If they find her, our DEA friend assures me he will inform us where she will be taken."

Mendez nodded once. "Very good . . . make arrangements to have a team ready to respond, and remind them I want her alive. Have you taken care of the other matter? Will I soon have the company of Miss Starr?"

"Vargas and his crew are working out the arrangements as we speak, Colonel. And the place where the authorities will receive their surprise has already been selected. The Colombians are using their boatyard for storage of their powder."

Carlos's lips drew back in a smile. "I think it honorable, dying while trying to do one's duty . . . it is a fitting end."

Raul nodded, then motioned to the green. "Your opponent just missed his putt, Colonel. I trust you'll win."

Mendez took the ball from his pocket and winked. "I always win."

FBI field office, Atlanta

Ashley set the color photograph in front of the old woman who was seated holding a cup in which she spat her snuff. "Officers found his body two miles from his home, Mrs. White. He was tortured."

Halley White glanced at the photo and shook her head. "That ain't Duwane."

Ashley dropped another photograph on the table. "That's a close-up shot, Mrs. White. That's the clothes and boots he was wearing when we interviewed you both this afternoon. It's him, all right . . . we ran a dental check and confirmed it."

"Oh, Lordy . . . poor Duwane." Halley lowered her head. "Why . . . why they burn his face like that?"

"They used a handheld propane blowtorch to make him talk, Mrs. White. The people who did this wanted information, and you can be sure he gave them what they wanted. Take a good look, Mrs. White. The people responsible for this are still out there. We need your help in finding them. Please tell us everything you know about the woman who is missing."

Halley wiped away a tear from her cheek with the back of her hand. "She ain't missin' . . . she's probably with Mr. Teddy."

Ashley exchanged looks with Faraday, then turned on the small tape recorder. "Please start from the beginning, Mrs. White."

8:10 P.M., Residence Inn, Miami, Florida

Eli stood holding the phone to his ear, listening to Ashley brief him on what Halley White had said. He let the information sink in, then asked: "You said Bonita Rogers had a visitor almost every night?"

"Yes, Mrs. White called him Mr. Teddy. She said he was a private investigator, but we checked and there's only two P.I.'s within four hundred miles with a first name of Ted, and none of them fit his description: Caucasian, six-two or -three, mid-forties, and muscled up like a weight lifter. We don't think he was a P.I. We've got a description of his vehicle, and Mrs. White remembered a partial on his license. Ed is checking with the state vehicle registration office. We'll have something pretty soon."

"We're too late, Sutton. You can bet this Ted guy and the others have already left the country with the money."

"You're probably right. Just so you know, Tanner, you, Ed, and me are out of it. We're done."

"What d'ya mean, we're done?"

"We're done, as in we're out of the investigation. The SAC thanked us for our efforts this evening but now it seems he doesn't need us anymore."

"Sutton, are you messin' with me? I haven't been told to pack up and go home yet."

"Tanner, protecting Miss Glamour News isn't part of the investigation. You've still got the job until you convince her to come home. And guess what? You're soon going to have some help. Just so you hear it from me first, Ed and I got a new assignment. We're coming down to help you. I volunteered us for the duty. Ed and I will be catching the early bird tomorrow and will be there by seven."

"You volunteered? Sutton, I thought I taught you better than that."

"Couldn't help myself, Tanner. Since my job was done up here, I couldn't stand the thought of you pulling such horrible duty all alone. Since Miss News is from Georgia, I talked the SAC into having Ed come along to help you convince her to go home. I knew you'd appreciate it."

Eli sighed. "Yeah, I'm sure Ed really appreciated you volunteering him. Guess I'll see you two in the morning, then, huh?"

"Yeah, Tanner, you will. You missed us?"

"Yeah, kinda . . . my temp partner doesn't bitch enough. I really miss that, you know?"

"Are you sayin' you miss me, Tanner?"

"See you in the morning, Sutton."

"Tanner, I've kinda missed you, too. See you in the morning."

Interstate 95, northern Florida

Ted sat behind the wheel of the conversion van, his attention focused on the road ahead. Seated beside him in a captain's chair, Bonita unwrapped a Big Mac. "This sure is comfortable. I've never been in a van like this before."

Ted glanced in the rearview mirror at the dog on the back of the folded-down rear seat. "Looks like the hunter likes it."

Bonita handed Ted the hamburger. "You still upset at me for coming back?"

"I'm not upset, Bo. I'm worried about you is all. Those guys back at the score site have told Mendez about you by now. He won't rest till he finds you."

Bonita popped a french fry into her mouth. "It doesn't matter, Teddy. He would have looked for me even if I hadn't gone on the raid."

Ted took a bite, chewed awhile, and swallowed. "I . . . I missed you, Bo."

Bonita reached over and patted his leg. "It's nice, isn't it? It's like we're on a vacation and heading for Disney World, just like regular people."

"We're not goin' on vacation, Bo."

"I know, but we can pretend for a while. You and me and Baby, the family getting away for a while. It's a nice thought. Don't spoil it, Ted. Let me pretend for a while, okay?"

"I always did want to ride that Space Mountain ride and the jungle cruise . . . and see that castle up close, you know, the one where Sleeping Beauty stayed."

"It's Cinderella's castle, Ted."

"Yeah? I'll be damned. What ride we gonna take the hunter on?"

"We'll find a nice place for him to stay, and just you and me will go. I want to do it all. See everything, Pirates of the Caribbean, Frontierland, Adventureland, and the new places they built . . . We'll stay in one of those ritzy hotels right there in the park . . . eat at the nicest restaurants, make love in the morning, and go see everything during the afternoon."

"What we goin' to do in the evening?"

Bonita leaned over and put a french fry in his mouth. "We'll go dancing and look at each other in the candlelight. Make eyes at each other and get ourselves all worked up."

Ted nodded. "Yeah, that sounds good."

"Then I'll take you back to the hotel and we'll stand on the balcony and look at the fireworks and the Tahiti canoes on the lake and we'll slowly undress each other, and then we'll . . ."

Ted kept his eyes on the road and kept nodding, but he was no longer listening. He was thinking about Carlos Mendez.

CHAPTER 16

9:10 A.M., Monday, Miami airport

Eli slowed his steps and motioned ahead to the waiting area for Delta's Gate 19. "Her plane should be here any minute."

Ashley rolled her eyes after taking a sip of coffee from a plastic cup. "I bet you can hardly wait, Tanner."

Eli gave Ed Faraday a consoling look. "I told you Sutton was a joy to work with in the mornings."

The detective nodded. "You were sure right about her not being a morning person—she's been actin' bitchy since we left Atlanta this morning."

Ashley glared at the two men through her unbandaged eye. "You want to see me really bitchy, just keep it up, you two."

Eli motioned to the waiting area. "I think it's time I broke the news to Miss Lopez. Both of you follow me."

Eli strode into the waiting area and approached an attractive woman seated in the smoking section. "Excuse me. You're waiting for Miss Stacy Starr, aren't you?"

The dark-haired woman lowered the magazine she was reading. "Who are you?"

Eli took out his ID. "Special Agent Tanner, FBI, ma'am. You are Miss Rita Lopez from Channel 2, correct?"

Rita's eyes narrowed. "What is this?"

"This is a request, Miss Lopez. I need to talk to Miss Starr. It has to do with an investigation we are running. I will be picking up Miss Starr when she arrives and you can follow us to the hotel. You have her checked in at the Coral Gables Hyatt, right?"

"Big Brother is watching, is that it?" Rita said, snuffing out her cigarette. "How did you know we had Stacy checked into the Hyatt?"

"Your station manager told us, Miss Lopez. We know you are going to be working with Miss Starr in a cooperative effort on the story."

"What if I refuse your 'request'?"

"I was being nice; it's not really a request. It's going to happen just like this: When Miss Starr arrives, me, my associates here, and you will escort her to the baggage area. Once she's got her things, she goes with us. You can follow us in your van to the hotel."

"That's it? There's nothing I can do about it?"

"That's it, Miss Lopez."

Rita motioned to the plate-glass window where, outside, a DC-9 was approaching the gate. "She's not going to like this."

Minutes later Stacy stood in front of Eli. She slowly shifted her gaze to Faraday then Ashley and shook her head. "I don't believe this is happening."

Eli wrinkled his brow. "Believe it, Stacy. We'll talk in the car and I'll explain everything."

Stacy turned to Rita with a frown. "It's all right. I'll ride with them. I think they're holding all the cards right now."

Stacy sat in the backseat with Eli beside her as the rental car came to a stop in front of the Coral Gables Hyatt Regency. Stacy's eyes were locked on Eli. "You've certainly done a good job of scaring me, but it would help if you could be more specific. Do you have a suspect or don't you?"

"I can't tell you that, Stacy. The SAC's instructions were to tell you what we were up against in the hope you would back off of your investigation. It doesn't matter who the suspect is; these players are all the same when it comes to their privacy. They don't like people asking questions about them, especially the media."

"Are these men so powerful that they can't be touched?"

Eli thought that maybe his past twenty-minute update was having an effect. "Some of them are, Stacy. One of them I know for sure is very smart. He's mostly legit now, and the way he's organized, with others doing all the actual dirty work, we can't get to him."

"Unless one of his people talks," Stacy said. "If somebody inside his organization talks, then you'd have him, right?"

Eli frowned. "That's not likely. There's probably no more than a half dozen inside people who actually talk to him. And they're all very loyal and tied to him by blood. In ninety, when I worked the case, I found out pretty quick that over half of his employees had never actually even seen him. Think of him as the CEO of Ford Motors—he makes the major decisions but others actually make the cars. One division makes Thunderbirds; another makes Escorts. In his case, one division handles all his legit business and another is the dirty division that launders his money. The dirty division is made up of subdivisions spread out throughout the southeastern United States. The Yona Group could have been just one of many of his subdivisions. You have to understand, Stacy, this guy in particular isn't like the players in the movies who wear flashy clothes and go out dancing and partying every night. He's all business and controls his operation with an iron fist. When we picked up his people, they never said a word to us. . . . They knew if they said anything they'd be dead, and so would their relatives. That's how this guy worked. He went after the families as a lesson to others. You asked if the players were *that* powerful— remember, one of them had Senator Goodnight and his family murdered, and we're not even close in trying to prove it."

"Isn't it frustrating for you, Eli?"

"It's more than frustrating; it's maddening. These guys have big money, and money can buy you anything, including people inside the Miami Police Department and most likely even in our government agencies. It's the only explanation for why some of them know so much about how we operate or when we're getting close. Look, Stacy, that's strictly off the record, as is everything else I've told you about these people. Now I think you understand why we want you to back off the story—it's too dangerous."

Stacy shook her head. "I can't do that. I have a duty; the people have a right to know."

Seated in the front passenger seat, Faraday turned in his seat. "Jesus, Miss Starr, Tanner just told ya why ya gotta drop it. These guys kill people. If you start asking questions, none of them are goin' to think twice about having you knocked off."

Stacy's face was set in determination. "Our system of justice has failed us, Detective. I heard what Eli said. He said, in effect, the Justice Department doesn't have the necessary tools to bring the one responsible for the senator's death to justice. Doesn't that bother you? It does me. What is wrong with our system, that it allows such men to stay in business? Don't you think the people have a right to know their system has failed?"

Seated behind the wheel, Ashley spoke, trying to contain her anger. "Is it worth risking the lives of Miss Lopez, the news crew, and possibly us? Is getting your story out worth that much?"

Stacy returned Ashley's glare. "The truth is worth the risk, Agent Sutton. The system has failed us all. Perhaps when the truth is known, people will demand changes to our laws." Stacy shifted her gaze to Eli as she reached for the car door. "Tell Donny, no deal. I'm doing the story, but I won't use anything you just told me. I'll get what I need on my own."

Eli took hold of Stacy's arm. "If you do this, the three of us are going to be with you every step of the way. Our job is to protect you."

"What if I refuse your protection?"

"You're too smart to do that, Stacy. We're the reason

you're refusing to back off your crusade. You figure if we're protecting you, the players won't try anything. Maybe you're right. Then again, maybe you're wrong. You're betting your life and the lives of others on your chance to tell the world what you think the truth is.'

Stacy held his gaze a long moment before lifting her chin. "Let go of me, Eli. I have work to do."

Eli kept his grip. "Fine, but there's rules to play by. First, you'll never be alone. One of us will be with you at all times. Second, you'll tell us your schedule to give us time to have backup wherever you go. Third, no secrets. We hear everything you hear, and that goes for telephone conversations. Fourth, you will heed my advice and do whatever I say is necessary to ensure your protection. That means you don't question me or balk when I tell you to do something; you just do it. That's how this is going to be played. You understand?"

Stacy nodded once. "I agree to your rules, but I have a job to do. The first interview is in an hour. People won't talk to me if you three are standing over me. At least dress like you're members of the crew. Don't flash your IDs and guns around and don't be obvious."

"We agree to that," Eli said, "as long as we don't perceive there's a threat to you. From this moment on you'll introduce me and Ed as your personal bodyguards. Agent Sutton is your hairdresser. That's our cover. You got it?"

"Yes, I have it."

Eli kept a somber expression. "Ed, escort Miss Starr inside. Agent Sutton and I will join you in just a minute and explain the deal to Miss Lopez."

Stacy got out of the car but leaned back inside and touched his arm. "I'm sorry, Eli, but I have a duty, too. I hope you understand."

Eli took the cell phone from his blazer pocket. "Yeah, Stacy, I'm afraid I do." He sat up and said, "Park this thing, Sutton, while I call the SAC and tell him the bad news."

* * *

Eli still sat in the backseat of the rental car after completing his call to the SAC. Ashley began to open her door but Eli raised his hand. "Hold it a minute."

She turned with a one-eyed questioning stare. "What's going on?"

Suddenly the back passenger door opened and a tall, well-built man slid into the seat beside Eli.

Eli raised an eyebrow. "Well?"

The man shook his head. "You first. She going to drop it?"

"Nope, she says the people have a right to know. What did you find out?"

"You were followed, all right. We spotted two pairs. One pair is parked across the street in the gray minivan. The other pair parked in the lot and is inside in the lobby keeping an eye on Miss Starr. We've got them covered and I've got a tech team monitoring the cell phone bands if they use a cell phone to report in."

Eli motioned to Ashley. "Howie, this is my partner, Agent Ashley Sutton. She and Detective Ed Faraday of the GBI are the ones I told you about."

The agent nodded to Ashley. "I'm Agent Howard Parker, your stand-in partner for Tanner. He's said good things about you."

Ashley's unbandaged eye bored a hole into Eli. "What's going on, Tanner?"

"Sutton, it's what it looks like. Howie tailed us from the airport to see if we were followed. We were, just like we thought we would be."

"Who are they?" Ashley asked, looking at Parker.

"We don't know who they're working for, but it's local contract surveillance boys, not hitters, which is good news. I've got a squad parceled out watching both pairs, and they'll report all their movements."

"You get the stuff I requested?" Eli asked.

Parker smiled. "I'm way ahead of you. You'll find the equipment in your room. And like you requested, your room is next to Miss Starr's."

Ashley relaxed her stare. "Sounds like you two have been busy. I'm impressed."

Eli opened his door. "Come on, Sutton, it's time to go to work. We'll let Howie keep an eye on our backs."

Ashley quickly got out of the car and caught up to Eli, who was already heading for the hotel entrance. "Tanner, why didn't you tell me about Agent Parker?"

"Didn't have time. I had to get you and Ed up to speed on what the DEA knew before Stacy arrived."

"What's this about your room being next to Miss News? You planning on visiting your lady friend after dark?"

Eli smiled as he kept walking. "Well, Sutton, if I do pay her a visit, you'll be the first to know. You're staying in the room with her."

"What?"

"You heard what I told her—one of us will be with her every second. While you're staying with her, maybe she'll pass her beauty secrets on to you."

"Keep it up, Tanner. I know you're enjoying this. Keep the surprises coming—you're really trying hard but you're not getting to me."

"Just doing my job, Sutton. I didn't volunteer to watch her."

"Tanner?"

"Yeah?"

"What did you mean that she might show me her beauty secrets? I look nice most of the time, don't I?"

"Drop it, Sutton."

"What is it? My hair? More makeup?"

"Drop it."

"Clothes?"

Less than three miles from the Hyatt, Ted stood on the balcony of a fourth-floor apartment just off Dixie Highway. If he stood in the right spot, he could see between two high-rise hotels and actually see Biscayne Bay and, out much farther, Key Biscayne. Sitting beside him, Baby nuzzled Ted's hand with his nose. Ted broke his gaze from the distant key and patted the dog's head. "She's sleepin', huh? Sorry, but I can't take ya for a walk, either. I gotta get some sleep, too."

Glenn walked out onto the balcony. "I'm getting worried about you, Ted. You were talkin' to that mutt, weren't you?"

"He's no mutt. He's got better breeding than all of us put together. Ya couldn't sleep?"

"I will, just had to wind down after that long-ass drive. So that's it, huh? Key Biscayne out there?"

"Yep, that's where he is. According to the maps Gee gave us, his place is straight across the bay on this side of the key. He's probably sittin' on his tiled patio havin' breakfast and lookin' across the bay at all us poor folks."

"We've got eleven mil of his money, Ted. We're not so poor."

"It's poor when he's sittin' on over half a billion. The rest of the guys sleepin'?"

"Yeah. Ted, we have to talk about Bonita."

"I was wonderin' when you'd get around to it."

"What are we goin' to do with her, Ted? When it's over she's still going to be hunted by Mendez's people. They won't rest till they find her, and when they do, they'll make her talk."

Ted faced his friend. "Glenn, I've decided that when it's over, she and I will take off together and hide out someplace down in Mexico. Sorry, but I guess we won't be startin' that business together after all."

"You're going to stay with her?"

"Yeah, I am. I made up my mind when we drove down here together—don't worry, if they do come after her, they'll have to go through me first."

"Ted, there is no *if* about it. They *will* keep looking for her. You'll both be running for the rest of your lives."

"At least we'll be together. It's fate."

"Fate?"

"Yeah, fate. We're supposed to be together. Look, Glenn, I've made up my mind on this. I'm goin' to stay with her and protect her. She needs me. And don't start in on that mistletoe thing . . . she's not like that."

Unable to take Ted's stare, Glenn lowered his eyes. "You're right, Ted; she's not like that. I see she really cares for you." He slowly raised his eyes. "She going to stay here while we do the op?"

"She's goin' with us, Glenn. She'll stay on the boat and keep an eye out for trouble. It'll make it safer for us. We won't have to surface to take a look around for reinforcements. We can stay under and go straight to the target."

"You're putting her life in danger doing that."

"It's already in danger, Glenn. She wants in—plus it's better all around. Once it's done, we won't need to come back here—we'll head up the coast to Boca Raton."

Exhaling, Glenn looked once again toward the bay. "I'm going to miss you, Ted."

Ted put his arm around his friend's shoulder. "We gotta a lot to do before we part ways, Glenn. Better get some sleep. Later this afternoon I want you and the guys to go buy the boat and the rest of the gear we'll need. Tonight we'll make a recon to firm up our plans. I wanna make sure the hull of that yacht hasn't been reinforced in some way."

"I can't believe it, Teddy, the day has finally come. Tomorrow night we get that son of a bitch."

Ted joined him in looking out toward the bay. "Tomorrow night it finally ends."

Across Biscayne Bay, seated on his patio in a silk robe and sipping orange juice, Carlos Mendez glanced up from the latest issue of the *Horticulture Journal*.

Raul approached with a smile. "Colonel, arrangements have been made for you to meet Miss Starr, but there is a complication. She is being protected by the FBI."

Carlos set down his glass. "How many?"

"Three that will accompany her and two others that will follow at some distance. It's not a problem. Our good friend who is helping us says she can ensure only one agent is with Miss Starr when Vargas makes the move—it's all arranged. We have the schedule of her interviews; Vargas will have her by three this afternoon."

Mendez sighed as he looked out toward the bay. "Such fools they are—it is hardly a game worth playing anymore. Inform Vargas the FBI agent who is with Miss Starr is not to be harmed. I am curious as to what they know. I'm sure the agent will enlighten me."

"I'll inform him, Colonel. There is some other news . . . but I'm afraid it is not good. Our people have not been able to find who the man was who visited Bonita at the lake cabin. Our people checked, and he was not a private investigator as the security guard had said. I assume he used a false name, as did Bonita, which means they planned in advance very well."

Mendez's attention quickly shifted back to his chief of staff. "I'm becoming very concerned about this, Raul. The use of false names and the professional execution of the raid tell us we are dealing with those who can think. What is of concern is what else they know—they knew of my arrangements with the group and knew the investment would be moved."

"Perhaps someone in the group told them of the investment, Colonel."

"No, they would not have known of our plans to move the money. We can rule out the authorities, for they would have seized the investment. We can also rule out a Mafia connection—they would have ensured that Inez and the others didn't talk. They are stupid but not that stupid."

Raul raised an eyebrow. "Perhaps an associate of ours?"

"None would dare be so bold as to defy me. No, I believe the key is Bonita. She made a mistake in going to the veterinarian . . . it was a stupid mistake. It is obvious to me she was not behind this. It was someone else . . . someone who thinks, collects facts, and weighs his options then acts decisively. Remember, Raul, only four men were involved. That tells us much. They must be very confident of their abilities . . . and confidence comes only from training and experience. They are also disciplined. They killed only when necessary and left no trace of themselves. The key is Bonita—she is the weak link. She made a mistake and she will again. Pull out the team that is looking for her accomplice—he is too smart to make an error in judgment now. Concentrate all our efforts on Bonita . . . and her dog. She would not have left the animal behind."

Raul took a step back from the table. "I'll send a description of the animal to all our people who are looking for her."

Mendez rose from his chair. "It is time for me to visit my children. . . . I will dine with Miss Starr on board tonight. Have the chef prepare stone crab for the occasion. Tourists always enjoy stone crabs."

"And what of the FBI agent, Colonel?"

"No need to set a place for the agent, Raul. After the officer answers my questions, he shall be permanently retired. . . . Terrible how many tourists try to swim the bay, isn't it? They really should know better."

Raul nodded without a smile.

CHAPTER 17

2:15 P.M., Little Havana, Miami

The news van pulled to the curb. Wearing an ear radio receiver, Eli got out and looked up and down the side street, checking for suspicious people on the sidewalk. Seeing none, he raised his hand and spoke into the miniature mike pinned inside his blazer sleeve. "We've arrived at the newspaper office."

Another van pulled in behind them, and Ed Faraday and Ashley quickly got out and walked directly toward the entrance of the stucco building in dire need of paint. Ed stopped at the door and took up position as Ashley entered. A full ten seconds passed before she came out and nodded.

Eli returned the nod and slid open the news van's side door. "It appears clear. Remember to stay close and to the left of me until we're inside."

Stacy Starr stepped out of the van with a frown. "We've done this twice already, Eli. I know what to do."

Rita Lopez stepped out behind Stacy and rolled her eyes. "He's really into playing the part of a bodyguard, isn't he? I think he likes the control."

Eli ignored Lopez as he walked Stacy toward the entrance.

Once inside, a small middle-aged man wearing an open-neck panama shirt approached. "Miss Starr, I am Hector Ramirez, editor of *La Voz*. It is a pleasure to finally meet you."

Stacy smiled as she shook the editor's hand. "It is my

243

pleasure, Señor Ramirez. I hope we have not inconvenienced you with the security requirements."

"Not at all, Miss Starr. Rita called and explained the concerns of your station manager. As you can see, the office is empty. I released my employees for a late lunch per the instructions. Please come with me to my office, where we can talk."

Eli stepped in front of the editor. "Sir, I'll need to check the office first."

Stacy kept her smile. "I'm sorry, Señor Ramirez, this is Mr. Tanner. He is in charge of my security."

"Of course," Ramirez said. "Please follow me, Mr. Tanner. My office is back here. I followed all the instructions and . . ."

Two minutes later Eli shifted uncomfortably from one foot to the other as he stood leaning against the wall, listening to the interview. The editor, Ramirez, sat at the head of a small table, flanked by Rita Lopez and Stacy, who held her open notebook.

Ramirez put down his coffee cup and leaned forward in his chair. "Why is it the gringo media always believe Cubans are involved in such activities? Yes, it is true a few Cuban-Americans are involved in the illegal drug business, but their number is very small and they are ostracized by the Cuban community."

Stacy looked into the editor's eyes. "Señor Ramirez, the man identified as the leader of the team that assassinated Senator Goodnight and his family and led the attack on the FBI office was a Cuban. His name was Jorge Orlando and he was from Miami. Is it not true that he has worked for Cuban drug lords?"

"Miss Starr, sadly, you have been misinformed. Jorge Orlando worked for anyone willing to pay for his services. I have received information from a reliable source that Señor Orlando was recently in the employ of a man who was laundering money through a company in your state. The source's employer was *not* Cuban; he is a Colombian."

Stacy's expression betrayed her surprise. "Have you told the authorities of this?"

"Miss Starr, I only received this information very recently, and I am not a fool. The Colombian I am speaking of is quite well known and extremely ruthless. His people would surely kill me if he knew I had knowledge of his affairs. Why do you think I did not allow you to record this interview, and requested the majority of your people stay outside of this office? If you were to name me as a source, I would be dead within twenty-four hours."

"But you are telling me now, señor. Why?"

"I made it clear to Rita on the phone, Miss Starr, that I would speak to you only on the condition of anonymity. I trust my life to my belief that you and Rita will honor our agreement. I agreed to see you and tell you what I have learned so that the truth will be known. It is obvious you and the authorities assumed Orlando was contracted by a Cuban. It is not so. And I can prove it."

Stacy glanced at Eli before pinning the editor with a questioning stare. "What is your proof?"

Ramirez folded his hands in front of him. "My source is a young man who returned only yesterday from your state, Miss Starr. This young man, along with three others, was involved in recovering eleven million dollars of drug money. The young man and the others were successful and returned the money to its owner, but it seems the owner considered these four men a liability. Three of the men were killed and the young man barely escaped with his life. He was very scared, as you can imagine, Miss Starr, and he sought refuge within our community. Some friends of mine have talked to this young man, and he identified his employer to them. But before I tell you who he is, Miss Starr, I am sure you are aware that neither the FBI nor the DEA has released any information concerning the loss of money from the bank in Dahlonega, Georgia. That alone should persuade you this young man is telling the truth . . . and to add even more validity to his story, he told my friends that others were hired by his employer to assassinate Congressman

Richards of your state and the Yona Group CEO, Henry Cobb. The reason, of course, was to eliminate them before they could incriminate his employer in his involvement in a money-laundering scheme. There is one thing more, Miss Starr, and this should interest you very much. The young man states he knows for a fact that his employer hired Jorge Orlando to assassinate Senator Goodnight. He says he knows this because he personally delivered weapons to Señor Orlando before he and his men departed for northern Florida to perform their mission. The young man says the weapons included Mac-10s and M-72 antitank rockets."

Stacy kept her eyes glued to the editor. "Who is it? Who was the young man's employer?"

"Eulalio Terres, Miss Starr. A well-known Colombian drug dealer here in Miami."

Using every ounce of his self-control, Eli forced himself not to move a muscle or show any expression as Stacy asked, "Can I talk to the young man and confirm this information?"

"Of course, it is the reason I agreed to see you, Miss Starr. But as I have explained, the young man is very scared. He wants federal protection and assurances he won't be prosecuted."

Again Stacy glanced at Eli before shifting her gaze to Ramirez. "I have contacts with the FBI, señor. I can arrange his protection, and if what you told me the young man said is true, I'm sure they'll grant him immunity. When can I talk to him?"

Ramirez motioned to the cellular phone on his desk. "He is awaiting your call, Miss Starr, but Rita will have to talk to him for you. He does not speak English. There is one more thing, a condition. He wants to meet with you before you contact the authorities. It was my suggestion. As a Cuban-American, I want to ensure that his information is made public. As I have stated, I am concerned that the authorities have already made up their minds as to who was responsible for these murders. The single-mindedness of the federal agencies is all too well known to us, Miss Starr. Your meeting with the young man, first, ensures that the federal authorities will listen to him, and, second, that his information is acted upon."

"Are you saying you don't trust the FBI?" Stacy asked.

"Please, Miss Starr, we are both well aware that the FBI and DEA are under extreme pressure to find the one responsible for the deaths of the senator and others. Such pressures cause expedient suspect theories. I need only remind you of the security guard in your hometown of Atlanta during the Olympics. The FBI asserted he was the one who planted the pipe bomb in the Olympic village; he was later cleared. 'Trust,' Miss Starr? It is not a matter of trust but rather a concern. It is clear that you and the authorities believe your suspect is a Cuban-American. . . . My concern is that federal officers have already made up their minds. Such officers might not be open-minded to the truth when it is presented to them."

Stacy looked at the cell phone on the desk. "I agree to his condition. Please call him."

Rita held the cell phone to her ear as she spoke to Stacy. "He says he'll be waiting for us at Versailles, a restaurant on Calle Ocho, Eighth Street. He says you and I are to be dropped off in front of the restaurant so he can see we are alone when we enter. He'll allow us to tape the conversation and you may call the FBI as soon as we arrive."

Stacy saw Eli shaking his head. She said to Rita, "Explain to him we can't come alone as he wants—my bodyguard must accompany me or it's no deal."

Rita spoke in Spanish into the phone and waited for a response. Seconds ticked by, then she nodded, spoke again in Spanish, and set the phone back on the table. "He agreed to one bodyguard accompanying us inside the restaurant. The other must stay outside. I told him we'd be there in twenty minutes."

The editor rose. "Miss Starr, I hope that I have helped you. I respect your work greatly and I know you and Rita will ensure the truth is made public."

Stacy shook the editor's hand again. "Señor Ramirez, you

have been most courageous for talking to us. Rita and I will do everything possible to expose the man responsible for the murders."

Eli spoke into the miniature mike. "We're coming out. Check the street and bring up the vehicles."

Thirty seconds later Eli slid the van door shut once Stacy and Rita were inside. He spoke into his mike. "Papa, this is Tango. Did you hear all of it? Over."

A block away, seated in a communications van, Agent Parker responded. "Roger, Tango. We heard and taped it. Your receiver is working five-by. I've informed the office and have a green light for us. The scramble button is pushed and agents are responding as we speak. Did you believe Ramirez? Over."

"Papa, he certainly knew things that haven't been released, but I don't like it—it's too easy. It smells like a setup to me. Will you have a bomb team check the vehicles in front of the restaurant? Over."

"Roger, dogs are already en route from Dade County resources as well as undercover detectives. ETA is ten minutes. You'll be covered. The boss also approved a team to watch the editor. We'll pick him up once we have the informer. Over."

"Roger, I have good copy," Eli said. "We'll move slowly to allow time for the reinforcements to get in place. Out here."

Eli turned to Faraday and Ashley, who stood next to him. "You heard everything on your ear mikes so there's no sense in going over it. Just stay close behind us and stay ready until we stop in front of the restaurant. Once we're inside, take your instructions from Agent Parker."

Ashley shook her head. "I don't like it, Tanner. Ed and I should go in the van with you."

"We've been over this, Sutton. With all the news gear, there's no room. Like I said, just stay on our rear and be ready. Okay, that's it; load up, we're moving out."

As soon as Eli climbed into the front passenger seat,

Stacy attacked. "Is Congressman Richards dead? Neither you nor Donny said a word to me about it."

"He's missing, Stacy. We—"

"Donny broke the deal we had, Eli. My God, that means the informer is real. How else would he have known about Richards?"

Eli turned in his seat. "Calm down; this could be a setup. We're taking precautions and checking it out now. I want you both to listen to me very carefully. The young guy we're supposed to meet may or may not be the real thing. We're going to play it safe. Agents will be in place in the restaurant and a search for a bomb will be conducted very passively so as not to spook him. If he's real, he'll be there. If our people don't see a possible suspect, it's off; we don't go in."

Rita quickly leaned forward in her seat. "You don't know what he looks like. How will your agents know if he's there or not?"

"Our people know what to look for, Miss Lopez. If he's real and there, he's going to be in a position to see the street and he's going to be one nervous customer—believe me, we'll know. All right, listen. If he is there, we'll enter the restaurant—I'll lead. When he approaches, don't make any move toward him; keep your distance. When I know he's clean of weapons I'll nod, but you still keep your distance from him while we walk to his table. Agents or undercover detectives will be at most of the tables by the time we get there. I'll direct you two to sit with your backs to the nearest wall. I'll sit to the guy's right. Don't sit until he does. If we get that far without trouble, then chances are we're home free. Got it?"

Stacy dipped her chin. Rita silently nodded as she slowly moved her hand to the hem of her skirt. Eli faced the front again and spoke over his shoulder. "I'm going to go over it one more time anyway. If it's a go when we arrive, I lead. If he—"

Rita pulled free the small automatic that was taped to her inner thigh, jerked the weapon up, and pressed the barrel against Stacy's temple, saying in a whisper, "Don't move a muscle." Then she spoke calmly in a regular tone. "Agent Tanner, excuse me for interrupting, but who will carry the recorder?"

Eli turned to answer her and froze. Rita lifted a piece of paper with her left hand and handed it to him in silence. Eli read the printed words: *You say a word, she dies—then you die. With your left hand pull out your radio and give it to me now!*

Eli slowly moved his left hand and pulled the small radio free from his belt, disengaging the wires to his ear receiver and sleeve mike.

As soon as Rita saw that the radio was free from its wires she snapped to the driver, "You know what to do, Pablo. The turn is just ahead." She grabbed Stacy by the hair, pulled her head down to her lap, and barked, "Put both hands on the dash where I can see them, Agent Tanner, and brace yourself."

Seated in the front passenger seat of the trailing van, Ashley pressed her ear receiver. "Ed, I'm not getting anything, are you?"

Faraday leaned forward in the backseat. "I'm not picking him up eith—what the—ohh shit!"

Seeing the news van in front of them suddenly make a hard left turn, Ashley squealed to the driver, "Follow them!"

Despite the red light, the driver accelerated and was about to make the turn when he had to slam on the brakes to avoid hitting a large refrigerated produce truck that had sped up and suddenly braked in the middle of the intersection, blocking the way. Faraday slid the van door back and yelled into his mike as he ran around the truck. "Parker, news van suddenly made left turn on . . . on . . . Christ! What the hell is the name of this street?" Faraday turned, searching for the street sign, and blurted, "Southwest Fourth Avenue heading north. We're blocked and can't follow! Get on it! I can still see them. They're still heading north— Wait, they just turned west . . . they're out of sight!"

Eli was thrown against the door as the van made a skidding right turn just after completing a left. Suddenly, the van seemed to leap into the air as it hit a speed bump leading into a parking garage. The van hit the pavement and bounced; the driver slammed on the brakes and skidded the vehicle to a bone-jarring halt.

Partially dazed from hitting his head on the van's ceiling when the van had landed from the bump, Eli tried to sit up and see where he was. Then his door opened and a huge man dressed in black wrapped his arms around him. Eli felt like he was being crushed and jerked his head back, feeling a horrific stinging sensation on the side of his neck. Kicking and squirming to free himself, he abruptly felt numb. His eyes blurred and became so heavy he couldn't keep them open. Feeling as if he were falling into a giant black hole, he heard a woman's voice say, "You're dead, Agent Tanner—got it?"

CHAPTER 18

The van stopped in the street, joining police cruisers and FBI vehicles in front of the parking garage. Seated in the front passenger seat, Ashley lowered her head. "Ed, I don't think I can do this."

Ed Faraday opened the van's sliding door and got out. He opened Ashley's door and put his hand on her shoulder. "I understand. I'll find out, then come back and let you know."

Ashley leaned back in the seat, wiping the tears from her cheek. Abruptly, she unbuckled her seat belt. "No, I have to know now. Just stay close to me, Ed; please stay close."

Together they walked toward the garage entrance, where a young police officer lifted the crime scene tape for them.

Seeing Agent Howard Parker approaching, Ashley braced herself.

Parker motioned behind him at the news van. "No bodies were found inside," he said.

Ashley closed her eye for a moment. There was still a ray of hope.

"Any witnesses?" Faraday asked.

Parker nodded. "We've got a woman who saw two black minivans leaving the back exit in a big hurry. She gave us a partial on one plate. We're running it now."

He turned and gestured to a pile of clothes. "They were smart. They stripped them; the transmitters we put on Tanner and Miss Starr are still attached to their clothes. It was hurriedly done ... the clothes were ripped from them. We figure the driver, one Pablo Fernandez, video man on Rita's crew, was in on it. He's been with the station for two and a half years. No priors—seemed clean, until now."

Ashley took a step toward the van. "Signs of struggle?"

"No blood, if that's what you mean," Parker said. "What we don't like is how the driver got the drop on Tanner. We're thinking maybe someone got in the van while it was parked outside the newspaper office. No evidence to support the theory as yet, but we did find a place behind all that equipment where somebody could have hidden."

"What about Rita Lopez?" Faraday asked.

"Her clothes are in the pile with the others, but we're doing a background check on her anyway. Right now we're going with the driver and a second person who got in the van. It's the only way we see it going down. The driver couldn't get them here alone. Once here, it looks like a crew was waiting for them. Had to be a minimum of three to four, probably more. Based on the time our witness said she saw the minivans leaving, it took them no more than two minutes to subdue the passengers, strip them, and move them to the other vehicles. The driver of the produce truck that blocked the intersection came clean—it was what you two thought, planned. He was paid five hundred dollars for his part. He was parked in the alley off the main street. He received word over a cellular phone to move onto the street and wait till the news van turned. When it turned, his instructions were to block the intersection. Bottom line is, this whole thing was well planned—pros for sure."

Ashley looked into the front passenger seat. "Why didn't they kill them?"

Parker shrugged. "We're asking the same question, and haven't come up with any answers, unless they want to make a trade for something."

"You guys don't trade," Faraday said.

"Yeah, that's common knowledge, so we're back to Agent Sutton's question: Why didn't they kill them?"

"Information," said a well-dressed man stepping up beside Parker. "They're keeping them alive to see what they know."

Parker gestured to the stranger, who had an unlit cigar stuck in one side of his mouth. "Agent Sutton, Detective Faraday, this is Agent Sam Ortiz from the DEA. He's the chief of the Organized Crime Division here in town."

Ashley pinned the DEA agent with a stare. "It was Mendez, wasn't it?"

Ortiz rolled the cigar to the other side of his mouth before looking at her. "Carlos Mendez is on the sixteenth fairway of his country club."

"You know what I mean," Ashley said.

"Yeah, I know, but you're wrong. I went over this with Agent Tanner yesterday—Mendez is inactive. This could have been done by one of three dozen crews in town."

"Jesus H. Christ," Faraday blurted. "Surely you've got a couple of big boys who are suspects."

"We do, Detective, and we're workin' it," Ortiz said.

"Who's your number one?" Ashley asked quickly.

"Terres," Ortiz said, "a Colombian who's come up through the ranks in the past three years."

An agent holding a radio ran up to Agent Parker. "Howard, the police just received a call from a man who said he just witnessed a man and woman being shot just off an access road to Hammock Park—he said four men dressed in black did the shooting then got into two dark minivans and drove back to the highway and turned north."

Ashley reached for Faraday's arm.

Brickell Key Marina, Miami

Ted nodded as he looked at the forty-eight-foot cabin cruiser gently rocking in its berth. "Looks good—how's the engine?"

Glenn stepped from the pier to the cruiser's deck. "Virgil checked it out and looked over the maintenance records, says it was overhauled only four months ago."

Ted stepped onto the deck and headed for the pilot's cabin. "How much you pay for it again?"

"Fifty-five five—it's a steal for that. The lady's husband died last month; she's moving back to New Jersey to be with her daughter. She wanted seventy but took my first offer. The lady said they took her out no more than a dozen times in the past two years, and I believe her. Take a look below; it looks like it just came out of the showroom."

Ted took the steps down into the plush paneled cabin and made a quick walk-through inspection of the galley and small bedrooms before nodding again. "Ya done good, Glenn. Get all the equipment stowed aboard and have one of the guys do some shopping to stock the galley—don't forget to tell 'em about dog food, canned, the good stuff. And some treats. Also rig us a diving platform that can be attached to the stern, portable, so we can break it down easy."

"I got us a prefab aluminum one when I bought the scuba gear this afternoon. Also got us some racks for the tanks that we'll install on the deck."

"What about the fishing gear?" Ted asked.

"Since it's just for show, I picked up six rigs real cheap from a pawnshop. And to make it really look good, I bought some sleeves for the railing to hold the poles so it looks like we're really serious fishermen. Anybody looking at us when we're under way will have no doubts what we're going to be doing."

"Charts and navigation equipment?"

"Got it. She's equipped with the ML-8000 II Loran Navigator, Edson radar, and Titan communications—all of it worked great when I took her out before I bought it."

Ted walked up the steps into the pilot's cabin and stood behind the wheel. "I'm goin' back to the place and pick up Bonita. You and the guys be ready to shove off at 1600 hours. We'll take her out a little ways and get Virg and Ramon checked out in their gear and take 'em on a practice dive to make sure they don't drown out there."

"Ramon says he's dived before; it's Virg I'm worried about. He says he can do it, but the look on his face tells me he's not all that confident."

"I'll take Virg down; you take Ramon. Once they see how

shallow the bay is, they'll both do fine. The problem will be getting them used to the boards. Tonight, you and me will do the recon and check out the yacht. Tomorrow we'll take 'em down again and have 'em use the boards until we know they can handle them. They'll be ready for the real action tomorrow night."

Glenn allowed himself a small smile. "It's almost ironic, Ted. You know what the name of this boat is? *The Revenge.* The lady said her husband named her that because his company fired him from his job because of his age. He sued them for discrimination, he won, and this baby was his present to himself. I never thought the day would come, Teddy. We're really close to doing it, aren't we?"

Ted stared vacantly toward the bay. "Yeah, Glenn, tomorrow night it's finally going to be over. Mendez will wish he never messed with Team Two-two. We're back, and this time it's our turn."

Matheson Hammock Park, Coral Gables

Seated in the backseat with Faraday in Agent Parker's car, Ashley felt guilty about her giddiness. Still several miles from the scene, she already knew the male seen being shot was not Eli. Agent Parker had a radio set to the Dade County police frequency and had listened to all the reports. The first arriving officers at the scene described the dead male as fully clothed and Hispanic. After checking the contents of his clothing, they had ID'd him as Pablo Fernandez, the news van driver. The female victim was Rita Lopez. She had been lucky. She'd been shot twice, in the side and in the shoulder. Unconscious but under paramedic care, she was en route to the hospital.

Parker was following a police cruiser and turned off the highway into the park's parking area. Two minutes later Ashley stood in shin-high saw grass looking down a low embankment at the driver's still form. A balding M.E. squatting beside the body glanced up at Parker. "He took two pops in the base of the skull, a .22. Officers found the casings. No exit wounds, very clean."

A park police officer approached Parker. "Sir, I found Miss Lopez over there . . . ten yards from the male. I recognized her immediately. She was nude and had sustained two gunshot wounds to the—"

"We heard your radio report, Officer. Where is the witness?"

"Actually, sir, there are ten of them. As you can see, this access road is clearly visible from the northern part of the park. We have four locals who were drinking beer just over there at that picnic table, and six others, tourists, were sunbathing just beyond the table. One of the locals had a cellular phone and called it in, but when I arrived I found all ten had witnessed the shootings. They all say pretty much the same thing. The two vans pulled in and drove down the side access road and stopped over there. Four Hispanic men dressed in black got out along with the male victim and Miss Lopez. It was Miss Lopez's being nude that got everybody's attention. The witnesses say the male was walking in front of the others when one of the men dressed in black placed a small pistol to the back of the victim's head and fired. They say it was so muffled they aren't sure if they heard one or two reports. Many of the witnesses thought it was staged for their benefit because it didn't sound real. Miss Lopez was being kept on her feet by two men; the witnesses say she appeared unconscious. The two men held her up and a third shot her twice. All the witnesses agree they heard the two shots. The bodies were left where they fell, and the four men got back into the dark vans and backed up, turned around there, and drove onto the highway, heading north."

"Any of the witnesses see anybody else in the vans?" Parker asked.

"No, sir, I asked all of them. Both vans had dark tinted glass. I also asked about plates. We have the last van's complete plate number and I already called it in. The second van was so close to the first they couldn't see its plate."

"Any witnesses touch the victims?"

"They didn't touch the male because he was obviously dead; Miss Lopez is a different matter. When I arrived, three of the males were bandaging her wounds with towels to stop the bleeding. The rest of the witnesses were pretty shaken up and were staying back. I got here within five minutes of the call, sir."

Parker motioned to two agents who had just arrived. "Get written statements from the officer here and the witnesses. And start on descriptions of the shooters." He walked over to a lone paramedic who was standing by an ambulance. "You from the attending team?"

"Yes, sir. The officer told me to wait for the FBI. I guess that's you, huh?"

"Yeah. What was the status of Miss Lopez?"

"Good. None of the bullet wounds was life-threatening. If you're going to be shot, those were the places to be hit. I'd say she didn't feel a thing . . . she was doped up on something; she was out like a light. All her vitals were normal when we arrived, and stayed that way until my team left with her."

"Exit wounds on both hits?"

"Just the side wound. In and out clean. No exit on the shoulder hit. It was a .22 on her, too."

"You can go now. Thanks for waiting," Parker said. He turned to Ashley and Faraday. "They execute a near perfect abduction, then drive out here in broad daylight and shoot their inside guy and Miss Lopez in front of an audience. Why doesn't that make sense to me?"

Ashley looked in the direction of the picnic table. "They had to have seen the beer drinkers sitting there—maybe they *wanted* to be seen."

Faraday wrinkled his brow. "They make a pro hit on the driver with two in the back of the head but botch shootin' Lopez. Uh-uh, they didn't want her dead. Nobody said nothin' about the guys in black being masked—in fact they said they were Hispanic. Are they that stupid? Lopez can ID them."

"She was drugged," Ashley said. "Maybe she *can't* ID them, but I still agree with you both; it stinks. We need to talk to Lopez and see what she says."

Parker nodded and said, "Maybe Tanner and Starr were drugged, too—that's good. It gives them more time. Whoever wants them is going to have to wait until they come out of it."

"Then what?" Faraday asked.

Parker looked at the detective for a moment, lowered his eyes, and started walking toward the car.

Eli finally managed to open his eyes. Having to squint because of his pounding headache, he saw a blurry figure directly across from him. He closed his eyes, took a deep breath, then forced his eyes open wider. It wasn't a horrible dream after all; the nude form of Stacy on the carpeted floor across from him told him it was real. She was facing him, her arms behind her, her face partially covered by her dripping wet hair. *Somebody splashed her with water like they did me,* he thought. *I can feel the drops rolling down my neck and shoulders. And I'm naked, as she is.*

Eli tried to move, but a sharp pain slashed down his neck into his shoulders. That was when he figured out that his hands were tied behind him. *Okay, what about the rest of you?* he said to himself. *Are you hurt? Wiggle your toes . . . okay. Now your fingers . . . okay. Nothing so far, nothing must be broken. Where . . . where are we?*

Taking in another breath, he exhaled slowly and tried to scan the small room. *A boat . . . we've got to be on board a boat of some kind . . . a big one because I don't feel any rocking. A cruiser maybe . . . a nice one, but old. Teak paneling, polished brass portholes . . . yeah, I feel the vibration of the engine now but I don't think we're moving . . . maybe it's the generator. Do they have generators? Okay, you're moving your head all right now. Let's try your hands . . . no. They're tied to something behind me . . . what? Doesn't matter, can't see it. Is Stacy all right?*

To his left he heard a door open and a moment later a big

man wearing black slacks and shirt leaned over and looked into his eyes. "*Bueno*, you wake."

Turning, the big man walked over to Stacy. He leaned over and swept the plastered hair back from her face. "Señorita, wake, *por favor*! Señorita must wake! *Ahh ... bueno! Habla español?* No? No *problema*, I speak good *inglés*. I see you on TV ... you lookin' good. I think maybe you lookin' better now." He smiled as he gently cupped her right breast and squeezed. "No plastic *aquí. Bueno* ... good, very good."

Stacy jerked back like a frightened animal.

"Lea-Leave her alone, asshole. You wanna practice your *inglés*, talk to me," Eli croaked, finding it difficult to speak; his throat and mouth felt like a desert.

The man faced Eli. "Tough *hombre*, huh? You call me asshola, huh?"

"I called you an ass-*hole*, not *hola*."

Still smiling, the man walked over and looked down at Eli. "Okay, ass-hole, how my *inglés* now, *hombre*?"

"Improving. So you goin' to tell us what we're doing here?"

"Don' know, ass-hole."

"Where's Miss Lopez, genius?"

"Andres shoot her."

"Really?"

"*Sí*, bang bang."

"And the driver? Pablo?"

"I shoot him, bang bang."

"Okay ... I can see you're really feelin' bad about it, too. Can the lady and I have something to drink? And how about some clothes?"

"Pepsi?"

"Two, please ... and some clothes, okay?" To Eli's shock, the big man nodded and walked out of the room.

"Don't look at me ... please don't look at me," Stacy said weakly.

"Move your arms, Stacy. Are you tied to something?"

She leaned forward and slowly moved back. "Yes, wha-what happened to us?"

"The guys who took us drugged us. We're on a boat of some kind . . . must be anchored someplace away from people or they would have gagged us. Stacy, listen to me. Do whatever they want . . . cooperate fully with them, you understand?"

"What do they want? Oh God, what are they going to do with us?"

"Hey now, calm down . . . if they were going to kill us, they would have done it by now. . . . They want something. You have to stay calm to keep your wits about you. Don't fight or argue with them . . . do everything they ask of you. We've got to buy some time."

"Rita . . . Rita helped them. He said he shot her. . . . Are they going to shoot us, too?"

"Cooperate, Stacy; you have to cooperate and be cool. All we need is time."

"Take his advice," said a twenty-something Hispanic guy who entered the room holding two Pepsis and two bowls. Dressed all in black, like the big man, he set one bowl in front of Stacy, opened a Pepsi can, and poured the contents into the bowl. "I apologize for making you drink this way, Miss Starr, but we cannot unchain you. I'm afraid your request for clothes must be denied; we have orders. I'll see if there is a sheet or blanket in the other cabin that I can use to cover you."

The young man rose and set the second bowl in front of Eli. "Agent Tanner, do not provoke my friend again. In your position, it would be very unwise. You should follow your own advice and cooperate fully with us."

"Keep the big boy away from the lady—he played doctor and upset her," Eli said.

"I'll ensure he doesn't touch her again, Agent Tanner. Drink; it will help you feel better."

"What's the deal here? Are we hostages?"

"I don't know, Agent Tanner. I merely follow orders. I'll see if I can find a covering for Miss Starr and yourself."

"Did you guys really shoot Rita and the driver?"

"Yes. As I said, Agent Tanner, we follow orders. I shall return shortly."

As soon as the young man disappeared, Stacy whimpered, "They're going to kill us, Eli ... you know it ... we've seen their faces; they'll have to kill us."

"They shot the others but not us, Stacy. There's a reason for it, and it's keeping us alive. Look up at the porthole above you. I can see the sun ... it's going down. It means we were taken hours ago. Every cop and agent in town is looking for us. Every minute we stay alive gives them more time to find us. Hang tough; you gotta hang tough."

5:30 P.M., Jackson Memorial Hospital

Seated in the waiting room, Ashley held a thick gold chain in her hand as she prayed. Faraday walked up holding two cups of coffee. "It's not bad stuff."

Opening her eye, Ashley accepted a cup and began to put the chain back into her purse.

"That's Tanner's gold chain, isn't it?" Faraday asked, sitting down beside her.

"Yes, I got it from the pile of clothes along with his weapon, billfold, and boo ID wallet," she said. "When we find him I know he'll want his necklace back ... he told me it was his good-luck charm ... hasn't taken it off since Vietnam."

Faraday set down his cup and took the chain from her hand. He looked at it a moment, then put it over her head. "You wear it for him; he needs all the luck he can get."

Ashley lowered her head. "Is Lopez still out?"

"She's awake. No, don't get up. We won't be talking to her for a while."

"Why? What's going on, Ed?"

"The doc's removed the bullet in her shoulder ... it was no big deal, used a local on her. She's fine, but she won't talk to Parker and us until her station manager and video man get here. She's got a Cuban lady in with her now fixin' her hair and doin' her makeup. It's goin' to be a regular dog and pony show, I guess."

Flushed, Ashley tried to get up, but Faraday put his hand on her shoulder. "Just take it easy. I've done enough pissin' and moanin' for the both of us. There's a lawyer standin' outside her door. A real know-it-all who's been spoutin' legalese to Agent Parker and me about Miss Lopez being a reporter. She's under obligation to report *first* to the station, *then* us. Parker threatened the bastard with obstruction, but the legal eagle has a damn signed judge's order in his hand."

"They can't do—"

"Seems they can. Miss Lopez is behind it all. Soon as she could talk, the first thing she asks for was the lawyer, then she conveniently feels too much pain to talk again until he got here. I'll tell ya, Ashley, if that bitch knows something and didn't tell us, I'm gonna ring her scrawny neck."

Ashley motioned to the hallway. "Looks like we'll know real soon. That must be the station manager and his news crew." She rose and set her shoulders. "If she withheld from us, Ed, I'm going to help you wring her neck. Come on. Parker is motioning toward us."

". . . and he suddenly appeared from behind the equipment, pushed Stacy over in her seat, and stuck a pistol in the back of Agent Tanner's head. He then whispered in the agent's ear. Agent Tanner immediately took off his radio, unplugging the wires. Then the gunman spoke to Pablo, our driver. He said the turn was coming up. Seconds later Pablo made a hard left turn and we sped up the street very fast and made another turn, then another into a parking garage. Suddenly a man opened the side door; he was wearing black slacks and shirt, and looked young, maybe mid-twenties, Hispanic. He held a pistol and told Stacy and me to get out. Stacy screamed, and then I saw two more men. One was very big, over six feet and broad-shouldered and heavy like

a football player. The other was tall but thinner and wore
glasses. Like the young man, all of them wore black shoes,
socks, slacks, and shirts. I got out, following Stacy, and—"

"Hold it, Miss Lopez," Agent Parker said. "Did the young
man speak in Spanish or English?"

"He spoke English, very little accent. He sounded well
educated."

"What about Agent Tanner; what happened to him once
you stopped?"

"I don't know. With all the wild turns, I was thrown forward in my seat, then back . . . then the door opened and all
my attention was on the young man's gun. He was pointing
it directly at me."

"Can you describe the man who appeared from the back
of the van and put his weapon on Agent Tanner?"

"He was behind us. When he pushed Stacy over, I ducked
down, too. I never saw his face, but I do know this: All of
them were Colombian. Let me explain. They stripped Stacy
and me and made us get into a black minivan, a Toyota, a
new model. It even smelled new. They forced us onto the floor
behind the front seats and then they sped out of the garage. I
heard the driver talking to the front passenger. He said,
'Sergeant, Corporal Zapata is driving too slow.' The passenger then said, 'He is following orders, Corporal. This is
not Medina; we must obey the traffic regulations.' Then
Stacy screamed. She was yanked from the floor by her hair.
The front passenger spoke angrily and said, 'Corporal
Bedoya, be gentle with her. Terres will cut your balls off if
she is marked by you. Show the discipline of the Lancero
you are.' "

"Lancero?" Parker repeated. "What's a Lancero?"

DEA agent Sam Ortiz was listening at the open door and
stepped into the room. "Lanceros are the Colombian Army's
equivalent to our Army Rangers. Miss Lopez, are you sure
the man in the front seat said the name Terres?"

"Yes, I'm sure. I had heard that name only a half hour
before from the editor, Señor Ramirez."

Parker rose up from his chair, facing Ortiz. "Sam, I'm conducting this interview. I'll ask the questions."

Ortiz shifted his unlit cigar to the other side of his mouth. "Not anymore. We've got an open case on Terres, so from this point on this witness is mine."

Parker growled at the cameraman, "Turn that off!" Then his eyes narrowed. "Sam, don't pull this shit on me."

"You can stay if you want, Howard, but consider it pulled. Miss Lopez, I'm sorry for the interruption. Please continue."

For a long moment Parker looked at Ortiz as if he were going to cut his heart out, but he finally stepped away from the bed and backed up against the wall beside Ashley and Faraday.

Ashley leaned over and whispered, "Can he really do this?"

His facial muscles twitching, Parker nodded once in silence.

". . . then the man in the backseat pulled me up and I felt as if I had been stung by a bee on the neck. I felt suddenly woozy and I guess I passed out. I don't remember anything after . . ."

In the hospital corridor Sam Ortiz lowered his cellular phone and looked at Parker. "I've got my people en route to run a surveillance of Terres's estate and boat company."

"You bought her story?"

"It fits. I did some checking after I heard the editor's interview tape you sent me. I've got an informer who corroborates that Terres had three guys whacked yesterday in the 'glades . . . a fourth got away. Terres's people have been looking everywhere for him."

"We checked the restaurant, Sam. The young guy wasn't there."

"I know. The reason he didn't make it is that he's dead."

Standing next to Parker, Ashley narrowed her eye. "How do you know that?"

"A young man with a Lancero tattoo on his forearm was

found an hour ago in a Dumpster one block from the restaurant. His tongue had been cut out and nailed to his forehead. It's the way they mark those who have talked, Agent Sutton."

Ortiz took the cigar from his mouth. "Look, Howard, six months ago a squad of Lanceros in Colombia were investigated for being turned by the druggies they were supposed to be hunting down. The entire squad disappeared. We had rumors they were in this country but had nothing firm until now."

Faraday stepped closer. "What puts these commandos with Terres?"

"The squad was supposed to be hunting for drug labs— they were Terres's labs. His brother-in-law runs the farming, collection, and labs in Colombia. Terres has the distribution and sales side of the operation here in the States. Like I said, it fits. Do you want to help me on this or not, Howard?"

Parker sighed and nodded. "Yeah, where do you want to meet and discuss the coverage?"

"My office. See you there in thirty minutes," Ortiz said. He put the cigar back in his mouth, dipped his head toward Ashley, and walked toward the elevators.

Ashley stood staring at Parker. "That it? You're going to support Ortiz?"

Parker looked into Ashley's unbandaged eye. "Face it, Agent Sutton, the editor was right about us—we jumped on Mendez being the one and didn't look at other possibilities. We screwed up. I just hope it's not too late for us to get turned around and focused on Terres." He took the cellular phone from his jacket pocket. "Excuse me, I've got to call my SAC and tell him I was wrong."

Parker turned and walked down the hallway, leaving Ashley and Faraday in the middle of the corridor. Ashley shifted her stance, looking at the stocky detective. "Have we been wrong, Ed?"

Lowering his head, Faraday let out a long sigh. "Maybe we have. But one thing I know for sure. Tanner said it was Mendez . . . his gut told him so. Tanner's gut feelings mean a lot more to me than what that Lopez and the DEA guy said. Hey, where you goin'?"

Ashley spoke over her shoulder as she walked toward Rita Lopez's room. "I'll be right back."

"What are you doing here?" Rita asked, setting down a pad she'd been writing on.

Ashley spoke to the nurse beside the bed. "Excuse us, please. You can come back in just a few minutes. This won't take long."

The nurse was about to protest, but Ashley held the door open. "*Now,* please. It's an FBI matter."

As soon as the nurse walked out, Ashley shut the door and faced Rita. "Miss Lopez, this is a warning to you. If I find that anything you said in your statement was a lie or misleading I will come back and personally arrest you."

"Are you threatening me?"

"No, Miss Lopez, I am stating a fact. If it is found you gave perjured testimony, you will be charged with obstruction of justice, conspiracy, and three counts of murder. One of those counts of murder will be for a federal officer, my partner. That count alone will get you a life sentence and the good possibility of a death sentence."

Ashley opened the door. "Miss Lopez, you had better pray I don't walk back into this room again." She walked out, shutting the door behind her.

Faraday raised an eyebrow. "What was all that about?"

Ashley kept walking. "Girl talk. Come on, we're going to the field office and look over everything we have on Mendez again."

"So you trust Tanner's gut, too, huh?"

"No, I trust *my* gut, and it says Rita Lopez lied."

Biscayne Bay

Virgil Washington surfaced and spit out his mouthpiece. "Where's all the fish? On TV there's always pretty fish."

Ted took the regulator from his mouth and pushed back his mask. "Ya gotta get around coral, where they hide. Ya did good for your first time. Let's work on clearing your mask if it fills with water."

"Wait, before you show me, tell me somethin', Ted."

"Sure."

"Ya know that movie *Jaws*? I know it was just a flick, but do—"

"Naw, Virg, there ain't no Jaws in this bay. The only thing you gotta worry about tomorrow night is you. You get scared and start seein' things underwater, you'll get yourself drowned. There's nothing as bad as you in the water. Trust me."

"I trust you, Ted—no Jaws, huh? Okay, I can do this. Shiiit, it ain't near as deep as I thought. I can see the bottom no sweat. I got it. I can do this. I can be a squid like you."

Only thirty yards away Baby ran up the steps and bolted out of the open door onto the deck. Behind him Bonita yelled, "Get back here; I'm not finished yet! Ohh . . . you've dripped dye on the carpet. Ted is going to kill me. Come here, darn you!"

Bonita stepped out of the cabin and searched the deck with her eyes. "There you are. You can't hide from me, buster. Ohhh, look at you. You're shaking. Come to Mama. I'm sorry. Come on, honey. That's my boy. I'm so sorry, but we have to disguise you. Black is beautiful . . . well, right now you're not so beautiful, but I'll get it right. Just look at Mama. See how my hair looks. . . . That bad, huh? Yeah, I think so, too. When Ted sees us, he'll throw us both overboard. Come on, it won't be much longer and you'll be all done . . . thatta boy. We have to finish you up and dry you off before the frogmen get back. Won't they be surprised."

CHAPTER 19

7:00 P.M., Biscayne Bay

The sun had just turned burnt orange and had lost its strength as Ted, Glenn, Virgil, and Ramon sat in plastic chairs on the deck of *The Revenge*. Bonita set a tray of soft drinks on the table in front of the team and picked up two empty snack bowls. "Dinner will be ready in thirty minutes," she said softly.

Without looking at her, Ted unfolded a sketch he'd made. "That's fine; this is just an overview planning session. We'll be done by then."

As Bonita walked toward the cabin, Ted pointed across the bay. "Guys, over there, four miles away, is Key Biscayne and the estate of our target, Carlos Mendez. Lying at anchor just a quarter mile from his place is his yacht. Tomorrow evening our boy is going to be enjoying the company of a couple of ladies on that yacht, and that's when we're going to take him out."

Ted motioned to the table where he had placed the sketch. "Bonita gave us all the info, and here's what we're up against. Mendez keeps himself protected at all times. He has a covered walkway from the back entrance of his estate all the way down to his private docks. He'll take the walkway and board a small cruiser with his bodyguards and ten security guards, then be escorted to the yacht by four cigarettes, speedboats, that each have four men, all carrying automatic weapons. Once he and his guards board his yacht, the four cigarettes take up position in a box formation around the yacht. Nobody is allowed within two hundred yards; the perimeter boats make sure of it. If a boat heads in the direction of the yacht, the closest cigarette immediately responds and warns the skipper to change course—you don't argue with guys holding Macs. The perimeter boats are the first line of defense. The second line is the ten security guards who stay on the yacht when Mendez is there. Two are positioned on the lower aft deck, two on the lower forward deck, and two constant rovers. Two spotters are on the bridge and there are two that monitor radios in the communications room located on the bridge. The guards are rotated every eight hours by a new crew that comes out from the estate. The third and final line of defense is Mendez's bodyguards. Four of them always stay close to him. Each carries two automatic pistols. Like the security guards, they're rotated every eight hours while he's on the yacht. All tol', we're talking about thirty armed men whose job it is to protect their boss. And they have help. The permanent yacht staff is made up of fourteen people. It includes the skipper and his crew of eight, a chef, his assistants, dishwasher, stewards, maids, and even a gardener—Mendez likes plants; he's got a slew of them on board. The point is, all of these people have eyes and ears and are a passive security measure to reckon with. That's the bad news. The good news is the staff lives belowdecks. Also, most of the security guards are stationed on the second deck. Mendez's quarters and entertainment area are on the first. That means once Glenn and I get to the first deck, we only have to deal with four bodyguards to get to Mendez."

Ramon shook his head. "Yeah, but you gotta get to that deck first, man. You and Glenn ain't invisible."

"We will be," Ted said with a small smile.

"Hold it, back it up," Virgil said, leaning forward in his chair. "Let's go back to those cigarette boats that form the perimeter. You told me and Ray this afternoon we were goin' to be responsible for taking them out. . . . How we goin' to do that if there are four boats all spread out and only two of us? Especially since ya said they all gotta be taken out at the same time."

"Piece of cake," Ted said. "We've got digital timed-fuse igniters. Once the charges are in place all you have to do is push the right button at the right time."

"That's a piece a' cake?" Virgil responded. "Sure, I went underwater with you today, Ted. I kinda liked it even, but shit, man, we're talkin' about me and Ray scuba-dubin' on our own, at night when it's black as a witch's tit. You said we gotta stay under and don't surface through the whole thing—how the hell we gonna find them boats when we're underwater? And even if we do find 'em, how we gonna see where to put the charges and how we gonna know what damn button to push when it's darker than two feet up a bull's ass? Piece a' cake? You smokin' dope sayin' it's a piece of cake."

Ted smiled again as he pointed above him. "In a couple of hours there's going to be a full moon up there. And when it does get up there, we're all going in for a dive just to prove to you it's not as dark as you think underwater. And to-morrow mornin' startin' at oh dark thirty we're going to rehearse this op a dozen times. You'll be able to do it blind-folded. And if it clouds up tomorrow night for the op, it's not a problem. The NVGs we got are made for underwater use. You'll be able to pick up a dime off the bottom at mid-night if you want to. Relax. I know what I'm doin', and you're goin' to do fine."

His face grim, Ramon pushed back in his chair. "Why we doin' all this high-speed plannin'? When Mendez gets on board, why not just blow the fuckin' yacht out of the water and be done with it?"

"We're not like them," Ted snapped. "The permanent staff aren't dirty—we're not killin' innocent people."

"You tellin' me they don't know the guy is dirty? Give me a break, man. You sittin' there sayin' there's thirty bad-asses with automatics protectin' him. Look around you, man. I count four of us. Thirty against four—let's see, my math ain't so good but it don't take that many brain cells to figure out what our chances are with them odds. Fuck the crew and the maids and his whores, man. None of them people on that boat are turnin' down his paycheck. Blow the fuckin' thing out of the water and let the fish eat 'em."

Angry, Ted stood. "You should have joined Mendez; he doesn't mind killing innocent people, either."

Ramon lowered his head, looking at his hands before his eyes rose to Ted. "I got a little carried away, maybe—I don't wanna kill no innocent people. I just don't like the odds, Ted. Thirty fuckin' people is just too damn many. It takes just one to get lucky and it's over for all of us."

"You haven't heard the whole plan yet, Ramon," Ted said as he retook his seat. "I'm not a glory-seekin' officer or dumbass planner with no experience. I've trained for these kinds of ops for years; so have you. You know what we've got in gear and weapons, and you know each of us. We're all pros here. Listen to the rest of the plan and wait till you make a couple rehearsals tomorrow. Then, tell me if you think the odds are still too high."

Ramon dipped his chin. "Fair enough . . . but after all that if I still think it's fucked up, I'm tellin' you, man. I told you the first day I met you, I don't do fucked-up missions."

"Fair enough. Once we've had supper and done our practice dive this evening, we're pulling anchor and moving into a position about a half mile from the yacht. Glenn and I are going under to make a recon to confirm the depth, take a look at the yacht's hull, and make sure there'll be no surprises for us. But right now let's get back to the plan and some specifics. Tomorrow night we'll all be carryin'. . . ."

Ted pushed his empty plate back and glanced at Bonita, who was taking the leftovers into the cabin. He leaned over to Glenn. "What's with her? She hasn't hardly said a word ta me all evenin'."

Glenn raised an eyebrow. "You should have said something to her about her hair."

"What ya want me to say? 'Bo, you look like that witch on *The Munsters*'? That black hair looks like shit on her and you know it. And ya see what she did to the poor hunter? Poor guy looks like a damn tiger the way she streaked him up with that dye."

Overhearing the conversation, Virgil leaned closer to Ted. "Teddy, you'd best talk to her and be nice. When this op is over you don't be needin' to go back to Atlanta to check out the Little League and soccer fields for classy mommies—Bonita got 'em all beat."

"Christ'a'mighty, Virg, I'm tryin' to run an op here. Being a sophisticated guy makes you know all about women now?"

"Just tryin' to help you, Ted. You gotta talk to her and make her feel better about her hair, man."

Glenn nodded in agreement. "She did it for us, Ted . . . thought a disguise would lessen the chances of being spotted. It was me who screwed up. She told me to get some hair dye for her and for Baby. I got cheap stuff and the wrong color. Talk to her and tell her she looks good."

Ted leaned back, eyeing Glenn. "Wait a minute. *You,* of all people, are worried about her feelings? You don't trust her, remember?"

"She's good people, Ted. Like I told ya this morning, I was wrong about her—she's trying real hard and been good to all of us. We're a team, Ted, and she's a part of it. Talk to her."

Ramon stood, walked around the table, and patted Ted's shoulder. "The guys are right, man. You gotta be nice to Bonita—she's been nice to us. Dinner was good, man, and she's workin' hard for us."

"Christ'a'mighty, you too?" Ted shook his head in disbelief. "You guys worry about the op and let me worry about Bonita. But I will talk to her—I'll lie about her hair and won't say nothin' about her screwin' up the poor ol' hunter."

Ted pushed back his chair and took a deep breath. He stood, exhaled, rolled back his shoulders, and walked toward the cabin.

"Remember, be nice," Virgil whispered.

Bonita was washing dishes in the small sink when Ted

stepped up behind her. "Supper was good, Bo. You didn't need to go to all that trouble, you know."

Bonita kept her back turned to him and continued to rinse off the plates. "I wanted to do something helpful."

"Uh . . . I couldn't help but notice you colored your hair. It—it—"

"I know it looks terrible—you don't have to lie to me, Teddy. And I'm sorry about Baby . . . I'll try and fix him tomorrow."

Ted put his hand on her shoulder. "Bo, I don't care about your hair—you could be bald and you'd still look like a million dollars in my book."

Bonita set down the plate and covered his hand with hers. "Promise me you'll come back to me, Ted. Promise me."

"I promise, Bo. And I promise somethin' else, too. One day you and me are gonna be on a balcony watchin' the canoes and fireworks at Disney World. I still wanna see Sleeping Beauty's castle up close."

Bonita faced him and rested her head on his chest. "It's Cinderella's castle, Teddy."

Peeping through the doorway, Glenn smiled, turned, and raised his thumb to Virgil and Ramon. Both men raised their hands and slapped them together in a high five.

The young man in black held a Sig 210 nine-millimeter pistol to Eli's head as he unlocked the bike chain. "Keep your arms spread and head on the floor, Agent Tanner. It's time for you and Miss Starr to make a trip."

"Where to this time?" Eli asked.

"I don't know, Agent Tanner. We are giving you and Miss Starr to others."

"Look, before we go, would you let Miss Starr and me please use the latrine? We've been here a long time. I'm about ready to bust."

"You may sit up now, Agent Tanner. Good. Yes, you may visit the facilities, as may Miss Starr, but neither of you will have privacy."

Eli felt the thin chain around his wrists and could see the

chain around his ankles. He knew escape was impossible but managed a nod. "Thanks for your consideration."

Abruptly, he was lifted to his feet and the piece of sheet that had been covering him fell to the floor. The big man leaned over and spoke into his ear. "I take good care of you, ass-hole."

Eli glanced at Stacy as she was lifted to her feet and her sheet also fell to the floor. The young man picked it up and wrapped it around her shoulders again. "Please walk slowly; the chain around your wrists is also tied to your ankles. It will be difficult, but if you walk slowly, the chain will not rub your skin raw. That's it; walk slowly."

"Please don't do this—just leave us here and go," Stacy said, sobbing.

"Come now, Miss Starr, my associates and I were paid to do a job. We take pride in our work."

Ten minutes later Eli sat beside Stacy on a cushioned seat below the deck of a sleek cigarette boat. They were chained to each other and to the bulkhead. The big man was seated across from them, wearing a Walkman; he was rocking his shoulders back and forth to a beat only he could hear.

Eli whispered, "You okay?"

"Na . . . no, I'm not okay. I'm scared to death. Aren't you?"

"Not yet—giving us to someone means more time for us. You're doin' real good, Stacy. Just keep it up. Our people will find us—I know it."

"Oh God, we're moving. Ohh . . . why do they have to go so fast?" Stacy asked in a whimper.

Eli winced and closed his eyes tightly. "I hate boats . . . my stomach is already doing somersaults. Why did it have to be in a damn speedboat?"

Stacy glanced at him. "You're pale . . . you're serious, aren't you?"

"I almost drowned once . . . yeah, I'm serious. I . . . I really hate this."

"Eli, we're nude, abducted by armed men, going God

knows where, and they're probably going to kill us—and your stomach is upset because we're in this boat?"

"I hate being on water ... I just told you I almost drowned once."

"I think we have more to worry about than being on this boat. What are we going to do once we get to where we're going?"

"I ... I think I'm going to be sick."

"Are we really going to get out of this?"

"Our people will find ... oooh ..."

The big man wrinkled his nose as Eli lurched forward and vomited on the floor between them.

FBI field office, Miami

Ashley turned from the window. "It's getting dark, Ed; we're running out of time."

Faraday motioned to the papers spread out on the table. "We've been over everything twice ... I don't know what else to do. I just know sittin' here isn't helping Tanner any."

The office door opened and Agent Parker stormed in. "We've got a break! A DEA snitch came through. He says he saw two dark vans drive into Terres's boatyard about four-thirty this afternoon."

"I thought the DEA had surveillance on those yards," Ashley said.

"They didn't get into position until five. The DEA is staging their Tac Team close to the yard and sending up a chopper to see if they can spot the vans with night-vision scopes. I'm going to the yard—you two coming?"

Ashley exchanged looks with Faraday before shaking her head. "No, we'll monitor the radios in the ops room to keep up with events. We're working on a few things on our own."

"You still think Mendez is the one, don't you?"

"I think we've all been taken for a ride by Lopez, so yes, I still think he's behind all this."

"I'll be at the yard if you change your mind." Parker turned and walked out.

Faraday started collecting the papers. "We can go over this stuff a third time in the ops center. What time is it now?"

Ashley glanced at her watch, then turned and looked out the window into the darkness. "It's almost nine."

His chin caked with dried vomit, Eli felt too weak to move when a uniformed man in khaki took hold of his arm and said, "Stand up."

Stacy took hold of Eli's arm and pulled him to his feet as she stood. "You've got to do something," she whispered.

Standing in his bare feet in his own vomit, he felt the rocking motion of the boat. Another wave of nausea surged through him. He began to fall backward but was grabbed by the guard and pushed toward the open hatchway. Eli wondered if they were going to be transferred to yet another boat. They had been transferred to a second cigarette thirty minutes before, and new people were guarding them. He hoped this would be another transfer, which would mean spending more time away from their final destination. But his stomach hoped they were finally at the last stop.

Once on the deck, Eli took in deep breaths of the fresh night air as he looked up at a huge white hull. There was a whirring sound, and a stairway with an overhead canvas cover was lowered into view. Stacy brushed her shoulder against his. "It's a yacht, Eli. They've brought us to a yacht."

Too sick to speak, Eli thought, *I don't care as long as it doesn't rock.*

A uniformed guard took hold of Eli's chain and led the couple toward the stairway. At the yacht's polished wood deck, the couple was met by five men. The one in the middle was thin, middle-aged, and wore a white linen suit. He ignored Eli, nodding toward Stacy instead. "Good evening, Miss Starr. Welcome to the *Princess*. I am Raul, your temporary host." Raul shifted his gaze to the guard. "Unchain her."

Once she was free of the chains, Raul handed Stacy a robe. "I apologize for the embarrassment and discomfort we have caused you, Miss Starr. We shall do our best to make amends. These two gentlemen will escort you to your stateroom, where you can shower and freshen yourself. You'll find everything you need. A dinner gown has already been laid out for you, and should you need anything else, don't hesitate to let these gentlemen know. They will be outside your door."

Stacy quickly put on her robe. "You said you were my 'temporary' host?"

"You'll have the honor of dining with Colonel Mendez tonight, Miss Starr. He is very much looking forward to meeting you. Please, gentlemen, be so kind as to escort Miss Starr to her accommodations."

Stacy held her ground as two of the khaki-clad men stepped forward. "Will Agent Tanner be dining with us?"

Raul wrinkled his brow as if apologetic. "Miss Starr, the agent will be dining alone this evening. Please don't be concerned for his welfare. He will not be harmed in any way. Like you, he is a guest. Now please, you must not delay any longer. You are expected for dinner at ten."

Stacy looked at Eli, who nodded. She held his eyes for a long moment, then stepped forward and was immediately flanked by the two men, who began walking her down the deck.

Raul wrinkled his nose as he looked at Eli. "Take him to the holding room and see that he is washed. He stinks."

"Don't I get a robe and stateroom?" Eli asked as the remaining two guards stepped toward him.

Raul waved his hand. "Hurry, his smell is making me nauseous."

Standing on the deck of *The Revenge*, Bonita stared at the distant yacht with Baby at her side. Virgil stood beside her. "Don't be worried. Ain't none better than Ted and Glenn when it comes to snoopin' and poopin' underwater." He glanced at his watch. "They should be reachin' the yacht in ten minutes or so."

Getting no response, Virgil glanced at her face. Tears were rolling down her cheeks. "What's wrong, Bonita?"

"He's on board," she said almost in a whisper.

"Who?"

"Carlos. He's on board. The lights in his stateroom came on a few minutes ago—he's there."

Seated in a plastic chair sipping a Coke, Ramon had heard the conversation and immediately stood. "He's not supposed to show up till tomorrow night."

"Yeah, it's probably somebody cleanin' his room or some-thin'," Virgil said.

Bonita maintained her distant stare. "He's there. He's entertaining. All the second deck's lights are on—they are never on like that unless he's on board."

"Never?" Virgil asked.

"Never. He's there, all right, and that means he's brought all his security," Bonita said, finally breaking out of her trance. "We've got to warn Ted and Glenn."

"How we goin' to do that?" Virgil asked. "Come on, Bonita, so what if he's there? The guys are just makin' a look-see recon and comin' right back. It's gonna be all right."

Ramon looked out toward the distant yacht. "I can just make out the perimeter boats. Ted and Glenn will see them and know he's there. No sweat, Bonita. Relax."

Bonita began pacing. "How much longer till they come back?"

"They said it'd take them twenty minutes to get to the yacht, fifteen minutes for the look-see, and twenty back. Let's see, they've been gone about fifteen minutes; that means they should be back in about forty minutes. Come on, Bonita, relax. Virgil was right; them squids know what they're doin'. They'll be back."

Bonita nodded absently, and looked once again toward the lighted yacht.

*   *   *

Eli sat nude in the middle of a room lined with shelves for sheets, towels, blankets, and cleaning equipment. He was still dripping from being hosed off ten minutes before, but at least he was no longer sick. The door opened and the guard seated in front of him stood.

Carlos Mendez entered the room and nodded toward the guard, who immediately exited the small room. Mendez studied Eli a moment before taking a seat in the guard's chair. "I have been anxious to meet you. I understand from my associates your name is Eli Tanner. Please let me introduce myself. I am—"

"I know who you are, scumbag," Eli said.

"Please, Agent Tanner, refrain from movie dialogue. It is unbecoming in a professional such as yourself. But it does intrigue me that you do know me. How is that?"

"I worked you, Mendez—I ran an investigation on you in ninety. You killed those grocery people who were laundering for you—and you killed my partner."

"Interesting. But I assure you, Agent Tanner, I killed no one."

"You had them killed, just like you had the senator and the others killed, you son of a bitch."

"Please, Agent Tanner, you are becoming upset. And for no reason. You see, the *killers*, as you call them, are as we speak being surrounded by your DEA friends. Not far from here actually. I understand tomorrow morning at exactly seven o'clock they will assault the killers' base. Oh, I see you doubt me. No, it is quite true. Mr. Terres, a Colombian who can be quite disagreeable, will no doubt be very surprised and agitated by the appearance of these armed, uninvited guests."

"You set Terres up, didn't you?"

"Me? Come now, Agent Tanner, I'm a businessman. Men such as Terres are of no concern to me. What does concern me, however, are those who steal from me. Perhaps you can help. I'm sure you are aware that money was stolen from me. A former friend of mine was involved, a woman. She, I will take care of, but I am concerned about the others who were with her. Perhaps you could tell me what you know about them?"

"What do I get in return, Mendez? I know you're not going to let me go."

"In return? Let me think a moment . . . yes, I have it. I will assure you Miss Starr will have no reason to fear death or injury."

"Don't play games; you're going to kill her, aren't you?"

"I said she will not have any reason for fear, Agent Tanner. I will keep my promise—she will not know it's coming. It will be quick and painless for her . . . that is, if you tell me what you know."

Eli bored holes into Mendez with his eyes. "We don't know anything about them—that's the God's honest truth. We know about Bonita Rogers because we got her prints from the lake cabin . . . that's all we've got."

"Pity, I thought as much. I would have hoped for more from the Bureau, but it appears your organization is as inept as always."

"I told you what I know . . . you'll keep your part of the bargain, won't you?"

"But of course, Agent Tanner. I am a man of honor. Miss Starr is quite beautiful—and I appreciate her like all of nature's beautiful things."

Mendez began to rise but paused and shifted his gaze back to Eli. "You are not going to beg for your life, are you, Agent Tanner?"

"No way."

"You are a realist. That is good. I have often wondered about the men who pursue me. You seem a worthy adversary—are there many like you?"

"Yeah, and they're going to get you, Mendez."

"I think not, Agent Tanner. Yes, I'm sure others will attempt to do so, but their time is running out. You see, I am ending my old business dealings; the game tires me now. I have other interests that give me greater pleasure. Do you like tropical plants, by chance?"

"Going legit won't help you, Mendez; you've stepped on

too many toes and killed too many people. If we don't get you, somebody seeking revenge will take you out. You know what I'm saying is true . . . you can't stop them; people like that don't care. They have a single purpose in life—it drives them and makes them the most dangerous animals on earth. They're out there, Mendez . . . you created them with your drugs, contracted hits, and corruption. They're out there and they'll always be coming for you."

Mendez smiled. "Very good. Spoken from the heart. Earlier you accused me of being responsible for your partner's death. I assume you are one of those animals you speak of. Pity, look at you now, but, for your efforts, I shall let you in on a secret. Tomorrow many of your associates will be staging their assault on Señor Terres's estate and his boatyard. Those waiting to assault the boatyard will encounter a horrible surprise—a very destructive surprise. The event will anger and transform the survivors into revenge-seeking animals, just as you described. Terres's men inside the boatyard will receive no quarter."

"You're going to set off a bomb?"

"Actually, I understand it will be several. I'm quite proud of the plan. You see, once this catastrophe occurs, your people will have no doubt of poor Señor Terres's guilt. They will assault his estate, perhaps even capture him alive—but that is very doubtful. I have taken precautions to ensure he is eliminated should that possibility occur. In any event, sufficient evidence will be present to make his guilt undeniable. The case will be closed, and although saddened by the huge loss of life, the participants will take solace in the knowledge that justice was done."

"You son of a bitch!"

Mendez sighed as he stood. "It would disappoint you if I were otherwise. Tomorrow, at seven o'clock, when these unfortunate events are happening, Miss Starr and I will be at my estate receiving a new specimen for my collection, Agent Tanner, a quite rare plant known as a Tiger plantiutim. It is from Papua, New Guinea . . . very fragile. Requires delivery in the early morning before the heat builds.

If it were to occupy the rear of a sweltering truck for more than ten minutes, the beauty would surely perish. I have looked forward to this delivery for some time. . . . I have already prepared a place for my new family member and will delight in finally being able to spoil her with my love and devotion. I'm sure Miss Starr will appreciate the opportunity to be present."

"What are you going to do to her?"

"I promised you she would not be in fear or distressed in any way, Agent Tanner. I'm afraid I cannot promise the same for you."

Mendez opened the door. Two men entered. One placed a piece of duct tape over Eli's mouth. Mendez canted his head toward Eli. "A pity you won't have an opportunity to dine on my stone crabs. I would make the offer, but it is unhealthy to eat prior to swimming." He smiled and strode down the passageway.

Raul was sipping a gin and tonic as Stacy stood looking out the dining room's plate-glass windows toward the lights of Miami. Raul rose from his chair when Mendez walked into the candlelit room. "Colonel, it is an honor for me to present Miss Stacy Starr."

Stacy turned and eyed the approaching man dressed in a white military-style tuxedo. "Where is Agent Tanner? Is he all right?"

Mendez bowed. "It is an honor to meet you at last, Miss Starr. I assure you Agent Tanner is perfectly fine. In fact I spoke to him only minutes ago and answered his questions concerning your welfare."

"I want to see him."

Mendez stepped closer. "I'm afraid that is impossible. I ordered him moved to another location, Miss Starr. It is dangerous for me to have you both here. I'm sure you understand that."

"Where have they taken him?"

"To a place that has a lovely view of the bay. Please, Miss Starr, enough questions. Won't you join me at the table?"

* * *

Standing beside the stern rail, Eli knew the day and time had finally come. Nude and with his hands still chained behind him, he closed his eyes as a guard wrapped a rope around his ankles. Tied to the other end of the rope was a forty-five-kilo York weight, the kind used in gyms.

Another guard standing several feet away commanded, "Over with him."

Two guards lifted the heavy weight and rested it on the railing as two more lifted Eli and set him up on the narrow rail beside the weight. Eli glanced down at the dark water fifteen feet below and immediately shut his eyes. He had always thought he would die while on duty. A bullet was what he'd hoped for, a good clean shot, instant, with no pain. But that wasn't going to happen. Water was going to claim him after all. Fate was so damn unkind, he thought.

A guard took hold of the weight and smiled. "How long can you hold your breath?" He pushed the weight over the side; Eli followed feet first.

Under the hull, Ted and Glenn had night-vision goggles pulled down over their masks and were looking at the yacht's exposed propeller shafts. A sudden *ka-thunk* startled both men. They spun just in time to see something dark sinking quickly to the bottom, and attached to the dark object by a short length of rope was a naked man.

Ted closed his eyes for a moment, thinking maybe his eyes had deceived him. He opened them again and looked down. Nope, there he was, big as life, wiggling like an elongated worm, doing everything he could to try to wiggle himself back to the surface.

Glenn poked Ted and pointed east. Ted began to nod in agreement that it was best to get the hell out, but something made him look down again. The naked man was just a green blur, but he could still see the poor son of a bitch struggling to hold on to life as long as he could. *Ahh shit, nobody should die that way,* Ted thought. He pulled the knife from the sheath on his leg and dove down.

CHAPTER 20

Carlos Mendez eyed his dinner guest, who was staring vacantly at her plate. "You don't like the stone crabs?"

Stacy set down her fork. "It's difficult to eat when you know you're going to die."

Mendez patted her hand. "I promise you will see the sun rise tomorrow, Miss Starr. I have no intention of hurting you."

Stacy pulled her hand away. "I'm not a fool. I know you can't let me live."

"You certainly are not a fool, Miss Starr, but your assumption is incorrect. You see, I'm leaving the country tomorrow. I'm going to return to Cuba. Fidel has invited me home again."

Stacy lifted her eyes to her host. "What's going to happen to me?"

"You will leave with me, of course . . . but only until we have arrived safely in my country. Then I will release you. You'll have a wonderful story to tell, Miss Starr. I'm sure your viewers will be impressed."

"And what of Agent Tanner, Mr. Mendez?"

"Once we are in Cuba, I will send word for him to be released as well."

Stacy looked at the succulent claw meat on her plate, then at Mendez. He smiled as he picked up her fork and handed it to her. "Dip the flesh in the melted butter . . . the taste is beyond description."

Stacy accepted the fork.

* * *

Virgil Washington knelt by the nude man lying on the deck. He felt the man's neck, checking for a pulse, and nodded. "He's alive, all right; his heart is beating okay."

Bonita averted her eyes from the naked man and looked at Ted as he took off his tanks. "My God, Ted, where did you find him?"

Ted handed his tanks to Ramon and tossed his night-vision goggles and mask to the cushioned seats. "They dropped him overboard. I just couldn't let him drown. The son of a bitch almost drowned me, though. When I got to him, he was almost gone. I put my regulator in his mouth and he clamped down on it so tight I couldn't get it out again. If Glenn hadn't come down to help me I'da been a goner for sure."

"How'd you get him back?" Ramon asked, taking Ted's weight belt.

"Glenn and I buddy-breathed off his regulator—it wasn't easy draggin' this bozo with us, I can tell ya. Virg, throw some cold water on his face and let's see if we can wake him up. Glenn, you and Ramon get the anchor up and get us out of here—put in where we were this afternoon."

Standing over the unconscious stranger, Baby sniffed his wet hair, then his face. Virgil bent over the man again. "Uh-oh, what we got here? Take a look at this scar on his chest . . . this guy is a vet."

Bonita leaned over. "He's got one on his forehead and arm, too—they both look recent."

"What d'ya mean he's a vet?" Ted said. He stepped closer.

Virgil motioned to the chest scar. "I seen scars like this before on the old-timers. This guy was in some shit. I bet he was in the machine."

"Christ'a'mighty, Bo, don't be lookin' at him. Get somethin' to put over him. Virg, the guy probably owed Mendez money or somethin'."

Virgil shrugged. "Whatever he did, he musta really pissed the man off."

"Just get the cold water like I said, and let's see if we can get him to come to."

"Ted, he's been underwater with you squids. I don't think more water is gonna do it. What made him pass out? I thought you said he was suckin' up all your air."

"He was, but I guess he ran out. We were almost here when he started kickin' and jerkin' and then he up and goes limp on us. I thought maybe he had a heart attack or somethin'."

"There's smelling salts in the first-aid kit; that'll wake him up." Virgil turned and walked toward the cabin.

Ramon stepped up beside Ted. "We got the anchor up . . . the dude come out of it yet?"

"He look like he's awake to you?"

Ramon stepped closer. "Check it out. Baby likes him; he's lickin' the dude's face."

Eli opened his eyes and stared into two huge black eyes. Something soft and wet stroked his cheek again and he turned slightly and could see the stars. Suddenly, dark faces appeared.

Ted leaned closer. "Just stay where you are and don't move, buster. Who are you and why were you on the yacht—you work for Mendez?"

Eli heard the words and couldn't help but smile. It wasn't a dream; he was really alive.

Ramon leaned over. "I think maybe his brain is fucked up—look at the shit-eatin' grin on his face. Lack of oxygen will do that, won't it?"

Ted tried again, and this time poked the man in the chest. "Hey, I'm talkin' to you. *Look at me!* Who are you and what were you doin' on the yacht?"

Eli kept his eyes on the stars as he savored each breath of fresh air he brought into his lungs. *I'm really alive . . . I'm lying on a boat deck . . . there are people and a dog beside me. The dog likes me. My God, those stars are beautiful . . . so beautiful.*

Bonita dropped a towel over his lower body and bent over

the man. "Mister, you want to sit up? Come on, I'll help you. There you go."

"Watch it, Bo!" Ted said.

"His hands are chained behind him with a bike chain, Ted. He can't hurt me. Come on, mister. Who are you?"

Eli looked into the angel's face and said in a whisper, "You're real, aren't you?"

"I'm real, all right. Look, we need to know who you are. Please tell us."

"I'm Eli Tanner—special agent, FBI."

Ted's mouth dropped open for a second before he quickly dropped to his knees, staring into the man's face. "No way. You're kiddin', right? Tell me you're kiddin'."

"Did you save me?"

"Just answer the damn question! You're not really a G-man, are you? Tell me you aren't."

"Yes, I'm a special agent. Thank you . . . I thought . . . I thought I was dead and—"

"Prove it!" Ted blurted. "Hell, you could just be sayin' it. Prove you're a damn agent."

"You can call the Miami office . . . ask for Agent Howard Parker. Or you could call the Atlanta office; that's where my SAC is. . . . I'm sorry, a SAC is the special agent in charge. I'm the resident agent in charge of the Columbus, Georgia, office but I work for the SAC in Atlanta, who is—"

"Shit!" Ted said, shaking his head. "I don't believe this! I should have let him drown . . . a damn FBI agent? I pulled up a damn fed?"

"Cool it, Teddy, you couldn't let him drown," Bonita said.

Ramon threw up his hands. "Great, just fuckin' great. Now what're we gonna do? This guy can make us all. We're screwed."

Virgil leaned over Eli with a glare. "Why was you on the boat? FBI or not, you worked for the guy, didn't you?"

Eli dipped his chin toward his ankle chain. "You think I'd be wearing these if I worked for Mendez? He had his people abduct Stacy Starr, Rita Lopez, a van driver, and me. His boys shot the driver and Lopez. He kept me alive to find out what I knew about . . . about . . . wait a minute. You're the ones he wanted to know about. Ma'am, are you Bonita Rogers? Yes, sure you are—you've dyed your hair—and you, you've got to be Ted, the pretend P.I."

Ted reached down and pulled Eli to his feet. "That's it, you're goin' over the side right now."

"Stop it, Teddy," Bonita growled. "Agent Tanner, you said they shot Rita and the driver. Where is Stacy?"

"On board. Mendez has her. He's going to kill her tomorrow along with a bunch of DEA agents unless you people free me right now."

Bonita looked into Ted's eyes. "Oh God, Teddy, I'm responsible for Stacy being on the boat. We can't let him kill her."

Virgil took hold of Eli's arm. "Ted, he's not going over— he's a fed—we're not killin' a fed."

Ramon threw up his hands again. "Great! Jus' fuckin' great! We're fucked. I knew it; we're fucked."

Eli spoke calmly. "Ted, I owe you my life. I don't know what you were doin' under that boat and I don't care. All I know is you did the right thing and saved me from drowning. Keep doin' the right thing and let me go and let me get my people in here so we can get Stacy and keep all those DEA agents from being killed. You let me go, I swear to you I'll never tell anyone about any of you."

Ramon shook his head. "You can't trust him, man. He's a fed."

Eli kept his eyes on Ted. "I give you my word of honor."

"Yeah, right," Ramon said. "He's gonna let us walk away from this? No way. Feds don't do that."

"It doesn't matter. The news lady is going to die anyway," Glenn said as he hopped down from the flying bridge. "I've heard most of it. Agent Tanner, you have a big problem. Even if Ted decides to free you and you talk to your FBI friends, who is going to believe you? And even if they do, by the time you mount a rescue operation, Miss Starr will be dead and Mendez will be out of the country. He has informers everywhere. Ask Bonita there. Ask her about the

DEA informer Mendez has. Hell, ask Ted and me. We know it for a fact. We lost six of our team members six years ago because a DEA fucker told Mendez we were doing an op. Free you? Sure, I believe you won't tell your friends about us, but it won't do you any good. Stacy Starr is as good as dead right now."

Eli looked at Virgil. "Let me sit down."

Virgil kept his grip on Eli's arm but walked him back three steps to the cushioned seats.

Bonita kept her eyes on Ted. "We can't let Carlos kill Stacy."

"Christ'a'mighty, Bo, how we gonna keep him from doin' it?"

"Do the operation tonight. He's there."

"We can't, Bo. Virg and Ramon need more time in the water; they haven't practiced with the demo boards and—"

"You were reconning the yacht, weren't you?" Eli said. "That's why you were under it."

Ted pointed his finger into Eli's face. "Saving your ass tonight was a big mistake. You just sit there and keep your mouth shut. You've screwed things up enough for us."

"Why? Why are you planning to kill him?" Eli asked anyway.

"Because he killed my team, that's why! Now shut the fuck up."

Eli nodded. "I'll help you do it."

"What?"

"I'll help you take out Mendez tonight."

Ramon rolled his eyes. "I'm not believin' this guy. Now he wants in. He's gotta have brain damage, man."

Ted took a deep breath and let it out slowly before speaking. "Thanks for volunteering but it's a no-go for tonight. There's no way we can do it without a bunch of rehearsals to get the timing right. We'll have to stick to the original plan and do it tomorrow night."

"Stacy will be dead, Teddy." Bonita began to cry.

"So will a bunch of DEA agents," Eli added. "Mendez has set up a Colombian to take the fall for the Senator

Goodnight assassination and the others he had killed. He has a couple of bombs hidden in the staging area for the assault on the Colombian's boatyard. He's going to blow those bombs at seven in the morning—Mendez told me before he had me tossed overboard."

"What about Stacy; when is he going to kill her?" Bonita asked.

"She dies tomorrow morning, too. Mendez wants her to see—wait a minute, that's it. The plant delivery."

"I told you he had brain damage," Ramon said. "He's talkin' crazy."

Eli stood. "Listen to me, Ted. Mendez told me that tomorrow morning he was expecting some kind of rare plant to be delivered to his estate. Don't you see? It's a way in. We find out who is delivering the plant, replace the driver with one of you, and the rest of us hide in the truck."

"They'd check inside the truck," Ted said.

"We take the checkers out quietly," Eli said. "It's going to be early; most of the guards will be sleeping. We'll have the element of surprise on our side."

Glenn stepped closer. "I see us getting in with the truck, but how do we get out? The dead guards will be found sooner or later. They'll just shut the gate and trap us inside the compound."

"By boat," Bonita said. "The back gate leads to the dock. I could be there waiting for you in *The Revenge*."

"Hold it, Bo," Ted said, lifting his hand. "This is crazy. We don't know anything about the compound. We don't know the number of guards, where they are, where Mendez will—"

"I know all those things," Bonita said. "I can draw you a map and tell you everything you need to know. You have to do it, Teddy. We can't let Carlos kill Stacy."

Ted began to speak, but Bonita turned to Glenn. "Once you're inside it should be easy. Only one shift of guards stays in the compound during the day, and half of them watch TV in the guard quarters. And all the security cameras are on the walls and gates to ensure no one gets in uninvited. There's no cameras inside the estate."

"When does the guard shift change?" Glenn asked.

"At eight in the morning. The guards and most of the house staff don't live in the compound. There's quarters across from the main house where the guards change into their uniforms, rest, and watch TV. At seven in the morning half of the shift will be sleeping in the quarters; the others rove the estate grounds."

"How many guards on a shift?" Virgil asked, stepping closer.

"Twenty. Ten will be sleeping; six will be roving in two-man teams. Three will man the main gate, and one watches the monitors in the security room in the gatehouse. The sleepers went off duty at midnight."

"How do you know so much about the guards?" Ramon asked.

"I walked the estate grounds many times when I got bored waiting on Carlos to come back from playing golf. I can count."

Ted growled. "Wait just a damn minute here! I'm runnin' this show and I don't think there's enough time to get a plan thrown together to—"

"It'll be a quick-strike mission, Ted," Eli said. "Mendez said he was meeting the truck to personally oversee the unloading; we don't have to go looking for him. We drive in, take out the guards, go to the greenhouse, take out Mendez, get Stacy, and run out the back gate to the dock, where we get away in this cruiser. It's the last thing they'd expect, we'd have surprise on our side. If we do it quick and quiet, we've got a good chance of getting out with no problems."

"Oh yeah, there's a problem all right," Ted said. "The problem is you. See, I don't get it, Agent Tanner. Why are you riskin' your life and your career on this? Everything you're talkin' about is illegal."

Eli looked into Ted's eyes. "Mendez was responsible for my partner's death when I was working out of Miami. And I also had responsibility for Stacy. It's my duty to get her back . . . I can't let them kill her. This is the only way to save her."

"What about those DEA guys Mendez is plannin' on blowin' up?" Virgil asked.

Eli nodded. "I need to make a call. We can't do this by ourselves. We need help, and I know two people who will help us. One will warn the right person to make sure the DEA agents get out in time. The other will find out who is delivering the plant in the morning."

"Whoa," Ted said. "These friends of yours know you were taken?"

"Yeah, of course."

"Where are they now?"

"Probably the Miami field office."

"Too risky, then. You callin' 'em, they're going to go nuts when they hear your voice. Glenn was right. Mendez has people everywhere. You have someone else outside the Bureau that can contact these two friends of yours?"

Eli began to shake his head but thought of someone. "I know somebody who will talk to them—better yet, I'll have the person pick them up and take them to the marina to meet me. I'll need to explain in detail what I need without getting them into trouble—they aren't like me. They need to stay clean of all this."

"How do you know they'll help you?" Glenn asked.

"They're my friends. They'll help."

Ted held up his hands. "Everybody shut up a second and let me think. . . . Okay, the way I see it there are three options. The first is to stick with the plan and do Mendez tomorrow night. If we do that, the agent stays tied up and we release him after it's over. It also means the Starr woman will most likely be dead along with the DEA guys. Option two. Try to go in tonight—I say that's not an option 'cause it's suicide, since half the team isn't ready for the mission. Option three is we do what the agent says. We use the plant delivery truck as a way to get inside the estate. The agent gets the Starr woman and we get Mendez. The problem with option three is time—we don't have much of it."

Ted looked at Glenn. "What option do you vote for?"

Glenn glanced at Bonita, then Eli. "I vote for three. Use the truck and get inside."

Ted turned to Virgil. "And you?"

"Three. It happens on dry land. I'm Army; I like the idea of not havin' to breathe through a hose."

"Ramon, which option?" Ted asked.

"I say there's a fourth option, man. We get the fuck outta here right now. Let the agent go, and let him worry about the news lady."

Bonita stared into Ramon's eyes. "We're responsible for her being on that yacht—we leaked information to her."

"We? *I* didn't give her anything—ahh shit, okay, okay, option three."

Ted faced Bonita, who nodded once. "You know my vote, Teddy."

Ted exhaled and set his shoulders. "Virg, get Agent Tanner out of those chains and find him something to wear. Glenn, take us to the marina. Bo, get the agent your cell phone and start drawin' us a sketch of the compound. Ramon, get below and start bringing up the gear we'll need. We'll need the commo gear, silenced Mac-10s and grenades, smoke for sure, and fragmentation. Let's move, people! We got an op to get ready for."

11:15 P.M., Miami FBI field office

In the corner of the operations room, Ed Faraday sat slumped in his chair staring at the distant wall as he held a cup of cold coffee. Beside him, Ashley leaned forward in her seat, her head resting on the table.

A woman walked up to the table and tapped Ashley's shoulder. "Excuse me, are you Agent Sutton?"

Ashley sat up and looked at the woman, who she judged to be in her late forties. She was wearing a visitor's badge. "Yes, I'm Agent Sutton."

The woman motioned to Faraday. "And is that Detective Faraday?"

"Yes," Ashley said.

The woman scanned the others in the room before lowering her voice. "I'm Alice Wade. Agent Tanner was my late husband's partner here in Miami. They worked the case on Mendez together. Would you two please meet me outside in the parking lot? It's not safe to talk here. It's about Mendez—I have information for you."

Ashley reached out for the woman's hand. "Mrs. Wade, I hate to be the one who informs you of this, but Eli has been—"

"I know about Eli, Agent Sutton. Please meet me. I'll be in a dark blue Ford station wagon parked in the first row, lower level. Please hurry; it's a matter of life and death."

The woman held Ashley's eyes for a moment, then turned and walked from the ops center.

Faraday set his coffee cup on the table. "What the hell was all that about?"

Ashley stared at the doorway the woman had passed through. "It was Eli's partner's wife—you see the look on her face?"

"What can she know?"

"She knew about Eli, and it hasn't been released to the press yet."

"Lopez could have told the whole world by now and we wouldn't know it, being in here."

Ashley stood. "Come on, let's go talk to her."

Ashley leaned over and looked through the open window at the woman seated behind the steering wheel of the station wagon. "Mrs. Wade, what did you want to tell us?"

The woman started the engine. "Please, both of you get in. I've been asked to take you to the marina to meet someone."

Ed Faraday shook his head. "Ma'am, just tell us what this is all about."

"It's about Eli. He's alive and safe. He called me about

forty minutes ago. He needs to talk to both of you; he needs your help."

Faraday put his hand on the butt of his pistol. "Lady, freeze. Let's see some ID."

The woman nodded. "He told me you wouldn't believe me, so he told me to tell you this, Detective. 'Ed, you barbecue rib–eatin' S.O.B., get in the damn car. You gave up your tickets to the Falcon game for this.'" The woman shifted her gaze to Ashley. "And he told me to tell you, Agent Sutton, he was wrong—you could give Miss Starr lessons on looking nice."

Ashley exchanged shocked looks with Faraday, then both grabbed for the rear passenger door handle.

Ashley and Ed got out of the car and stood in front of the wagon's headlights. Ashley searched the empty parking lot with her good eye, then shifted her search to the marina's docks. She saw a woman and a dog walking down the first pier but scanned past them to the boats rocking gently in their slips. The woman and dog passed beneath a pier light and Ashley saw that the woman had dark hair, as did the dog. She was about to shift her feet and look down the other piers, but the woman changed direction once off the dock and headed straight for them.

Faraday rested his hand on the butt of his pistol again and spoke in a whisper. "I don't like this. If she makes a sudden move I'll take her."

The dark-haired woman stopped ten feet away. She looked past the couple toward the road, then said, "It looks like you weren't followed. . . . Are you Agent Sutton?"

Ashley spoke warily. "Yes, who are you?"

"Bonita Rogers. Agent Tanner said you have been looking for me. Come on, he's waiting on the boat for both of you. Follow me."

Ashley wiped a single tear from her cheek as she stepped aboard the cruiser. He was standing on the deck with that irritating smile of his. Faraday grinned, hopped to the deck, and slapped Eli's shoulder. "God, am I glad to see you're still kickin'!"

Eli smiled but kept his eyes on Ashley as she approached. "Been a long day, huh, Sutton?"

Ashley stopped two feet from him. "You scared us, Tanner."

He lifted his arms. "Come here, you two." He stepped forward, hugging the couple to him. "God, it's good seein' you two again."

Bonita cleared her throat, then said, "Agent Tanner, we're on a time schedule, remember?"

Eli stepped back. "Look, I know you two have a lot of questions. Sit down. I have to make this quick. Like Miss Rogers says, we have a time schedule to keep to. First, let me tell you what happened, then I'll explain what I want you both to do for me. We don't have much time. . . ."

When Eli was finished explaining, Faraday rose from the cushioned seat. "I'll take care of my end, don't worry. I'll make sure Parker pulls the guys back. Maybe Parker's boys will find the bombs first and get 'em defused."

"It's got to be done quietly, Ed. Remember, somebody in the DEA is on this—the guy won't be in the staging area, that's for sure, so Parker has to ensure that the DEA boys don't get on their radios. If the informer finds out they're pulling out, he'll contact Mendez and tell him his surprise is blown. You and Parker can't let that happen."

"Got it, Tanner. I'll have Gus's wife take me to the staging area right now. Parker and I will take care of it."

Eli patted his friend's shoulder. "Be careful, Ed. I'll see you when it's over."

Faraday stepped to the pier and nodded. "Yeah, Tanner, when it's over." He set his shoulders and began walking down the pier.

Eli shifted his gaze to Ashley. "Call me as soon as you get the information—Customs will have records of the plant coming in from Papua, New Guinea—can't be that many shipments from there."

Ashley lowered her head. "Eli, I know why you're doing this, but it breaks all the rules. There's got to be another way."

"Don't you think I haven't tried to think of another way? I've run it over in my head a hundred times but it all comes down to Mendez killing Stacy if we play by the rules on this. It has to be this way. I'm sorry I'm involving you—just say you were following your senior partner's orders. I might be able to use the temporary insanity thing. God knows enough of them think I'm nuts. Just get me the info we need and make the call if you hear shooting. If there is a firefight inside the compound, we're going to need the cavalry, and fast. According to Bonita, we can hole up in the west wing of the main house, where we might be able to hold them off till the cops respond. Keep your distance from the gate but keep your ears peeled. You'll see us go in and—"

"I know, Eli. You told me. Be careful; I thought I had lost you already once today. I don't want to lose you again. I . . . I . . ."

Eli stood. "Time for you to get going. Here's the keys to Ted's van; it's there in the parking lot."

"No heroics, Tanner. Just get Stacy and get the hell out of there, promise me?"

Eli patted her shoulder. "I promise. See you when it's over. Just stick to your story and you'll be fine." He led Ashley to the pier and gave her shoulder a light squeeze. "I missed you, Sutton. See you later." He released her and stepped back onto the cruiser's deck.

As Ashley walked away, Bonita stepped up behind him. "You know she cares for you, don't you?"

"She's my partner—of course we care for one another, Miss Rogers."

"And I thought you FBI people were smart. If you can't see it's more than that, then I guess you're not only dumb but also blind. Never mind, Ted and the guys are waiting in the pickups with the equipment. All we need now is the information about the delivery. You think your partner will find out in time?"

"Miss Rogers, she'll get it. I guarantee it."

"It's after midnight. Where is she going to find somebody who will answer her questions?"

"She's FBI; she'll wake people up and get answers. Agent Sutton knows what to do."

Bonita leaned over and patted Baby's head. "Where were you staying in town, Agent Tanner?"

"Coral Gables Hyatt, why?"

"I . . . I don't want anything to happen to Ted. He thinks he can protect me from them. He can't. When this is over I'm going to turn myself over to you. . . . Ted doesn't know. Once I know he's safe, I'll sneak away from him and go to your hotel and find you."

Eli looked across the dark waters of the bay. "Did you kill those men at the lake cabin?"

"Yes, I shot two of them. I . . . I didn't want any of this to happen; you've got to believe that. I didn't want anybody to get hurt."

Eli turned and looked at her. "Miss Rogers, we'll talk about it when it's over. Getting Stacy comes first. It's time for me to join Ted; like he said, we have an op to run."

Aboard the *Princess*, Carlos Mendez took the wineglass from Stacy's hand. "It's time for us to depart for the estate."

"Oh no, I've had enough moving around for one day, thank you."

Mendez rose from the couch. "You'll love my estate, Miss Starr. I insist you accompany me, for I must be present for a very special delivery that arrives early in the morning."

"Mr. Mendez, I'm tired, and I'm still frightened of you despite your assurances. Please let me go to my room and sleep. Send for me tomorrow and I'll be most happy to accompany you to Cuba or anywhere else you want to go as long as you keep your word and release Agent Tanner and me."

"Come now, Miss Starr. I have no intention of sleeping alone tonight. We can—"

Stacy bolted from the couch. "Don't think for a moment I would sleep with you. I would rather sleep with a dog."

"I can arrange that, Miss Starr, if I am permitted to watch."

"Don't come any closer! Stay right where you are!"

Mendez stepped toward her. She grabbed the wine bottle by the neck from the table and smacked it against a corner, shattering the bottle. Backing up holding the jagged neck, she hissed, "Come near me, and I'll cut your balls off!"

Mendez smiled and snapped his fingers. Two of his body-guards stepped inside with smug expressions. "You see, Miss Starr, you will do nothing of the sort. Come, we must go, and we'll discuss this matter further in my bedroom." He turned to his men. "Please escort her to the craft."

Stacy stuck her arm out. "I'll die first, Mendez, you hear me! I'll slit my wrist right here and now if they come near me!"

Mendez wrinkled his brow. "Such a pity—I had hopes of videotaping our coupling. I would have thought you a realist, like the agent was."

"Was? You killed him? Oh God, no."

"Rogelio, bring her down to the boat once you take that ridiculous weapon from her. And give her a lesson for me."

Stacy spun around, but it was too late. A huge man grabbed her wrists. Another stepped up and knocked the bottle neck from her hand, then backhanded her across the face, knocking her off her feet.

Mendez sighed. "So much for my video. Perhaps tomorrow, after the delivery, she will be more accommodating. Rogelio, get a napkin from the table to stop her bleeding on my carpet . . . it is a Kabistan."

CHAPTER 21

2:00 A.M.

Parked in a lighted parking lot in front of a small boat dry-dock and repair company, Ted and Eli kept watch as Virgil and Ramon loaded bullets in Mac-10 magazines.

Ted handed Eli a silenced Beretta. "You'll need it."

Eli racked the weapon, chambering a round, and shoved the pistol into the waistband of the slacks Glenn had given him. He glanced at Ted. "Your teammate said you and him knew for a fact a DEA agent warned Mendez of your mission. What's your fact?"

Ted slipped a magazine into his Mac-10. "It was six years ago when I ran a SEAL team. We were doing some trainin' in Panama and got word to get ready for a secret joint op. A day later some high muckety-mucks in the DEA showed up and gave us a full dog and pony mission brief . . . showed us pictures of Mendez and explained how he was the honcho of a dope-smuggling organization. They yacked on about how important the op was because Mendez was going to be at the transfer site . . . they were going to catch him dirty and finally bring him down. They said Air Force aircraft had been keepin' track of a commercial fishing fleet out of Barranquilla, Colombia, that was fishin' the waters off Honduras and Belize. Only thing was, they weren't doin' much fishin'. Their intell guys said they were really haulin' Mendez's cocaine. The fishing boats, ten of 'em, were anchored in a protected bay in one of them little islands off the Honduran coast. They said Mendez had cruisers inbound to the

301

bay to pick up the stuff from the fishing boats. Ya see, the civilian cruisers were goin' to pick the stuff up and head for Florida. Once they got within six miles, Mendez had cigarettes pick up the dope from the cruisers and bring it in to places on the coast. Them cigarettes could outrun anything the feds had on the water.

"Anyway, the DEA told us Mendez was going to be personally overseeing the transfer because it was his biggest haul ever. The DEA guys gave my team the mission of sneaking in at night to the bay, IDing Mendez's cruiser to make sure he was there, and making sure he didn't escape when the Coast Guard made their raid the following morning. The plan was for us to disable his cruiser just before dawn . . . a small charge on the propeller. It would be a piece of cake for me and my guys. They flew us into Hondo for staging, and just minutes before we were to load our insertion chopper this DEA guy shows up and says our mission has been changed. He says Mendez isn't gonna be there after all and neither are the cruisers . . . they had anchored in a Belize port. Our job now was to sneak in, go ashore, hide out, and report the fishing crew's activity. He gave us a map and told us exactly where to go ashore and the place to hide out that would give us observation of the bay.

"It was a setup. That fuckin' DEA guy had to be Mendez's boy. We were choppered to within two miles of the island and did a water insertion . . . you know, jumped out of the ass end of the chopper with all our gear, including our Zodiac boats. Once we got on board the Z's, we headed for the island. We were usin' those new supersilent outboards. We beached our Z's on a tiny island in the mouth of the bay, hid them, then continued into the bay usin' our scuba gear. It was a good thirty-minute swim for us 'cause the bay made a dogleg right. We surfaced about 0200 hours close to shore, and guess what? Cruisers were everywhere. I signaled my team ashore and was tryin' to break out my radio to report the cruisers when wham, the whole shoreline seemed to explode all at once. I'm not talking about a pop here and a pop there; it was a slew of automatics that opened on us. When they hit us we were in knee-deep water—we didn't have a chance. Barry went down, then Wendall. Tommy was next, shot in the gut. He screamed and kept screaming as Paul dropped, tryin' to help him."

Seated in the back of the pickup, Glenn nodded solemnly. "I still hear his screams, and Andy's, too. He was hit right after Paul bought it."

Ted lowered his head. "I got hit in the leg. Glenn and Gee pulled me back into deeper water. I didn't want to leave my guys, but . . . but they were past needing help."

Eli looked up at Glenn. "You sure the DEA agent set you up?"

"There was at least a mile of shoreline around that bay. We could have gone in anywhere—and yet they were waiting at the exact spot where he told us to go in. He set us up, all right. Tell him the rest, Ted."

Ted sighed and glanced toward the road entry into the parking lot. "The DEA said there was never a mission change. I told 'em bullshit, the agent came and told us there was. They said what agent? They showed us pictures, but none of them was him. When we couldn't point him out, they figured we made up the story to cover our fucking up the operation. We didn't fuck it up . . . that hippie-lookin', cigar-chompin' son of a bitch set us up."

Eli's jaw muscles tightened. "Cigar-chompin'? What'd he look like?"

"It was dark when he came into the staging area; we were adjusting our eyes for the op, usin' red-filtered lights so as not to screw up our night vision, but I know he was average height and had a scraggly beard and mustache. He also had this half cigar in his mouth the whole time he talked to us. He never lit it. I know 'cause he stood right beside me when he gave me his map and told me where we were supposed to go ashore. He was using a red-filtered light, too."

"You ask him for ID?"

"Christ'a'mighty, he walked into our staging area, which was inside a fenced-in Navy base. Nobody walks into a base without being checked. . . . I assumed he had been ID'd. I was busy tryin' to get ready to load our gear in the chopper, remember?"

"And you gave his description to the other DEA people who questioned you?" Eli asked.

"Of course we did!" Glenn snapped, leaning over the side of the pickup. "Trouble was, we didn't talk to the DEA people until two days after the ambush. Ted, Gee, and me were all that was left of the team, and we'd all taken hits—we barely made it to that island where we left the Zodiacs. None of us could get one into the water—we stayed the rest of the night watching those cruisers and fishing boats unass the bay. Coast Guard came in the next morning, found us, and evacked us to the Hondo military hospital. It took another day before the DEA people came around asking what the hell happened."

"Could the beard and mustache have been a disguise?" Eli asked.

Ted shrugged. "Could have been . . . like I told you, it was dark."

Eli took the cell phone Bonita had given him from his pocket and quickly began pushing keys.

"What are you doin'?" Ted asked.

Eli lifted the phone to his ear. "I'm going to tell my detective friend your story. I think I know who your DEA informer was. . . . Ed, this is Eli, listen very carefully. . . ."

Several minutes later Eli closed the cell phone flap. Ted was staring at him. "You really think it could be him?"

"I don't know, but Ed will find out soon enough. Ed says the guy is there at the staging area. If he makes some excuse to leave before seven A.M., then we can be pretty sure he knows about the bombs."

The cell phone rang in Eli's hand. He answered with a simple "Yeah?" He listened for a full minute without saying a word and finally said, "Good work; see you there." He closed the flap and looked at Ted. "The plant arrived on a flight from Sydney an hour ago. Customs has already cleared it and sent it to the U.S. Agricultural Department holding area. It's six miles from the airport on Palmetto Way . . . I know where it is. Hold it, there's more. The company picking up the plant is called the Tropic Zone Import Company. Agent Sutton is already at the Agricultural Department's holding area and says the company has been notified and is having a truck make the pickup at 0600. There's some good news for us. The plant is big; it's actually a small tree of some kind, so they'll need to bring a good-size truck to haul it. The other good news is that Sutton talked to the department inspector. He says the company has picked up plants before for Mendez. The company usually sends a driver and a helper. The driver collects the papers and pays the department's charges for inspection, handling, and storage."

Ted stood and smiled. "Looks like we're in. Saddle up, time to ride."

4:15 A.M.

Special Agent Howard Parker and Detective Ed Faraday stepped up into the back of the semi trailer that was being used as the DEA command post.

Standing only a few feet away, DEA Agent Sam Ortiz turned away from a map posted on the trailer wall. "There you are, Howard. I was looking for you earlier. Take a look at this map and I'll go over how we're going in."

Parker walked to the map. Ortiz took the unlit cigar from his mouth and used it as a pointer. "We're going to make a simultaneous strike. The units here in the staging area will move into assault position close to the boatyard at 0645 hours. At the same time my Bravo unit will move into position around the Terres estate down here in South Miami. Choppers will come in at exactly 0700 and lay down a cloud of persistent gas. Following the smoke birds will be two assault birds with teams on board that will rappel into the boatyard and onto the main building's roof. At the same time we've got a ram truck that will speed in and bust open the chain-link fence gate to allow the ground units entry. We'll have snipers in position and spotters for the ground units. It'll be over in a couple of minutes. The same goes for the assault on the estate; it's the same basic plan but the estate grounds are smaller and will take even less time . . . they won't have time to shit their pants."

Parker studied the map a moment before speaking. "You pinpoint where Miss Starr and Agent Tanner are being kept?"

Ortiz used the cigar and pointed at a hand-drawn map pinned next to the bigger map. "Based on the body-heat scan, we're pretty sure they're here in the boatyard supervisor's office. The scan showed two hot spots side by side. Other hot spots are here just outside the office door. We're sure it's their guards."

Parker raised an eyebrow. "You're going to run both missions from here?"

Ortiz motioned to a seated man behind a radio. "Bill is going to run the boatyard mission from here. I'm going to be with the Bravo unit at the estate. I want to make sure we get Terres alive."

Parker raised an eyebrow. "You guys in the DEA sure run things different than we do. The AIC always stays with the majority of his men. How many in your Bravo unit . . . twenty or so? You've got at least thirty here, not counting what's coming in on the birds."

Ortiz stuck the cigar back in his mouth. "I run it my way, Parker. We need Terres alive."

"Yeah, and I want Starr and Tanner alive, Ortiz. Seems to me your priorities are screwed up. The hostages come first."

"We'll get them, Parker, don't worry. You can go in with the assault team if you want. I'm sure my people can find you a gas mask and a vest."

Parker gestured toward the door. "Come outside a minute and let me show you something. Detective Faraday walked around your staging area earlier and found something you need to see."

"I don't have time; I've got a mission to—"

Faraday stepped behind Ortiz, stuck his snub-nose .38 barrel in his back, and whispered, "Look natural for your boys and just walk to the fuckin' door. You're gonna make time. Move it."

Once outside in the darkness, Faraday cuffed Ortiz's right wrist, swung it back, and cuffed his left. Parker knocked the cigar from Ortiz's mouth with one hand and with the other slapped a piece of tape over his mouth. He then grabbed his arms and shoved him toward a parked car beside the trailer. Faraday opened the rear door, pushed Ortiz inside, and followed him in. Parker got in behind the wheel and started the engine. He backed away from the trailer and weaved his way through the DEA vehicles until a chain-link fence came into view in the headlights. Stopping the vehicle, Parker turned and held up a small black box with a digital display.

"You know what this is? It's the device somebody was going to use to blow the thirty pounds of C-4 we found in the side panels of that rusted abandoned van over there beside the fence. It's really a neat device . . . it had wires attached to it that led to a blasting cap stuck inside a block of the C-4. Sam, you wouldn't know anything about this device, would you?"

Faraday reached over and pulled the tape from Ortiz's mouth. "Yeah, Sam, you wouldn't know about that thing, would you?"

Ortiz growled, "I don't know what you're talking about. What the hell is going on? What is this?"

"Funny, I thought you'd say that," Faraday said as his head bobbed. "Well, I got news, Sammy boy. We know you know. We did some checking on you. You know that young guy, the Colombian you said the cops found in the Dumpster close to the restaurant? Guess what? The body ain't in the city morgue. We talked to the morgue guys, though. They say a guy was brought in from a Dumpster, all right, but he was in his forties . . . and he didn't have any Lancero tattoo like you said he did. You figured since you were runnin' the show nobody would check you out, didn't you? Wrong. So, Sammy boy, looks like we got you. Now me and

Agent Parker here been askin' ourselves how we should handle this. We thought maybe we should do the right thing and turn you over . . . but then there's that assassination of the senator to think about. His family we gotta think about, too, and the others your friend knocked off to protect himself. It was the family that made it easy for us. Guess what? We decided not to turn you over. We got somethin' better in mind. Show him, Howard."

Parker turned the car around and drove in the opposite direction across the parking lot.

Ortiz blurted, "You two are certifiable. I don't know what in the hell you're talking about. I didn't have anythin—"

Faraday slapped the back of Ortiz's head. "Shut up and enjoy the scenery. We'll let you know when you can talk. Oh, look, Sammy boy. Look at that old boat up on stilts just beyond that chain-link fence up ahead. By the way, you're sick, came down with somethin' real sudden . . . at least that's what Agent Parker is going to tell your boys. Your second in command is going to take over. In about twenty minutes your second in command is going to be called by your boss and told to put the operation on hold and fall back to another staging area. Guess where you're going to be? Yep, you guessed it. You're going to be right here in your car, lying in the backseat, and the car is going to be parked next to the chain-link fence. . . . Yeah, beside that old boat."

"You can't do this to me!"

Faraday slapped the man's head again. "I didn't tell you it was time for you to talk."

Parker pulled in beside the fence, turned off the engine, and turned in his seat. "I'm sure if we told your people you'd sold them out they'd do a lot worse to you. Detective Faraday and I are giving you and your agency a way out of embarrassment. Gosh, we didn't know there was another bomb, did we, Ed?"

"Heavens, no, Howard, we didn't know. We were worried, though, when we found the one in the abandoned van, and pulled everybody back just in case. . . . Oh damn, we didn't check Sam's car, did we? Oops, we thought somebody took him to the hospital. Too bad about that. That bomb inside that old boat was made really good, too. Had bags of nails lining the inside hull, then the C-4 was laid in blocks over the bags, kind of like a giant claymore mine. Guess ol' Sam never felt a thing. I hear all they found of him wouldn't even half fill a sandwich Baggie. Real shame."

"You're wasting your time; you're not scaring me," Ortiz said. "I don't know what you're talking about. I just know you both are in big trouble."

Parker said, "You hear that, Ed? He says *we're* in trouble."

Faraday patted Ortiz's shoulder. "Attitude, that's your problem, Sammy boy. I saw it right off when I first met you. You got a real attitude problem . . . holier-than-thou type, ya look down your nose at everybody. And you know what else? You're dumb. You thought you could get away with it. Dumb, really dumb."

Parker got out of the car and opened the back door. Faraday shook his head. "So *we're* in trouble, huh? I guess that means you're really in some deep shit, then, Sammy boy. Not talking anymore, huh? I understand. I'd be thinkin' about all those nails, too. Okay, time for me to go . . . oh, I almost forgot."

Faraday suddenly grabbed Ortiz by the back of the head and slammed his head forward into the back of the front-seat headrest. Pulling the stunned man back, he slammed his head forward again, then pushed the dazed man to the car floor. Parker slipped a plastic tie around Ortiz's ankles as Faraday took off the handcuffs and replaced them with another plastic tie that, once tightened, could only be removed by cutting it with a knife or scissors. Faraday wrapped another tie around the front-seat floor mount and passed it through the tie around Ortiz's wrists. Finished tightening the plastic band, Faraday patted Ortiz's face. "Sick boy, you're all set for the big boom."

Parker taped Ortiz's mouth, then set the small black device on his chest. "Take a look at the digital readout. It's counting down the time for you so you know when to shut your eyes before the boat bomb goes off."

Parker then hissed, "This is for Gus, and everybody else you sold out. Burn in hell." He shut the car door and joined Faraday. The two men exchanged nods and began walking toward the distant trailer.

Parker slowed his steps after ten paces. "You think he knows we disarmed it?"

Faraday shook his head as he kept walking. "Uh-uh . . . he pissed his pants while I was tying him to the mount. I figure he'll be Jell-O in another few minutes."

"You goin' to tell me how you found out he was dirty?" Parker asked.

"I told ya."

"No way you just had a hunch and checked the morgue for that body . . . it was something else. Come on, who told you he was dirty?"

"I told ya, Howie. It was a hunch."

"Well, how about using your hunching ability and telling me where to find Starr and Tanner."

"I told ya Agent Sutton was working it—but hers ain't a hunch . . . she calls it *intuition*. She'll call if her *intuition* checks out."

Parker halted and took hold of Faraday's arm. "You two are hiding somethin' from me. What is it?"

"Ah, now, Howie, we wouldn't do that. You'd better get goin' and get his DEA bunch stood down before they really screw things up by shootin' up the wrong people. I'm gonna borrow your car and see if I can help Sutton with her *intuition*."

Parker released his grip. "If I find out you two were holding out on me, I'll . . . I'll kick your ass, Detective."

Faraday held out his hand. "Give me your keys, and pray her intuition is right."

U.S Department of Agriculture, Miami office

In the driveway behind the building, Ashley handed Eli his ID wallet. "I forgot to give you this when I saw you last. It's a reminder, Tanner, of who you are and who you represent."

Eli took the thin wallet. "I told you there was no other way to do this, Sutton. Stacy was my responsibility . . . it's my duty to get her out of there."

She held his gaze for a moment before motioning to the lighted loading dock behind her. "I've got it all set up. The inspector thinks we're working a drug case. Once the Tropic Zone people sign the paperwork, pay their fees, and load the plant, I'll do my act. You and that bunch behind you stay out of sight until I have the inspector ask the driver and his helper into the back room for my questioning. If they're wearing some kind of special company clothing, I'll bring their clothes out to you along with the plant's papers."

Ted stepped up behind Eli. "Thanks for helping us, Agent Su—"

"Shut up and step back," Ashley snapped. "Your deal is with Tanner, not me. I don't want to see your face or hear your voice. Get the others away from the light, too." She gave Eli a one-eyed glare. "I just hope you know what you're doing. Ed called just a while ago and said it *was* Ortiz, just like you thought. Parker is taking care of him and has the DEA operation on hold. Ed is on his way here. I'm going inside again and talk to the inspector before the delivery people get here. I'll signal you when you can come in." Ashley softened her stare. "Damn you, Eli Tanner— make sure you don't get yourself killed." Turning, she strode toward the loading dock steps.

"She always that bitchy?" Ted asked as he stepped up beside Eli.

"She's not a morning person. Come on, we'd better get the vehicles out of sight and get ready."

Five minutes later, after moving the vehicles, the team sat leaning up against the outside back wall of the Department of Agriculture building.

Virgil leaned forward, looking at Eli in the darkness. "You a vet, aren't ya? I saw that scar a' yours on your chest—ya get that in Grenada or Panama?"

"Vietnam," Eli said. "I was with the 101st Airborne in seventy-two."

"I knew it," Virgil said with a smile. "I knew you'd been in the machine. I'm ex-Army, too, SF."

Ramon slapped at Virgil's shoulder. "Why don't ya jus' give him your Social Security number while you're at it. He's a *fed*, man."

Virgil slapped Ramon's shoulder in retaliation. "He's a vet first—he's a brother."

"You two sophisticated guys cool it," Ted snapped. "Keep focused on the op. Let's go over it again. Virgil, tell us your part one more time. Picture the sketch Bonita made for us and talk us through it so I know you've got it down."

Virgil closed his eyes, trying to remember the drawing. "We go down the drive and come to the first gate. There's a speaker box there and a security camera. I say we're there for the delivery of the plant. The gate slides back and we drive about forty feet to the next gate. Two guards will come out of a small side gate. They'll be carrying poles with mirrors attached and will check under the truck for bombs and shit like that. They'll check me and Ramon out and will want to see what's in the back of the truck. I get out and walk back to the rear of the truck and unlock the back door. Soon as I open it, Ted and Glenn take the two guards out. As they're doin' that, Ramon goes in the side gate and goes into the gatehouse; the panel is on the left. He hits the green button to open the gate, then walks into the security room and takes out the guy monitoring the compound's security cameras. Ramon gets back in the truck with me and we drive through the gate into the compound.

"The main house is on our left; guards' quarters are on the right. The chopper pad is just beyond it. We watch for the three pairs of roving guards Bonita says are always walking the grounds. We drive around to the far side of the main house, the west wing. The greenhouse sits alongside the wing. I back up to the greenhouse, stop, and Ramon and me get out. Mendez should be there and probably all four of his bodyguards. I give the paperwork to Mendez while Ramon is opening the back. He opens it and Ted, Glenn, and Agent Tanner are standin' there holdin' Macs with a drop on everybody. I grab Mendez. Ramon grabs me a Mac from the back of the truck, and he grabs the sniper rifle. He gives me the Mac and then he goes straight to the rear gate that leads to the dock. His job is to hold the gate for us. If the news lady isn't with Mendez, the rest of us move everybody inside the greenhouse and get Mendez to tell us where she is. The agent goes and gets her. Once he has her, we take her and Mendez out through the back gate and radio Bonita. She brings in the cruiser and picks us up and we take off."

Ted nodded. "Good, you've got it. Glenn, tell us what happens if we get in a firefight."

Glenn looked up at the stars. "If it turns to shit, we toss smoke grenades to hide us while we make for the rear gate. Ted and I will stay to cover the rest of you. Once you're through the rear gate, we'll take up position just outside the gate and cover while everybody runs down to the dock, where Bonita will come in with the cruiser. Virg shoots up the cigarettes at the docks to make sure none of them can be used to follow us. Ramon uses the sniper rifle to cover Ted and me while we head for the docks."

Eli leaned forward. "Remember, if it turns bad before I find Stacy, I'm staying. I'll take my chances on Agent Sutton getting the cops to the compound."

"You won't have much of a chance," Ted said.

"And Stacy won't have any chance at all," Eli responded.

Ted shrugged. "Your funeral. Okay, I think everybody's got it. Remember, we plan on something going wrong, so Glenn and I will be wearing packs full of claymores and grenades. While we have everybody in the greenhouse, Glenn sets up the mines just in case. And remember, too, once we have the drop on them, everybody puts on their radio headsets. Bonita will have hers on in the cruiser, and I'll tell her when to head in for the docks."

Ramon leaned forward. "Any chance there's guards on the docks?"

"Bonita said they monitor the docks with a security

camera, remember? With Mendez bein' at the estate, nobody should be in the cigarettes, either. But just in case, if Bo says she sees people, she'll tell us on the radio. Ramon, you'll take them out with the sniper rifle."

Ramon nodded. "Piece of cake, man."

Glenn motioned at the approaching headlights of a white panel truck. "Show time."

CHAPTER 22

6:30 A.M., Mendez estate, Key Biscayne

Holding a cup of coffee in one hand, Raul knocked lightly on the bedroom door with his other hand. He knocked again, opened the door, and entered the huge room.

Mendez sat in a wing-back chair putting on his socks. "Good morning, Raul. I trust you slept well?"

Raul set the coffee cup on the table beside his boss. "It's early for me, Colonel. The delivery company called a few minutes ago and said they will be here at seven as promised. I also checked in on Miss Starr. I'm afraid her lip wound opened again during the night and is quite swollen. She is very distraught."

Mendez stood and slipped his feet into tasseled loafers. "She is a disappointment to me. I would have thought a woman in her profession would have been more accommodating. No matter, I'll not let her spoil my morning. Have Arturo stay with her in her room. Once the delivery is made, tell Arturo to take her fishing. . . . He'll also need to collect the FBI agent from beneath the *Princess*. Drop both their bodies into the Atlantic for the stone crabs. Come, I have time for breakfast before my new child arrives."

Raul smiled as he walked alongside his boss toward the door. "The DEA is in position to assault the Colombians. It won't be long, and they will no longer be a problem for us."

Mendez clapped his hands. "Excellent, it is a fine morning indeed."

* * *

Holding her breath, Ashley drove past the stucco-walled estate as Faraday shook his head. "It's a damn fortress. How's Tanner gettin' in there and out alive?"

Ashley continued down the road. "He says they have a plan. He wouldn't give me any details except for needing the truck." Slowing, she made a turn, stopped, backed up into a driveway, and pulled forward again. In seconds she was back on the road, heading toward the estate again. A quarter mile from the compound she pulled to the side of the road and rolled down her window. "Now we're supposed to wait. Once the delivery truck gets in—and that's a big *if* in my book—we're supposed to listen for gunfire. If we hear shooting, we're to call the local police and tell them we hear shots being fired inside the Mendez estate, then hang up. That's all he wants us to do."

Faraday rolled down his window and let out a sigh. "He's in way over his head on this. He say why he's doin' it?"

"Yeah, I asked him. He said it was his *duty*. Starr was his responsibility, he says, so he has to get her out of there."

"She might already be dead. He'd be puttin' his life on the line for nothing."

"He thinks she's alive, Ed. You know him; it's like talking to a rock when his mind is made up."

"What about the others who are with him? What's their reason?"

"I don't know, and I didn't ask, but I think they want to take Mendez out for personal reasons . . . it's a vendetta of some kind."

"How many of them are there?"

"Four plus Eli are going in."

"Four? Look at the damn place! It's huge! Mendez must have guards and dogs and no tellin' what else in there for security. Tanner must not have seen what he was up against. Four people and him . . . uh-uh, no way."

"He said they had a plan."

"Yeah, they got a plan, all right. A plan to get themselves all killed. Come on, Sutton, you think they have a chance?"

Ashley looked at her passenger. "They have Tanner."

"Yeah, and he's eaten up with the duty-and-honor thing. It's going to get him killed. The hell with waiting for the sound of gunfire. If the truck makes it through the gate, we're callin' right then and tellin' the cops all hell is breakin' loose over there. It's goin' to take some time for the cops to react, but at least they'll get here sooner and give whoever's inside a reason to worry. You agree? We call as soon as the truck makes it in?"

Ashley motioned up the road. "We're going to know if it makes it in real soon. Here it comes. Get ready to make that call."

Seated behind the steering wheel, Virgil glanced at his passenger. "That's it just ahead."

"I see it, man. Be cool."

"I'm scared shitless, Ray—sorry, but I am."

"No sweat, man. I ain't goin' to let nothin' happen to you. We're sophisticated rich guys now. . . . Think of all them ladies we're goin' to score, man."

"Yeah, the ladies." Virgil turned into the short drive and came to a stop in front of the gate. He rolled down his window and looked into the security-camera lens as he pushed the button on the speaker box. Immediately a voice said, "We been expectin' you. Drive in."

The gate began sliding back and Ramon smiled. "A piece of cake, man."

Virgil shifted into first and rolled through the gate.

In the back of the truck Ted brushed the leaves of the plant away from his face and stepped toward the back door. Holding a silenced Mac-10 in his hand, he glanced at Glenn beside him. "Team Two-two is back, Glenn. This is for them."

Glenn nodded as he raised his Mac. "For them."

Holding the Beretta Ted had given him, Eli stepped up beside the two men and said to himself, *This is for you, Gus.*

Virgil slowed as they approached the second gate and brought the vehicle to a gentle stop. Two men dressed in khaki uniforms opened a side gate and walked toward the truck.

"Where's their poles with mirrors?" Virgil asked out of the side of his mouth.

Ramon whispered, "Be cool; they're smilin' at us."

Both guards approached Virgil's side of the truck. The bigger of the two men motioned with his hand. "The man be waitin' on you. Go on." The gate began sliding back.

"This ain't the way it's supposed to go," Virgil whispered. "You gotta get inside the gatehouse."

Ramon whispered back, "Don't move." He opened his door. "Hey, amigos, I gotta take a shit first. You gotta john in the gatehouse?"

The big guard motioned again. "The man waitin'; go on."

Ramon hopped to the ground and hunched over. "I'm in pain, man; you ain't gotta john, I'm gonna shit over there by the wall. Ya got some paper?"

The two guards exchanged looks before the bigger guard nodded. "We got a john. We show you."

Ramon waited for the two men to step in front of him before he dug into the crotch of his pants and pulled out the silenced Beretta. He stepped up behind the bigger guard, placed the fat silencer against the back of the man's head, and squeezed the trigger. As the guard fell, Ramon took a step sideways, aimed, and squeezed the trigger again. The weapon coughed and sent a bullet into the side of the second guard's head. Stepping over the bodies, Ramon hurried through the small gate and entered the gatehouse. A guard sitting behind a console rose from his chair, trying to get his pistol from his holster. Ramon shot him in the face, then spun and fired at another guard, who had just poured himself a cup of coffee from a Mr. Coffee machine on a table. The coffee drinker grunted as he twisted around. Ramon shot him again as he hurried past into the security room. A wide-eyed young guard sat behind a bank of security TV monitors. He reached out to slap a red button on the console. Ramon fired from the hip and the young guard's head snapped back, then rolled forward. He sat perfectly still, as if he'd fallen asleep. Ramon turned around, walked back into the other small room, and studied the console a moment. There were two green buttons and two red. Not knowing which green button would open the second gate, he pushed both and ran for the truck.

Virgil put his radio headset on and spoke into the small mike in front of his lips. "Ray is back, the gate is open, and we're movin'. I'm takin' off the headset now."

In the back of the truck, Ted relaxed his taut shoulders and turned to Eli. "Ramon had to modify the plan a little. The guards were going to pass us through without checking the back. Ramon got inside anyway and took out the guards watching the monitors. We're back on track."

Outside the compound, Ashley had driven up closer to the estate to see if the truck had made it through the second gate. Parking on the side of the road opposite the front entrance, she exchanged looks with Faraday, seeing that both gates were open and the white truck was rolling forward into the estate's grounds.

Faraday lowered the cell phone. "The cops should be here in a couple of minutes. Looks like they can pull right in as long as nobody shuts those gates."

Ashley closed her eye for a moment, speaking to herself. *Come on Eli, do it and get out safe . . . come on. Do your damn duty and get out of there.*

At the entrance to the greenhouse, Carlos Mendez smiled as the white panel truck approached.

Raul glanced at his watch. "Colonel, our surprise for the DEA should be going off in seconds. We might be able to even hear it from here."

Mendez ignored him as he stepped out and patted the shoulders of his two bodyguards. "Stand back so I may see my new baby when they open the back of the truck."

Both men backed up and joined the other bodyguard, standing at the entrance of the greenhouse.

Looking into his side mirror, Virgil backed the truck

toward the greenhouse and whispered, "There's two guys in suits. Which one is Mendez?"

"Don't worry about the suits . . . worry about them three big guys behind them. They're carrying. And we've got two security guards walkin' up on my side . . . rovers come to see the show."

"Ooh shit. What are we goin' to do about the rovers?"

"Be cool. I'll take care of them."

Virgil braked, turned off the engine, and took a deep breath. Taking the clipboard from the dash, he exhaled slowly and opened his door.

Stepping to the crushed oyster-shell drive, he smiled and walked toward the two men in suits. "As promised, we're on time. Who is Mr. Mendez? I need a John Henry for the tree."

Ramon was already at the back of the truck and took hold of the latch.

"A tree?" Mendez said, stepping forward with a scowl. "It is not a tree. It is a—"

Ramon swung both doors back, ducked, and pulled his pistol from inside his shirt, aiming at the closest uniformed security guard, who, with his other rover, had stepped closer to see what was in the truck. "Don't move, either of you!" Ramon barked.

Standing in the back of the truck with a Mac-10 in his hands, Ted barked, "Freeze! Don't anybody move!"

Flanking Ted, Glenn and Eli both held identical weapons and had their pistols in their waistbands. They swung their Mac barrels left and right, covering the five men they could see. Glenn commanded, "Raise your hands so we can see th—"

The bodyguard closest to Mendez grabbed for the machine pistol inside his jacket. Virgil saw the movement and dived to the ground. Ted fired a short burst that sounded like dull thunks. The bodyguard's face and neck sprouted crimson mush as he jerked back and fell. Behind him greenhouse glass shattered from stray rounds. The bodyguard on the other side of Mendez ducked down and pulled his automatic. Glenn fired, stitching the crouching man from thigh to neck, knocking him back. With a sickening high-pitched shriek, he crashed through the lower greenhouse glass and wood frame. As more glass fell and shattered, the remaining bodyguard charged toward the truck like a maddened bull, but Ted squeezed off another burst and the wild-eyed man staggered under the impact of bullets that tore into his chest and shoulders. His eyes lost focus, then rolled upward as he crumpled to the ground.

Raul Ortega stood in openmouthed shock, afraid to move. Mendez had sunk to his knees and was staring at Eli in disbelief.

Ramon approached the two roving security guards. "On your faces! Now! You want what they got? Do it now!"

Ted hopped to the ground and commanded, "Virgil, get your Mac and watch those guards for Ramon. Ramon, get the rifle and get to the rear gate. Glenn, get out the claymores; somebody's bound to have heard that damn glass shattering."

Eli had already hopped to the ground and jerked Mendez to his feet. "Where is Stacy?"

"Y-You. No, it can't be you."

"It's me, all right. Where is Stacy? Where is she?"

Mendez closed his eyes tightly and shook his head from side to side. "No, no, this cannot be happening."

Ted stepped up and backhanded Mendez across the face. "Where is she?" he hissed.

Mendez reeled from the blow and sank to his knees. Eli jerked him back to his feet. "Talk!"

Mendez's eyes opened but were unfocused. Ted wrinkled his nose and slapped him again. "Shittin' your pants ain't goin' to help you! Where the hell is she? Talk or I'll blow your fuckin' balls off right now!"

Bleeding from the nose and mouth, Mendez suddenly stiffened, staggered back a step, and fell like a tree face first onto the pavement.

Ted viciously kicked him in the thigh. "Don't faint on me, you son of a bitch!" Bending down, he pulled Mendez onto his back and was about to slap him when Eli grabbed his arm. "Look at him; he didn't faint—he's having a stroke."

Ted grabbed Mendez's lapels, jerked his limp body up to a sitting position, and yelled into his pale face, "You can't do this! I'm going to kill you, ya bastard! You can't die on me!"

Eli turned and pressed the silencer into Raul's forehead. "You'd better know where she is!"

"Up . . . upstairs, se-second floor, third room on the right," he stammered.

"Show me," Eli said as he grabbed Raul's arm and pushed him toward the entrance.

"Down!" Virgil yelled as he threw himself to the ground and fired toward the guards' quarters.

Eli pulled Raul down just as bullets zipped overhead and struck the greenhouse windows that were still intact.

Glass fell like rain, shattering again on the pavement as Virgil and Glenn rose to their knees and fired their entire magazines toward the half-dressed men streaming from the building fifty paces away.

Ted leaned over Mendez, holding the barrel of his Mac against his head. "Look at me, damn you! You killed them and now you're goin' to pay! Look at me!"

Eli grabbed Ted's shoulder. "Ted, he's dying! You gotta have the team cover me. Stacy is inside the house!"

Ted squeezed the trigger and held it back for a full second, letting the weapon buck in his hand. Splattered with blood, he lowered his Mac and stood looking into what was left of Mendez's face. Turning slowly, he wiped his eyelids of the blood and barked, "Glenn, smoke and frags! Virg, you and me cover Tanner when he tries for it."

Taking cover behind the truck's right rear tires, Glenn was already pulling grenades from his pack as bullets hit the truck like hailstones. He pulled the pin on a fragmentation grenade, tossed it underhand toward the guards' quarters, and immediately pulled the pin on a smoke grenade. "Wait till the smoke builds to make a run for the house entrance!" he yelled.

Above the din of incoming fire, wide-eyed, Raul screamed in Eli's face, "You'll get me killed going that way! There's another entry into the house through the greenhouse! I'll show you!"

The first grenade exploded with an ear-shattering *crack*.

Eli yelled to Ted, "He says there's a way inside through the greenhouse. Cover us!"

Kneeling beside Glenn, Ted slapped in a fresh magazine and yelled to Virgil, "Ready?"

"Ready!"

Ted nodded, then he and Virgil rose, took a step out from the protection of the tires, and fired toward the guards' quarters.

Eli pulled Raul to his feet and, hunched over, both men ran toward the greenhouse door.

Outside the compound, sitting in the van, Ashley winced and shut her eye, hearing the shooting and the second loud cracking explosion.

Beside her, Faraday slapped the dash. "Christ, it sounds like World War Three in there! Where are the cops?" He suddenly pulled his .38 and reached for the door handle.

Ashley grabbed his arm. "Don't be a fool!"

"I can't sit here and do nothing!"

Ashley released him and turned the ignition key. "Hold on!"

"What the—"

Ashley floored the accelerator; the van spun in the gravel for an instant before shooting forward onto the road. She made a hard left, crossed the other lane, and barreled down the drive, through the open gate.

Inside the compound, Ted kneeled alongside Glenn as he inserted a fresh magazine. "Glenn, their firin' is slackin' off . . . the smoke is workin' for us."

"It's the grenades that's got them shook up. I figure no more than six or seven are left that are makin' a fight of it. The rest are dead or hiding."

Ted spoke into his mike. "Ramon, you in position?"

Thirty yards away, hidden by hedges and huge ferns,

Ramon spoke as he knelt by the open rear gate. "That's a roger. It's clear and so is the dock. I can see it good from here. Your lady is on her way into it—about four hundred yards out. You get him?"

"Roger, he's history. We're waitin' on the news lady."

"Roger, I'll be waitin'."

Another grenade exploded, sending a tremor through the pavement. Virgil ducked down after tossing another. "Not many heroes over there, Ted. They don't know shit about fire and maneuver."

"Just keep tossin' them grenades and keep 'em down, Virg," Ted said. "They'll be gettin' over the shock soon enough."

Holding her issue Sig Sauer nine millimeter in the ready position, Ashley knelt behind the van parked to the right of the second gate. She peeked around the corner of the van and ducked back. "I see two bodies by the small gate."

Faraday peeked around the other side. "I can only see thirty yards into the compound. Green smoke is covering what's going on. You mind telling me why you drove in here like that?"

"We have to make sure the gates stay open for the cops. I'm going to make a run for the small gate. There's got to be a control panel inside the gatehouse. Cover me."

"Hold it! In that smoke, we don't know who the good guys and bad guys are. Just stay where you are. The gates are open; the cops can get in just fine."

Ashley rose. "Can't chance somebody closing them. Cover me." She broke into a run, jumped over the bodies, passed through the gate, and flattened herself against the outside wall next to the gatehouse door. She took in a deep breath and was about push off the wall when Faraday rushed past her and entered the gatehouse in a shooter's crouch. She followed him inside. Both had their weapons held in both hands and turned left and right, searching for a threat. Ashley looked past the dead men sprawled on the floor and nodded to the open door leading to another room. Faraday nodded, motioned to himself, and whispered, "Cover me."

He entered slowly and seconds later backed out. "It's clear . . . one body. It's the security room."

Ashley nodded to a closed door leading out into the estate grounds. "They'll have to come through there to—"

The door suddenly burst open and a khaki-uniformed man holding a pistol rushed inside. Ashley screamed, "Freeze! FBI!"

The startled guard turned to fire, but Faraday fired first and kept firing until the guard fell. Shaking, Ashley watched the man in disbelief as he squirmed on the floor, making a sickening gurgling sound. She looked up, raised her pistol, and fired at a second guard who appeared in the doorway. Lifted off his feet, he fell backward with arms extended, like a kid making a snow angel.

Faraday pushed Ashley out of the way, kneeled in front of the door, and yelled above the sound of an explosion: "They were trying to get out of here! They must be losing the fight!"

Inside the house, Eli held Raul's arm tightly as he walked him down the upstairs hallway. "Is anybody with her?" he asked in a whisper.

Raul pointed ahead. "There . . . she's in there. Arturo is guarding her."

Eli lifted his pistol. "You're going to yell toward the door, 'Arturo, take the woman to the dock; we're escaping.' You got that?"

"Yes."

"Good. Now once you yell it, back against the wall and squat down. I'm going to be right behind you, so don't try anything funny. Okay, yell it out."

"Arturo, bring the woman; come quickly, we're escaping . . . take her to the dock!"

Several long seconds passed, then the door opened. A large man holding a machine pistol stepped out and froze, seeing Eli pointing his pistol at him. "Don't move!" Eli said.

Arturo tried to duck back inside but Eli's bullet tore through his cheek and out the back of his jaw. He fell backward while spasmodically jerking the trigger of the machine pistol. The spray of bullets ripped into the hallway ceiling, the doorjamb, then the bedroom ceiling as he collapsed on his back.

Eli stepped through the doorway while putting a single bullet into the bodyguard's forehead. Looking up, he saw her sitting up in bed, staring at him in disbelief. For a split second he didn't recognize her; she seemed to have aged twenty years, and her upper lip was blue-black, split, and swollen to the size of a golf ball.

With tear-filled eyes Stacy raised a trembling hand and spoke. "I . . . I thought you were dead."

"Me, too," Eli said as he hurriedly strode toward her. "Come on, let's get out of here."

A metallic click sounded behind him. Eli spun and fired. Raul jerked back and fell on his buttocks with a stunned expression. The machine pistol of the dead bodyguard thumped to the floor, and Raul slowly lowered his eyes to his own chest, to the small hole in his left breast. He tried to lift his hand to touch it, but toppled over on his side, his head on the carpet, his open eyes fixed and lifeless.

Eli took hold of Stacy's arm. "Come on, get to your feet."

"I . . . I can't," she said, beginning to sob.

He leaned over, propped her on his left shoulder, and rose. "We're going to make it. I promise. Hold on tight to the back of my trousers . . . we're goin' home."

In the gatehouse, Ed Faraday canted his head. "About damn time! That's sirens I hear."

Ashley turned and looked out the back door. "They're coming through the first gate. . . . I'm goin' out and show my ID and stop them from going in. They'll need a Tac Team to go in."

"Have 'em keep their sirens on," he said.

Glenn heard the sirens and turned to Ted. "We have to get out of here right now!"

Ted spoke into his mike. "Tanner, where are you?"

On the first floor at the bottom of the stairs, Eli spoke into his mike. "I've got her. You all get out. I hear the cop sirens . . . we'll be okay. Get out."

Ted said, "We still got that deal?"

"I made you a promise," Eli said. "Go."

Ted rose and barked, "Glenn, you and Virgil get to Ramon . . . I'll cover."

Glenn shook his head. "I'll cover! You and Virgil go."

Virgil yelled: "Bullshit, you squids go. I'll cover!"

"Fuck it! We're all goin'!" Ted said, pulling the pin of an incendiary grenade. He tossed it into the cab of the truck and broke into a run.

Glenn and Virgil fired off the rest of their magazines toward the guards' quarters and broke into a dead run, following their leader.

The police officer lifted his megaphone mike. *"This is the Dade County police! Throw down your weapons and walk out of the smoke toward the front gate! You are surrounded! This is the Dade County police. . . ."*

Faraday stood back from the officers and looked at Ashley. "Are you the praying kind?"

Ashley nodded and closed her eye.

Faraday lowered his head. "Me, too."

As Ramon saw Ted and the others running toward him, he glanced over his shoulder toward the bay and froze. *No. Mother of God, no!*

Out of breath, Ted came to a halt beside the kneeling Cuban, who pointed toward the distant yacht anchored in the bay. "I just saw it—it's heading for Bonita."

Glenn and Virgil halted by the gate as Ted grabbed Ramon's sniper rifle. A cigarette boat was racing across the water toward *The Revenge*.

"Oh, Christ, where'd it come from?" Glenn asked.

"It came from the other side of the yacht," Ramon said. "I never saw it until it—"

Ted fired.

Virgil shook his head as he pushed Glenn forward. "Ain't gonna hit nothin' at this range. Come on, let's get to the dock and get us a cigarette and stop 'em!"

Glenn, Virgil, and Ramon were already running down the covered walkway as Ted resignedly lowered the rifle. The cigarette was within fifty yards of the cruiser, and he could see puffs of smoke coming from the weapons the three men on board were holding.

The green smoke had turned to a fine mist as members of the SWAT team cautiously moved forward. Ahead of them a fire roared and sent flames skyward, where they were lost in a thick black boiling cloud. Ashley moved to the right. Her line of sight no longer blocked by the SWAT team members, she saw that it was the panel truck burning. To her right lay the bodies of four guards. The windows of the guards' quarters were shattered, and SWAT officers were escorting khaki-clad men in handcuffs. To her left the entry of the huge main house was open and other officers were leading out staff members, maids in white uniforms, and men dressed in black trousers and white shirts. She paused and searched their frightened faces for a moment before spotting Faraday at the door. His look made her lower her head.

He stepped up beside her. "They've cleared most of the house. Doesn't look like they're in there, but there's two dead guys upstairs . . . both from gunshots. One is in an expensive suit; his ID says he's Raul Antonio Ortega. The other was ID'd by a maid as one of Mendez's bodyguards. They found blood on the pillow and sheets in the bedroom where the bodies were found—the blood was dry and didn't come from the dead guys. Maids weren't allowed upstairs this mornin' so they don't know who was in the room."

Faraday paused, took a breath, and let it out. "There are more bodies ahead but they're too close to the burning truck to check out. We'll have to wait until the fire department gets here." He put his arm around her waist. "I'm sorry, Ashley, I—"

"Hey, that's my partner! Get your rib-eating paws off her!"

Ashley and Faraday looked up at the front door. Eli smiled tiredly as he followed a SWAT officer down the short flight of steps. Behind Eli another officer held Stacy in his arms.

Ashley wiped the tears from her cheek and strode toward him. "You're a bastard, Tanner! Why didn't you yell or break a window and wave a sheet or something to tell us you were all right? Huh? Why didn't you?"

"My hands were full, Sutton."

Ashley glanced at Stacy as a paramedic took her from the officer's arms. "She all right?"

"No, but nothing time won't heal." He stepped closer, patted Faraday's shoulder, and took Ashley by the arm. He whispered, "I got a story cooked up. You two haven't seen me till right now. I was moved here with Stacy from the yacht last night . . . got it?"

Faraday glanced around before replying in a whisper: "How you goin' to explain what happened?"

Eli shrugged. "I don't know what happened . . . I was locked away in the greenhouse when I heard shooting. The two guys guarding me ran out, and I went looking for Stacy. That's all I know. Must have been competitors of Mendez that made the hit . . . decided to take him out. Lucky for Stacy and me, huh?"

"What's Stacy know?" Ashley asked.

"Nothin'. She thought I was dead . . . she didn't see a thing except me deal with the two guys upstairs. I'm goin' to say I snuck up on 'em and took one of their weapons. I did good."

"Yeah, a regular hero," Ashley said, glaring at him. "You done now, Tanner? You finished with your *duty*?"

Eli looked toward the burning truck. "Yeah, Sutton, I'm done."

A police officer walked up to Ashley and pointed skyward. "Agent Sutton, our chopper has spotted two boats behind the estate in the bay not far from the docks. The spotter says there are bodies in the water by one of the boats."

Ashley asked, "What kind of boats are they?"

"A cruiser and a cigarette, ma'am. The spotter says he sees three bodies in the water. We've cleared the grounds, so if you want, you can walk down to the docks. The rear gate is back there about forty yards. Just make a wide detour around the burning truck . . . it's hotter than hell even within a hundred feet of it. Coast Guard is on the way to pick up the floaters."

Eli had already broken into a run toward the docks.

A Bell Ranger helicopter settled down to within a few feet of the shoreline, and Agent Howard Parker jumped from the skid to the beach. The chopper immediately lifted and shot forward over the bay. Parker walked up to the pier and stopped beside Ashley and Faraday. "Where is he?" he snapped.

Ashley motioned to the approaching small Coast Guard cruiser. "He went out to check the bodies. They found a survivor."

Parker saw the waiting paramedics standing by and looked out at the bay. "I heard the report about there being two boats. . . . I see the cigarette but I don't see the small cruiser."

"It sank," Faraday said. "Happened just five minutes ago. Tanner and a couple of the Coast Guard guys were on board and got off just before it went down."

Parker stepped closer to Ashley. "How'd you know Tanner was here? And don't give me that crap about it being intuition."

Ashley shrugged. "I had a hunch, then."

"That's not going to cut it, Agent Sutton. I want answers."

"You've heard the best answer you're likely to get, Agent Parker. Back off. You know I never believed this was a Colombian deal."

Parker turned as the Coast Guard cruiser bumped against the dock tire bumpers. Standing on the deck, Eli squatted down and picked up a wet dog wrapped in a blanket. He stepped onto the pier, holding the limp animal. "He's been hit in the back," he said to a paramedic.

The medic shook his head. "We don't take animals."

Eli growled, "You will this one. He's a material witness. Get him to a vet. Now!"

Parker flashed his ID to the still skeptical medic. "Do it. Get going and call the FBI office when you get there. And it'd better be quick."

The paramedic took the animal as Parker smiled and patted Eli's shoulder. "Sure good to see you . . . I thought I'd never see you alive again."

Eli returned the shoulder pat. "Good to see you, too, Howie."

"What did you find out there?"

"Three of Mendez's guards," Eli said. "I figure they were from the yacht and when they heard all the shooting got in their cigarette and took off to see what the problem was in the estate."

"What about the cruiser that sank?" Parker asked.

"Howie, this is pure speculation on my part, but I think at least a part of the crew that made the hit on Mendez was probably trying to make good their escape in the cruiser. The guards in the cigarette saw them and fired them up. When we got to the cruiser, she was about gone, but we did see blood on the deck; the guards sure hit somebody. We were about to reboard, but I heard a whimpering and found the dog in the cabin, barely able to keep his nose above water . . . poor mutt was in the middle of it. I'm thinking there was another boat with other hitters who came to the rescue of the cruiser crew. The cigarette was shot to hell and so were the bodies. By the number of shell casings in the cigarette, it must have been some shootout. Obviously the rescuers won—they killed Mendez's people and got their dead or wounded off the sinking boat."

Eli turned and scanned the bay. "There must be five, maybe six hundred boats on the bay right now. . . . We're not going to find the hitters anytime soon."

Parker stepped closer to Eli. "Can you describe any of the hitters?"

"Didn't see any of them." Eli kept his eyes on the bay. "I was being guarded by two of Mendez's boys. When the shooting started, the guards left me to go protect their boss. I got the rope off they had me tied up with and went looking for Stacy. By the time I found her it was over and they were all gone. At least I think they're gone . . . maybe they left some dead behind in the estate, I don't know."

Parker motioned to Ashley. "Your partner says she had a gut feeling you were here—you were lucky."

Eli faced Ashley, looking into her unbandaged eye. "I've always considered myself lucky having Agent Sutton as a partner—she's the mother-hen type . . . tries to keep me out of trouble."

Parker patted Eli's shoulder again. "I'm going up to the house to take a look at those bodies and see if Mendez is one of them. Stick around; I want to ask you some more questions later."

Ashley waited until Parker was out of hearing, then lowered her head. "You think the guys in the speedboat killed Bonita?"

"I don't know." Eli shook his head. "But it doesn't look good for her. There was blood all over the deck, and she wouldn't have left the dog if she'd been conscious. I figure Ted and the others got in a cigarette and went out to exact some revenge on the shooters. They got them, all right, but it was a helluva fight."

"You think Ted has Bonita's body?"

"She wasn't on that boat. I checked. I saw the dog in the cabin but he appeared dead. Only when we were about to leave did I hear him whimpering. The water must have revived him when it flooded the cabin."

Ashley looked at the billowing dark cloud forming over the estate before lowering her head. "Poor Bonita . . . I guess Mendez won after all."

Eli shook his head. "Nobody won . . . everybody lost."

Faraday placed his hands on Eli's and Ashley's shoulders.

"Talking about losing reminded me of something. Agent Sutton, I know somebody you made a promise to. I think you'd better get goin' . . . you wouldn't want somebody else to do it."

Ashley's eyes narrowed. "Thanks for reminding me. . . . See you two later. I have business to attend to." Setting her shoulders, Ashley strode up the walkway.

With a loud pop the smoking motors stopped. His hands sticky with blood, Glenn let go of the wheel of the shot-up cigarette and looked out at the open sea. Virgil patted his shoulder. "You tried, Glenn. How's your arm?"

Glenn glanced at the bullet gash across his forearm and turned, looking at the two men lying on the deck. "I'm okay. How're they doing?"

Virgil lowered his head. "They'd both make it if we could just get 'em to a hospital. I stopped Ramon's sucking chest wound . . . lucky for him he's unconscious now. Ted's just lost too much blood. He should have never helped us search for Bonita."

Glenn got up and leaned over Ted, looking at the bullet hole in his stomach. He took Ted's hand into his own. "It's over, Ted . . . the motors are shot. I'm sorry, buddy. Looks like this is it."

Ted rolled his head back and forth and spoke weakly. "I killed her, Glenn . . . I killed her. I shoulda never let her go with us."

"She loved you, Ted. She wouldn't have left you."

Ted closed his eyes. "It wasn't what I thought it would be, Glenn—killing him didn't feel good. It was all for nothing. . . . Oh God, Bonita, I'm so sorry . . . I'm so damn sorry."

Virgil poked Glenn's shoulder and pointed. "We got a cigarette coming up fast toward us."

Glenn picked up his Mac from the deck. "I guess this is it, Virg."

Virgil slapped in his last magazine and released the charging handle, chambering a round. "I guess it is, Glenn.

Never thought I'd buy it in a damn boat, though. Guess it's okay—at least my mama won't have to worry about no funeral expenses."

Glenn flicked off his weapon's safety. "Better wait till they get close. I've just got what's in the mag, and it's not much. I've got a frag left—I'll save it for us. I don't want them to get Ted and Ramon."

"That's okay with me. If I'm still standin' just let me know; I wanna shut my eyes and pray a little."

Glenn stood erect and watched the boat approach with his finger resting lightly on the trigger. Suddenly the sleek maroon cigarette slowed and a man climbed up on top of the bow deck with a bullhorn.

"Glenn, it's me, Gee. Do you need help?"

Glenn smiled and tossed his Mac overboard. He climbed up to the bow deck and began waving his arms.

Virgil canted his head. "Who the hell is Gee?"

"An angel!" Glenn shouted. "An ugly squid angel!"

Rita Lopez dropped her TV remote when she saw who opened the door and stepped inside the hospital room.

Ashley walked slowly to the bed. "I guess you didn't pray hard enough—I'm back. Miss Rita Lopez, I'm arresting you for obstruction of justice, conspiracy, and one count of murder in the third degree. You have the right to an attorney. If you cannot afford an attorney you . . ."

As Ashley spoke she took out her handcuffs and slapped them on Rita's wrists. After Mirandizing her, Ashley picked up the remote and tossed it to the floor. "You'd better call your hairdresser and makeup lady; you're going to be making the news instead of reporting it."

Ashley leaned over and whispered in Rita's ear, "By the way, Mendez is a crispy critter—he won't be paying for your lawyer." Ashley stepped back and opened the door. Two agents and a police officer walked in, followed by an orderly pushing a gurney.

Ashley faced Rita again. "We're moving you to a room across town that has bars." She motioned to the television screen. "Don't worry, I saw it, it's a repeat. The good guys win. Get her out of here before I puke on her clean sheets."

It was almost midnight when Genesse walked into the small, dimly lit room.

Glenn and Virgil rose from their chairs.

Genesse nodded. "The doc says they're both out of danger."

Glenn lowered his head. "Thank God."

Virgil looked past Genesse. "Can I see Ray?"

"Sure, but he's sacked out."

"That's all right—I'll just sit with him awhile."

When the black man left the room, Glenn raised an eyebrow. "You're taking a big risk doing this, Gee."

"Risk? Naw, you guys took the risk. I had a couple guys watchin' the yacht. When Mendez's boys fired up your cruiser, they contacted me. Good thing my guys followed you and kept me informed by cell phone or I never would have found you."

"What about the doc and this place?" Glenn asked.

"No sweat, Glenn, relax. The doc owes me a favor, and nobody lives near his old house. Tomorrow I'll have my guys drop by a big van, a nice one with a foldout bed. The doc will tell ya what to do as far as how to take care of Ted and the little Cuban until they're on their feet. He says a couple of weeks for the Cuban and a little longer for Ted. The bullet just missed his kidney. He was lucky."

Glenn shook his head. "He wasn't so lucky, Gee. He and Bonita got tight and—"

"I know," Genesse said. "He told me a few minutes ago. It don't figure, you know. A guy like Ted and a broad like that."

"She was no broad, Gee. She was a lady—Ted had a good thing going with her."

Genesse put his hand on Glenn's shoulder. "I'm sorry I couldn't have been there when you iced that bastard. At least it's finally over."

"Maybe for you and me it's over, Gee, but for Ted it's just

begun. He loved Bonita. He never said it, but I know he did. It'll never be over for him."

Genesse's hand slipped from his former teammate's shoulder. "I gotta go, Glenn. I won't be seein' you again. Take care, huh?"

Glenn forced a smile. "Thanks, Gee, for everything. Team Two-two was together again, at least for a while. Mendez finally paid."

Genesse nodded and walked toward the door.

It was just past midnight when Ashley heard the door open. Eli entered the hotel room, shut the door, and froze, seeing Ashley seated on the bed.

She got up, took a bottle of iced beer from the bucket on the nightstand, and handed it to him. "Sit down, Tanner. It's wind-down time."

Eli screwed off the top, looked at the bottle a moment, then took a long drink. Lowering the bottle, he sank onto a chair. "God, I need this—thanks for remembering about my wind-down thing."

She sat on the bed again. "Sorry, I looked for a Garth Brooks tape and a Walkman, but Miami isn't into country music. Couldn't find his tape with 'The Dance' on it."

Eli put the cold bottle against his forehead. "You tried, Sutton, that's what counts. You get Rita put away?"

"Yeah, her station came up with a lawyer, but once they heard the facts they withdrew him. Seems they don't like her as much as they thought. What about you? You been to the hospital?"

"Yeah, the dog is goin' to be okay. The vet says the bullet missed the spine. Poor mutt is goin' to lose a rib, but otherwise he's goin' to be fine."

"Tanner, I wasn't talking about the dog. I was talking about Stacy. You go by and see her?"

"I'll do it tomorrow."

"You went by to see the dog but not Stacy?"

"The dog liked me, okay? We kind of hit it off."

"Are you sayin' you and the news lady didn't hit it off out there?"

"It's wind-down time, Sutton. No more questions."

Ashley lowered her head. "So it really was duty . . . I thought maybe you put it on the line for her because you—" She stopped herself, reached out, and touched his hand. "Take another drink, Tanner. I have some bad news for you."

Eli shifted his eyes to her. She rose from the bed and walked to the window. "The Coast Guard found one of Mendez's cigarette boats in the mouth of the bay about three this afternoon. It was shot up very badly. From the blood found in the boat, we think the people who had been inside were wounded severely or had been killed. No bodies were found, but the Coast Guard is still searching. Parker is working it. He thinks whoever was in the boat transferred to another. He's checking the hospitals for people admitted for gunshot wounds."

Ashley turned from the window. "I'm sorry, Eli, it doesn't look like Ted and his team made it—you were right; everybody lost."

Eli leaned forward and stared at the bottle in his hand. "I guess I should retire, Sutton. I broke all the laws I swore to uphold. I lied to Parker and will have to keep on lying. It's not my style. I never liked liars, and right now I don't care for me very much." He got up slowly from the chair and sank down onto the bed. "I'd like to be alone, Sutton."

Ashley was searching for the proper words when someone knocked on the door.

Eli tiredly shook his head. "I don't want to answer any more questions. Do me a favor and tell 'em I took some sleeping pills and sacked out."

Ashley walked to the door and opened it a crack to see the visitor. She took a step back in shock. *Oh, God.*

At Ashley's silence, Eli rose and walked toward the door just as Bonita entered the room.

CHAPTER 23

Looking as if she'd gone through a car wash in a convertible, Bonita hobbled across the room and fell back on the bed.

Eli closed his open mouth and sank down in a chair, still not quite sure whether to believe his eyes. Ashley stood over the prone woman. "My God, Bonita, how . . . how'd you get away?"

Bonita kept her eyes closed and didn't move as she spoke. "I saw the speedboat coming. I cut the engine and ran down into the cabin to get a gun . . . then everything seemed to explode in little pops around me. Baby whined . . . poor Baby . . . he didn't understand why he was dying. He lay there looking up at me. So pitiful . . . so helpless, then he was gone . . . just laid his head down and—"

"How'd you get off the boat?" Ashley asked, pressing the woman as tears formed in the corners of Bonita's eyes.

"They kept shooting and I knew I had to get out. I crawled out of the cabin onto the deck. I could hear them circling and firing. I began crawling around the side of the cabin and saw one of Ted's scuba tanks. He had used it the day before and it was still rigged with the regulator. I thought maybe I had a chance. When they were on the other side of the boat, I jumped overboard. Oh, God—I was so scared . . . I couldn't see anything. I kicked and fought to stay under but it was like a giant hand was pushing me up. I finally got the regulator in my mouth and that helped. Once I didn't have to hold my breath, I managed to stay under. God, the noise of that boat passing over me . . . it was like nothing I've heard before. I knew the propellers were going to tear into me any second . . . it was all going to be for nothing."

Ashley sat down beside Bonita as she continued. "When I heard that horrible sound going away, I put on the straps of the tank but didn't know which direction to go. Everything was just a blur without a mask. I told myself to be calm and think. Then I saw it . . . the brightness. The sun, I guess. I knew it rose in the east and that was the way to shore. I headed for the brightness."

Ashley patted Bonita's hand. "Go on. You got to shore, then what?"

"I made it, but not to shore. . . . I knew I was heading back in the direction of the estate. Once I got close to shore I headed south, and kept going until I ran out of air. I got rid of the tank and kept going south, keeping my head just above water, and walked along the bottom. My feet . . . my feet hurt so bad. Finally I saw some people on a small beach, a family. I came ashore and told them I fell out of my boat and would they please take me to a gas station so I could call my brother. They were nice people . . . tourists from Maryland. They insisted on taking me home. They wrapped my feet in towels and drove me to the safe house off Dixie. I soaked my feet . . . and decided I'd still do what I told Agent Tanner I would. . . . I'm turning myself in."

Eli rose and took another bottle from the ice bucket. He put the beer in Bonita's hand. "Baby is okay," he said.

Bonita shot upright. "What?"

"Your dog is okay. I found him in the cruiser before it sank. He's at a vet."

Bonita covered her face. "Oh, sweet Jesus, I thought he was . . . oh, God, I left him, I left him." She suddenly lowered her hands. "Ted? He and the team made it out, right?"

Eli exchanged looks with Ashley before he wrinkled his brow and lowered his head. "They made it out of the estate okay, Bonita, but they went after the guys that fired you up. We don't know for sure what happened, but it doesn't look good. The Coast Guard found the cigarette they used. It was shot to hell and the blood inside says most if not all of them were probably hit. I'm sorry."

Bonita's chin dropped to her chest. Slowly, she fell back on the bed and covered her face with her hands again. "No . . . sweet Jesus, no."

Eli put out his hand to Ashley. "You have the keys to Ted's van."

Ashley raised an eyebrow. "Yes, but why?"

"Give them to me."

Ashley looked at him a moment before leaving the room. She came back a minute later and handed them to him. Eli sat on the bed beside Bonita. "Bonita, it's over. Mendez is dead. It's not going to happen like you thought. His people won't keep looking for you. He was the glue that kept his organization together. They'll be in a fight for what's left and they won't think twice about you. If you change your name and move out west, you won't have any problems making a new life. You have someplace you can go?"

Bonita spoke between sobs. "Ted . . . Teddy told me . . . to go to Kansas if something happened. He had a friend there who would take care of me for a while."

"Take the keys and go there, then. Agent Sutton will tell you where the van is. Get in it and go."

Ashley eyed Eli, but he lifted his hand. "I made a promise to Ted and I'm keeping it. Get up, Bonita . . . go start a new life."

Bonita gazed at Eli. "I don't care anymore, Tanner."

"You will," he said. "Scars heal." He took her hands and pulled her to her feet. "Agent Sutton will give you my phone number in Columbus. In a month, call me. I'll have your dog and ship him to you. I'll also tell you everything I've found out about what happened to Ted. Come on, you have to go now. Agent Parker could come over at any time. Agent Sutton will walk you to your van."

Ashley took Bonita's arm and led her to the door. Bonita stopped and looked over her shoulder at Eli. "Why . . . why are you doing this?"

"Like I said, I made a promise . . . a life for a life. Ted

gave me a second chance at life, and now I'm giving you that chance. It's his gift to you. Take it."

Bonita lowered her head and walked out the door with Ashley.

Eli lifted his beer bottle toward the empty doorway and whispered, "I hope you can find happiness."

Ashley walked back into the room and saw him sitting on the chair with his eyes closed. She sat down on the bed across from him. "She's gone, Tanner."

He nodded in silence. Ashley fell back on the bed and looked up at the ceiling. "She had two million dollars under the backseat of the van, Tanner. Two million."

"Nice way to start over, huh?" he said.

"She wanted to give me a million . . . a million dollars. I refused, of course . . . I didn't even look at it, just shook my head and told her to go. Jesus, Tanner, a million dollars."

"You're a good agent, Sutton."

Ashley turned her head, looking at him. "And you're a good agent, too, Tanner. Just so you know . . . I would have done the same thing if I'd been in your shoes—let her go, I mean. It had to end, and this was just as good as anyplace to start. You did the right thing."

"I hope so, Sutton. It felt right, anyway."

"Your gut tell you it felt right?"

"Nope, my heart."

Ashley sat up and took his hand. "You have a good heart, Tanner, a good strong heart. It's what I like about you."

Eli squeezed her hand. "Thanks, partner. I like your heart, too."

He rose, sat on the bed beside her, and kissed her forehead. "I never kissed a partner before, but it's my way of saying thanks."

He leaned over, laid his head on the pillow, and shut his eyes. "I gotta sleep now, Sutton. Turn the light off when ya leave, okay?"

Ashley rested her head on the other pillow and closed her eye, savoring the feeling of his kiss. "Sure, Tanner, you sleep now . . . I'll turn it off." She began to get up but her heart told her something else. She smiled to herself, leaned over, and turned off the light. Pulling up the blanket, she rested her head again on the pillow and closed her eye again. After a few minutes she knew he was sleeping soundly, and put her arm over his chest and snuggled closer. *Don't worry, Tanner,* she said to herself. *I'll be gone when you wake up. It's a new start for me, too . . . a new start.*

CHAPTER 24

One month later, Saturday, Columbus, Georgia

Eli opened his apartment door and Baby scampered past him and shot out the door. "Damn, Babe, just knock me down, why don't you? Hey, get back here!"

Eli watched as the golden dog ran down the walkway with his nose to the pavement. "Those squirrels been in the flower beds again, huh? Yeah, you sniff 'em out and scare 'em back to their trees."

Eli walked to his pickup and unlocked the door. Baby was back at his feet when he opened it and bounded up into the seat.

"Nope, we're not going anywhere, buddy; just got to get this paperwork here. Don't give me that look. Uh-uh, get out. I've got work to do. Come on, I'll give you a treat once we're back inside."

The dog hopped out and ran for the open door of the apartment. Eli smiled. "You sure know what 'treat' means. Okay, I'm comin', I'm comin'."

Holding the folder with his request for retirement, Eli left the pickup and walked back toward his apartment. Reaching the doorway, he was about to enter when he felt something hard press against the small of his back. A voice said, "Don't move."

Eli slowly raised his hands. "What do you want?"

"Christ'a'mighty, get your hands down."

Eli turned and gasped.

Ted smiled and lowered his crutch. "No, it ain't no ghost. It's me, your old teammate. How you doin'?"

"Jesus, Ted. I . . . I thought you were—"

"Naw, almost, though . . . nearly lost my left kidney. The worst is over now. All of us made it. Damnedest thing, that dog of yours looks just like—"

"It's him, Ted."

Ted eyes widened. "It can't be . . . I saw him layin' on the cabin floor when me and the guys searched for Bonita."

"It's him, Ted. I took him from the cabin before the boat sank. I would have thought Bonita told you."

Ted's eyes narrowed. "What the hell you talkin' about? You sick or somethin'? You know Bo is gone to her maker."

"No, Ted, she's alive. She went to Kansas just like you told her."

Ted was staggered. "A-Alive . . . she's alive? It can't be . . . I searched the cruiser for—"

Baby came out the door wagging his tail and jumped up on Ted. Eli smiled. "Come in, Ted, come inside and let me tell ya how she escaped. You'll be proud of her; she used your scuba gear and—"

Ted shook his head and began hobbling backward. "Bullshit, 'Come inside.' I'm goin' to Kansas."

Eli stepped out and caught Baby's collar. "Take him with you."

Ted looked at the dog, then at Eli. "You saved him, Tanner—a life for a life, remember? I saw and heard you talkin' to him. Everybody needs somebody, and I can see you got that somebody right there. I gotta go, Tanner. I got me a somebody in Kansas. Oh, and Tanner—the reason I came was to thank ya. We were a team, Tanner . . . a real team. I won't forget you."

Eli nodded. "Yeah, Ted, we were a helluva team. Go on; go find her."

Minutes later Eli sat on his couch with Baby beside him. He stared at the phone in his hand and finally started pushing keys. Putting the phone to his ear, he waited a few moments while he heard the rings. "Come on, be there . . . please be— Hey, Sutton, it's Tanner; whatcha doin'? . . . Nothing? Good. Why don't you come over here and let's cook some steaks on the grill, then how about us takin' in a flick . . . I know I haven't asked before but somethin' just happened, Sutton. The day just became brighter and I feel great. Come on over and let me tell ya all about it. I . . . I don't want the feeling to end. . . . Will ya come over? I want to share this wonderful day with you . . . No, I'm not sick, damnit! I . . . I'm trying to tell ya I'd like you to come over because . . . because . . . ah, hell, Sutton, never mi— You will? Great! Me and Babe will be waitin'—hey, could you pick up some steaks on the way and some dog bones, you know the Milk-Bone kind that . . ."

Monday, Orlando, Florida

Ted held a beer as he stepped out on the balcony that overlooked Lake Sweetwater. He took in a deep breath and let it out slowly as he looked at the distant castle on the far shore. Wearing a robe, Bonita stepped out on the balcony and joined him. She rested her head on his shoulder and sighed. "Isn't it beautiful?"

Ted put his arm around her and motioned toward the lake. "There's the canoes . . . tonight we'll be able to see the fireworks. The guy downstairs said they shoot up behind Sleeping Beauty's castle over there across the lake."

"It's Cinderella's castle, Ted. Come on back inside . . . let's start some fireworks of our own."

"Christ'a'mighty, Bo, we just got here."

Bonita let her robe fall from her shoulders. "Teddy."

Ted quickly set his beer on the rail. "Christ'a'mighty, Bo . . . hell, yeah, let's get them fireworks started."

Waikiki Beach, Oahu, Hawaii

On the private beach of the Royal Hawaiian Hotel, Virgil handed Ramon a towel. "You best keep that bandage covered so sand don't get in it. You shoulda waited longer, ya know? We coulda come next month when you was healed better."

"And miss this, man—you loco? This is what I need. Sun, sand, and ladies. Man, check them two over there . . . they hangin' out all over, man. Oh wow, they checkin' us out. Be cool now. Lift your arm like you waving off a fly and show off that new gold Rolex . . . yeah, that got their attention. Fishin', man . . . we sophisticated dudes doin' some lady fishin' now."

"Hey, Ray, the sunburned one is making eyes at me."

"No, man, she's makin' 'em at me. The dark-headed one is lookin' at you."

"Ray, the sunburned one is *lookin'* at me."

"Virg, forget them, man, check out the two at our three o'clock. Now that is some serious bad la-dies."

Virgil smiled as he flicked away another imaginary fly. "Hey, Ray, it's been some ride, huh?"

"Yeah, Virg, it's been some ride, man."

SOMETIMES IT'S HARD TO TELL
WHERE RIGHT ENDS
AND WRONG BEGINS

SOLEMN DUTY
by *Leonard B. Scott*

FBI agents Eli Tanner and Ashley Sutton
have been exiled to the backwater of
Columbus, Georgia—but they soon find
themselves in the middle of a chilling series
of killings tied to a betrayal in Cambodia in
1969.

Published by Ballantine Books.
Available in bookstores everywhere.